SEVEN DEVILS

SEVEN DEVILS

ELIZABETH MAY
& LAURA LAM

GOLLANCZ

LONDON

First published in Great Britain in 2020 by Gollancz
an imprint of The Orion Publishing Group Ltd
Carmelite House, 50 Victoria Embankment
London EC4Y 0DZ

An Hachette UK Company

1 3 5 7 9 10 8 6 4 2

Copyright © Elizabeth May and Laura Lam 2020

A CIP catalogue record for this book
is available from the British Library.

ISBN (Hardback) 978 1 473 22514 5
ISBN (Export Trade Paperback) 978 1 473 23114 6
ISBN (eBook) 978 1 473 22516 9

Printed in Great Britain by Clays Ltd, Elcograf S.p.A.

www.orionbooks.co.uk

For the underdogs among us, those who hold
the lines, and protest, and write, and speak out.
Empires only topple brick by brick.
And for Hannah, who was always there to
help us smash the patriarchy.

1.

Present day

Eris got the call from her commander while she was killing a man.

The guard slumped against her, dead in under thirty seconds from a blade to the throat, a stab in the carotid artery. Fast and quiet. The sharp, tangy scent of his blood wafted toward her as she hauled the guard's still-warm body against hers and slowly lowered him to the spacecraft's floor.

Could she have prevented this death? If she were honest with herself: yes.

But there was no time for guilt. She was doing her job.

Her Pathos, the communication chip embedded within her cerebrum, echoed through her skull with the most irritating musical tune. Commander Sher had chosen it because he knew Eris couldn't ignore it. *<Riiing riiiing this is important,>* the tune sang. *<Listen to meee and remember don't murder people!>*

<I'm busy,> she sent back through her Pathos.

Most Pathos only had a range of a planet, half a solar system at most. Sher was outfitted with a beta design that could bounce its signal off satellites as far as it pleased as long as he knew her rough coordinates.

It irritated the shit out of her. She had a spacecraft to commandeer.

Scylla was larger than most of the ships she'd taken in the past. It had the capability of growing large amounts of hydroponic food, and if there was one thing the Novantae resistance was short on, it was food, followed by weapons.

Eris grabbed the guard's identity card and cut off his finger with a swipe of her blade.

Almost every ship the resistance had was taken through force or subterfuge, and Eris was damn good at her job. She slid the identity card through the slot, pressed the guard's severed finger against the pad, entered the code, and hurried down a second hallway that led to the main corridor. Five seconds to get through this section before the alarms sounded.

<Riing riiiing this is important—>

Eris gritted her teeth. Shoved the identity card in. Pressed the finger. Entered the code.

The door slid open. *Oh, shit.*

Eris rolled to the ground as the high-pitched blasts of laser bullets stung her ears. They dotted the metal of the ship above her head with a deafening *clang clang clang.* She shoved herself behind one of the storage containers before they could correct their aim and riddle her body with seared holes. Of *course* there would be soldiers on the other side. *Of course.* She would have been better prepared had it not been for that stupid—

<Riing riiiing this is important—>

Son of a bitch.

She commanded her Pathos to answer the godsdamn call.

<Finally,> came the commander's voice.

<You had better be dying,> she said to Sher as she pulled the gun out of her holster.

Eris peeked over the storage containers and hid again just as more blasts rained and exploded like stars. Eight against one, six blasts left in her antique gun. If she ever smiled genuinely, she would have then. Challenging odds—her favorite. Otherwise, she wouldn't bother running around with a weapon so old most people didn't know what the flame it was. She had back up weapons, of course—five knives and two Mors—but this was her baby: a gorgeous filigreed limited-edition RX

Blaster from the turn of the last century. She was a beauty. Updated with little add-ons to keep her blasts deadly, but the shooting style was all old-school skill. No lasers to help aim.

<We need you back at Nova,> Commander Asshole in her head said. *<Now.>*

<I said I'm busy,> she replied, lifting her blaster.

One, two, three down. Lasers in the Mors weaponry might be more accurate, but her little baby had a beautiful curve to its fall that lodged the blast right where she wanted it. It had charm. It had character. She liked its quirks.

And, yes, she felt sentimental about it.

<Get un-busy,> Sher said.

<I am>—she pointed her gun—*<in the middle of>*—one shot to the head of a soldier—*<a job>*—one shot to another's torso—*<and you are>*—another soldier down—*<destroying my focus. And now I'm out of shots.>*

<So use one of your other weapons.> He sounded impatient, as usual. *<And try not to shoot them all in the head this time.>*

<I got a few in the knee and a few in the gut.> Only *some* in the head. *<If you called just to give me a lecture, I'm turning off the Pathos.>*

The soldiers yelled—calling for reinforcements from the other part of the ship. More loyal Tholosian soldiers would be flowing into bullet crafts, speeding through space to close off her exits. Eris had to seal the doors and disable the comm system, or she'd never take the command center.

She could practically hear his sigh through the Pathos. *<I've got another mission for you.>*

<Are you kidding me? I'm in the middle of commandeering a ship.>

She only had the blade in her boot left and less than three minutes before the other soldiers arrived. She'd told her other superior, Kyla, that she was looking for something challenging. Eris could never decide if the other woman was obeying her wishes or deliberately trying to kill her.

<Kyla says you're usually faster than this.>

Eris paused. *<She did not.>*

<She's telling me that if you don't finish your mission in the next fifty seconds, it'll be your slowest run time—>

<If you'd shut up>—she lunged from behind the metal container—*<for one>*—threw her blade into a soldier's gut—*<godsdamn>*—dove to avoid a spray of laser blasts that exploded into white lights behind her upon impact—*<second.>*

Eris leapt onto the last soldier, tore the Mors from his grip, and slammed her fist into his face. Her body modifications were a godsend, giving her strength unmatched by a common soldier. Her punch cracked the bones of his face. He staggered, spitting blood onto the floor. He didn't manage to recover before she snaked an arm around his throat and snapped his neck.

Sorry, Sher. Sorry, Kyla.

She heard another bullet craft anchor to the hull. The screech as doors opened. The patter of footfalls above her as more soldiers—twenty at least—came to try their luck at killing her. Eris sprinted to the door that opened the command center. The captain was unprotected, vulnerable.

"Wait," he only just uttered before Eris grabbed his shirt.

"Disable the doors." When he hesitated, she seized his arm and squeezed until he cried out. *"Do it."*

His fingers moved fast on the controls as he sent the commands. Captains were trained in rudimentary defense tactics, but not more than the guards stationed outside. He would have seen her through the monitors, known his skills were no match for hers. If this had been one of her captains—if she were still called *General*—she would have either killed him or sent him back for more training. No weakness. Only sacrifice.

So far, Eris could justify the corpses left in her wake tonight. Kill or be killed. This man wasn't attacking. Kyla told her to end a life only if necessary, save as many as possible. Eris should at least try to keep her word.

"There." His voice trembled. "It's done."

"Good," Eris said.

She saw the exact moment his Oracle programming kicked in. The rapid eye movement and dilation of his pupils, the curl of his lips as his hand reached for his belt. His snarled words barely sounded like the voice he used before: *"For Tholos."*

The captain lunged with a blade. Eris smacked the weapon away and pivoted, but he came at her and slammed her into the ground. His hands were on her throat, a tight squeeze. Eris saw stars. The Oracle's programming was a benefit and a curse. Right now, it was pumping adrenaline through his body and running code through his brain until all that remained was the Oracle's commands: *God of Death, I kill for Thee. In Thy name I give my body.*

Nothing else. No consciousness. No choice.

No autonomy.

She hit him, aiming for his kidneys. Just enough to get him off her. But it was no use; the Oracle had taken over. The programming all Tholosians had hardwired into their brains since birth was bad enough, but the chip at the base of his skull gave the AI control over his body's motor functions.

He was so far gone, he might never come back. Shorted out into what the Tholosians called gerulae. Mindless servants. Human drones.

Eris edged the knife out of her wrist sheath and struck. She aimed for his arm, and shoved him hard enough to knock him on his back. "Captain? Captain, come on. You've got to fight through the—"

"In His name," he murmured, grasping the hilt of the blade. He yanked it out of his arm in a single move.

"*Captain*—" Eris scrambled to her feet.

"I give my body."

The captain slit his own throat.

Eris stopped short, shutting her eyes at the sight. "Fuck," she breathed. "Fuck, fuck, *fuck*." She reached into her pocket, closed her fingers around her small animal figurine. The weight of it helped her breathe. But it was a poor replacement for the man who had given it to her.

<Eris?> Sher's voice came through the Pathos. *<Is it done?>*

She closed herself off to feelings. There was no place in her line of work to mourn the dead. There was only this: small moments after a mission. Taking stock. A quiet moment to tally up her kills.

Even the ones she'd intended to save. Or the ones she'd given quick deaths.

Did the captain count?

<Yeah,> she told Sher, trying to keep her inner voice light even as a heavy weight settled in her chest. Guilt had become too familiar. *<Tell Kyla I beat my personal best for a ship this size.>*

<Well done,> he said. *<Now report back to Nova. Kyla will brief you on the way.>*

<Fine. Be there as soon as I can.>

She pulled out of the call, stepped over the captain's body, and entered a command into the ship's computer. She might have killed to take the ship for supplies, but sacrificing the few to save the many was the way of the resistance. It was sure as shit more merciful of an end than those the Empire gave. The ship's survivors would have the chips at the base of their skulls removed and be deprogrammed of the Oracle's influence. They'd be given another chance on Nova. And who survived was simply the luck of the draw.

The God of Death did not have favorites. He simply took.

Eris locked the other soldiers in and directed the ship back to Nova headquarters. Maybe some of the soldiers would be freed of the Oracle's programming and could be turned to the cause. Most would fail, and she was delivering them to their death.

She unclasped the necklace at her throat, with its tiny metal scythe, and bent over the captain's corpse. She might not have been able to save him, but she could offer last rites. The ones she would have given in her previous life. His fate would be decided in a level of the Avernian underworld, all seven the realm of a different god. For the Tholosians, the gods and devils of the Avern were one and the same. Light only shown by the dark.

And her patron god was Letum, the most powerful of their pantheon. Death Himself.

Eris whispered a prayer to her insatiable god.

In His name.

2.

CLO

Present day

"Dinnae do this tae me, ye temperamental piece of silt," Clo cursed.

Last night was a late one. *Chrysaor* had given up yesterday, and Clo had been dragged out of bed closer to midnight than dawn. The weather had been humid and hot, and the water system was completely bogged. She'd spent an hour cursing the mechanic who had let it go dry.

But that was the resistance—never enough of anything to go around, equipment held together with little more than tape, strategic welding, and a prayer. Clo had managed to fix the damn thing and the ship had taken off for its mission. Less than five hours of sleep and she was back at it again.

Every pore was drenched in sweat, sand, and engine oil. If she got hungry, she could probably cook an egg on the flagstones. Clo had been working on this engine all morning beneath the Novan sun. The sand dunes rising around the compound were a gradient of orange, yellow, and red ablaze in the light.

It was another world to the damp, marshy swamplands where Clo had grown up. She never thought she'd miss the smell of sulfur, peat, and stagnant water. Sometimes, the resistance itself seemed as dried out as this empty planet they'd claimed as their own—a movement that could crumble into dust.

Clo wiped the sweat from her forehead. The Valkyrie X-501 in front of her should be flying like a dream, but the damn ignition wasn't lighting up the engine.

Ugh. "Useless," she muttered.

Maybe if she changed tactics, cajoled instead of insulted, the thing would listen to her.

"We need yer wings, my snell one." With only the metal of the spaceship to hear, Clo always slipped back into the Snarl dialect of her youth. "Wouldn't ye rather be out among the stars than mired on this blarin' rock?"

A frustrated curse drew Clo's attention.

On the next landing pad, Elva battled her own engine. Like Clo, she worked alone—but unlike Clo, it wasn't by choice. Elva's skin was stippled with swirls that branded her as different from Clo or the other Tholosians at Nova. The markings fell down Elva's neck like stripes and curled around her collarbones. She had told Clo that the pattern followed the lines of cell development in the skin.

Clo had become very familiar with those dappled marks one night in her bunk. Their intimacy hadn't repeated itself, instead giving way to an easy friendship. One mechanic to another.

Elva was one of the few Evoli in the resistance. Her people had been at war with the Tholosians for over five hundred years, the two empires competing for resources across their separate galaxies as their populations expanded. With the Tholosian resource-rich planet Charon experiencing a mass die-off as a result of an asteroid strike, the Empire's food stores were strained to support all their citizens. They were desperate to conquer the farming planets owned by the Evoli.

Elva's knowledge was vital to the resistance; the Evoli tech she wove into the machines made them sing. Though the Tholosians at Nova had been deprogrammed of the Oracle's influence, superstition ran deep, and some still whispered that the Evoli were majoi, especially their leaders, the Oversouls. Sorcerers that knew your every thought and emotion. They claimed no secret was safe. That they'd eat children, sucking the marrow from their bones.

Elva didn't even eat meat.

"Elva!" Clo called. "Can I borrow your welder? Mine's sunk!"

The woman nodded, crossing over to pass it to Clo. The sun highlighted the darker dapples in her red-gold hair, throwing her features into sharp relief. They were a pretty people, the Evoli. Taller, almost ethereal, even when covered in engine grease. Unfair.

"You need a hand?" Elva asked, her Evoli accent soft.

"Nah, I got it. Just need to threaten her a bit more."

Elva flashed a grin and loped back to her work.

Clo reconnected the wires, even though she'd already done it three times this morning. Maybe if she tied them up extra tight. Her fingertips were callused and nicked with scars from endless hours in machines. Clo climbed out of the engine and swung herself into the cockpit, grunting as too much weight hit her bad leg. She had a hole in the left knee of her trousers—Kyla would be right brackish when she saw it—and the dull silver of her prosthetic caught the artificial lights. She rubbed the part where skin met metal. She could never tell how much pain was physical and how much mental.

Clo started the flight sequence, whispering a halfhearted prayer to whatever gods were listening—if any—then tapped her left shoulder, an old good-luck movement from her childhood. She'd tried to translate it to her commander once. Closest she got was: *Never let the water level of the swamp go above yer shoulder, or ye'll be head-deep in shite.*

The engine fired to life. And then it purred.

"Yes, my beaut!" Clo called, slapping the walls.

While the spacecraft quivered, she tapped her mech cuff and ran diagnostics, watching the readings with bated breath. Green lights. Atmosphere fully regulated. The temperature cooled from the inside of an oven to perfectly pleasant. Clo could smell herself, like old cooked onions. At that moment, she didn't care. Her ship worked.

She tapped out a message to the guard at headquarters that she was giving the Valkyrie a test run and got the all clear. She fired up the launch sequence and the Valkyrie gathered speed, skimming along the fire-gold sand before swerving up, up, rising above the ocher and brilliant orange mountains of Nova and into the purple of the sky.

Clo let out a whoop, hands dancing across the controls, and the ship moved like an extension of herself. She sluiced through the atmosphere and up into the stars. Nova grew smaller in the distance.

It was only up there, in the darkness of space, that she felt truly at home. More than the old Snarled swamp of her childhood, more than the sweltering Novantae desert. One circuit of the planet, and then she'd touch back down and make sure everything was still functioning. Or maybe she could chance two orbits. A little more fun.

Clo probably should have shrugged into a pressure suit in case the ship's atmosphere gave up, but she'd been too impatient. Kyla had basically grounded her since she lost her leg. No more reconnaissance, no more stealing ships from Tholosians. Much as she loved fixing engines, she was bogging bored.

She was a quarter around Nova when she got the call. "Cloelia," Kyla said, voice crackling over the ship comms. "I'm switching over to Pathos. Answer it this time."

Clo had a habit of ignoring her Pathos when she was working on engines, even though Kyla yelled at her not to. <*Hey, Kyla,*> Clo said, cautiously, all traces of Snarl gone from her voice. She sounded just like any other vial-grown Imperial. She shouldn't be in trouble. She'd gotten the all clear.

<*Touch back down. We need you at headquarters.*>

<*Right now?*> Clo asked, fighting down annoyance. No second orbit for her.

<*I have a mission for you.*>

Clo's pulse sped up. <*About time. I'll just finish my circuit.*>

Kyla let out a short laugh. <*We'll see how happy you are when you find out what it is. Have fun.*>

Clo's hands tightened on the controls. From above, the planet looked even more like fire. The oranges and rust of the mountains, the yellow sand. All of it interspersed with the dusky blue of small, rare pockets of water dotted along the planet's surface.

Most of Nova was practically uninhabitable due to the massive storms that covered almost the entire planet's surface in dust. Novan headquarters were nestled in a valley surrounded by high desert mountains, protected from the brunt of the winds. Even then, the occasional storm rocked the facility. The resistance was forced to pump most of their water from deep underground.

A tiny, overheated planet in a forgotten corner of the galaxy. The stronghold of the resistance, hidden in the outermost quadrant of the Iona Galaxy—still Tholosian territory, but barely acknowledged. Full of stubborn, fierce fighters, determined to be a thorn in the Empire's side.

There were no illusions on Nova. It would take time and effort to topple the Imperial family. But maybe, if the resistance grew and flourished, they could make a difference. Skirmish by skirmish, ship by ship, soldier by soldier freed of the Oracle's programming.

One. At. A. Time.

And maybe, she thought wryly, *long after my aged corpse is launched intae space, those shitegoblins will be off the throne.*

Clo landed right where she'd started. The Valkyrie X-501 set down like a dream. As she swung out of the cockpit, she uselessly patted at the shirt of her oil-splattered uniform. There was sand in the creases of the fabric, and her buttons were tarnished despite a polish from the harsh wind. She looked a damn mess.

<Do I have time to wash and change clothes?> Clo asked Kyla as she motioned for Felix, one of the other mechanics, to bring the Valkyrie back into the hangar.

<No,> Kyla said.

<Seriously? I stink. Like sweat and oil.>

Clo could practically hear Kyla's annoyed sigh. *<Now, Cloelia.>*

She broke into a reluctant run, grumbling at the use of her full name. Only her mother had called her Cloelia, and only when she had been well salted with her daughter.

Clo opened the barracks door and stamped in, shaking sand from her boots. Sher and Kyla stood together; this must be one Avern of a mission for both Novan co-commanders to be there. They were often apart—training recruits, checking ongoing missions, or surveying their growing spy network.

Clo's face softened at seeing Sher. He'd been away too long. Sher was technically her commanding officer; he'd been the one who plucked her out of the swamp water and given her something to believe in.

Though she'd never tell him, she thought of him as a sort of older brother or uncle. The closest thing she had to family.

Sher was tall and lean, muscled from his past training as a soldier for the Empire. His dark brown hair was in desperate need of a cut and his stubble was longer than usual, meaning he'd probably been at some silthole of a forgotten outpost for the past month. His face was still unlined, his skin a light, golden brown, but he was older than he appeared—one of the first cohorts of soldiers completely genetically engineered and programmed for fighting. He'd been among the only survivors of that particular crop of infants, along with Kyla.

Kyla stood taller than her co-commander, even in flat-heeled boots. They were genetic siblings—born from vials within minutes of each other. After being forced to present as male during her time in the military, Kyla transitioned after escaping Tholosian rule fifteen years ago with Sher. Her skin was a warm brown, and her hair fell in long, black curls that no pin or hair tie could tame. What always struck Clo first was Kyla's eyes: black as ink and so piercing, they made even the toughest soldier squirm.

"Okay," Clo said. "I'm here. Hey, Kyla. Welcome back, Sher. And—wait a minute—" She reached for his face—an insubordinate move for anyone but her. "Look at that fuzz! You trying to grow a full beard?"

Sher dodged her hand. "Shut up, Alesca."

"You are! Look, how patchy."

"I was going for *distinguished*."

"Of course you were." She leaned in to him. "Distinguished. I'll bet you're trying to look all serious and broody for the troops, too."

Kyla hid a smile.

Sher rolled his eyes and gave Clo a side-on hug—then immediately wrinkled his nose. "What's that smell?"

Clo glared at Kyla. "*See*? What did I tell you? She wouldn't even let me wash, Sher. I've been at the engines since dawn."

"This is more important," Kyla said, serious again. "Before I brief you, I'm going to need you to remember your training: keep a clear head; stay calm; don't act without thinking; don't—"

A throat cleared behind her. Clo twisted, taking in the small woman in fragmented pieces before her mind put them together. Delicate features, deceptively doll-like, skin too pale for the harsh desert, hair night-black. But those eyes weren't really green.

The last time Clo had seen that face up close, those eyes had blared a luminous gold. The cold, brutish expression was just the same.

If I ever see ye 'gain, I'll drain ye t' the dregs, Clo had vowed the last time they met.

She felt Kyla's hand clamp hard on her wrist before Clo's hand could stray to the blaster at her belt.

Clo hated Eris. She hated everything the other woman stood for. Clo hated that she'd been drawn into Eris's lies, that she'd let herself care for a murderer. No matter what good Eris did for the resistance, it would never erase that stain of what she'd done before.

And Clo hated Eris, most of all, for saving her life.

3.

ERIS

Present day

Clo had tried to pull a Mors on her. Eris glanced at where Kyla still had her fingers around Clo's wrist hard enough to bruise.

"Still a slow draw, I see," Eris said.

She skated near a lie; Cloelia Alesca might not be the sharpshooter Eris was, but what Clo lacked in skill she made up for in sheer raw anger and tenacity. Sometimes, that mattered more.

"Let me go, Kyla," Clo snarled.

"Absolutely *not*." Kyla's grip tightened. "What did I just say? Clear head. Stay calm. *Don't act without thinking.*"

Eris let out a short laugh. "Good luck getting her to do that."

Clo lunged at her, stopped short only by Kyla's interference. "Nice face you've got there," she said. "Is it permanent now or can I still fucking tear it off?"

"*Alesca,*" Sher snapped.

Eris kept her expression even. The last time she had seen Clo, she'd worn a shifter over her true features. Her old face had been replaced by a new, unrecognizable one. It went with a new identity and life with the resistance. Clo, for all her annoyances, had been part of that life at the start. All it had taken was one glitch, and that was over.

The three people in this room were the only ones who knew Eris's true identity—and that she was still alive.

"I figured I'd make this one permanent," Eris said mildly. "Like it?"

Clo's lip curled. "You can change your face, but you can't hide who you are."

When Eris was around Nova headquarters, Kyla and Sher let them both know each other's schedules so a chance encounter never happened. It had been a dance, a successful one. It created the facade of harmony, of union within the rebellion. It wouldn't do to have the kind of infighting that resulted in their best agent and their best mechanic trying to murder one another. But it was pretty clear to everyone with a pair of working eyes and ears that Clo hated Eris.

Eris had told Kyla as much, when she'd delivered the stolen Imperial ship and its crew of survivors. But she kept her true thoughts to herself: Kyla and Sher had lost their godsdamned minds if they thought Clo would agree to this.

"I told you this wasn't a good idea," Eris told Kyla and Sher. "She can't follow orders because you're both soft with her. You treat her like a sibling, not a subordinate."

Eris didn't admit that watching Clo, Sher, and Kyla had stirred something inside her that had to be squashed down and destroyed: jealousy. She'd had that camaraderie with Clo once. She'd had it with someone else, too, and that person was long dead.

She pressed her palm to the firewolf carving. The animal figurine was a reminder that she was alone, same as always.

Sher straightened. "Don't pretend like you haven't been disobedient with me. I let it slide because you do good fucking work."

"There's a difference between permitting occasional disobedience and being too soft. Besides"—Eris's eyes lingered on Clo—"she's reckless. A liability. You ought to keep her on Nova. Better yet, send her someplace else."

"I'd rather be a reckless liability than a cold-hearted mass murderer," Clo ground out. "They should have killed you."

Eris heard Clo's unspoken words: *I should have killed you.*

It didn't matter that Eris had saved Clo's life. What was one life spared compared to so many others taken? The scales had been tipped long before. *Cold-hearted. Mass murderer.* These were all things Eris had heard before, spoken by the other rebels at Nova when they'd celebrated the anniversary of her former self's death—because none of them knew that death was as fake as the face of their new recruit. Eris had tried not to show how much those words hurt.

After all, she could be honest: they were kinder descriptors than she deserved.

The mechanic was right to loathe her: Eris used her old skills for a different purpose. She was still the Servant of Death, and always would be. Didn't matter which side she fought on—Empire or resistance—killing was dirty work. Few people liked to sully their hands or minds with it.

Few people liked to acknowledge that it didn't matter how good your intentions; in order to overthrow an empire, murder was a necessity. Someone had to do it.

So Eris did. And she let herself be feared and hated and never told anyone about her guilt. She'd never told Clo how much she hated her own past, her family, those tallies she kept nightly of her dead as she recalled every last rite she ever gave.

The Servant of Death is always alone. And you deserve it.

Kyla and Sher both stared at Eris. Eris had always figured they agreed with Clo. But they didn't have to like her—they had a use for her. That was all she offered them.

"Stand down, Cloelia," Kyla said.

"I don't think—"

"I said *stand down.*"

Clo jerked her arm out of Kyla's grip, her hand resting on the handle of her weapon. "I take it this mission has something to do with *her.*"

"Hand off the Mors, Alesca," Sher said. "You're not shooting anyone."

"Oh, but if we all aimed at the same time . . ."

Eris scoffed, impatient. "Can we get on with the brief?" she said to Sher. "Kyla gave me the basics. Details, please."

"Let me know so I can formally turn it down." Clo crossed her arms over her chest.

Sher shot Clo a look. "A ship is about to leave Tholos called *Zelus,*" he said. "It looks like your typical cargo ship, standard S-model space-craft. Records say Legate Atkis and his crew are delivering to a military outpost and will be taking up a position there. Nothing out of the ordinary, according to the paperwork. It didn't even register with our intel until we saw these."

He passed Eris his tablet and Clo edged closer to the screen with a resigned sigh. Eris studied the ship's schematics with a practiced gaze. She knew every trick her father and brother had in their employ, every secret, but even she didn't know how Sher and Kyla had managed to obtain a copy of the Oracle's coding on this spacecraft. Whoever they had hacking into the Tholosian ships' computers was damn good.

"That's one flame of a coding structure," Eris murmured. "The Oracle is keeping a close eye on this one. Could be weapons." She tapped the screen to get a closer look. "One watches ships like this if they're sending in supplies to the front lines, especially for a critical battle. There hasn't been that kind of fight with the Evoli for a few years, but Tholosian resources have been strained since Charon got hit by the asteroid. Food is going to get low if they don't find another planet that can pick up the slack, and stealing one from the Evoli is a desperate option. Maybe high-risk materials. Something they'd have good reason for the Oracle to watch over. The AI's programming has become better about detecting supply strains."

"You'd know, wouldn't you?" Clo muttered, her lip curling.

"Not helping," Sher snapped at Clo. He flicked his finger across the screen to bring up an image of the ship at port on Tholos. "What do you think now?"

Eris let out a breath at the image. A typical cargo ship like that shouldn't have so many soldiers on guard, even for the usual weapon shipments. Her father would have depended on the Oracle's space scanner to make sure the ship couldn't be commandeered while in flight. But this? Eris would have used this kind of security to ensure the weapon she had was delivered safely to the battlefront.

For a big win. Possibly Empire-altering. Something that would kill a lot of people.

"That . . . is concerning," Eris said.

"Understatement," Clo said. "Hey, Sher, remember how excited I was about a mission before? Scratch that. Assign me to a backwater planet to avoid the slaughter before it starts."

"And have you miss out on all the fun, Alesca? Wouldn't dream of it. Stop whining."

Eris passed the tablet back to Sher. "What do you want us to do?"

"Impossible to infiltrate," Kyla said. "Your favorite. We need you to intercept the ship when it docks for fuel. Sneak on board, gather intel, hide a tracer inside so we can track its movements, and get out." Kyla's gaze was hard. "*Get out* being the end goal here. Don't stay aboard. Don't commandeer the ship. Do not, under *any* circumstances, kill anyone. We need to know what the cargo is, who it's for, and the ship's final destination. Cloelia will accompany you to ensure you make it on."

Eris tried not to let her irritation show. "I know how to break into a ship, Kyla. I did it just before you called me in."

"Clo knows these types of ships inside and out, and I'm not taking any chances. Questions?"

A pause as Clo and Eris looked at one another. Then at the same time: "Who's in charge?"

Sher grinned. "Told you," he said to Kyla. "Hand over the scratch and nobody gets hurt."

"Oh, shut up." Kyla dug in her pocket, came up with a few coins, and smacked them into his hand. "I'm disappointed in you both."

"You deserve it," Clo said. "You shouldn't have bet on us. Answer the question."

"Eris has done more ITI missions, so she takes the lead. Clo, follow her command."

Clo curled her lip. "Do you hate me? Did I piss in your breakfast this morning without realizing? Has everyone here forgotten what happened last year, or do you need a refresher?" She gestured wildly to Eris. "*She tried tae kill me.*"

Eris rolled her eyes. "Don't be so dramatic. If I had actually tried to kill you, then you wouldn't be here irritating me. I saved your life."

"Only after nearly taking it to begin with." She looked at Sher and Kyla, swallowing back her Snarl accent. "You can find someone else to do my bit, right? You have other mechanics and pilots. I'll train one to get around the Oracle's watch. I'll take a shittier mission. But I can't be around her."

"No," Kyla replied tightly. "This is nonnegotiable. You're both going. And if one of you ends up killing the other, I'm leaving the survivor in the middle of the desert for the birds to pick at."

Clo tried a different tack: "Sher, please. I don't understand why—"

"Because it's stopping for fuel on Myndalia. In Kersh."

Clo's head shot up, her nostrils flaring. *"Excuse* me?"

Sher's expression softened. "I'm sorry. You're the only two we have with advanced levels of training who spent extended time on Myndalia. You both know the different sides of Kersh, so you'll look like you belong." When Clo stared at him, he sighed and reached for her shoulders. "Look. I know the city brings back bad memories. But you won't have to go into the Snarl, just the transport hub. You and Eris worked well together before Sennett, and I trust you more than any other mechanic we have. I need you both on this."

Eris glanced at Clo. She only knew scant details about Clo's past before Nova. Those who lived in the Snarl, a regional name for the slums of Kersh, were the only citizens in the Empire not engineered in birthing centers or under the Oracle's influence. The Empire made up for this weakness by clustering the natural-born in densely populated urban areas, and carefully controlling the citizenry with drugs and heavy military presence. The existence of such communities had forced the Empire to implement mandatory sterilization five years before. Every citizen in the future would be engineered rather than born.

Clo's upbringing would have been immensely different from Eris's. Eris had spent years in the high-rises above Kersh. As long as the floating cities didn't hover over the Snarl, they had glorious views of the sun reflecting off the marshlands that dotted Myndalia. But like everything about Tholosian society, there was no sense of kindness in that place, nothing more than constant studying and fighting. Every activity was framed by physical and mental deprivation disguised as a lesson.

You have to learn to think quickly in a war, when all hope is lost, and when you haven't slept for days, her prefect, Mistress Heraia, had once told her. Eris had once gone six days without sleep in response to Mistress Heraia's words, just to prove she could, and trained every day on top of it. Eventually, even with her body mods, she'd collapsed. They'd nursed her back to health and congratulated her.

Clo sighed. "All right. I'll do it."

Sher and Kyla both looked at Eris. She shrugged. "I already signed on. ITI mission, remember? Little chance of success, high chance of death. My favorite."

Clo's eyes met Eris's. "Yeah. I'm familiar with Eris's favorite hobby. It cost me a leg."

4.

One year ago

"I've got another mission for us." The breathless voice made Clo glance up with a grin. Eris was in the doorway of Clo's quarters at Nova, her hair messy from the run clear across headquarters to find Clo.

"You're back," Clo said. "I thought you'd be off for a few moons, stealing ships and kicking ass."

"I prefer to steal ships and kick ass with you, though."

Clo's grin widened. It'd taken her ages to convince Kyla to let her go on a proper mission after Sher had dragged her back from Fortuna, traumatized and broken but alive. Sher had stayed with Clo as she healed from her wounds, comforted her when she woke up in the middle of the night with nightmares of fleeing Prince Damocles. It was Sher who lured her back to training, sweating out all her fear and anger and heartache.

When the worst of the grief had passed, Kyla had eased Clo back into work gently—surveillance, reconnaissance, the occasional tampering with a ship's engine while planetside.

Six months before, Kyla had paired her with Eris for the first time. The other woman had been quiet and intense when she first came to Nova—a deprogrammed soldier from the front lines, Kyla said. She kept her head down, did her job, but didn't offer up much in the way of herself or her past. That'd suited Clo well enough. She could get plenty sparkish herself when people pried too much into her background.

They'd found a good balance, the two of them. Clo could count on Eris not to do anything stupid that would get them killed. Quick with a blade, but didn't like Mors guns. Kept to her silly anachronistic weapon, but Eris was sharp enough with it.

The others at Nova found Eris odd—the way she took everything in without blinking, how she kept to herself. How she spoke in curt orders. She wasn't making friends, or at least not with anyone else.

The first few times, Clo had knocked on Eris's door, holding up a bottle of moonshine from the mechanic's quarters. They'd drunk in silence, mostly, watching the sunset over the golden sands of Nova. Each visit, each bottle, loosened a few more secrets. When the bottle was nearly empty, Eris once mentioned that the Empire had taken her siblings. Her whole family was nothing but a sacrifice. Clo had given the barest sketch of what happened to her in the slums. They'd clinked their glasses and killed the rest of the bottle. Let loose a few more details of the lives they'd left behind.

Clo would wake up with a sore head but the strange pride that Eris had chosen her. Before Clo quite realized it, Eris was her closest friend on that desert rock.

"Show me," Clo said, gesturing to Eris's tablet.

Eris settled beside Clo at her bare desk and tapped a few icons until she pulled up the mission particulars. "Challenging," Eris murmured.

"My favorite," they said at the same time, smiling at each other.

Kyla was going to drop them straight into enemy territory.

Their task was clear. Land on Sennett. Blow up the factory that processed parts for a large percentage of starships in this quarter of the galaxy. That would slow down the Empire's ability to send out ship after ship of soldiers throughout the Empire. It was an advantage the Novantae needed.

Clo had never been to Sennett, but that wasn't saying much. She'd barely been anywhere that wasn't a complete silthole backwater planet. Yet there on Sennett, everything was clean, despite the crowds. The streets were tidy and swept.

Still too fluming hot.

Clo waded through people, the air so thick and stifling that she fought the urge to pant with every breath. Her baggy shirt and tall boots—both worn to cover the Mors tucked into the small of her back and a few knives and lockpicks at her ankles—only made the humidity worse.

More than half of Sennett was covered in dense rainforests. The amount of foliage meant lots of cover, yet also plenty of opportunities for others to creep up on them. At least the Tholosians, in their thirst for draining the bogging galaxy dry, had killed most of the large predators on the planet. Most. Clo loved how the air smelled, though. Loamy, dark, and dangerous.

Their target city was Alina. A large swathe of jungle had been flattened, the city built from black metal, studded with the bones of the large, catlike aliens that had been there before the Tholosian conquest. Tall buildings of black and white, with curling green vines like clasping fingers twined along the sides. The streets were narrow and high, blocking out the sunlight, almost purplish with the haze of the atmosphere. The city projected countless moving advertisements onto the sides of the buildings, the images dancing in the gloom. They praised Sennett's famed fruits and vegetables as jewels taken from the black earth.

Peppered through those swirling colors were the reminders that the planet was loyal to the Tholosian Empire. The double scythes, the dark circle between them. The icons of the Emperor, his face smooth and serene, and of General Damocles, the new Heir Apparent. The memorials to the former Heir Apparent, Princess Discordia of Tholos. Sleek blond hair that fell to her ribs, pale skin, the same royal golden eyes she'd shared with her father and brother, narrowed in the certainty that the entire galaxy would someday be hers.

But Princess Discordia was dead and gone, and Prince Damocles would take the throne and her galaxy instead.

Good riddance.

One less member of the royal family. Though her brother was, if anything, worse. Heir Apparent Damocles was a slimy, useless muskeg lag, to use one of her favorite insults from her childhood. Unlike his sister, he hadn't earned his place, the galaxy whispered. Damocles was not loved by the people, and he knew it.

They passed an eight-foot icon of him, gazing down his aquiline nose at his subjects as they scurried through the dusk. His eyes shone like coins. He was even paler than his sister, his skin cream against his platinum hair. If these icons had bothered with accuracy, his hands would be covered in blood rather than so white and clean.

He'd once tried and failed to murder Clo. The memories of Jurran swirled up like a murky whirlpool. Her throat closed. *Dinnae think of Briggs. Dinnae think 'bout warm blood freezing on the hangar floor. Dinnae think of those months on Fortuna.* No.

A few gerulae emerged from the buildings to scrub the already-spotless icon. Clo had only seen them from afar; they weren't common on backwater planets. Gerulae were convicted criminals who had been reprogrammed so extensively by the Oracle that they no longer had thoughts of their own. They existed as drudges, performing menial work throughout the Tholosian empire.

There were other classes of cohorts; the aedifex were the architects and makers of the Empire. Opifex were the artisans and craftsmen, including courtesans. Militus were soldiers, commanders, killers. Servitors for servants. Clo had found it deeply unsettling when she'd first realized just how deeply the Empire engineered people down through their bones.

Tholosian propaganda claimed the gerulae class was a second chance for those convicted of the petty crime of acting against their initial birth programming. Sometimes, it was for something as little as refusing a superior, or stealing food when hungry. Clo was one of the few born without an implant. If she'd been caught thieving as a child, they'd likely have just killed her. Maybe that would have been a kinder fate.

"Clo." Eris's voice startled her. "Come on."

Eris ignored the gerulae, as if they were no more interesting than the stone behind them. She wore a long hooded coat to cover her concealed weapons. It must have been boiling. Her hair stuck to her temples with sweat, but otherwise, she seemed unfazed by the planet and the Tholosian propaganda swirling around them in the haze.

Clo resisted the urge to take another second and spit at Damocles's feet. She passed Eris, letting nothing show on her face.

"You all right?" Eris asked.

"Fine. Just some memories best left forgotten."

"I have plenty of those." Eris reached out, softly grasping Clo's shoulder. "The sooner we're done, the sooner we're gone. I have a bottle of brandy back at base with our name on it."

Clo nodded, one hand straying to the small of her back.

The factory wasn't far from the city center. Plumes of blue smoke rose above the streets of Alina. They passed the market, and the air filled with the scent of ginger and other spices. Clo's mouth watered. After a childhood of stolen scraps or bog berries foraged in the marshlands, she was always hungry.

Eris walked so smoothly that she disappeared into the crowd. Clo found herself craning her head before Eris startled her.

The other woman lifted her chin. "Stop staring at the food." Her voice was quiet but commanding. "I need you to focus."

Clo ground her teeth together. They worked well on missions, but Eris could throw barbs at Clo as easily as the others at Nova, unaware how they could sting. Eris might try to hide her past, but her amount of confidence—that unafraid way of walking through streets—spoke of a childhood with money.

They circled the factory. Shift was over, the workers streaming from the doors. Machines would be left to do some of the simpler tasks, and the Oracle was always there, the ever-watchful eye of the Empire. A program threaded through the fabric of the Empire, reporting back to the Archon. Ensuring order, compliance.

The Oracle was considered to be so powerful that they referred to the program as One. The Oracle was more than a thing, an artificial intelligence. One was an entity.

The Oracle's programming was downloaded into the brain of every citizen engineered and bred by the Empire—and if that person's will proved stronger than most, the Oracle controlled motor functions through a tiny implant embedded in the base of the skull, close to the brainstem. The Novantae had their work cut out for them trying to undo One's influence. Deprogramming was messy at best, fatal at worst.

The Oracle originated in the palace on Tholos but was everywhere.

One was the AI on all ships. One was on every Tholosian planet. One was in every soldier's mind, keeping them loyal. *One of the many*, people would whisper of the Oracle, in corners where the cameras could not see or hear.

And here were two members of the resistance, hoping to trick the Oracle into not noticing them.

Eris reached under her coat and took out the explosive. It was such a small thing. Clo didn't think it looked dangerous enough to kill one of the rats in the Snarl, but appearances could be deceiving. If they miscalled this, they could kill people. That didn't seem to bother Eris. Shouldn't it?

<How close do we have to get?> Clo asked on their closed Pathos loop.

<A bit farther and we'll throw it from there,> Eris replied. *<Then we'll get the seven devils out and watch the fireworks.>*

<We're going to . . . throw a bomb?>

Eris gave something resembling a smile in the growing darkness. She looked feral, her white canines pointed. She was pretty, but something about her face was too symmetrical. Her green eyes were dark pools in this light. *<Do you have a better idea?>*

<Not throwing it?>

<Fine, I'll place it down like it's a newgrown right out of the vat,> Eris said. *<Then I'll set off the pulse to kill the factory's power. We'll have about five minutes to get this as close as we can and bail. You can hang back, if you want. It's a risk. I've got this.>*

<No chance,> Clo said, flashing her own wild grin. Eris returned it, and Clo felt a flush of camaraderie.

They picked their way through the foliage. Clo took the explosive from Eris. She set it down gently in a small hollow in the ground, nestled among the twining roots of a tree with a yellow cast to its bark.

Crack. A footstep breaking a twig near them.

"Shit," Eris breathed.

Both women stumbled into the underbrush near the un-activated bomb. Clo tripped in the dark, smacking into Eris. The other woman hissed.

Two Tholosian guards made their rounds. Clo fought down a surge of panic. They'd plotted the guards' routes—they should have had ten minutes at least without having to worry, and Eris's initial electromag pulse had taken out any nearby cameras.

A horrible thought pulled at her like quicksand: *is this a trap?*

Clo could make out Eris crawling through the underbrush. She was low to the ground, inching toward the explosive as the guards headed away. If Eris activated it now, those two men would die.

Clo wished she could turn off the ability to care, like Eris seemed to. They couldn't save every guard programmed with loyalty to the Empire. They would still kill Clo and Eris without blinking.

All's fair in war.

Eris reached out and pressed the small button on the side of the sphere.

<*Go!*> she yelled in Clo's mind, crawling back. <*Four minutes and thirty six seconds.*>

But in the darkness, Eris's face had changed.

Clo stopped, fascinated and horrified, as the features she knew so well amended subtly. It took her a second to realize what had happened: shifter technology glitched during electromag pulses.

Eris wore a false face.

And Clo had caught a glimpse of her true one.

The other woman's hair was still dark, but blond showed at the roots. The shifter had altered the bones of her features, the effect melting away to reveal their true shape: wider nose, blunter chin, high cheeks and brow. The most startling difference was her eyes—they glowed yellow-gold, luminous in the darkness. Gold as royalty. The spit of the icons that dotted on every street corner on Sennett.

That face was blasted across the galaxy.

Princess Discordia had infiltrated the resistance. The ultimate spy in their midst. Everything Clo and Sher and Kyla and all the other rebels who risked death to break free of the Empire—they would all be dead.

And Clo had *defended* her. Drunk with her.

Become friends with her.

The Empire took my siblings, Eris had said, the neck of the bottle clinking against the glass as she refilled it.

She'd neglected to mention that *she* had done most of the killing.

Eris read the change in Clo, but she wasn't quick enough. Clo had the Mors from the small of her back pressed against the princess's head before she could blink. Gods, there was four minutes before the bomb went off. What was she supposed to do now?

One shot. Discordia was supposed to be dead anyway. One shot, then Clo could run and disappear. Worst case, she blew herself up and died a godsdamned hero.

But she didn't want to be a hero. She just wanted to live.

"Let me go," Eris—Discordia—hissed. "We have to get out of here. There's no *time*."

Clo hesitated.

Discordia jabbed her elbow into Clo's stomach. Clo wheezed, her grip on the Mors loosening. Discordia ducked and sprinted away from the bomb. Clo followed. She gained speed as she moved through the tangled underbrush as easily as she'd darted through the slums of her homeland.

She caught Discordia, tackling her to the ground. She shoved the Mors into the small of Discordia's back. Were they far enough? How much time?

"Shoot me, then," Discordia's voice was low, almost a growl. She still sounded so much like Eris. "Kill the person who's best placed to help take down Tholos."

"No royal would turn their back on the Empire. Especially the Heir."

Discordia's expression went hard. "Well, I did."

"You're lying," Clo said, her finger tightening on the trigger. "Kyla—"

"Kyla knows," Discordia said. "So does Sher. Both of them helped me stage my death."

A rushing in Clo's ears. They knew, they *knew*. And Kyla had kept it from her. *Sher* had kept it from her.

"You lied to me."

"*Clo*, there's no—"

A warning beep blared in the dark. Discordia turned toward Clo, eyes wide. Clo had thought they were far enough away. But if they heard—

A boom, so loud it reverberated in her chest.

The world burned bright as the flames of the Avern.

Clo went flying and slammed into the trunk of a tree. Leaves, debris, and heavy branches rained down. She couldn't think. Her ears rang, the world roaring like spaceship engines. She saw only the brightness of fire, then the warm, almost-red blackness. She let out a moan. Everything hurt.

Movement above her. Clo couldn't turn her head.

"Come t'kill me proper?" Clo managed to mumble through swollen, bloody lips, Imperial accent forgotten in pain.

Princess Discordia crept closer, her face illuminated by the dying fires. She was lacerated with small cuts that were already healing over. Nanites like that were only for royalty.

The shifter had half-kicked back into place, her features a blend of the Eris she knew and the Discordia she feared. One iris was still green as forest moss, the other luminous as a sun. They were steady, no ocular dilations to indicate activated programming. Royalty, like Clo, were not influenced by the Oracle.

Which meant that every life taken by Discordia had been a choice.

"Tempting, after what you just did." A pause, her mismatched eyes flickering down. "Your left leg is trapped by debris. You wouldn't want to see it. By all rights, I should leave you here. You let emotion overwhelm you, and you jeopardized this mission."

"D'it, then," Clo said through a mouthful of blood. She'd lost a tooth or three. "Leave me or kill me."

Discordia gave a frustrated huff. "You're not going to thank me for this." She rummaged beneath her oversized coat, bringing out a large, very sharp knife.

That was how Clo would end, then. Cut open, her blood feeding the twining vines beneath her. No marshland burial for her.

Discordia made an incision along Clo's upper thigh, and Clo hissed in a breath. One more stab of pain on top of so much more.

Discordia sliced her own wrist and pressed their wounds together.

"Whit're ye doin'?" Clo asked, consciousness beginning to blur around the edges. She felt weak, floating. She'd lost a lot of blood.

"The nanites will stay localized for a few minutes." Discordia took off her belt, tying it tightly above the shallow gash. "They'll help."

"Oh, no," Clo said as her mind worked through Discordia's plan. "No, no." A futile wriggle. She was stuck.

Discordia leaned close again. "Do you want to die here, in the dirt, your bones left for the bugs? Do you want this to be your last day in the universe?" She didn't blink. Clo didn't see Discordia in that gaze.

"No," Clo whispered again, the word catching on a sob.

"All right. Bite down on this." Eris shoved her scarf into Clo's mouth. "For what it's worth, I befriended you for real. And I have chosen this side. I'm not a spy. I don't care whether or not you believe me."

Eris brought the knife down, her strength enough to break through the bone.

Clo screamed through the gag, the pain taking over every cell in her body. She spit out the gag, panting. She wanted to tear off her own skin to make the pain stop.

"If I ever see ye 'gain, I'll drain ye t' the dregs," Clo managed with the last of her breath before all went dark as the void.

5.

CLO

Present day

At least they got to use Clo's favorite ship.

It was one of their smallest ones, called *Asteria*. Class C. Repurposed from the Empire, like all of their ships. Agile and moved like a dream, with an engine that hummed. The cloaking tech was so good, it could sneak up on almost any craft. Over the past few years, Clo had taken it apart and put it back together more times than she could count. She knew this hunk of metal better than anyone, even the myriad pilots that took it on missions.

Asteria had sentimental value. This ship had saved her life.

Clo set her hand on the side, patting it like a friend. She opened the hatch for Eris. "After you, my . . ." She gave a pause. "Former potential sovereign."

"Thank you." Eris looked the ship up and down. "This craft barely looks like it could get off the ground." She swiped a finger across the dash, wrinkling her nose at the resulting dirt. "Seven devils, how long has this been sitting here? Longer than I've been alive?"

Clo glared at Eris and patted the ship's dash. "Shh. She doesn't mean it, sweetheart," she whispered to her craft. To Eris, she said, "You still carry around that ancient junk blaster with the fancy etchings? This ship is like that to me. Sentimental. Say one more bad word about it and I'll deck you."

Eris didn't even look up from the dash. "I was giving you two hours for your first show of insubordination, and you displayed it in fifteen minutes. Congratulations."

"I agreed to the mission. Kyla made you leader, but that dinnae mean you're *my* leader."

"Look," Eris sighed. "I'm just as unhappy about this as you are. But we're stuck together and I need to know you're going to follow my orders and not shoot me in the back at the first opportunity."

"Your *orders*? Ohh, but it's *so* tempting." At Eris's glare, Clo rolled her eyes. "Fine. No back-shooting. No front-shooting. No shooting, except in emergencies."

Clo thought Eris might argue with her, but the other woman only nodded once. "Fine. I'll take it."

"Good. 'Cause that's the best you're gonna get from me." She stood. "I'll check over the engine. The sooner we're out, the sooner we're back, the sooner we can go our separate ways and I'll stop thinking about shooting you."

"Fair enough. Is your Pathos on?" Eris asked.

"Of course."

They took a moment to sync their devices by turning back to back and gently touching their heads together. Clo stiffened at the contact with the other woman. She hated even being near a member of the Imperial family after everything they'd done—not just to Clo but to others throughout the galaxy. Eris might not have been personally responsible for the deaths of people Clo cared about, but she'd hurt so many others.

There was a reason Discordia had been known as the Servant of Death.

The microchips embedded within their brains' cerebrums connected the software with a soft *<beep>*.

Clo jerked away. Eris didn't seem bothered, but then, she was as emotionless as a statue.

<Testing,> Eris said in Clo's mind.

"This is such a bad idea," Clo said out loud with a grimace. "Just hearing your voice in my head makes me want to flip a table."

"I don't want to be killed because you're too stubborn to communicate. Now test the damn thing."

<*I hate you.*>

"Loud and clear." <*And I don't like you, either.*>

Clo narrowed her eyes.

Eris shook her head and completed an inventory of supplies. This mission would only last one week. Seven days. Clo could last that long. She'd have to.

Less than an hour later, *Asteria* fired up and blasted into the sky toward Myndalia.

———

Home hadn't changed at all.

Myndalia rose in the distance, a small dot growing larger as Clo navigated through the stars. It'd taken fourteen hours and one hyperjump from Nova to reach the planet. Clo and Eris did their best to avert conflict by avoiding each other. They'd had one brief sleep on opposite sides of the ship, respective doors bolted tight. Clo had slept in the pilot's seat and had a crick in her neck.

"I never thought I'd see this silthole again," Clo muttered as she maneuvered *Asteria* into the asteroid belt near the planet.

Though the Novantae had employed hackers to hide their ships from enemy detection, the thick layer of rock and debris would help protect against scavengers looking for parts to steal. It was easier to take the smaller pod to the transport hub. It was a military issued minicraft with forged permissions the Novantae hackers had put into Tholosian detection systems for situations exactly like this.

Just a quick, easy jaunt into the enemy's territory. Get in, get out.

"Me neither," Eris said. "Can't say I missed it."

Clo scoffed. The princess's experience on this planet wouldn't have been anything like Clo's. She would have grown up far above Clo's rundown slums in that golden and opulent academy, which circled around the city of Kersh like a second sun. Clo had looked up at that building every day of her childhood, wishing for even one hour up there. Eating fine foods, being clean, not having to look over her shoulder.

Eris had that upbringing—she and her monster of a brother, Damocles. They'd grown up scheming together, right over Clo's head. She stared at the other woman. *Did you know? Did you know what your brother did on Jurran? Did you approve?*

She kept these thoughts from Eris, out of the range of the Pathos. It was a skill, to keep from projecting thoughts. It didn't always work.

Eris caught her look. "What?"

This spoiled woman had everything, and she'd walked away from the whole damn galaxy. What made her run? She wondered if Eris had told the truth about losing someone. That question had kept Clo up at night, those first days in the Novantae hospital, numb below the waist as they fixed the remnants of her leg.

She'd decided it was a lie.

"Nothing." Clo turned her head. She slid the ship into a perfect place in the asteroid belt and unbuckled the chair's straps. "You didn't see much of the slums, did you?"

Eris flattened her lips. "If this is another dig—"

"Assumption." Clo stood. "And I'm guessing a correct one. The Snarl was only something that ruined the pretty view from your floating palace when there was a break in the clouds."

"Floating palace," Eris murmured with a bitter laugh. "Yes, I suppose it must have looked like paradise to you."

Clo's expression hardened. "There was so much gold on that building that it heated the ground below. Sometimes, it melted the pavement, if the light went through glass." She glanced again out the window as they flew closer and closer to her former home. "Don't try to make this mission into a bonding thing. We may have both spent time on Myndalia, but you don't know a fluming thing about where I lived."

"I'd watch your assumptions," Eris said, coolly. "I may not have stayed there, but I did go down to the Snarl. I killed one of my brothers there."

Uncertain of how to respond, Clo focused on their landing point.

Most of Myndalia wasn't solid enough to build upon, and what little land there was wasn't exactly habitable. Arable land was used for farming food Clo had barely been able to afford on her mother's meager benefits. Most of the planet was nothing but swamp and bogs parents warned their children about. Monsters lived down beneath the water, they whispered in the night, and loved to snatch tender morsels. Clo had never seen anything bigger than the fishes, but the tales had worked. She'd always kept to dry land.

The planet looked beautiful from above, all green, blue, and purple swirls, like a marble Clo had stolen from the market half her lifetime earlier. The parts of the planet not covered in swamps were rich in natural resources. The Empire grew crops and exotic fruits, enough food to feed dozens of other planets.

Those crops had become more strained since Charon's mass die-off; that planet had been a huge source of the Empire's food. The farmers on Myndalia were trying to pick up some of the slack, but the planet didn't have enough arable land. What resources they did have? They were sent to the floating palaces or other Tholosian planets. The inhabitants of the Snarl, many of whom worked in the fields, received the same food given to gerulae: gelatinous nutrition made from ground-up bugs, cheap oil, and cheaper grains.

From their hands, the Empire was fed. And the workers were starved of the very crops they helped grow.

Clo fucking hated this place.

Growing up, she'd never known how beautiful Myndalia could be. All she'd ever been there was a small cog in the machine of the Empire— like everyone else who lived in the Snarl. The Oracle couldn't weave One's tendrils into the slumrats; they were the last natural-born humans, created within the womb instead of engineered in birthing centers. One's programming hadn't taken well within the Snarl. Too many people were left comatose.

After losing too many farmers to programming experimentation, the Empire decided to control those in the Snarl through other means: addiction to drugs supplied by the Empire to keep them "docile to influence." Meant the slumrats were constantly off their face. Clo's mother protected her from those drugs. That was the only reason Clo had been able to run away.

Once the natural-borns had all died out, Clo figured the Empire would let the swamp take the Snarl back. It'd sink into the bog as if it had never existed at all, just another forgotten place in an insatiable, vast Empire. The farming would be left to the gerulae.

"Let me do most of the talking once we arrive," Eris said as they got ready.

Clo lifted a shoulder. "Fine by me."

Clo watched as Eris made sure everything on her uniform was perfectly in place. It all had to be. Guards were trained to notice the small, imperfect details that betrayed a Novan spy who wasn't born into the role they were playing.

The threads on Eris's cuffs were the brown and purple of a middle-ranked Publican. In contrast, Clo's uniform was a dark gray, embroidered with a silver chain around her own cuffs to mark her as a mechanic.

Over both of their left breasts, right across the heart, were the crossed scythes of the Tholosian crest, the blades dipping down like harpies' wings. Between them rose the black circle symbolizing that death claimed all in the end. Eris's hand kept creeping to it, as if she wanted to rip it off. Clo longed to do the same.

Publicans had the power to conduct surprise inspections, with the assistance of a mechanic to check the engines for any unapproved tracking, and then collect any fines or extra taxes. They would not be the guards' favorite people, but they should command respect and a little dose of fear. Just what they needed.

They walked through the dusty *Asteria* to the transport room, stiff and silent. It'd been a long fourteen hours with a weapon always within reach. The small shuttle down in the hold looked like every other military emergency transport vehicle. It was an oblong craft that could barely fit two people. It looked like a bullet. Or a coffin.

Eris and Clo settled into the pod and Clo prepped the coordinates. She wasn't nervous, exactly, but she was sparkish—it had been so long since her last mission. If Eris was on edge at all, it didn't show. Clo remembered Eris as a chameleon, able to shift into someone else at a moment's notice. She'd seemed to thrive on that knife's edge of danger, as if it made her feel alive.

But as the lights in the craft dimmed, throwing the other woman's face into sharp relief, Clo heard Eris release a shaky breath. Maybe the perfect princess had her own nightmares from this place, after all.

"Takeoff in ten seconds," the ship's calm voice intoned.

"Let's go spy on the Empire," Eris said. Clo didn't reply, her fingers tightening around the throttle.

The ship's computer gave them their final warning. "Three, two, one."

Clo shoved the throttle forward and the pod burst out of the ship and toward Myndalia.

———

It'd been a long time since Clo had barreled through the atmosphere in such a small craft. She'd forgotten how much she hated it.

The interior grew warmer, until the controls were almost too hot to touch. A halo blazed around the small ship. The world grew clearer, closer, the ground seeming to rise up to meet them. A few thousand feet from the ground, Clo swallowed hard and wrenched the controls, slowing their descent and making sure the cloaking tech was engaged.

They landed, the craft skipping the swamp mud until it slowed to a stop on mostly dry land.

Clo powered down the engine and took off the safety belt, stumbling from the ship. The smell of the planet hit Clo first, and her stomach heaved. Too many memories. The dampness of the mud, the rotting stench of decomposing greenery and algae on stagnant water. The sulfur. The far-off scent of too many people living together in such a small space.

Her boots squelched in the puddles as Clo staggered to the edge of the path. There, she bent over and threw up the scant remnants of her breakfast.

Godsdamn transport sickness.

Clo was fine with larger beasts of ships, but these little bullet craft sometimes made her violently ill. It'd take a few minutes for her stomach to catch up with the rest of her body. She hated feeling weak. She was a bogging pilot.

After she finished, Clo wiped her streaming eyes and straightened to look over at Eris. The other woman was standing, hands on her hips. She looked perfect, no trace of sickness. Of course.

<Ugh, I hate you and your steel stomach.>

Eris caught Clo's message through her Pathos, and she lifted her lips in a hint of a smile. "Do you need the med kit or something?"

"I'm fine," Clo said, shortly, steadying her ragged breath. Myndalian air was so heavy; it tasted like lead at the back of her throat.

"I'll bring it anyway. You almost puked on my boots."

I wish I had, Clo thought to herself as she rubbed at her false knee. The temperature shift affected the metal and squeezed her skin.

Eris's eyes flickered to Clo's hand, and her expression briefly faltered. *Aha.* It seemed the princess felt a little guilty. That was something, at least.

As if hearing Clo's thoughts, Eris looked away. "Grab your shit and let's go."

Clo clenched her jaw and reached into the ship's side compartment for her tool belt—mostly filled with unscannable weapons, of course— and her Tholosian mechanic's jacket.

"Oh, and Clo?" Eris reached into her pocket and tossed something at the other woman. Clo caught it. "Take one of those."

Clo's eyes narrowed in suspicion at the small blue case. "What is it?"

"Neutralizers," Eris said sweetly. "Your breath stinks."

6.

PRINCESS DISCORDIA

Ten years ago

The training academy on Myndalia was a prison made of gold and glass.

"*Up!*"

A slap across the face jolted Discordia awake. She shook her head to clear it. "Sorry, Mistress Heraia."

The papers blurred in front of her eyes. She had been awake for four days in this room, with its single desk surrounded by the glass walls of the training academy.

It overlooked the clouds, tinged pink and orange with the rise of the twin suns. Sometimes, Discordia wished she could open these windows, spread a pair of wings, and fly.

Mistress Heraia snatched the book off the desk. "Recite chapter five for me. Precisely."

Tholosian history—the reign of the fifth Archon. He had expanded his Empire well beyond the Tholosian solar system, ruthlessly conquering planet after planet. It was his idea to engineer a cohort of royal children, each with the potential of becoming his successor. Natural-born male Heirs were too risky. All it took was one spoiled lackwit with more bluster than sense to lose control over the Empire he'd built.

No, the fifth Archon decided his royal cohort should be engineered to his exact specifications, trained up to his brutal standards, and forced to compete for the throne until only two were left standing. One to be Heir of the galaxy. To lead the charge against the Evoli threat and defeat their enemy once and for all. The other the trusted right hand, still royalty, but no Archon. The Spare.

That had been the tradition for hundreds of years, down to Discordia's own father. The tenth Archon.

After more than one hundred years as ruler, Discordia's father began growing his potential successor. The first three batches of one hundred were failures. The first two never made it out of the vats. The third survived and grew to age sixteen. They began dueling as they should, for the title. An Heir and Spare were named, but they killed each other less than a year later. That was not supposed to happen—they were meant to respect the final decision, to set aside their bloodlust and work together.

Discordia was part of the fourth cohort. One hundred children had been grown in vats—fifty assigned male at birth and fifty female, just like all the others. Only fifty-one had survived through childhood.

Discordia was the only female left.

Mistress Heraia, as cruel as she was, had placed her bet on Discordia precisely because she was the only female to make it past age six. She instructed Discordia in all areas—intellectual, physical, and emotional—that would lead to her becoming the best candidate. The strongest. The fastest.

The one who lived.

Discordia shut her eyes and recited the chapter verbatim.

Her prefect didn't smile. She didn't congratulate her. Mistress Heraia gathered her bag and digital tablet before saying, "Come with me."

"Where?" Discordia just wanted to sleep.

"Where else?" Mistress Heraia raised an eyebrow. "To the gymnasium."

Discordia pressed her teeth together against the urge to beg for sleep. "Practice?"

"To start." The prefect's gaze sharpened. "Combat training this morning. History and philosophy this afternoon. And this evening, you run."

"When can I—" Discordia pressed her lips together. She hadn't meant to ask aloud, to betray how vulnerable she was.

"Sleep?" Mistress Heraia finished. Her eyes narrowed and she pressed her fingers to the desk. "There will be no rest in war, Discordia. Every soldier will depend on you to keep your mind sharp when you're most exhausted. So, you will run until I tell you to stop. And when your breath threatens to choke you, you will recite chapter five for me again. Then, once I'm satisfied, I'll *consider* letting you sleep."

Discordia ran until the suns reached their zenith in the Myndalian sky. They shone through the windows of the gymnasium and the trees planted to create the illusion of an outside.

Not once did Discordia fall. Not once did she pause and give Mistress Heraia the opportunity to thrash her for her failure. Not like her siblings; all of them had, at some point during their training, allowed their prefects to beat them into unconsciousness. Just for sleep.

Every sibling except for Damocles.

After Discordia recited the chapter through her hard, heavy breathing, she looked up at the raised observation deck. She knew Damocles would be there. Every child of the Archon was encouraged to watch each other train in the small amount of free time they were given. First, to find each other's weaknesses. Then, eventually, to exploit them. Though they were not permitted to kill each other at the academy, it was where the royal cohort began viewing one another as competition.

And as potential victims.

Their eyes met. Damocles nodded once and held up one finger, then another. A message passed down from the Archon to all of his potentials.

Damocles wanted to form an alliance.

He came to Discordia's room later, after another grueling day of training. Mistress Heraia had finally allowed her to eat and then sleep.

Discordia opened the door shortly after dinner. She froze when she saw him. Though still a fourteen-year-old growing into his gangly limbs, he towered over her. His gaze was penetrating, a beam sharper than any Mors laser. He constantly measured the people around him.

Whether they were a danger, or—more likely—how quickly he could kill them.

She scanned the hallway and ushered him inside. "Hurry."

"You were awake for five days," he said as she closed the door. He sounded almost accusatory. "How did you do that?"

Discordia kept her voice cool. "Sheer force of will."

Damocles scanned her room—clean, white, and sterile as a prison cell. The only personal object she kept in her room was the round za-trikion board on the desk, still in the same positions that she and Mistress Heraia had left them. The prefect always played the King, and Discordia the Queen. It was a game of strategy, of careful calculation meant to reproduce the moves one might make in war. She had another twelve hours to make her decision. If she won, she ate again. If she didn't, she starved. This was how they played, and Mistress Heraia was a master at it.

"Do you play?" Discordia asked, noting how he studied each piece.

"Not often." Accusatory again. "It seems my prefect is useless."

Every prefect was a former member of the royal guard, all trained to be the best soldiers in the Empire. Each one had picked their trainee among the royal cohort—and those who had first pick always went with the male children. A woman had never been Archon. A woman had never made it through training without dying.

But soldiers all had vulnerabilities and strengths. Some prefects emphasized battle. Some emphasized strategy. Mistress Heraia was determined to teach Discordia everything—and if she ended up dying, then she wasn't strong enough to begin with.

"You indicated you wanted to form an alliance," Discordia said, impatient. "Did you mean it?"

"Would I be here if I didn't?"

"Then who would be the Heir?" Her unasked question was just as important: *Who would be the Spare?* The other was lucky enough to live, but they would never be as valued, never as vital, never as recognized.

Damocles shrugged, as if it didn't matter. Didn't fool her. "Whoever was better."

He kept staring at the zatrikion board, never at her. Finally, she grew impatient. "Do you want to play?"

"Yes. Yes, I do."

They sat there afternoon after afternoon between their own training—often exhausted—strategizing and figuring out each other's weaknesses.

She learned that Damocles didn't like losing. She learned that he considered it a weakness. She learned that he grew impatient easily, and that when he sensed he wouldn't win, he made stupid mistakes.

And she learned that he hated hearing her say the same words when she won every game.

Regina regem necat. Queen kills King.

7.

Present Day

As Clo and Eris trudged to their destination, they kept to the muddy path, their boots splashing in the shallow water. The trail grew so narrow in some places, they had to go single file. One wrong step might cause a stumble into the swamp, where bogs could be three times as deep as a person. The hidden currents dragged people down in the undertow, to tangle in weeds and never be seen again. Monsters or the thick sludge of water would kill anyone just the same.

The hangar was on the outskirts of the slums. Technically, the city was called Kersh, but everyone in that cesspit called it the Snarl. The outskirts were solely for the transport centers where commercial and private spacecraft came, to either refuel or drop off the rich to go up to the silver and gold floating palaces. High above the clouds, they never heard the constant roar of engines as the ships landed or took off.

The poor had no such luxury. Clo's childhood had been punctuated in three-minute intervals. The ships landed and took off with perfect precision. Eventually, the roars had faded into the background like the stench of lead, garbage, sulfur, and fuel. When she'd first left Myndalia, she'd found the relative silence and the huge open spaces on Nova terrifying. She'd downloaded engine rumbles to her newly fitted Pathos to help lull her to sleep.

Eris must have looked down on the Snarl, through breaks in the clouds, and thanked her stars she'd never had to live among the scum like Clo. Clo had told Eris where she'd grown up, late on those booze-soaked nights. It wasn't until much later that Clo realized Eris had barely shared anything in return. That she'd said just enough about training and military to fool Clo into thinking she'd been a soldier.

A spacecraft flew low over their heads, the sound drowning out all thought. From above, they wouldn't be seen. They would time their entrance with a big Tholosian carrier crawling with hundreds, thousands of soldiers and passengers.

Clo's Pathos read the details of the spaceship—an Empusa V-900, nice—and fed it into their forged paperwork. The resistance had updated the Pathos since her last mission. Whoever designed their tech was brilliant. A Publican and a mechanic could now pretend to be on the passenger list.

"Hurry," Eris said. "Let's make this one."

"Another one will come in less than ten minutes," Clo grumbled, but Eris had already taken off, her steps quick and sure despite the slick sludge.

Clo forced herself into a run. Every step hurt. Some was the prosthetic, but mostly it was that ghostly feeling of a crushed leg, long gone, burned and scattered along the soil of Sennett. She placed her feet as carefully as she could. One wrong slip and her prosthetic could disappear down a bog, then Eris would have to carry her back to the craft, mission failed before it even began. And it'd be her own damn fault for lying to Kyla and Sher and downplaying the pain.

At hangar IV, they stomped the worst of the mud from their boots and crept around the back. They timed it perfectly. Floods of people from the Empusa streamed out, waiting for smaller craft to take them either to other planets or up to the floating palaces or resorts.

Clo had worked freelance jobs in these hangars when she was young. She'd hated being employed by the Empire—even briefly—but morality never entered into the choice between eating or starving. Her meals as a child had been meager as it was. No one would recognize her after being well fed for years. Her formerly thin arms were thick with muscle.

No one could call her scrawny. No one could call her weak.

<Two guards,> Eris said in her mind. <Palm panel entry. Retinal scan. Let's hope the paperwork holds.>

<You'd know better than me if it will,> Clo said, and got a sharp look in return.

Eris adjusted her uniform, tightened her ponytail of long, dark curls. Clo felt drab in comparison but comforted by that. All eyes would be on Eris.

They approached hangar IV as if they had every right to be there. Eris strode with her chin up, shoulders back, her movements stiff and officious.

The guards watched their approach. Eris sent their false paperwork ahead, and the guards checked their tablets.

"An inspection?" the guard on the left asked.

"Yes, to ensure all is in working order for the might of Tholos," Eris said.

The accent Eris put on was completely different. It was clipped and flat, abrasive.

The guards' lips thinned. They both wore black jumpsuits similar to Eris's, but their buttons and threads of blue ranked them as military guards. Their dark hair was cropped close to their heads, their beards short and tidy. Bred for service since before their birth. Loyalty further unshaken by the threads of the Oracle commands woven into their minds. The Oracle tamped down their fear—as well as most other emotions—and made their patriotism unwavering. Guards always gave Clo the creeps.

Eris's chin stayed raised, her gaze imperious. The guards' stances didn't change, and their fingers strayed close to their Mors, their hands steady.

"An inspection for certain ships or the entire hangar, Publican?" one of them asked, his tone respectful.

"Every craft landed in the past three days. It's just a routine look at the engines and cargo."

Clo had forgotten just how good Eris was at deception. Her accent, her expression, the way she held herself, all transformed with the role she was playing. Everything about her—from her boots to the top of her head—demanded deference.

The guard glanced back into the hangar. "We've got fifteen new craft. Where would you like to start?"

Eris slid her finger down the surface of the tablet to draw up the list. "*Zelus* just arrived for refueling half an hour ago, no? We'll start there and work our way through." She let out a breath that shuddered with exhaustion. "We have to check six hangars before nightfall, then we're off to three other planets to do the same thing by next week."

Damn, she was good.

The guards softened, just slightly. They knew grueling schedules, long shifts. "All seems to be in order," the one on the right said. They moved aside, and the doors embossed with the Tholosian scythes opened for Clo and Eris.

<*What was that accent?*> Clo asked Eris as they entered the vast, open space of the hangar.

<*Tholosian Publicans are trained on the same planet as a lot of military commanders. It's remote on purpose, so their accents are very distinctive. Not easy to mimic.*>

Not for the first time, Clo was struck by just how vital that intel was to the Novantae. Clo had yet to be on a mission where she'd interacted with many high-up officials. She'd only met another member of the royal family once, by accident, and it hadn't ended well. Eris had detailed, insider knowledge about so many aspects of the Empire. No wonder Sher and Kyla had insisted on keeping the Archon's only Heir alive when she defected.

They made their way through the empty space toward the hulking craft at the far side of the hangar. Their footsteps echoed against the metal floor.

<*Watch the guards while I'm in the ship,*> Eris said. <*One of the men at the door seemed less certain of me than the other. He'll make a call once we're inside, just for due diligence.*>

<*How do you know?*> Clo asked.

<*Because he's hungry to prove himself.*>

They reached the ships. These were smaller than the vast transport crafts that usually passed through. Clo's attention was drawn to the stark, unmarked craft. It was all sharp angles, the front built like the point of a knife.

So, this was an S model? She hadn't seen anything like it. By gods, it was beautiful. If they weren't on a mission where she was meant to be a stiff, upright Tholosian, she might have whistled in admiration. Their target could slice through the atmosphere like a blade through skin. Clo itched to get her fingers around the controls of *Zelus*, to have a look at how it all worked.

"You start on the engine and I'll inspect the interior," Eris said aloud, keeping the strange accent and disinterested tone. *<And turn off the comm hatch on that wall there,>* she added, her gaze flicking to it. *<Just in case.>*

Clo nodded. She'd settle for laying her hands on that gorgeous engine.

The hangar was oddly beautiful, with high arched ceilings, the wall in front of them made of thick sheets of glass made to withstand Mors weaponry. Clo angled toward the comm hatch. There were no guards this close to the crafts when all entrances were covered. She switched off the comms to stall any outgoing messages. It wouldn't help for long, but if things went south, a minute or two could save their lives.

Clo opened up the hatch. The engine was still warm. They couldn't have timed this better. The inhabitants of *Zelus* should have just disembarked on a shuttle up to the floating buildings above. Not enough time to take out the cargo. A few minutes before or later, and this would have been much trickier. Clo thanked the gods for that flicker of luck.

<That's strange,> Eris said. *<We mapped our identities and the Oracle should have taken them no problem, but I haven't heard any confirmation. It's as if One is turned off. >*

<Might have powered down when they landed,> Clo replied, her fingers dancing along the metal wires. If only she could fly it.

<Shit.> Eri's thought was quiet but strained.

<What now?> Clo asked, making a show of checking the engine, her heartbeat quickening.

<People are still on board. I thought they'd be gone. Usually, the crew at least go for a meal somewhere. They must be resting.>

<What's the plan, then?>
<Do what I do best: lie.>

Eris fell silent but kept the line open; her voice was muffled as she spoke to someone, but Clo couldn't follow. A movement out of the corner of her eye—a guard, making a slow circuit of the space. His body language was relaxed, but Clo was aware of how closely he watched her.

<There's a guard here. He's making me nervous,> Clo sent.

No response, just more murmurs. Was Eris speaking to Legate Atkis? He was a diplomat; Eris might even have met him before she defected. Knowing that didn't comfort Clo.

The guard drifted closer to *Zelus*. He might be the same one that Eris worried was desperate to prove himself. It was hard to tell. The same cohort of soldiers were engineered to look so similar.

"Hey," she said to him, aiming for nonchalance. "You got any oil around here? The hinges on these hatches are godsawful. Wouldn't want it taking off again like that."

"The supply room is over there," he said. He moved as if to show her, but his gaze caught on the comm hatch. "Those lights shouldn't be off." He frowned, pressing a button. Nothing.

"I can fix it for you," Clo offered, still hoping she came across as relaxed. "It's probably just a loose wire." She could take it apart and fiddle with it long enough for Eris to finish.

The guard hesitated. His Oracle programming had taken over—his pupils were dilated. One overlay ran through the scenarios, statistically determining her likely motivations and the threat of danger. Clo wondered what he would have been like without it. Maybe those brown eyes would have been warm rather than cold. He was a head taller and outweighed her by a good sixty pounds. She might still be able to take him.

"Yes," he said, eventually. "Proceed."

"Thank you." But as Clo bent to grab the rest of her tools, the guard bolted.

"*Silt.*" She'd been half-prepared for it, but still.

He sprinted for the comms unit on the other side of the hangar. Clo went back to the one by *Zelus*, deepening the jam so he wouldn't be able to send anything for a mile in either direction. It was going to cause problems—any incoming passenger or freight craft would have to be redirected to different hangars, and it wouldn't take long before the other guards realized their system was compromised.

Too late.

The guard reached the comm but realized what she'd done. He took off running in the opposite direction, shouting to the second guard, "Grab the woman!"

The other guard came after her. All Clo had to defend herself with was the wrench in her hand; her tool belt was the only thing she could get through the hangar without the Oracle's scan immediately flagging her.

There was no time to prepare. The guard was on her, his Mors pressed against her skull. He gripped her wrist so hard he might break it. "Drop the wrench."

"Up yer hummock," Clo snarled. His eyes widened at her dialect before Clo kneed him in the groin and ducked just as the weapon fired. The laser blast hissed and the gun hit the metal floor.

Alarm lights flashed and blared. *Silt, silt, silt.*

Her Pathos beeped. *<What in the seven devils did you do?>* Eris demanded.

Clo shifted her weight to her good leg and slammed her wrench against the guard's skull. He crumpled to the ground, but his enhancements would have him awake again soon. Clo took his Mors and shot him in the leg, wincing at the sizzle of flesh.

One guard down. Now the next.

<I'm taking care of it,> Clo said. *<Just find out what's on the fluming ship.>*

Clo left the hangar. She could just make out the guard as he darted from the edges of the compound into the Snarl. He'd know her comms jam couldn't spread far. If he reached the other side of the slum, he'd sound the alarm.

Clo sped up, grunting with effort, as she followed him into the crooked buildings of her old home.

It was as if she passed from daylight to growing dusk. The buildings were built so tall and close together that little sunlight penetrated the bottom levels. Lights flickered overhead, dangling on precarious wires.

Above her were rickety rope bridges and laundry drying in between crooked windows. The ground was uneven, the cement pitted and cracked. People moved through the narrow spaces with packages balanced on their heads. It was barely wide enough for one person to pass in either direction. So many people spoke or yelled at each other that it blended into a senseless cacophony. The air smelled of human bodies, dirt, smoke, and fuel, cooking food and laundry soap.

She was home. So many memories lay in these close quarters. The tiny room she'd shared with her mother was only a few floors above her and to the right. What did it look like five years later? Who lived there?

It didn't matter. Her mother was long gone, but the memories hadn't died with her.

This place was in Clo's bones.

8.

CLO

Five years ago

Clo slunk home at nightfall, lugging her bag of parts to sort and salvage in time for the markets tomorrow. She laid out her finds on the table. She didn't like fixing weapons, but the sparked-out Mors would fetch plenty of shale if she could bring it back to life. They needed the dosh.

Mam was in the corner, wrapped up tight in a threadbare blanket, and Clo's work was punctuated by her wracking, pained coughs. Clo winced at each one, knowing they were marking down the time her mam had left. Once someone had Snarled lungs, it was only a question of how long, how comfortable. How much medicine they could afford.

Clo's head snapped up when someone knocked at the door.

"Let them in, Clo," Mam wheezed. "We're expecting them."

Clo let out a soft swear. "Ye promised nae strays."

More hacking coughs. No way to pretend they weren't home. "Just open the door, Cloelia."

Clo scowled and picked up the broken Mors for show. She was a scrawny fifteen-year-old and couldn't scare a marsh cat, but the gun might give whoever was behind the door pause.

The flickering light in the hallway showed a hulking man, face angry as storm water, supporting a slimmer bloke drenched in sweat and blood. The hale man met her eyes, and she flinched away. She didn't want anybody remembering her face.

He whispered to Mam and they both helped the other bloke to the bed. Mam went to work right quick—cutting off his clothing, cleaning him best she could with hot water, bad whisky, and clean scraps of cloth. The larger man shifted from foot to foot, awkward in such a small space. He had big hands that were scarred here and there. A mechanic, maybe, like Clo.

"Hey," he said softly to her. His face was not as stormlike now.

Clo ignored him and slurped down her noodles, hunching over her bowl protectively. The man took out some nutrition bars and crammed two down his gullet before offering her one.

She snatched it from him, tore off the wrapper, and took a big bite as she headed back to her workstation. She wasn't one to shun free food, and this tasted pure gleyed. She could snarf another half dozen, easy.

He laughed deep in his throat. "Don't eat it too fast, kid." He watched her tinker with the Mors. He didn't mention she'd near brandished a broken weapon at him. "You're soldering that part half an inch too high."

She glared at him, but the bogging sinkhole of a man was right. She adjusted the part.

"Briggs," he said to her, holding out his hand once she'd finished the welding. After a long pause, she took it. His hand was warm. "You do good work."

She bent her head over the Mors with a grunt. She focused on it with all she had, never mind the curiosity about the resistance burning in her gut.

Dinnae talk to strays, she reminded herself. *They dinnae stick around long and often end up bloated bodies in the bogs.*

Sure enough, he left not long after. She ate more of the nutrition bar, shutting her eyes at the sweet taste. She saved half for Mam, even though her stomach still rumbled.

Clo eyed the stray in the bed. It had been months since the last one. She had started to hope Mam would stop letting them in, stop giving them food they couldn't spare or shale that could buy medicine. *Go to*

Petra's, folk whispered to strangers—rebels—seeking shelter or help in the Snarl. *She'll fix ye up right proper.*

Sometimes they paid her back. Often they didn't. Mam always said this was the last one. She always promised.

Mam's face was harsh under the swinging bulb of the lamp. Clo saw her home anew when a stray washed in, knowing how they must judge. Stained walls lined with scant possessions—boxes of spare parts, the med kit, their patchwork clothes Mam had stitched as neatly as she sewed up flesh. Teeny kitchen and bathroom. Cracked, concrete ground with threadbare rugs, the shared bed in the corner.

A bed currently full of a muscled man, his stomach bandaged, blood already soaking through the white. Clo glared at him, then at Mam.

Mam opened her mouth, but only coughs came out. She covered her mouth with a rag, and Clo wanted to snatch it from her, check if it were flecked with blood and pus. Her mam always hid it from her.

When she recovered, Mam's voice was raspy. "Come on, Clo. Don't give me that look."

Mam always spoke Imperial instead of Snarl, even though it wasn't natural for her. So formal and clipped, like speaking with your nose pinched shut. Clo's tongue tripped when she tried.

"No' givin' ye any such look," Clo countered. "What's with the dipwell?"

Petra gave a resigned sigh. "No cursing. And he's the last one, I promise."

Her mother looked pale. Too thin, with bags under her eyes, wispy hair tied up in an old rag.

Clo looked away. "Dinnae believe ye."

"Imperial, Clo."

"Nah."

Her mother cleared her throat, swallowing another cough. "He's hurt; he knew this was a safe place. You know they do the gods' work."

"Quag a mire, mair like."

"They don't bring trouble; you just need to keep your head down the next few days. Now go change his dressing so I can get some food."

Clo clenched her jaw. Didn't bring trouble? There'd be guards all over this cesspit looking for him. "Ye ha' shale, or no?" She glanced at the man in the bed. "Or did he nae bother bringin' any? Didnae see his friend offer none." She passed Mam half the nutrition bar just the same.

"Stop worrying about money, Clo. It's not about that. Go fix him up, please." She left the flat, her steps loud on the creaking stairs. Clo heard the coughing echoing down the corridors.

Clo groaned but did as she was told, approaching the stray. He was a tall man, muscled, but younger than she first thought. Skin a bit darker than hers, hair lighter. His eyes moved beneath closed lids, mouth hanging open like a swamp eel. He frowned in his sleep. She unwound the bandages, sliding them beneath his body.

His hand snapped out and grabbed her wrist. She startled back from him, ready to deck him if need be.

His eyes were a dark, dark brown, gaze blank until he focused on her face. "Sorry," he said, dropping her hand.

Clo forced a shrug, heart still hammering in her ears. "Nae bother. Shoulda asked first."

"You must be Cloelia," he said. "I'm Sher."

She didn't like that he knew her name. If Mam had told him before someone battered him, she'd be getting an earful when she was back.

His accent was perfect Imperial, not stilted like her mother's attempts. No, he was born and bred in the inner planets. Curiosity still burned in Clo like peat fire, despite herself—a man born from a vial, stronger and faster than natural-borns like her could ever be. A man programmed from birth to be loyal to the Empire, but he had smashed through it to join the resistance. She could admire that, much as it was a lost cause. Clo and her mam only escaped the same fate because Snarl was so packed full of folk, you could hide like pickled fish in a tin. Long as they seemed loyal, kept their heads down, they should be safe.

Taking in rebels wasn't safe.

"Clo," she corrected, dabbing the medicine on her palm. She slathered it on the wound. He hissed. Light Mors burn. Looked nasty but should heal clean. "Hold still," she snapped.

His eyes met hers. "You don't want me here, do you?"

"Don' matter. Nae my decision."

"It does. You're protective. I've already given her the money I had on me. She'll be buying a dose now. We'll make sure your mother is well compensated for giving me shelter. But I should find somewhere else to hide. The longer I stay, the more you're in danger."

Clo shrugged a shoulder. "Mire always lotic here."

"Can you speak Imperial?"

"I don't see the point of using it in my home," Clo said, enunciating clearly. "Can you speak Snarl?"

"If I tried, it'd be tragic."

"Try. Needa chuckle."

He cleared his throat. "Yer a muskeg lag."

Clo burst out laughing despite herself. "Ye blare muskeg, so aye!"

Sher gave a rueful grin. "And that's why I don't. Means I can't pose as a Myndalian when I come here. Have to pretend to be some off-world merchant. And then I get spotted."

"What ye doin' in Snarl, anywa'?"

"Stealing food, ships, weapons. Whatever we can."

Like me, she thought.

"Your mother's a friend to the resistance."

Clo flinched, eyes darting to the window. Even here, she wouldn't speak that word aloud. Whispers were one thing, but if the wrong ear heard, then it'd be soldiers at the door. A boot against the neck. Execution.

"Yer gonna get us fluming sunk," Clo hissed. "Ye no care a peat fer us Snarl berms."

Sher frowned, struggling to understand.

Clo made an impatient sound. "You're. Going. To. Get. Her. Killed," she said enunciating everything in insultingly slow Imperial, so he could understand her all proper-like. "You eejit."

Sher ignored her jibe. "Your mother's hidden me before, during the day when you were out. No one ever knew."

Clo scowled. So, Mam *had* told him her name. And Mam was *supposed* to tell her every time a stray came through the door.

Clo finished changing the bandage, then shuffled to her worktable. The broken Mors was still borked, and she didn't have the patience for it. She picked up the combustor for a hoverbike. Soldiers used them to skim over the swamplands between cities. She might be able to hawk it at the market for enough food to last them a week.

Sher watched her work. She didn't like it.

"Did you teach yourself how to fix this stuff?"

She ignored him. She sure did—plenty Snarl berms were clever, but he was discounting her like all the other vial-born. His gaze prickled the back of her neck as she unscrewed the metal plate to get at the mechanical innards. Least he was quiet. Strays usually got too chatty—like his friend, Briggs. It made her brackish.

Mam returned with stew from the market. The vegetables were only a little rotten. They ate, her mother glancing nervously between them, but smiling when Sher made a gentle joke. She didn't cough once the whole meal.

Clo made up the spare blankets into a nest for her and Mam in the corner. She curled around Mam, feeling the knobs of her spine. For the first time in weeks, Mam slept deeply. Clo turned, knowing Sher was still awake.

He stared up at the cracked ceiling, his eyes shining in the dark.

9.

CLO

Present day

Focus, Clo. Focus.

She wasn't fifteen anymore. Not a little girl. She wasn't stumbling through these buildings with Sher's hand on her arm, guiding her when she might have fallen. She wasn't some vulnerable kid.

Now *she* could hurt *them*.

Clo caught sight of the guard's sandy hair. He turned into another alley. Clo dove into the throngs of people, not bothering with apologies. She shoved through as if making her way into the thickest part of a peat bog.

Hard left. Another right. Past the tenements of families she once knew.

Focus.

She gasped with relief when she spotted the guard once more. He wasn't moving fast, having to push against the masses. Maybe he'd come through there a few times—passed into no-man's-land on the sly to buy his lunch from one of the many joints that served cheap food you ate at your own risk.

But this was not his world. It was hers.

The Snarl was a law unto itself. Tholosian guards were always nearby, if needed, but they didn't patrol the perimeter. Why bother? Outside the precious buildings was only dead swamp as far as the eye could see. Farms were guarded, as were transport centers, but otherwise, the Snarl was left to fend for itself. Residents formed a loose police force, run on bribes, and they had their own harsh sense of justice. It wasn't as riddled with crime as someone might expect. Only nearly so.

Someone screamed at her for treading on their toe. Clo threw a halfhearted apology over her shoulder. She could feel the language of the Snarl returning to her, twanging her vowels and dropping consonants. It'd taken so long to train herself out of it so she wouldn't betray where she came from every time she opened her mouth.

"Empire scum!" someone was bold enough to yell at Clo, noticing the patch on her jumpsuit.

People would remember seeing her, if authorities bothered to interview residents here after all of this. Not good.

You can't worry about that. Keep running.

One of the laundries emitted a plume of near-scalding steam. She fought her way through it, coughing. When it cleared, the guard had disappeared.

"Silt." Where would he have gone?

She was already nearing the distant side of the slums, not too far from the hidden craft that could take them back to the stars.

She paused for a precious second, imagining the various routes through the cramped buildings. The ground level there was tight, but a few floors up, it was usually lighter foot traffic. The guard must be making for the northeast exit—it was near the driest road, not far from another transport station.

The stairwell was fifty feet away and just as packed at the ground level. She didn't have room for a running jump, so she grabbed the nearest drainpipe and scrambled up. It meant attracting more attention than she'd like, but this was also far from the first time she'd done this. She'd climbed these condemned buildings every day in her youth. She'd just done it with two working legs.

Clo shimmied up to the second level and grabbed one of the rope bridges, waiting for one person to pass before jumping over. Her breath came hard. Despite regular training, her shoulder muscles screamed. She ignored the pain in her leg and started across the rope bridge. Some of the threading was badly frayed, wood partially rotted. The whole structure creaked.

"Please hold," she said aloud. If it broke, she'd fracture bones. If she was lucky.

On the other side, she jumped onto cracked concrete, grunting. A man peeling potatoes glanced up briefly, then went back to his work. A rat skittered across the damp floor. She jumped over it, jogging through the quieter corridor. She checked the ground out of every window, and out of the fourth she spotted their guard.

"Gods of Avern, thank you," she breathed. She'd guessed right; he was definitely making for the northeast exit.

She met him there.

As he passed the gate, Clo grabbed him, clamping her hand over his mouth and dragging him out into the swamp mud. A few people saw her but turned away. A tussle between two people in Empire threads—who'd want to be involved in that mire?

Clo jabbed her fingertips into his kidneys. *Wham!* She clocked him on the temple. He stumbled back, dazed. *Wham!* She slammed her fist into his face again. He went down.

Yes, she thought as she took some cables out of her tool belt. She tied his hands and feet, ripped the collar off of her mechanic's uniform and stuffed it in his mouth.

"Yer lucky I'm the one what caught you. My partner would have shot ye in the head," Clo said to him.

She left him in the mud. He'd be found eventually, just like the other guard.

Clo headed back through the Snarl toward the hangar. <*You alive?*> she thought at Eris.

Still no response.

Clo limped through her old home. It was both the same and entirely different. Here was the market where Nan Mel would look the other way when Clo filched some dried lentils. A few streets along was the mech market. Clo slowed, tempted to duck down and see what treasure was hidden among the dross.

<*Clo,*> Eris said. Finally. <*I need you to get back to the bullet ship and haul ass to* Asteria.>

<What? Why?>

<Because Zelus *is taking off, Clo. Just follow it, okay?>*

Clo sprinted in the direction of where they'd landed. She was already tired from running through the Snarl—her leg ached something fierce—but she kept going. She might hate the princess, but she had a job to finish. *<Where are you? Did you figure out what they're hiding in there?>*

A mental sigh. *<I'm in a bit of a . . . situation.>*

<What kind of situation?> Her mind whirred through the options. Eris could be held hostage. Arrested. *<Gods, you're not stuck in a swamp somewhere, are you?>*

A pause. *<I'm on the ship.>*

10.

CLO

Present day

Clo strapped herself into the bullet craft and loaded the launch sequences. She had about fifteen minutes to get back to the ship—if she was lucky—then another eight to dock and sprint her ass to the command center. *Zelus* would be long gone by then, gunning it into hyperdrive and slipping through space thousands of miles away. She'd have to track it with the tracer Eris took with her.

I should just leave her there.

Clo winced at the thought. Sometimes, she'd had to work with marshbrains. But one thing they believed in was loyalty, and when she was on a mission, Clo had never abandoned someone who needed her, even if that person went against everything she believed in. And she'd promised Sher and Kyla not to kill Eris. Letting her die was basically the same thing.

"Damn," she muttered as the bullet ship blasted up from the swampy ground. Clo took one last glance over her shoulder at the slums that had forged her, then kept her eyes on the stars. "I cannae believe I'm doing this."

She was actually going to have to save that spoiled princess.

<*Coming to get you,*> she said to Eris through her Pathos as the bullet ship docked on *Asteria*. It should still be within range, but if the ship jumped, they'd be cut off.

<Really?> The princess sounded skeptical.

<Aye. Don't make me regret it.> Clo's stomach roiled with guilt, not wanting to admit how close she'd come to doing just that. *<If the Pathos cuts out, just hang tight.>*

As soon as the airlock closed, Clo jumped out of the craft. Her skin broke out in a sheen of sweat, but she swallowed down the nausea and raced to the bridge.

She switched on the cloaking tech and hit the launch sequence. The tracer on *Zelus* indicated it was at least three jumps away—doable, but she was going to have to push this baby to its limits. *Asteria* shot off, then slipped into hyperdrive with beautiful ease. When she finished the third jump, *Zelus* was back within range.

<Clo?> Eris's thought sounded almost like a sigh, as if she had been calling Clo's name and had come close to giving up.

<Yep, I'm here. Can't shake me that easy. Where on the ship are you?>

One jump down. Two to go.

<Locked down in the storage bay. All the doors are sealed and I'm not sure if it's an extra security measure or— Shit.>

<What?>

Two jumps. The ship shuddered around her, the metal groaning. Clo's hands tightened around the throttle.

<What is it? Eris?>

No response. She followed the chaser, blipping through hyperdrive again. Too many jumps left Clo nauseated. Only so many times you can dissolve and put your molecules back together before it took a toll.

<Eris! Status update, princess.>

<I hear Morsfire.>

If Eris was killed, Clo would fail her mission. But if Eris was captured, the resistance was sunk. Eris might be hard as coffin nails, but everyone cracked under Tholosian torture. Everyone.

Clo couldn't lose concentration. Already, the ship shook all around her, losing its momentum. *<Just hold on. I'll follow you—>*

Zelus blinked out. Why was the ship doing so many little jumps? It was almost like it was trying to cover its tracks. Who the flark was flying that thing?

The hyperdrive blinked a red warning light.

Come on, sweet, she coaxed the ship as it prepared to jump again. *Come on. Remember how you saved me all those years ago? Just one more time. One more time.*

The ship jumped.

It came through with a shuddering, deafening groan, but it coasted into space right in clear view of *Zelus*.

"Yes!" Clo pumped her fist in the air. "That's my sweet," she patted the ship's dash. "That's my girl."

<I'm through,> she told Eris. *<What do you need?>*

<Hit the ship with a pulse. I've opened the loading bay door, so hitting it will keep that open and stall the engine. Be careful when you dock.> Eris was curt, but Clo could sense the princess's relief.

Zelus was in range. Clo blasted it with an electromagnetic surge. The ship slowed but didn't stop. She strengthened the shield, waiting for a return blast. Nothing. That was unusual. The pilot should have put *Zelus*'s shields up, hit her back with all it had. *Zelus* coasted like no one was at the helm anymore.

A thought jarred her. Eris said she'd heard Morsfire; maybe the pilot was dead.

<I'm out of the hold,> came Eris's voice. *<The Morsfire has stopped. I'll meet you in the docking bay to open the door for you.>*

<Don't get caught,> Clo thought back.

<Not planning on it.>

Clo blasted the ship again. In the black, peaceful quiet of space, *Zelus* went dark, and the engines stopped running. It moved through the stars on inertia alone.

If *Zelus* had a backup generator, it would switch on after a long-enough period of inactivity. She had to get Eris off the ship before it did.

A dark hole appeared on the side of the ship as the hatch opened. Smoothly, Clo guided *Asteria* to the loading bay. Her own ship had ceased its shuddering, but it wasn't in great shape and the electromagnetic blasts only worked for so long. Once the backups went live, the pilot could put the ship into hyperdrive—if they weren't dead—and they'd be dragged along with them. *Asteria* was in no condition for a dashing escape. Clo didn't even think it would make it back to Nova. They'd be stuck.

One problem at a time, Clo thought.

The ship connected, and the oxygen stabilized. Clo grabbed a few weapons—a Mors, a few blades, and Eris's ridiculous antique—and hurried down *Asteria*'s ramp.

The loading bay was quiet. On any ship this size, there would normally be officers performing the excruciatingly dull task of making sure that any area of the ship that could be docked was under constant watch. Piracy was rare since the Oracle's search mechanisms were perfected, but Clo had expected someone to be there.

No one. Not even Eris.

Clo held up her Mors and edged through the metal containers. She didn't relish the thought of killing, and hadn't pulled a weapon on anyone since that disastrous mission with Eris. Being planetside after losing her leg, she'd started to wonder if she'd gone soft. The idea of shooting someone had never sat well with her. She wasn't like Eris. Clo had heard the stories, seen the shrouded bodies carried out of the ships Eris commandeered and brought back. Someone else cleaned up the blood before Clo got her hands on the engines.

Eris must have used the last of the power supply in this sector to open the loading bay and close it after her. The interior door remained firmly shut. Clo was forced to return to the ship, grab a powered wedge, and pry it open until she could wiggle through.

The corridors looked so familiar, just like all the other stolen ships she'd seen at Nova. The workers at headquarters spent long hours removing the ornate frescoes of Tholosian conquests and replacing them with scenes of freedom. Clo's gaze caught on a mosaic of a soldier holding aloft the head of a conquered alien, its decapitated body sprawled beneath. She didn't recognize the species—gray and fearsome, with tentacles sprouting from their heads and the backs of their arms. A gorgon like the ancient myths, now permanently destroyed by greed for a fertile planet. Clo turned from the scene of death to pass so many others.

She rounded another corner and froze. *Oh.*

Five guards dead on the ground, each with a single shot to the head. A laser-burned bullet hole of a third eye. Whoever had done this had been quick, skilled. These soldiers hadn't even reached for their own weapons. Eris? Or someone else?

"Clo." A whispered breath of a voice made her look up. Eris. The princess barely glanced at the guards. "You all right?"

Clo gave a jerky nod and passed Eris her gun and holster. "Did you find anything?"

"You mean aside from the dozens of corpses littering the hallways?" At Clo's hesitation, Eris's gaze hardened. "These aren't my deaths."

Clo's pulse sped. "Then whose are they?"

"I don't know yet. I think someone is commandeering the ship."

"Commandeering the—*are you fluming kidding me*?"

"Wish I were." Eris buckled the holster around her waist and gestured with her fingers. "Come with me. You need to see this."

11.

Present day

Eris led Clo down the hallway, their footsteps quiet on the rubber floors. She knew what they were risking, staying aboard like this, but Eris was never one to give up easily. Kyla trusted her with ITI missions for one reason: because if she ever got caught, Eris had been trained never to give up her secrets. She'd die first—she'd *kill* first. Without hesitation.

Yet Clo wouldn't be able to withstand the torturers. Did she know what she might face?

"We should leave," Clo said. "You don't even know who murdered those guards out there, and the backup generator is going to turn on soon. We need to be on our ship."

"I *know* that." Eris's impatience sharpened her voice to a knife.

"Didn't you take images of the cargo?"

"There was no chance."

They passed another guard slumped on the floor. Three shots to the torso, one to the head. Military style.

Eris used to kill like that—back when her father forced her to play executioner. Clean, simple, no fuss. The Mors left barely any blood. It was so easy to forget the dead when they didn't bleed. When she switched to her old RX blaster or her little wicked blade, it forced her to acknowledge them, take responsibility for her sacrifices.

Eris stepped over the next body. Clo flinched at the pool of blood on the floor. Eris took in the way a small blade had ripped through the gap in his uniform just above his neck. How he lay on his stomach, head to one side, with his fingers curled up as if in supplication. But he had been granted no mercy; his face was a mass of blood, torn flesh, and flecks of broken bone.

"One of yours, I take it," Clo said, tightly.

"One of mine," Eris confirmed, gripping her necklace.

"Doesn't it ever affect you?" Clo made a sound in her throat.

Eris couldn't let it. She couldn't. When the God of Death chose his favorites, he expected them to deliver. Even though she had fled her life, her destiny, she could only deny him so long. Sher and Kyla never understood. Clo definitely did not. Killing had been bred into Eris. She'd murdered her first few siblings on the planet they'd just fled, and she'd only grown better at granting death since.

"I pray over them," Eris replied. "I always give them last rites. That's all I can do."

Eris hadn't had time to pray or hide the body before she'd heard the sizzle of Morsfire. She slid her fingertips across the scythe around her neck and thought the quiet prayer she'd whispered over him, over all of her victims.

Sleep, and may the God of Death take you in His embrace, and guide you to the seven levels of Avern . . .

Clo's mouth formed the words of the prayer silently, even though they both know she believed in nothing but the blackness of the abyss.

The echoing trill of another Morshot interrupted last rites. Another, closer. Firing on a ship was dangerous. Usually, the blasts weren't strong enough to pierce the hold, and the shields would seal any punctures, but the ship was powered down. No shields.

"That's near the bridge," Clo said.

"Shh." Eris paused, listening. "Surveillance is offline, and without it, they can't figure out who hit them with a pulse. We're fine for now."

"*Fine?*" Clo let out a low, short laugh and gestured to the dead soldier. "You're sluiced. I should have left you here and told Kyla you died from your own stubbornness."

"Stop whining and walk. I'll protect your delicate ass from danger."

Once, before Sennett, this would have been teasing banter between them, but anger and resentment bubbled beneath. She shouldn't miss being able to tease someone. It'd been a year; the delicate friendship they'd had had ended with a lie, a knife, and blood.

Eris strode down the hall, and Clo's limping, uneven footsteps followed.

"I don't want to die because of *you*," Clo muttered.

"Clo. If anyone is going to kill you"—she jerked the door open—"it's going to be me. Now get inside."

Eris shut the door behind them. Though just another storage hull, the Empire never spared details or expense in its design. How many times had she seen that depiction of the third Archon fearlessly conquering the planet Palatine? Palatine had been populated by aliens with long, sinuous rills that propelled their slight bodies through the air. The Empire had taken the planet, terraformed it for humans, and decorated the exterior of its buildings from the delicate bones of their victims. Like so many planets before, like so many planets after.

Tholos always claimed the conquered aliens were not sentient. Eris had been so young when she'd learned that was another lie of the Empire—that most of the ones she'd killed had pleaded for their lives in the only languages they knew.

Eris was responsible for so much pain; she knew that even as her father had told her it was all for Tholosian victory.

Every room on a Tholosian ship was intended to evoke her father's sense of patriotism and Imperial glory—at least on the surface. Its second purpose was to make sure every spacecraft, room, and building in the Empire had images to constantly re-trigger the Oracle's programming in its citizens. These were the images uploaded into their brain implants every night, depicted on walls so they were inescapable for those with enough natural resistance to have their implants illegally removed.

Eris turned away, tamping down the traitorous remnants of pride from those images of her ancestors' conquests. As royalty, she'd escaped the Oracle's programming, but that didn't mean Tholosian propaganda didn't leave its own marks. *It means nothing,* she told herself. *Don't forget Xander. Never forget Xander. Don't—*

"Holy silt," Clo breathed beside her. "Is that the Legate?"

Eris forced herself to look at the body. The fine clothing of gold, black, and silver. Those gleaming boots. That flawless, shining hair missing its pounded-gold circlet. It was a few feet away, crushed. The gaping red-black of his cut throat, the cooling blood already congealing on the metal floor.

"Whoever took the ship was willing to risk murdering a diplomat," Eris said, keeping her voice cool, detached.

"Evoli?"

She shook her head. "I don't think so. They may not be at peace with Tholosians, but relations have been relatively stable since the Battle of the Garnet."

"Yeah? Didn't your da just lose most of his agriculture when a giant fluming asteroid crashed into one of his planets? Tholosians are always fighting war over more resources."

Eris let out a dry laugh. "Fair enough. But losing Charon doesn't explain why *his* Legate is dead. The Evoli are fierce fighters, but it's always been in self-defense. The Oversouls don't start war."

"Then we have to leave," Clo said. "The last thing we need is to be caught in the middle of whatever this is." Clo's gaze flicked upward. "Where are the killers?"

"Hopefully, distracted enough not to notice the two unexpected stowaways checking out whatever was worth murdering Legate Atkis." Eris gestured to the storage containers.

"Kyla said they're probably weapons. I've decided I like that answer, so let's *go*. The mission is sunk."

Eris gave Clo an irritated look. "The Legate refused to let me in here. He wouldn't do that if they were just standard weapons, not during a routine inspection. He must have come down to protect whatever is in these containers and then—" She drew a line across her throat with a finger.

Clo let out a breath and shoved the heavy lid off one of the containers with a small grunt. Alarms blared, high and piercing. Clo clapped her hands over her ears until Eris shot the speaker. Her ears still rang in the heavy silence.

Eris grimaced. "That was—"

Clo's mech cuff vibrated. She twisted it, eyes going blank as the ocular display synced to her Pathos. "Reseal it," Clo told Eris sharply. "Whatever's in there is setting off the hazard detector."

"Does it say why?"

Clo scowled at the cuff and tapped it. "No."

"Then so what? Your suit has protection." Eris plucked a pair of gloves out of her pocket and put them on. "I'm just getting a closer look, then we can go."

Eris reached in and pulled out what looked, at first glance, like a chunk of silverite, a gray-colored mineral they used back at Nova in refractory material at headquarters. Only this was prettier, more iridescent. A meteorite of some sort? Eris twisted it back and forth, letting it catch the light.

"What is that?"

"Not sure," Eris murmured. "I was expecting something more exciting."

Lips pressed together, she peered around the storage hull before taking her small tablet out of her pocket. The screen fuzzed and then flickered off. Eris hit the power button a few more times, but it stayed dark.

"I'd wondered why there were no camera drones in here," she said. "Whatever this stuff is, it makes surveillance glitch. We'll have to take a sample with us." Eris wrapped the glove around the rock, delicately, and shoved the lid closed over the rest. She held out the swaddled object to Clo. "Put that in your pocket and let's go."

"That thing set off my cuff, and your plan is to take the highly dangerous, probably hazardous, unidentified rock with us? Really?"

"The Novantae need to know why it's so important."

Clo let out a long sigh and took the rock from Eris. "Fine."

They slipped back into the hallway and hurried toward the docking bay and *Asteria*. Eris almost told Clo to break for it—and risk being heard—but they needed a smooth getaway. They needed—

The hum of the backup generator echoed through the halls, and the lights flickered on.

"*Silt*," Clo said.

Eris grabbed her arm. "Run!"

They didn't even make it a few steps before a girl's voice boomed over the comm system: "Stop right there!"

They kept sprinting.

"I mean, you can waste the energy if you want, but I've just put your ship on lockdown, so."

Clo and Eris stopped. Eris had her gun out of its holster. "Why does that sound like a *child*?"

"I'm not a child," the voice said, affronted. "There's a camera station a few steps from you. Walk to it." When Clo and Eris hesitated, the girl added, "Your ship is trapped in the loading bay, so whatever you're thinking is pointless. Now go to the cam and turn it on."

Eris flicked the switch for the camera. It went over a few different views of the ship, then finally settled on the command center. At first, she could only see more Tholosian bodies, slumped in their seats or sprawled on the floor in pools of blood.

The first woman who came into view was dressed as a courtesan— all sapphire-toned silk, elaborate onyx hair, pale skin, and carefully applied cosmetics. The dress was blood-splattered. She turned and whispered to another woman with brown skin, dressed in a similar shade of blue. The cut of her clothing was less elaborate than the courtesan's, a strange imitation of Empire army threads, her hair tied back in a sleek bun.

The third—almost certainly the one over the comm—was a mere girl. Emphasis on *girl*. She was tiny, with black skin and black hair in an afro of corkscrew curls, her uniform styled similarly to the second woman's, though less martial in appearance. She looked about fourteen; it must have been her on the comms.

<*Novantae?*> Clo asked Eris.

<*If they are, they were deep undercover. They're dressed like dona. Offerings to be presented to a planet's governor as a gift for some service to the Archon.*> Her face twisted. <*Dona are almost always women of the opifex class. Once given, they continue their duties for the Empire, but unofficially, the governor is free to use them however he wishes.*>

<*That's fluming disgusting,*> Clo said.

Eris gave a fraction of a nod. A lot of things her father and brother approved of were barbaric. If she'd stayed, she could have changed it.

But she hadn't stayed.

Regret coiled painfully in her belly, but Eris shoved it down.

The small girl wiggled her fingers at the camera. "Hello. I'm Ariadne. Neither of you were on the manifest. Are you here on official business, or to try and commandeer our commandeered ship?"

Eris ignored the question. "Did you kill those guards? And the Legate?"

"Of course I didn't," Ariadne said. "I don't like killing. That was Nyx." She indicated the tall, military woman next to her. Then she gestured to the beautiful woman. "And this is Rhea."

Eris's mind whirred, trying to figure out how to play this. Whatever she'd been expecting, it wasn't three women, one of whom was chatting at them like it was a garden party. They should be completely taken over by the Oracle. They should be yelling their love for Tholos, then plunging knives into their bellies.

"Enough with the introductions," Nyx interrupted. "You should have let me kill them when I had the chance, kid. The Publican probably sounded the alarms already for backup."

Ariadne tilted her head. "She doesn't look like a Publican. Doesn't sound like a Publican, either." She gasped. "Are you Novantae? Resistance?"

"No," Eris said, though her heart rate ratcheted up. That little girl sounded very excited. What the fuck was going on here?

"Are you pirates, then?"

"Yes," Eris lied, then made a ploy. "But if you want the Novantae, I might know how to get you in touch."

Ariadne clapped her hands. "I've always wanted to meet a pirate. You're not here to kill us, are you? Because I've just decided I like you, but I take exception to someone trying to murder me."

Eris held up her empty hands at the camera. Never mind the blaster tucked into the small of her back. "I've no issue with you and yours. We have what we came for. We can just be on our way."

Too late, Eris noted the military woman wasn't on the screen. Gods, she'd moved like a ghost. Where—

The door slid open behind them.

<*Silt.*> Clo's soft swear sounded over the Pathos.

Nyx pointed a Mors at their heads. Her arms were marked with tattoos—Eris knew exactly what those meant. Tallymarks of her kills. This woman had seen battle—a lot of it—and those badges marked her as a royal guard.

Meaning Nyx might have once guarded Discordia or Damocles.

Eris still felt uneasy when encountering those from her other life. There had been too many royal guards for her to memorize them individually, but Nyx would have gone into training with Discordia's face giving commands on the vid-screens. Discordia's icon would have been projected at every military camp across the Empire.

Eris's new face felt like nothing more than a veneer. A sham.

<*Eris?*> Perhaps Clo had noticed how unsettled Eris was. <*Any bright ideas?*>

<*Yeah. Don't get shot.*>

"Come inside," Nyx said. "Let's talk."

12.

Ten years ago

Discordia watched her siblings train like a predator on a hunt. The academy was intended to keep them busy, more focused on their own practices than on each other, but Discordia knew there would come a time when they'd have to hunt each other down—with the entire galaxy as their dueling grounds. The chase was part of the challenge, and Discordia was preparing herself for the possibility of fifty duels.

Only the strongest two survive, Mistress Heraia had told her. *And if one of them won't be you, then put a blade through your throat right now and don't waste my time.*

Mistress Heraia gave Discordia more time to observe her siblings than the other prefects did. It wasn't cheating, precisely—they were encouraged to spot each other's weaknesses—but Mistress Heraia's methods were considered by the other prefects to be unusual. Too much emphasis on the cerebral and not enough on strength or battle.

Strategy, Mistress Heraia had told her, *is as much a weapon as a blade. Let the men use brute force. You shouldn't have to lift a finger to kill your opponent until the very end.*

All fifty of Discordia's brothers had varying degrees of skill. She had watched them from afar as they sparred with their prefects, and sometimes through the observation glass in the classrooms. She knew they did the same with her; the difference was that she never let her guard down. Every moment of her life was a performance, and her audience was fifty teenage boys eager to put a Mors blast through her skull. She counted Damocles among them; agreement or no, he would betray her in a moment if any other brother proved more competent.

No one there was worthy of trust. Not even allies.

Discordia crossed her arms, eyes narrowed at Adrian in his gymnasium below. Both the observation deck and the gymnasium were ringed with trees. It helped them feel like they weren't trapped on a golden ship, and the roots could also trip up an inattentive student. Adrian diligently switched through every combat weapon in the collection, displaying a familiarity with each one that made his prefect nod in approval.

Adrian was agile. Incredibly strong. The problem she spotted in him was a fatal one: he lacked focus. Badly.

A small rustle came from behind her. The shadow out of the corner of her eye moved.

Damocles still made stupid mistakes.

Discordia seized Damocles by the wrist and flung his hand away. "Clumsy," she said with a click of her tongue. "I'm not in the mood for games."

Damocles looked annoyed. "I should have brought a blade."

"You still would have failed."

He made a sound in his throat—loathing or an admission of truth—taking in the sight below them. Adrian was practicing with a quarterstaff: not a terribly effective battlefield weapon, but exceptional for honing reflexes. His prefect smacked him across the face with the staff and Adrian reared back with a fist that sent his prefect sprawling. Discordia almost snorted. He hadn't even bothered with his own staff.

"He has fists the size of boulders," Damocles murmured. "Formidable skills. Probably the best among our cohort."

"He might be big, but he's sloppy."

Damocles rolled his eyes. "Snob."

Discordia lifted a shoulder. "Stating facts. Adrian has six months to practice before we're permitted to fight duels. There's still time."

"You think he'll improve by then?" Damocles asked. His expression was hard. "Considering replacing me?"

"No," Discordia answered honestly.

"Good." His eyes burned fire-bright. "Because I'd punish you if you did."

Discordia went still. There was a promise in his voice, a dangerous finality. She'd always wondered if Damocles hated her. If, in the privacy of his room, he imagined ways of killing her. Theirs was an alliance based on survival, nothing more. Replacing him with a weaker brother wasn't an option. Perhaps, if Discordia became the first Archontissa, she'd find a way to deal with Damocles.

For now, she had to let Damocles live.

"Don't threaten me," she told him. "You're not being replaced."

"Good." He refocused on Adrian. "Then he'll be our first."

"Our first?" Discordia snorted. "I assumed you'd want to go after easy pickings. Leo and Marcus still can't beat their prefects at combat. Xander can, but doesn't seem interested in allying himself with anyone. That makes him vulnerable."

She peered down at where Xander trained with his own prefect— just beyond Adrian's gym.

Discordia scowled. She had yet to figure Xander out. Her other brothers were easy. Like Damocles, they wanted power by any means necessary—even weak ones like Leo and Marcus grew frustrated by their inability to overpower their own teachers. That made them defenseless.

But Xander, he had potential. And yet he seemed . . . bored?

Xander dealt a final blow to his prefect and left the trainer sprawled on the floor. Without a backward glance, her brother strode to the massive glass windows overlooking the clouds. He sat on a bench, tilted his head back against the glass, and shut his eyes.

Bored, yes. And . . . weary?

"What has you so captivated?" Damocles asked. He missed nothing. That made him a great ally.

That made him a dangerous enemy.

Discordia shuttered her expression. "I was thinking that Xander ought to be first. A brother who refuses an ally has no one to defend him."

"I prefer a challenge."

Damocles had gone back to watching Adrian. His small smile—the barest lift of his lips—was absolutely chilling. "Father will be so proud, don't you think?"

———

In the months that followed, Discordia began to wonder if she'd chosen the wrong brother.

This close to the ban being lifted, allied pairs were almost inseparable. Discordia spent most of her time with Damocles. He had become difficult to manage; his competitiveness was stifling and it made him violent. Lately, their games of zatrikion had grown turbulent.

"Queen kills King." Discordia uttered those same words—as she had done a hundred times before.

Damocles knocked the table aside and slammed his fist into her face.

They brawled on the floor of Discordia's bedroom. The zatrikion pieces scattered across the carpet as they punched and kicked and hit. Discordia flipped Damocles to the ground and had her blade to his throat, pressed to the flesh just over his artery. One wrong move, and he was dead.

"Either you calm down, or I make you my first sacrifice," she snarled. "Choose."

He huffed a breath, his eyes cold. "The ban doesn't lift for another two days."

"I'll risk it if you don't get it together," Discordia said, voice low. "Stop caring so much. Feelings are a weakness, and weaknesses get you killed."

Every potential Heir learned this from the moment they could walk. They all had tests to determine their flaws; Discordia's was deemed *excessive empathy*. She'd been given an Evoli nurse as a toddler. A majority of Evoli minds were incompatible with programming, but Livia had suffered a minor brain injury that rendered her mental empath defenses useless. As a result, the Oracle's programming was threaded through

Livia's mind even deeper than the average Tholosian. She was compliant. She was docile. She was kind. Discordia was purposely allowed to
bond with Livia for years, had come to love the nurse.

Do you think she'll still love you if I lift the programming? Mistress
Heraia had asked mockingly.

Yes, Discordia had said. She was still a child. So stupid. So foolish. *Yes.*

As soon as she was free of the Oracle, Livia had tried to smother
Discordia in her sleep.

And Discordia had killed the woman who had raised her to save her
own neck.

She blinked hard, bringing herself back to the present. "I need you
to be better than this. Do you understand me?"

Damocles's lip curled. "You're not my damn prefect." He sounded so
young, so petulant. Almost a man, still behaving like a boy.

"No, I'm not, and your prefect should have done his job." When Damocles didn't respond, Eris said, "You'll never make it if you keep letting emotion get in the way. It's why you're losing this game, over and
over. You want to make it to the final two? Stop. Caring."

She wondered if he'd hit her again. If he did, she would walk away.
One of her other brothers would ally with her. Maybe Xander; he was
still unpaired.

"Fine. Let's start the moment the ban is lifted." His lips curved into
an unexpected smile. "Lucky for us, Adrian is back from field training."

Startled, Discordia lifted her blade from his throat. "You're eager,
aren't you?"

"Eagerness has nothing to do with it. Father is leaving on the night
craft tomorrow."

There it was. During their training, they had so rarely seen their father; they had been raised in the academy since birth. He came only for
special ceremonies, Tholosian military grand tours after their victories,
and the occasional progress assessment. Once, Discordia had glanced
up from her sparring to the window of the observation deck to find him
watching her. She'd thought she had caught his nod of approval.

"You want him to see," she said.

Damocles raised an eyebrow, as if the answer were obvious. "Don't you?" He shoved her off and stood. "Meet me at Adrian's gymnasium tomorrow at sundown." As he started for the door, he said over his shoulder. "I can't wait to see the look on Father's face."

The next night, Damocles and Discordia hid behind the foliage at the edge of the gymnasium as Adrian trained with another of their siblings. Xerxes had a similar technique to Adrian's, a brutal fighting style that relied too much on strength. Damocles had hoped to find Adrian alone—but he and Xerxes were allied, and the dueling ban was too close to being lifted.

The time for solitude had passed.

"Fine," Damocles said in irritation. "Two at once."

He moved to stand, but Discordia grasped his wrist. "What are you doing?"

"Challenging our brothers," he said, as if it should be obvious.

Idiot, Discordia thought to herself. "We wait," she said, "until the dueling ban is lifted. Only another hour. Our brothers will still be here and they'll be more prepared. You said you wanted a challenge."

Damocles bared his teeth. "Father will be getting on the night ship any minute, and he'll come if security detects a duel," Damocles hissed. "I'm not waiting."

"It doesn't matter if he sees—*Damocles*—"

Her brother jerked out of her grasp and shoved his way out of the foliage. She heard his voice, high and authoritative: "Adrian and Xerxes, I challenge you—"

Discordia leapt through the foliage.

But it was already too late. He'd issued his challenge. The duels had begun.

Discordia darted into the melee, engaging Adrian while Damocles took care of Xerxes. Adrian recognized Discordia as a bigger threat than her brother, and he didn't waste time. He threw himself at her and swung hard. His massive fists were fast, barely missing her face as Discordia ducked and wove. She had trained for this. This was like breathing. This was like dancing. Mistress Heraia had taught her to move like water across rocks, and she did—oh, how she did. She spun away from Adrian's kicks and hits as if she were in a Tholosian waltz, every movement deliberate, smooth, beautifully orchestrated.

She played with him. She toyed with him. She teased him with the ease of her skill, with how easily she dodged, just waiting, waiting, for him to tire and slow from the force of his movements.

Adrian didn't see the blade until she struck. He managed a single word—her name, a ragged sigh—before she plunged her knife into his chest. Her aim was perfect: right through the heart. Quick, merciful. Mistress Heraia would have been proud.

Her brother collapsed to the ground, and Discordia looked over at Damocles's progress as she wiped her blade. Damocles stood over a prone Xerxes, who was bleeding out onto the hard floor of the gymnasium.

"You did it," Discordia said, breathless. "You—" She paused at Xerxes's struggle for breath, his eyes wide. Their other brother choked on Damocles's name. "He's still alive. Finish him off, Damocles."

Damocles stared down at their brother emotionlessly. "Father isn't here yet."

A chill went across Discordia's skin. "He's suffering. *Finish him.*"

His eyes snapped up to hers. "This is my duel. It's done when I say it is."

Xerxes looked at her, pleading. They were all taught to dispatch each other quickly. No prolonged, painful death, but a death with the respect given to fellow soldiers. Theirs was a difficult deity to please, but Letum did not reward torture. He only rewarded for the collection of souls.

This isn't right.

Discordia knew she and Damocles were never destined for a merciful alliance—their upbringing and expectations were too violent for compassion—but this? This was the only thing that came closest. This was what separated them from monsters.

One small act.

"No," Discordia said. "The duel is done when the God of Death gets his sacrifice."

Discordia dove to her knees. With a quick strike of her blade, she slid it into Xerxes's throat.

"*No!*" Damocles grasped her wrist hard, pulling the blade out. Their bloody hands gripped the knife as they struggled over it. "This was my duel. My death. *Mine.* You had no right to—"

Slow, steady claps came from behind them.

Discordia and Damocles startled. Their father leaned against the door frame. His body was so broad, he commanded the space of the doorway. His gaze was steady as he took in the two dead bodies bleeding out on the ground. If he cared at all for his two sons, it didn't show. He stopped clapping and lowered his hands, but the sound still echoed in the gymnasium.

The duo scrambled to their feet, bowing. "Father," they said at the same time.

The Archon came forward, his eyes only on Discordia. "Duels weren't supposed to be issued for another hour."

Damocles let out an almost panicked breath. "Yes, Archon, but—"

"Your excuses don't interest me." Discordia went still as the Archon reached out and grasped her chin. He studied her for what seemed like hours. He released her. "I'll be seeing more of you, I believe."

Without even a glance or a word to his son, the Archon strolled from the room and shut the door behind him.

Damocles stared at Discordia with an expression she couldn't place. Anger. Or hatred. Before she could decide, his features smoothed to indifference. "I'm going to my room," he said, walking away from her. Then, over his shoulder: "Say a prayer to the God of Death for me. He seems to favor you."

With a shuddering sigh, Discordia took off her necklace. She pressed the small scythe into her palm, and whispered her prayers over the bodies of her brothers. She tamped down the heaviness in her chest as their blood pooled at her feet. An unfamiliar feeling made her ache. A burden she didn't recognize. Didn't understand.

Years later, she would realize that was the first time she had ever felt guilt.

13.

NYX

Present day

"Put the Mors down and we'll come inside," said the woman with the piercing gaze.

Nyx recognized the shorter woman as a threat even through the screens. She didn't look at Nyx; she looked *through* her. The intensity of it did not match her youthful, doll-like features. Curls framed her face. Her belt emphasized her wasp waist and somehow made the godsawful Tholosian jumpsuit look flattering. Neither she nor the taller woman with the buzz cut looked older than Nyx's twenty-three.

The scavengers Nyx had seen caught and punished by the Empire were naturally resistant to the Oracle. They went through underground networks to get their chips removed and their programming wiped. Anyone who defected from the Empire and didn't join an organized group like the Novantae resistance was vulnerable and desperate. They were filthy, underfed, and—if their deprogramming had gone poorly, which they often did in those disgusting makeshift med centers— fucking bonkers.

By the time the Empire caught up with scavengers, it was all too easy for the Oracle to reprogram them into gerulae.

These women were well fed, clean, and clearly sane. She wouldn't lower this weapon until she knew who they were. "I wasn't fished from a vat in the Birthing Center yesterday," she said with steel in her voice. "You want off this ship with your life, then you talk. If you don't, I put a laser through your brain. Simple."

The women exchanged glances. A moment passed, as if a whole silent conversation occurred, before the smaller woman made a small noise of frustration. "Fine."

They edged through the double doors into the command center.

The taller woman had a Mors gripped in one steady hand, her shorn hair making her look harsh. She was shorter than Nyx but muscular, solidly built. Not a soldier—she didn't move or hold herself like one. Didn't take note of their weapons.

The other woman, despite being as delicate as a doll? Soldier. Every movement she took was a woman aware of exits, weapons, potential weapons. Training had taught Nyx never to underestimate an opponent, even if they seemed physically weaker or younger.

Nyx's gaze snagged on the odd piece of metal in her grip. Holy gods, was that . . . a *blaster*?

Nyx had fired every type of weapon she could get her hands on, but that thing had to be from the reign of the ninth Archon, which made it over one hundred years old. It must have been stolen from the Imperial Archives to be in such perfect condition. She wondered how far it could fire.

As if sensing her unasked question, the woman slid her finger to the trigger and bared her teeth in a false smile. A warning.

Nyx must have taken a step forward, because Rhea laid a hand on her arm. "Easy," she said. "No one else needs to be killed today."

Nyx's muscles relaxed, and she instinctively shook off Rhea's touch. She didn't know how the other woman did it, but she could calm anyone down. That sort of thing might have made her a damn good courtesan in the Pleasure Garden, but Nyx didn't like to be touched.

Curly Hair exhaled, frustrated. "If you're going to keep that Mors pointed at my head, I'm going to lose my patience." She lifted her blaster. "This may be old, but I'll bet I can get a shot off before you pull your trigger."

"Put that thing back in your holster," Rhea said to the woman. "Nyx, put your Mors down."

When Rhea was upset, she sounded disappointed. Like she'd expected better and you were the absolute worst for making her feel bad. Nyx had to hand it to her: it worked.

"Rhea's right," Ariadne said. "If they know how to contact the Novantae, we need them alive."

"Kid, we don't actually know if they can contact anyone," Nyx said, her Mors still pointed at Curly Hair. "A pirate? A fucking lie." She raked the strangers with a quick, assessing gaze. "I've seen scavengers. Neither of you look that desperate to me."

Buzz Cut narrowed her gaze. "And how would you know?"

Nyx ticked off the fingers of her free hand. "You're too clean, too well fed, too well spoken, you've still got all your teeth, *and*"—she craned to get a peek at the base of Buzz Cut's skull—"I don't see scars from some clumsy, back-alley attempt at brain surgery to get rid of the Oracle's implant. Now I'm out of gun-free fingers." She nodded to Curls. "That one is military. Takes one to know one."

That woman had dead eyes. Devoid of expression. She had the look of a thousand kills to her. Back in the barracks, they would have called her Blessed. It was always clear when the God of Death chose His favorites; they carried the burden of every life they took.

Nyx would know. She had been Blessed too.

Ariadne hesitantly raised her weapon and pointed it at Buzz Cut. Rhea—damn her soft heart—carefully stepped between everyone with her hands out.

"And me?" Buzz Cut asked. "What do you reckon my background is?"

"Nobody important. You slouch too much."

"Hey!"

Nyx lifted a shoulder. "You asked."

Curly Hair studied Nyx, pausing at her muscled arms. Nyx's tattoos were on full display, the black vines bristling with thorns. Every thorn represented a life taken for the Tholosian Empire. Yeah, definitely military—decorated, maybe. She assessed Nyx like she was choosing one of her officers: making sure her genetics matched up with what she saw.

Nyx knew they did. She had been the best example of her cohort, and they had all been hailed a triumph of genetic engineering. Each militus cohort had similar features—thirty different variants that made some look like siblings and others identical copies. Each was given a number before going into training that would serve as their identity. If they survived, they were named. A name was the first badge a soldier ever earned.

For Nyx, her name was special. They told her it meant *night* and *darkness*.

"You want to tell me who you really are and how you claim to be able to contact the Novantae?" Nyx didn't ask; she commanded. For she had earned her name and the reputation that went with it.

"Pirates," Curly Hair drawled. "Like I said. Natural-born escaped from the slums."

Nyx slid the safety off her Mors. In the quiet command center, that muffled *click* seemed as loud as Morsfire. "I might believe that about your friend, but not you. So, try that answer again, soldier. I'll give you five seconds."

"Nyx." The sharp warning came from Rhea.

But Nyx didn't care. They weren't safe out there in Tholosian territory. Flames, they weren't safe the moment they decided to flee the palace. "Five."

Ariadne spoke softly from behind her. "Nyx, maybe we should just—"

"Four. Three."

Curly Hair's hand tightened around her blaster, but she stayed quiet. She wanted a proper duel? Fine. Let them see who shot faster.

"Two. O—"

"All right." Buzz Cut stepped in front of Nyx's Mors. "Don't shoot. I'm Clo. Mechanic and pilot for the resistance. This is—"

"Godsdamn it, Clo," the smaller woman hissed. "I had it handled."

"Killing three women isn't *handling it*." At Clo's blunt response, the other woman's lips flattened. "Yeah, you don't even deny it. We both promised not to kill anyone on this mission, remember? You already broke that vow once."

Curly Hair's eyes slid shut briefly. "Fuck," she muttered. She took her hand off the blaster and addressed Nyx, Rhea, and Ariadne. "I'm Eris, formerly of the Tholosian military. The two of us were on a reconnaissance mission for the Novantae and I got trapped on your ship. My partner flew in after me."

Nyx scoffed. "No backup? So, you just walked into the hangar on Myndalia? I find that hard to believe."

Clo flashed her a smile. "We did, in fact." She gestured to Nyx's gun, which she hadn't yet lowered. "Are you going to put away your Mors or not?"

"Not," Nyx said. "Just because you made me pause my five count doesn't mean I believe you. Prove you're Novantae and I'll consider forgetting where I left off."

Eris let out an irritated breath. "Fine. I'm not reaching for a weapon, to make that clear." As the woman reached for the cuff of her uniform, Nyx couldn't help but tighten her finger on the trigger. Eris noticed Nyx's response, spreading her fingers to show her hand was empty. "Just watch."

She folded back the cuff of her uniform, showing two metallic bracelets—inorganic shifters. Nyx didn't have to turn her head to know Ariadne would have perked up at those. Eris typed in a few sequences on both bracelets, and the uniform threads changed color. She wore the same silver and gray as the military guards they'd just killed.

Ariadne was almost dancing with delight. "Oooh! They put shifter tech in the suits? How much can you change? Can you give yourself a tail? Can I have one?"

Nyx suppressed a sigh. She was the only one with a Mors still pointed between Eris's eyes.

"Why would I want a tail?" Eris asked. "What would I do with—"

"You can have a tail if you want," Clo interrupted. "Especially if you make her"—she gestured at Nyx—"lower the weapon."

Ariadne nodded. "Put the Mors down, Nyx," Ariadne said again, this time with more confidence.

Nyx bit her lip to keep from muttering a nasty swear. Trusting strangers over a godsdamn tail. Nyx couldn't believe this. But Ariadne and Rhea were both staring at her.

Nyx lowered her weapon very, very slowly, but she kept her finger near the trigger.

Eris still didn't move. "You aren't with the Novantae. Our leadership didn't mention another team assigned to this mission, and there is no way they'd appreciate two dozen corpses of soldiers that could have been deprogrammed."

Nyx tensed. All of them had been her kills. Nyx thought it was easier to leave them behind and do what she'd been born to do.

Nothing in Nyx's training had taught her how to spare someone. They only worshiped seven gods in the Tholosian Empire: Letum, Bel, Rem, Salutem, Phobos, Algea, and Soter. Death, War, Honor, Survival, Fear, Agony, and Salvation. There was no place in their pantheon for Mercy.

"We had no choice," Rhea said, hands folded in front of her skirts. She was good at playing demure and nonthreatening; that made her more dangerous. "We escaped to join the Novantae."

"So, let me get this straight. Your plan was to murder a Legate and his guards, commandeer a ship, and just . . . find the resistance?" Clo asked. "That's not even a plan. Seven devils, that's barely even a fraction of a plan. That's like a note to self after a night of carousing."

Ariadne bristled. "We knew where to go; we just needed a way to get there. We planned this for a year."

Clo's assessment had struck the kid's pride; Ariadne was nothing if not confident of her skills and knowledge. Without her, none of them would have made it this far. Nyx and Rhea would have been found out and executed, their heads left out on the fringes of the royal palace on Tholos as a warning to anyone who dared to rebel against the Archon and the Oracle's program uploads.

"And why did you think the resistance would welcome you?" Eris asked. "It's a nice ship, but if the Empire thinks the resistance was involved in killing the Legate, they'll redouble their efforts against us. You three might be more trouble than you're worth."

"We know our worth," Ariadne insisted, angling her chin up. "Rhea"—she pointed to the other woman, who gave a little curtsy—"is a magnificent, highly talented courtesan who is very prone to extracting interesting details post-coitus."

Nyx shut her eyes and muttered, "Please, seven gods of Avern, never let me hear that kid say the word *coitus* again."

Ariadne ignored Nyx and pointed at herself. "I happen to be an excellent engineer. There's nothing I can't hack."

Clo scoffed at that. "Nothing? Even the Oracle?"

Ariadne smiled, thin-lipped. "Even the Oracle. One is nowhere to be found on this ship. I made sure of it."

That got their attention. Good.

"Hacking the Oracle . . ." Clo echoed, almost awed. "That shouldn't be possible."

"I know." Ariadne flashed her teeth. "I'm marvelous. I even helped Rhea deprogram Nyx."

Clo's mouth hung open.

"Did you?" Eris asked. Eris remained expressionless, but Nyx caught her gleam of fascination. As if Nyx were some new species to be inspected, catalogued, and studied.

Nyx laid her hand on Ariadne's shoulder before the kid responded. "Yeah, she did. After my training, it wasn't easy, either. I was the best soldier in my cohort, and I reported to General Damocles directly. I rose seven ranks in two years."

Eris didn't seem convinced. "The courtesan would be easy enough to get approval for permanent transport from Tholos. But an engineer so good that she can hack the Oracle and a soldier skilled enough to report to the General don't seem expendable enough. I should think the Archon would want to keep you both close." She flickered a glance at Rhea. "Not meaning any offense to your work, of course. It's only that dona often come from the Pleasure Garden."

"None taken," Rhea replied. "I know that."

"We were never meant to leave," Nyx said. "Ariadne had never even left the Temple. She hacked the manifest and added our false names and identities as dona, and that was the easiest part of her job. So, don't pretend the Novantae wouldn't be desperate to welcome us into your ranks."

"Plus, we were going to come with a ship," Ariadne said, smiling more broadly at them. "A ship they already wanted."

"A mutually beneficial arrangement," Rhea added. "Safety and a new life for us, and in return we tell you everything we know."

"The resistance could have saved us a trip, if they had known," Eris said. She glanced at Nyx. "And if you ever point a Mors at me like that again, I'll put a bullet in you."

"With that ancient hunk of metal?" Nyx said mildly, nodding at the gun.

"I've got great aim."

"So do I."

"Enough dick-measuring," Clo said in exasperation. "We're interested in the cargo. Were you planning on using it as another bargaining chip to the Novantae?" She reached into her pocket. Nyx brought up her Mors again, and Clo made a placating motion with her free hand. She held up a swaddled object. "Someone tell me what the salt this is, please."

Nyx crossed her arms. "Looks like a dirty, wadded-up glove to me."

"*Thanks*, genius." Clo rolled her eyes. "I mean what's *in* the glove. We found a bunch of rocks in some containers near the back of the ship that set off my hazard detector."

"We aren't sure what they're for," Rhea said, coming closer. Her skirts swished against Nyx's leg as she passed. "We thought it was explosives, ammo, something. We checked it out before we boarded the ship, but Ari didn't have the time to look through the Oracle's system." She nodded to the covered glove. "Mind if we take a look?"

Clo eyed Rhea's dress. "Unless that flimsy thing offers protection against potentially hazardous materials, you might want to either step away or put something else on before I remove the glove."

Nyx sighed and holstered her gun so she could reach behind her and grab one of the military officer's coats hanging on the back of a nearby chair. Every boot, glove, and uniform in the Empire was designed with internal tech to withstand most of the dangerous shit planets could throw at them. "Here."

She passed the thick material to Rhea. The dead man's coat covered Rhea like a blanket, but it swathed her body to protect her. It was probably a lot warmer than that dress, too.

Clo waited until Rhea buttoned the coat, then uncovered the rock. Nyx edged forward to get a better look. She'd only seen it in the shipping bay days before they'd boarded, and the light hadn't been all that great; it had looked black. In the overhead lights of the comm center, the rock was gray with a sheen of blue, purple, and green, like multicolored feathers. The outside was rough and bulbous.

"Oooh," Ariadne said. "Pretty! We should turn the med bay into a lab and bust it open."

"Bust it open?" Nyx snorted. "Are you cracked? No. You don't even know what it is."

"But—"

Eris put up a hand before anyone could say anything else. "As much as I'd like to discuss the rock, we ought to put more distance between us and Myndalia first. Clo, can you prep the ship?"

"Fine." Clo held the rock out to Eris. "Here, take this stupid thing."

Ariadne slid between them. "Can I have it?" she asked brightly. "I love rocks. I'll take good care of it."

Clo pressed her lips together and gave Eris another meaningful look.

Eris muttered something that sounded like reluctant assent. Clo wrapped the rock again and passed it over to Ariadne. As she did, her arm brushed the courtesan's. Clo inhaled and pulled away as though the small touch burned, and Rhea's mouth curled into a smile.

Well, flames of Avern, Nyx thought. Looks like someone wasn't immune to Rhea's charms.

Ariadne stuffed the glove-covered rock in her pocket. "It won't be easy to start the ship up again."

Clo seemed flustered. "I'll go down and double-check the engines are okay after the electromag blasts. I take it you can sort the computers?"

The girl wiggled her fingers. "My specialty."

"I'll deal with the bodies," Nyx said, voice steady.

She knew none of the others would be able to. They'd avoided speaking about what had just happened. Rhea had small splatters of blood on the back of her skirt. She hadn't noticed yet, but she would when she undressed—and it would hurt her to see. Rhea wore her heart on her sleeve. So did Ariadne. It was Nyx who knew to tuck hers away, somewhere dark and quiet and deep inside.

Eris stepped forward. "I'll help, if you need. I'm not squeamish."

"No," Nyx mused. "I don't expect you are."

"Are you taking us to Nova?" Ariadne sounded so hopeful, Nyx almost winced.

Clo and Eris exchanged glances before the smaller woman answered. "I haven't decided. Make sure we're safe, and then we'll talk."

Nyx didn't ask what would happen if Eris decided she didn't like their *talk*. If she refused them safe passage . . . well, Nyx still had her weapon, and she wouldn't hesitate to use it.

Even if they reached the Novantae, the resistance might not be as brilliant as Ariadne had always hoped they'd be. The girl spoke about rebels like they were the last bastion of humanity and light in this dark, twisted universe. Nyx didn't have the heart to tell her that the resistance was likely as messed-up as the Empire. They'd have their own motivations. If that didn't suit her? Nyx would find some way to escape from them, too. She was done with her life being decided for her.

She'd be damned if she'd let someone else get inside her head or make her into their weapon again.

Nyx wore the tattoos on her skin. She had sacrificed to the Gods of Death and War too many times already. Her honor was in shreds.

Now she prayed only to Salutem. To Survival.

14.

Present day

Clo was glad to have the engines to herself. They didn't ask her to play a role; she never had to pretend around machines.

Every mechanism and part of *Zelus* was in harmony and song. She'd never been able to work on something so sleek before. The main engines were on their lowest power setting, the ship hovering in space until Clo directed them. After verifying the jump drive was in order, Clo searched for any hidden surprises. Sometimes, Empire ships installed extra trackers to make sure there were no unscheduled jumps erased from the logs. Ariadne might be confident that she hacked the Oracle, but Clo wasn't. She found a tracker and ripped it out, grinding it beneath her steel-toed boot.

For as long as she could spare, she sat, listening to the song of the machinery. She let her anger at having to work with Eris fade as much as it could. There, in the engine room, no one was around to hear her as she struggled to control her heaving breaths, her pounding heart, her shaking body.

So many dead men. Three women they were now responsible for. On a stolen ship. Mission sunk.

Eris's fault. Again.

She shook her head sharply. *Stop it. Just get through this.*

She stayed until she was calm once more. She carefully constructed her previous facade: working with Eris was fine. She could handle this. All she had to do was deliver the women to Nova, and she'd ask Kyla to give her another mission that involved flying ships out into the stars like she was meant to.

Yes, she'd stick with machines. Machines weren't capable of betrayal.

Back to the command center, she told herself. *Only a little longer.*

When Clo left the engine room, a flicker of movement out of the corner of her eye shattered her calm. The fear raced back, as if it had never left.

Clo unhooked the Mors from her shoulder and eased her way down the hallway, weapon at the ready.

When she reached the end of the corridor, there was only an Empire flag hung from the ceiling, the same as every hallway throughout the ship, with those familiar black scythes cradling the dark moon. Like the murals, they were another constant reminder of Tholosian patriotism. They'd even been everywhere in the Snarl, but no one had been brave enough to deface them.

The flag flapped in the breeze coming from an air duct. Her mech cuff showed no heat signatures in this quarter of the ship. She was alone.

Clo was losing it.

<*Eris. I'm moving* Zelus's *bullet craft, then I'll guide* Asteria *deeper into the loading bay,*> Clo said. <*I don't like it so close to the doors—a rough jump might damage our ship worse than it already is.*>

<*Good call,*> Eris replied, sounding distracted.

Right. She was busy dragging bodies to throw out of the airlock. Clo shuddered, glad she'd managed to dodge that job.

She rounded the corner into the loading bay, pausing when a soft *click* sounded to her left. It took her a split second to realize someone was climbing into the bullet craft—a man, sandy blond hair, pale skin, wearing a spacesuit dark as the night sky. Light reflected off the sleek helmet he held poised over his head. A spacesuit's cooling layers would mask a heat signature.

"Hey!" Clo pointed her Mors at him, her heart thudding but her hand steady.

"*Fuck*," he muttered, ramming the helmet on this head. He dodged behind a crate.

Clo sprinted after him and fired her Mors just above his head. The shots echoed through the metallic loading bay, sending sparks as the lasers sizzled across the metal. He didn't even pause.

<*Clo?*>

Clo ignored Eris.

The man had pried open the door to the bullet craft, but at her second shot, he ducked to the other side for cover. Clo crept closer, footsteps silent. The others would be coming her way for backup, but she hoped she could disable the straggler before they did.

And what then? A silent corner of her mind asked. *Would you kill him? Sink him like a stone in a marsh?*

She couldn't answer. She couldn't even *think* it.

Clo ducked low, her breath loud in her ears. With her Mors raised, she darted to the other side of the bullet craft. Nothing. She swung around, frantic, muscles tense. For all she knew, she was a sitting target, easily in range.

She jumped at the screech of the loading bay doors. Eris and Nyx burst in.

"What are you *doing*?" Nyx asked.

"There's someone in here." Her voice was breathless and wavering. Back in the Snarl, they'd say she sounded lotic. "I saw him try to break into the bullet craft."

Eris glanced around and hurried to Clo. Under her breath, she asked, "Where?"

Clo shook her head. "Dunno where he went. Didn't see a hatch."

"Shit," Nyx swore. "I was afraid of this. Someone from the manifest was missing when we threw the corpses out of the airlock. Ariadne just gave the ship an infrared scan a few minutes ago, but we didn't see anything. We'd assumed they'd stayed on Myndalia."

"Who was missing?" Clo asked.

Nyx looked wary. "The copilot."

Fluming great.

Eris straightened, in full general mode. "Clo, get to the bridge. Let's hyperjump out of here. After that, we'll tear this place apart until we find the bastard. The last thing we need is someone here still under the Oracle's influence. If he can't contact the Tholosians, he'll try to kill us to take back the ship."

"Someone better come with me," Clo said. "I've heard enough horror stories to know that the loner always dies first."

"I'll come," Nyx said.

Granted, Nyx was plenty fearsome herself. "Good." Clo glanced at *Asteria*. "Eris, can you shift our ship away from the doors and anchor it better? Then I can help Ariadne prep for a hyperjump."

Eris nodded once, sharp. "Right."

Eris following orders without question gave Clo a little thrum of power. Even if it was only to feign allyship in front of the other women, Clo would take it.

As Clo and Nyx headed for the door, lights flashed throughout the bay. Metal screeched, the overhead lamps flickering as more power went to the shields.

Clo grabbed her Mors from its holster. "Ariadne," she called, knowing the girl would hear through the comm system. "What is that?"

"Someone's opening the exterior hatch." Ariadne's breathless voice echoed through the loading bay. "Get out of the loading bay. *Now!*"

The three women raced for the door.

Behind them, the metal gears of the heavy hatchway whined. That damned gate only needed to open a fraction and the oxygen would be sucked from the room. Seconds later, they'd be blasted out into space. Dead. Gone. All because some brainwashed muskeg in an ugly space-suit wanted to return to his corrupt Empire.

Nyx reached the bay door first and bashed the button. She swore, low and urgent as the sluggish backup generators failed to respond. She hit the button a few more times.

"Move," Clo said, elbowing her way in.

She grabbed the powered crowbar still clipped to her tool belt and jammed it into the door. With a grunt, Clo heaved. The metal door only moved an inch. Not wasting any time, Eris wrapped her fingers around the crowbar to add leverage. Nyx slammed the button again, and between the force and that godsdamned generator waking up, the door finally, *finally* opened.

They all dove through. Nyx twisted to close the door and it slammed shut with a heavy, metallic *bang*.

Too close for comfort, Clo heard the roar of air leaving the loading bay. "My gods," she murmured, patting herself. "We almost died. I almost died. That fluming berm almost killed us."

"Get up," Eris said shortly, pushing to her feet. She leaned against the door to peer into the porthole. "Oh, *son of a bitch*."

They crowded around the window of the door. Both *Asteria* and *Zelus*'s bullet crafts were gone, the loading bay empty. The engines on smaller ships were so silent, they hadn't even heard them over the main hum of *Zelus*.

Clo gaped. "He's stolen my bogging ship!"

Ariadne's voice sounded through the speakers. "I can't tell if he's in the bullet craft or the other ship from here."

Clo shoved away from the door and sprinted as fast as her leg would allow down the hall back to the command center, the footsteps of the others echoing behind her. "He'll be in *Asteria*, definitely. It has the supplies. The bullet craft is a diversion."

"Should I fire at him?"

Clo paused. *Don't,* she wanted to say. *Try something else. Not* Asteria. *Not my ship.*

It wasn't just some stupid hunk of metal she'd pieced together. It was the only thing she had left of Briggs. She knew every wire, every nick on its nose, every twist of its corridors. She could point out each part that they had painstakingly added, and the purpose they all served. That part for speed. That part for emergencies. That part for luck.

Eris caught up to Clo, and a flicker of shock registered in her features. Clo didn't want to explain. How could she explain to a princess who was raised never to care for anyone? Who saw everyone and everything as disposable? A tool to be used or destroyed.

Clo swallowed the painful lump in her throat. "Fire," she said on an exhale, her voice breaking. "Kill the bastard."

She ran through a corridor that was not hers. *Zelus* was too big, too sprawling, too Tholosian. It wasn't safe. It wasn't *home*.

The ship shuddered as it fired.

She reached the command center. Ariadne was on her tiptoes, hands curled around the controls, tense. Rhea hovered behind her, resting her hands comfortingly on the smaller girl's shoulders.

"*Asteria*'s shields are down fifty percent, but they're holding," Ariadne said. "We need to hurry before he jumps."

Of course the shields were holding; Clo and Briggs had added the tech themselves. "He can't jump; the ship needs to rest from chasing *Zelus*," Clo said. "Let me do this."

Ariadne slid out of the way.

After *Asteria*, the controls of *Zelus* felt wrong. *Everything* felt wrong.

Clo shut her eyes briefly. "I'm sorry, Briggs," Clo whispered, and fired thrice. The turrets on the bottom of the ship powered up, and the ship shuddered as the projectiles released.

Asteria jumped. The blasts hit nothing; they zoomed out into the dark expanse of the galaxy.

The five women stared at the empty space where the ship had been. If the weapons had been just that much faster, Clo would have seen the hull of her ship glow with damage before that bright blast of kinetic and nuclear energy flared blue, leaving nothing but a dark husk behind.

Clo's favorite ship had disappeared into a bogging wormhole.

Clo sputtered. "He shouldn't have been able to— He just—" She made a frustrated noise and blasted the drifting bullet craft in frustration. It gave a tiny flash, and then it darkened.

"He might not have made it to the other side," Rhea whispered from beside Clo.

The other woman's voice was soothing. Clo didn't want it. She was fluming *furious*, and now they had to run because that bastard had probably alerted the nearest outpost.

With her ship.

Her godsdamned ship.

Clo rubbed the back of a hand against her eyes, blinking back tears. She shifted her hands on the controls, flipping switches. This was going to be rough. "Everyone buckle in and hold on." She couldn't keep the roughness from her voice. "We need to get the flame out of here before he can signal our coordinates."

"And if he left a tracker in the jump drive?" Ariadne said as she strapped herself into one of the chairs.

"I checked for them, found one and destroyed it, but I'll jump twice more in quick succession, just in case." She started mapping out the coordinates. Her hands shook, trying to do everything perfectly but quickly. "Get ready."

Clo turned on the hyperdrive. *Zelus* quivered. Time itself seemed to pause, and then the pinpoints of stars shifted from white to blue, then violet, then disappeared to ultraviolet. The hazy blue of cosmic rays came into view, then sharpened to white in the center. Clo let out her breath. She loved this feeling, jumping lightyears, bending time and space. It felt like magic, like she took the power of the seven gods for herself.

The ship slowed, stilled. Before them was the quiet of space. Clo let her heart rate calm before she started the whole process again. Up there, without true gravity and atmosphere, she felt no star sickness. There was only the joy of slipping through the void, of doing something that humans were not meant to do. To conquer the stars.

They jumped again, and Clo closed her eyes. She took her hands off the controls, just for a moment, to open her arms wide.

15.

Present day

"**S**ilt." Clo's Snarl swear was barely a whisper, but Eris heard it as loud as a Morsfire. "Silt, silt, *silt.*"

Eris unbuckled herself from her chair, glancing at the other women huddled across the deck, whispering among themselves. They seemed distracted enough not to cause trouble. For now.

"What is it?" she asked, stepping up beside Clo.

Clo gave a small shake of her head. "We might be in deep mud. I don't know yet." Clo had been quiet for so long as she raced the ship through space, but she was on edge again. "There's a call coming through the command deck. No identifier."

Damn. Eris had started to relax—they had passed outposts without incident for hours—every part of her tensed on high alert.

If the pilot managed to make it through his jump in *Asteria* alive, he might have been able to hail a Tholosian ship by now. The Oracle would be hunting for *Zelus*. As long as they were in Tholosian space, they weren't out of danger. Ariadne had put up a block for scanners, but Eris didn't know the girl's skills well enough to trust them.

"Can you track the signal?" Eris asked Clo.

"No." Clo pressed her lips together in frustration. "It's blocked. Could it be Nova? You contacted headquarters, right?"

"Hours ago," Eris said softly. "I'm not sure it went through. I didn't get a response." That wasn't exactly uncommon; Nova was constantly barraged by dust storms. She worried her lip. They'd have to pick up; they had no choice. If it was a Tholosian ship, an ignored call would alert the Oracle. "Answer it."

Clo looked at Eris sharply. "You're sure?"

Eris's hand crept to her blaster. She was subordinate, just another piece of the spy network, but aboard this ship, she was leader. A general of a small group of women who depended on her to survive.

She would not fail them.

"I'm sure." As Eris reached for the headset, she put her other hand on Clo's shoulder in a gesture of reassurance she'd used back when they were friends. "I'll handle it."

Clo stiffened at Eris's touch, then shrugged it off. "Fine." Her voice was hard. She nodded once as the call went through.

Eris put on a false voice as she spoke into the headset's microphone. "In Tholos's name, this is *Zelus*."

A familiar snort almost made Eris collapse with relief. Almost. "You've fucked up, haven't you?" Kyla asked.

<*Oh, thank the gods.*> Clo sprawled in her chair, relieved. <*I thought we were dead.*>

<*Don't be so sure. She sounds like she wants to kill us.*>

"We may have hit a small snag," Eris said to Kyla.

Clo's laugh was low. <*Small. Like, the way a* small *asteroid destroys all the life on a whole planet. Nice one, marshbrain.*>

Eris scowled at her.

"There are reports on Myndalia of several skirmishes, and videos of you and Clo have been put up all over the communication systems, Eris. It's only a matter of time before the Oracle finds out you've commandeered that ship and puts out notice that a Tholosian craft of interest has been stolen, so I'm going to amend my statement to a *monumental fuck-up*." She made a noise of derision. "Prepare the loading bay. I'm almost there and I'm going to dock. We'll talk then."

Kyla hung up.

"So." Eris removed the headset. "That went well."

"We're fucked, aren't we?" Clo asked.

"Yep. Once Kyla boards, she's going to ask where the crew went." Eris tipped her head back and heaved a sigh. "This is a mess."

"*We* made a mess," Clo said. "But the mission could have been salvaged. These three kind of made it worse."

Eris glanced back at the other women. The little girl—Ariadne—was animatedly discussing something, waving her hands around for emphasis. She elbowed Nyx, who reluctantly smiled back. Had Eris ever been that happy? She'd had moments of laughter—small, stolen ones with Xander. When she forgot about who they were, and that she was supposed to kill him. When she took his firewolf figurine out of its permanent place in her pocket and remembered someone in the universe cared about her. That was happiness, of a sort, too.

And she'd had them with Clo, before their last mission. Nights staring out at the sands of Nova. Alcohol to soothe the guilt.

Her friendships had a history of not ending well.

"They were scared," Eris murmured. "Running isn't a decision made lightly. Fear makes you do desperate things."

Clo gave her a sharp glance. "How would you know? Don't they train it out of you?"

"No. No, they didn't." She ignored the first part of the question.

A *beep* of an oncoming ship requesting to board sounded. The screen showed Kyla's craft anchoring itself to the loading bay. "Let her in. Let's get this over with."

Clo flipped the switches to open the shaft doors. "Done. It'll take her a few minutes to dock." She pointed her chin at the strangers. "What about them?"

Eris studied the three with a calculating, narrowed gaze. "The little girl and the courtesan seem fine. The soldier? Thinking about killing us."

Clo made a face.

"You know I'm right." Eris lifted a shoulder. "Let Kyla handle them."

As if sensing they were being discussed, the women all looked over. Eris didn't change her expression. Let them try and kill her. They'd just be three more in a very, very long line of corpses. The God of Death would only receive more offerings from His favorite subject.

"Just to let you know," Rhea called, "I have freakishly good hearing."

"Great!" Clo called back. She turned back to Eris. *<We need to convince Kyla to get them off this ship and take them with her.>*

<Ready for them to go so soon? I saw the way you looked at the courtesan earlier. I think sexy spy *is your type.>*

Clo's head reared back and she looked angry enough to hit Eris. *<Are you sluiced? Is this all a fluming joke to you? Maybe* you're *used to constantly being in mortal danger, but I'm not. If there are videos of us, then there's probably a bounty on our heads. We don't know these women. That courtesan is a very pretty liability.>*

Eris crossed her arms. *<So, you do think she's cute.>*

<Enough,> Clo said sharply. *<Between the courtesan's hearing, the tattooed one's glaring, and that little girl's smiles—which are way too friendly, and no one is that friendly—I'm going to snap. We're done for.>*

Before Eris could respond, Nyx snapped, "Okay, what the fuck is going on?"

Eris and Clo startled as Nyx strode across the command center, the other two women at her heels. The soldier had her eyes narrowed. "You two," she said, gesturing with a finger. "You stare at each other in silence longer than any people I've ever seen outside of an interrogation. What the fuck?"

Ariadne gasped in delight. "Oh! Oh oh oh! I know!" she clapped her hands. "You're using the Pathos, right? Oh my gods, this is so exciting."

"Uhhh," Clo said, glancing at Eris in panic. *<How does she know about Pathos? It's Novan tech.>*

<I have no idea.>

Ariadne came closer and peered around at the top of Clo's skull. Clo pulled back with an offended noise.

"Ohhh, your incision is so tiny. I wish I could see the device. It's my *favorite* design. Took me ages to get it right. I can't wait to run more testing on my new beta model."

<Her what?> Eris tried to hide her shock.

"Your *what*?" Clo echoed.

The walls shuddered as Kyla's ship fully anchored to the docking bay.

Eris released a soft swear. Great timing. Just great. "Hold that thought," she said to Ariadne. "My superior from Nova will want answers."

Ariadne smiled serenely. "Okay." When Nyx stepped forward, Ariadne put her hand out to stop the soldier. "It's fine, Nyx. We'll wait here."

That kid was starting to freak Eris out.

Clo strode after Eris. Once they were out of earshot of the other women, she hissed, "What the flark?"

Eris shook her head. "I don't know."

"Seriously. Who *is* that kid?"

"I don't know that, either."

But she planned to find out.

Their boots pounded across the metal walkway that led to the docking bay. Just down the long hallway, the doors opened, and Kyla strode through. Their commander was all business, as usual: hands clasped behind her back, a steely no-nonsense glint in her eye.

"Status update," Kyla said when she reached Clo and Eris.

Clo crossed her arms. "We're really confused, for a start."

"Cloelia, I'm not in the mood. My current level of patience is hovering around zero. If it dips any lower, I will put you on septic duty at Nova and you can clean up everyone's shit for the foreseeable future." Kyla looked at Eris. "Eris, update."

Eris barely suppressed a grimace. "I'll start with the bad news."

"Good approach. Improve my mood from there."

"There are three women still on board *Zelus*. They claim to be refugees fleeing the Empire and they want the Novantae's protection." At Kyla's intense expression, Eris added, "One of them murdered the entire crew, including the Legate."

Kyla's lips thinned. "So, what you're telling me is that my original assessment was an understatement. This is an *astronomical* fuck-up."

"Hey," Clo said defensively. "This isn't our fault. The crew was dead when we boarded."

"You shouldn't be on this ship. You—" Kyla inhaled and pinched the bridge of her nose. "Who are they and why are they running?"

"I don't know," Eris said. She gestured for them to follow her back to the command center. "They're each valuable to the Archon for their specific skills: military leader, engineer, courtesan. They claim they've planned for almost a year to escape and join the Novantae. Before we took them to Nova, we figured we'd call you." She let Kyla through the door of the command center first. "As for the cargo you asked me to gain intel on, that's just as much a mystery. You have to see it."

The three women's heads rose as they entered. Nyx's face remained unchanged—still stuck in a permanent, threatening scowl. Rhea gave Kyla a considering once-over, and Ariadne smiled lopsidedly.

Kyla studied the women with the ruthless gaze Eris remembered well from when she first defected. She recalled the weight of it, the way Kyla seemed to look deep inside her soul and somehow knew whether she was telling the truth or a falsehood. Eris had learned to lie well under her father's tutelage, but it was after she'd left the Empire that her skill blossomed. It was how she'd survived within the Novantae: to become so useful to the rebellion that they would never be tempted to replace her. A good-enough skill made a resistance fighter indispensable.

Still, Eris often wondered if Kyla was so good at detecting the truth that she saw right through her.

Rhea and Ariadne shifted uncomfortably under Kyla's assessment. Nyx took a small step forward, easing her body in front of the other two, as if she were ready to fight to protect them. As if she were ready to *kill*.

Any lingering suspicion Eris had wavered. That sort of instinctive gesture wasn't unfamiliar among Tholosian soldiers, but only with members of their own cohort—those who had been genetically engineered within the same group, with the same traits. Never for strangers—not unless the soldier was truly deprogrammed. That natural reflex to take a blast for them couldn't be faked.

Kyla smoothed over her own surprise. "I'm Kyla," she said. "Co-commander of the Novantae."

At that, Ariadne perked up. *"Kyla?"*

Kyla's expression didn't change. "I hope so."

Ariadne rushed over and thrust out her hand. "I'm Ariadne."

Eris had never seen Kyla actually blanch before. "Holy shit," Kyla exhaled. *"The* Ariadne?"

Ariadne laughed. "I hope so!"

Clo leaned closer to Eris. "I'm so confused."

"Gods," Kyla was still saying, even as she shook the other girl's hand. "*Gods*. I had no idea you'd be so . . ."

"Amazing?" Ariadne asked, looking like she was damn well about to twirl.

"Young," Kyla said bluntly.

Ariadne bristled. "I'm sixteen. Practically an adult."

The kid looked younger than that. Kyla glanced at Clo and Eris. "For the last few years, Ariadne has been responsible for a lot of our intel and technological advances. She's the only reason our spies have been able to get in and out of places without the Oracle detecting them."

Gods. "You really did design Pathos."

Ariadne tilted her head. "Of course! I'd never lie about my best invention."

Eris was still skeptical. The Novantae's tech and spy network had improved leaps and bounds over the last few years, but how could one person—a mere child, really—be responsible?

"Are you sure?" she asked Kyla. "Your tech person could be anyone."

Ariadne curled a lip. "Are you calling me a liar?"

Kyla held out her hands, placating. "Yes, I'm sure. I've never revealed Ariadne's name to anyone, not even Sher." She softened. "Why did you run? Are you in danger?"

A flicker of fear showed in the young girl's face. "I was becoming obsolete." At Kyla's frown, Ariadne forced a smile. "And I didn't like it there. So I'm here. We're here. Okay?"

Kyla nodded slowly. "Okay." She kept her voice low, soothing. This was more gentleness than Eris had ever seen in her superior. "Can you show me the cargo that was on board?"

"It's just some weird, hazardous rock," Clo said. "Ariadne has it."

Ariadne passed the glove-covered rock to Kyla, who donned another glove from the pocket of her jumpsuit. The commander examined the small stone, turning it this way and that. Eris thought she saw a bit of a glow emanating from the inside, but it could have been a trick of the light.

"What do you think, Eris?" Kyla murmured. "Could it be a weapon component?"

Kyla passed Eris her other glove. After putting it on, she took the rock from Kyla and smoothed her thumb across the rough surface. She held it up to the light and there it was. A faint glimmer inside, like fire trapped beneath foggy glass.

"If it is, it's not anything I've ever seen," Eris said.

"Or," Clo said, finally losing her patience, "it's literally *just a rock.*"

Nyx curled her lip. "Listen, jackass. It happens to be a rock that Prince Damocles ordered twenty of the Archon's best soldiers to guard. Does that sound like the kind of military resources they'd waste? Come on."

"Or," Clo argued, "how do we know this wasn't just some ruse to lure the Novantae out of hiding? Even if you're not spies, you could have accidentally lead them to us. Right, Eris?"

Eris had to concede that was a good point. "She's right."

Kyla reluctantly showed her agreement. "The Archon has been retaliating against the Novantae since we were blamed for Princess Discordia's death. Every pretender only makes him more determined to destroy us." She shook her head. "For all we know, another stupid, desperate woman made the mistake of claiming to be the long-lost general and was executed over it."

If Eris's father suspected she was actually alive and had defected to his enemies, it would be a disaster. She and the Novantae had had to stage her death in a ship crash with an asteroid. As it was, she'd barely made it out alive. The Tholosians recovered the wrecked ship, and the rumors began when her body was never found.

After that, many, many women tried to claim they were General Discordia. Facial shifters gave them the ability to change their features to resemble those of the princess—easily done, as her icons were in every city on every Empire planet in several galaxies. Some pretenders were said to be Evoli trying to gain entrance into the royal palace on Tholos to spy on the Archon and learn the secrets of the Oracle. Others were impoverished citizens from different slums who had a natural resistance to the Oracle's brain uploads, seeking what they assumed would be a better, more privileged life.

But the Archon knew his daughter. No one could mimic the results of how he'd trained her. To prove themselves, he would show pretenders the same brutality she'd endured once and survived without complaint, without tears.

Above all, without screaming.

No ordinary human would have survived such conditions. Not the engineered, and certainly not the natural-born who managed to escape the slums.

Eris shoved down the guilt she always felt when she thought about those women. *They shouldn't have done it. They should have just let me stay dead.*

"I would know if another pretender had come to the palace," Ariadne said. "All clearance went through me. Besides, I understand the Oracle. I grew up with One."

Eris blinked at her in surprise. "You *grew up* with the Oracle?"

If Ariadne had been at the palace that long, she would have seen Eris before she'd permanently changed her features. Eris had heard about One's Engineer, but . . .

"How long have you been Engineer?" she couldn't help but ask.

Ariadne looked uncomfortable. "All my life. The Oracle had my genetics designed to One's specifics, and had my brain altered after birth to enhance my logical-mathematical intelligence so I could check One's programming. I was the Oracle's—" She pressed her lips together and took a step back, shaking her head. "Look, I promise you: One had no idea we were on this ship. I was very careful. I didn't even risk contacting Kyla to warn her."

Rhea stepped in front of her. "And so were Nyx and I. We wouldn't have left if we feared discovery." She let out a breath and squared her shoulders. "You're just going to have to trust us on this."

"I don't care if they trust us," Nyx said with a scowl. "Let me just be clear here: my allegiance isn't to Tholos anymore, and it sure as shit isn't to the Novantae. I'm only here to ensure these two"—she jerked her head toward Rhea and Ariadne—"could bargain for a safe relocation on a planet away from the Empire."

That captured Eris's attention. Nyx looked to be in her early twenties, so when Eris escaped Tholos, Nyx would have still been undergoing the harsh training reserved for members of the royal guard. Eris's own training was similar but separate, and entirely under the devoted and ruthless attentions of her father.

Both lessons included eliminating weaknesses by having them beaten out of her. Affection was a weakness. Friendships were weaknesses, unless it was your cohort. All you had were loyalty and Tholosian patriotism, drilled into you until you no longer questioned or doubted the superiority of the Empire. Until you truly believed—with your entire heart—that everyone else who rebelled deserved to be executed, and every planet outside of it needed to be conquered.

"And you?" Eris found herself asking. "What do you want?"

She didn't look away when Nyx's harsh gaze met her own. "I want to go a day without executing someone," Nyx said. "I can't do it anymore."

Eris went still, remembering her words to Sher when she first defected to the Novantae. *I can't do it anymore.* Not after Xander. Not after the terrible things she had been commanded to do.

As stony and indifferent as Nyx's expression was, Eris recognized the same weariness. It was the cold, hard truth that no matter what either one of them did, or how many people they tried to save, it would never make up for the things they had done.

Eris studied the tattoos on the side of Nyx's face. The thick, jagged lines around her brow and across her cheekbone. Among the royal guard, it was an honor to wear the marks, but it also meant they could never defect. Never hide.

"Okay." Eris gestured to the tattoos. "Do you want those removed?"

"You can do that?" Though Nyx sounded impassive, her breathing hitched to a slightly ragged cadence.

If Eris had needed further proof that these women were genuine, that was it. No one still loyal to the Tholosian Empire would opt to have their tattoos removed; they'd die first.

Clo looked at Eris in surprise. "Seriously? She's *military.* Are we just going to forget the fact that those tattoos mean she's killed a silt-ton—"

"You should know better than anyone why that doesn't matter to me," Eris snapped. "I believe in second chances. Kyla?"

The Novan commander glanced up from the rock and assessed Nyx's tattoos. "Those will take at least three removal sessions. Maybe five. Still want them gone?" At Nyx's nod, Kyla said, "Clo, grab the laser and strap her down. Nyx, I hope you have a high pain threshold, because this is going to hurt like you've been sent straight to Avern."

16.

ERIS

Present day

Nyx lay on the reclining chair in the medical bay, two decks down from the command center. Clo lingered in the corner, arms crossed. Eris had secured the leather straps around Nyx's wrists and ankles to keep her still while Kyla painstakingly lasered the tattoos off her face. The laser sizzled, and the air smelled of burned flesh.

Eris had seen Kyla do this for various Novan crews over the years. It wasn't just royal guards who were marked for identification purposes. The Archon marked servants, soldiers, and prisoners. The gerulae wore the scythes on their cheeks. The marks were a message, both *I own you* and *You will never be more than this.*

Eris could count on one hand the number of people who made it through the multiple sessions required to remove most Tholosian tattoos. Her father and previous Archons did that on purpose; the heavy metals native to Tholos were used to create ink, spread with nanotech inserted through the needle so the tattoo went deep beneath the surface of the dermis and marked bone. Leftover scars would be visible on Nyx's face, requiring further treatments to smooth away.

Nyx's lips pressed into a thin line while Rhea gripped her cuffed hand. The soldier never moved, never hissed in pain. If Nyx twitched at all, Rhea smoothed a thumb across her wrist in a single, comforting stroke. Eris noticed Nyx grimace, and she couldn't tell if it was the pain or Rhea's touch.

"Does it hurt?" Clo asked as Kyla lasered the intricate design on Nyx's cheek.

Nyx's eyes narrowed, but she didn't flinch as Kyla ran the wand across her cheekbone. "What the fuck do you think?" she asked when Kyla paused.

"Nyx," Rhea chastised.

Kyla slowly slid the tip of the laser across the jagged lines that branched beneath Nyx's eyes.

"Most people pass out by now; that's all," Clo said.

"I'm not most people," Nyx said tightly, moving her mouth as little as possible.

"I suppose that's true." Eris craned her neck for a better view. At Clo's questioning look, Eris explained, "Members of the royal guard have training so strict and brutal, they consider war a respite. That laser is like trying to beat her unconscious with a spoon."

Even so, Nyx held the pain in better than most.

Stop it, Eris, she told herself. *It's not admirable. That training wasn't admirable. It was messed-up. Xander told you that, remember? He used to have nightmares. He used to—*

"How do you know that?" Nyx asked.

Eris kept her expression even. A soldier like Nyx would have been taught to recognize the slightest shift in features, anything that would give away emotion.

Kyla supplied the answer for Eris. "Intel," the commander said casually. "The Novantae know about the training for Tholosian soldiers. We have a few defectors, myself included."

Nyx turned her stony gaze on Kyla. "I've heard nothing about defectors from the royal guard."

Kyla continued her strokes down Nyx's cheek to her chin. The hum of the laser wand filled the silence. "Of course you haven't. Sher and I gave them new identities and staged their deaths. Made it look like they perished in skirmishes with the Evoli."

Nyx closed her eyes as Kyla ran the laser over where the tattoos dipped below her chin. After another minute, Kyla turned off the laser and leaned back. "That should do it for the first treatment." She undid the straps around Nyx's wrists and handed her a serum. It contained a pale echo of the nanites in Eris's blood. Not cheap, and not something the resistance could afford to give away. "Put this on to speed up the healing, and I'll start another treatment in a few hours."

They all returned to the command center to find Ariadne still laboring over the sample rock in a small glass side room usually reserved for pilot and copilot to rest between shifts. She'd snagged a massive dome light from the med center, and wore one of the ship's jumpsuits for an extra layer of protection.

"Any luck with that rock, or are we throwing it into space?" Eris asked.

Ariadne brushed the dust from the rock with one of her tools and peeked inside, the light reflecting off the visor of her helmet. "Well, the interior emits a luminescence," her voice said through her helmet's comms. "The basic tests came up empty, *and* it has unique, unidentified endospores that release with any hard impact."

Clo wrinkled her nose. "Translate that, please."

"Dormant bacterial morphotypes," Ariadne explained, as if that would help. "Resistant to tough conditions on certain planets. But that's it. I can't do much more without running it through an analyzer."

Nyx scoffed. "So. We have nothing so far."

Ariadne looked cheerful. "Not nothing. It's so shiny!"

"Kid, you're not helping."

A high chime echoed from the comms. Every ship in the galaxy was fitted with an announcer that received royal proclamations. Even the Novantae didn't dare remove them; they needed to see proclamations live just like everyone else. They were that rare.

Eris recalled the last proclamation vividly. Shortly after Eris had defected, she was in the medical suite at Nova, recovering from injuries sustained while staging her death. That ringing had sounded throughout headquarters—and the whole empire—a klaxon announcing her death.

Even though the Novantae had staged her ship's crash to look like an accident, the Archon used it as an excuse to blame the Evoli, retaliating and threatening to reignite all-out war.

How many deaths resulted? Eris was the one who chose to leave. She knew what she risked.

The chimes faded. The lights dimmed and the screen over the main controls clicked on. The live feed showed the Secretary to the Archon standing at the podium of the throne room, speaking the formal introductions. Behind him was the glimmering marble slab of the dais, with the simple seat from which her father took his appointments. The Archon sat, regal in his clean, pressed black military uniform and gold threads.

It was the first time Eris had seen her father in three years. He looked so much older, even with plenty of years left in his reign. Body mods reserved only for members of the royal family allowed them to live longer than humans did naturally; her father was approaching one hundred and eighty-six Old World years. But Eris didn't remember those gray streaks in his jet-black hair, or the sharp lines across his forehead. His expression was as stern as she remembered. Every bit as cold.

For a few years, she had known her father better than anyone. He was her captain, her trainer, and her tormentor. He only ever allowed a slight glimpse of emotion after she completed a training session. She'd be bleeding on the floor, and he'd approach, smooth down her hair, and whisper: *On your feet, Discordia.*

Clo tapped her metallic toes impatiently as the Secretary yielded the floor to the Archon. "What does he want?"

Rhea sighed. "He's made a difficult decision."

"How would you know?" Eris pressed.

Rhea gave her a look that said it all.

"Archons aren't supposed to take courtesans." Eris's words were hollow. She thought her father had honored that vow.

If Eris had continued on the path to become the first Archontissa, she would have taken that vow to the God of Death to be His Hand, and in that oath was a promise to forsake all others: family, lovers, friends. Death required impartiality, the knowledge that He would come for everyone at the right time, and it was at His will. Devotion to such a deity meant a ruler must sacrifice worldly pleasures that could lead to a deeper connection; a soul could not share space with the God of Death, for He owned it and in death it would be His.

Resentment tightened in Eris's chest. She'd accepted that her devotion to their gods was as flawed as a cracked vase. And in the end, her father was just as weak as she was. He was simply better at hiding it.

Rhea's face stayed smooth as glass. "We were rarely intimate in the way you're thinking—he had another courtesan for that—but he needed someone to listen. I was considered to be Damocles's, but the Archon came some nights. Often, I suspect, because he was curious about his Heir's chosen." Rhea nodded to the screen. "Out here, he looks calm. He could never hide behind that with me."

Eris's breath caught. Rhea had been her brother's chosen. He, too, disregarded the vow. As much as emotions warred within her, Eris already wondered how they could use this to their advantage. What weakness might her brother have divulged, whispered among satin pillows in the Pleasure Garden? How long had he gone to this woman? And her father? Rhea looked so young.

Eris tried to hide her troubled expression. "You're what? Nineteen?"

"Twenty-one."

Show nothing. Eris didn't want Rhea to assume she held judgment for *her* or for the other courtesans. No, all her feelings were reserved for her father and brother and what they must have done to make this woman risk death to run.

Still, she had to ask, "How can you sound fond of him?"

If Rhea was offended by that, she didn't show it. "He is a complicated man. But if I condoned the things he did, I wouldn't be here."

The Archon began speaking. Eris was distracted by his voice—the deep, rolling Tholosian accent that was deliberately intended to lull the masses. She knew she should hate him for everything he did—everything he did to *her*—but she didn't.

Until his words broke the spell. "—negotiating a truce with the Evoli leaders, the Oversouls. In just under a month's time, once our negotiations are complete, we will sign a formal declaration for peace at a ceremony on the Evolian planet Laguna. It will be broadcast across our galaxies, in every corner of our Empires. The Evoli and Tholosians have been at war for over five centuries. It's time we ended it."

The screen went black and they all stared at it in varying measures of shock.

"He's lying," Clo finally said, her breathing sounding a bit ragged. She looked wildly at Eris. "Right? I don't trust him. Do you?"

That drew a sharp glance from Nyx, who didn't miss anything.

"I don't know," Eris murmured. "With Charon no longer producing crops, the Empire's resources are too strained to support its population. The Evoli have more resource-rich planets in their galaxy."

"Then what would the Evoli get out of it?" Clo asked, incredulous.

Eris considered that. "Water. The Three Sisters have a great deal of fresh water between them," Eris said, referring to Tholos, Macella, and Agora, a trio of populous planets in the same system. "And perhaps the Evoli are tired of wasting supplies, time, and lives fighting. What do you think, Kyla?"

The commander pressed her lips together. "I need to make a call."

"I'm guessing your intel said nothing about a truce," Nyx drawled.

"No." Kyla was quietly furious. "No, it didn't."

17.

Present day

Ariadne wasn't sure what to think about the proclamation. She didn't know the Archon well enough to discern if he was lying, and her military experience was limited to ship comings and goings and their cargo. The Oracle had sheltered her from most things growing up—except the images of the dead.

See, Ariadne? One would have said. *This is what it's like beyond these walls. Death, destruction, war—humans are a violent species. One had these urges controlled in your synapses when One engineered you. You would never survive out there, child. And that's why One is keeping you.*

Ariadne's breath caught. "Well," she said, hoping no one noticed how she forced the brightness into her voice, "that was interesting." She lifted the rock in her glove-clad hand and stared at it through the visor of her helmet. *Focus on what you know.* "Maybe this *is* just a rock, then, if it's not meant to hurt the Evoli."

Nyx didn't look convinced as she approached the glass door of Ariadne's small nook. Ariadne could see why pilots and copilots liked resting in there between shifts. It was perfect for a blanket pile and some starwatching. Or makeshift rock tests.

Nyx gestured to the gemstone and spoke through the comm. "Just don't touch it and don't take off your mask when you're drilling at it. It might not be a weapon, but until we figure out what it is, consider it dangerous."

Ariadne smiled. "I'm going to name it Josephine. A pretty name for a dangerous rock."

Josephine was a good name. She would have added the rock to her collection of Named Things she kept on her desk at the Temple on Tholos, where she resided alone, surrounded by the Oracle's programming screens. Sometimes the Oracle, as sentient and clever as One was, sensed One's daughter was lonely and had the palace couriers bring gifts to the doorstep of the Temple: rocks, plants, dolls.

Ariadne named all of them. Stupid names, silly names, human names. Like Josephine.

Eris looked at her with a bemused expression. Ariadne still wasn't sure how she felt about her. She was a little scary, and not like Nyx. Ariadne could trust Nyx to have her back, to protect her. When Eris looked at people, it was like she was weighing the costs of either killing them or keeping them alive. Not comforting.

"You're not naming the rock," Nyx said, exasperated.

"Oh, but I am. I've decided," Ariadne said.

Ariadne placed the rock back inside the protective glove, wrapped it up tight, and put it in her pocket. The door gave a soft hiss as she came out of the glass room. Her helmet came off with an easy *click*. Rhea gave Ariadne an amused look and reached out to smooth down her hair. It felt *so* nice.

"Rhea." Ariadne smiled. "Do *you* like my rock's name?"

"Of course I do, sweet," Rhea said. "You came up with it."

Nyx rolled her eyes. "Can we get back to the topic at hand? I don't believe that bastard about this truce. The Empire's resources might be more strained, but that's happened before in the Empire's history. The Archon just conquers another planet, fights another battle. Kills a bunch of people. So, I'm still pretty convinced that the rock—"

"*Josephine*," Ariadne insisted.

"—is a weapon. And you want to give it a cute name?"

"It's a *good* name. I want to get a better look inside of it," Ariadne said. "It's shiny when I hold it to the light." Shiny, glittery, pretty. Definitely how she'd imagine a thing named Josephine would be.

"Are you cracked?" Clo looked like she wanted to confiscate the rock. "Who cares how shiny it is? It set off my mech cuff and you can't even identify what it is. If you open that thing up and your face melts off, you're on your own. We're locking you in the room with it."

Nyx looked at Clo sharply. "*We*? Speak for yourself. I'll shove you in a fucking room with it if you keep talking to her like that."

Clo's mouth snapped shut. Ariadne really loved Nyx. Really, really.

"If my face melts off, then you know it's a weapon," Ariadne insisted. Josephine was definitely going to be pretty inside; she'd seen a faint glimmer in it earlier, kind of like opal but with more light. "I can lay a few things out in the med center for a better makeshift lab and run a more thorough analysis once I open her up."

Clo shook her head. "I still think this is a bad idea." She gestured at Eris. "What do you think? You're supposed to be leading."

"This is important," Ariadne insisted. "We have to know why they were protecting this shipment."

The words tangled in her mouth; she wasn't used to speaking so much to people. Typing messages to Kyla back in the Temple was different. She could ponder her words and how they would be received. She could take her time, puzzle over the correct vocabulary.

Here? In person? Ariadne's vocal responses seemed insufficient to calm everyone. She didn't know how to make them happy. These women weren't Named Things, inanimate dolls or objects to sit on her desk that never had an opinion other than the ones she thought up for them. They were people—human beings—and she didn't know how to interact with anything but the practical thought process coded into the Oracle's mainframe that punished her for inefficiency.

Ariadne was just a girl. To a computer program a thousand years old, she was replaceable. Others had coded before her; others would after her. She survived by making herself useful, by being better than the others. She'd hoped that if she coded and improved the Oracle's sentience, that One would learn to feel things for Ariadne, to understand that she had needs, and wouldn't punish her if she got tired.

Lately, she was tired too often. *Obsolete.* Things that started to become obsolete ceased to work as efficiently.

That's when it was time to replace them.

Eris sighed. "Clo might have a point. We could have Kyla take the sample back to Nova and have someone in one of the labs at headquarters analyze it. They'd have a better idea of what it is."

No. No, no, no. Ariadne needed to prove her worth. She needed to make them realize she wasn't replaceable, not just some girl who had come to them begging for help like a lost pet, but intelligent, valued, important, efficient, *not obsolete*—

You're not here to make them happy. You don't have to please them with your responses or your work. They're not the Oracle. They won't punish you for failure.

She couldn't be sure of that.

Ariadne looked around wildly for Kyla. The co-commander had given her hope of escape. Of a different life. One still full of danger, but also with freedom. Away from the Oracle, from her Named Things that only offered company in the absence of anything better. It was all Ariadne could do not to propel herself into Kyla's arms and hug her around the waist as hard as she could.

But Kyla wasn't in the room, and she couldn't stop her breathing and it pushed too hard through her chest a *one to three four five in out in out in out* that started to *hurt*—

She felt a gentle hand between her shoulder blades. "Shhh," Rhea crooned. "You're fine. Me and Nyx are right here with you. Breathe."

Rhea smoothed her hand down Ariadne's spine, and a warm tingling spread across her skin. Her breathing calmed. Her heart slowed to a normal cadence. Ariadne could think again. Even so, she gave herself to that touch for a moment, to the comfort of it.

She'd never been touched before Rhea and Nyx. Not ever. She liked it. She *loved* it. The texture of skin—the whisper of it across her clothes in a downward stroke—soothed her more than the soft bed sheets back in the Temple.

"Thanks," she whispered to Rhea. Ariadne flushed when she looked at the others. Nyx had seen her have a panic attack once before, but not these strangers. "I need to look at the rock's interior," she said again. "With or without your permission. I'm doing it."

Eris considered her, those green eyes all too sharp and assessing.

Ariadne felt like she came up wanting. "All right. But if anything goes wrong, we're sealing up the lab and putting you in quarantine. Don't complain when you're stuck there."

Ariadne let out a little squeal, gathering materials and leading the way to the makeshift lab. It was in the little glass partitioned subsection of the med center with a series of metal work tables and instruments, there in case an onboard outbreak required quarantine.

"Nyx, can you come in with me?" The other woman was so strong, so imposing, that Ariadne felt just that little bit braver standing next to her.

Ariadne wriggled her gloved hands and donned her helmet once more. She waited as Nyx got into another jumpsuit and helmet.

Rhea, Eris, and Clo remained on the other side of the glass.

"Don't melt your face off," Eris muttered. "Kyla will kill me."

"We're taking proper precautions," Ariadne said.

"*Hopefully*," Eris said into the speaker from behind the glass.

"You worry too much," Ariadne sang. "We'll be fine. Josephine won't hurt us."

Eris rolled her eyes behind the partition before speaking into the microphone. "Josephine is an inanimate object of questionable origin. She can't make the decision. She can't make *a* decision." A pause, then: "And I can't believe you have me calling a rock *Josephine*."

"Alrighty, here we go," Ariadne said, putting on an affected accent. Nyx rolled her eyes, but Ariadne just grinned at her.

Ariadne sealed off the room and removed the rock from its protective glove. She turned it this way and that. She couldn't feel it, of course, but it looked completely unassuming.

"Josephine," she crooned, and then she picked up a low-heat Mors blade.

She started with the smallest cut, to ensure the interior was stable. There was a faint glow, the barest glimmer of startling topaz. She held it away, but the rock still felt cool and stable. She worked to carve a larger hole, but the Mors blade was having difficulty.

"Avern," Ariadne murmured. "This is going to take a while. The heat input on this is barely cutting it. The Mors blades back at the Temple are built for higher power consumption."

Next to her, Nyx shifted to get a better look at the microscope. "What are those?" she asked, pointing to the oblong shapes on the monitor.

"They're endospores releasing with the impact of the Mors blade," Ariadne explained.

"Anything we should be concerned about?"

Ariadne shrugged. "Possibly. They don't release with easy handling, but I wouldn't suggest doing this without a helmet."

For a few more minutes, she worked at carving into the rock, pausing only when the interior light increased. Through the glass, Rhea pressed her hands against the partition.

"Everyone all right?" Ariadne asked. Her question was pointed to Rhea, who had gone entirely still.

Rhea gave a small nod.

"So, if that thing is dangerous," Clo said into the mic, "what would happen to us?"

"Oh, who knows?" Ariadne gave a dismissive wave of a gloved hand. "But some substances can make you really sick from organ and bone marrow damage. Or you might start hemorrhaging. Or you can become incapacitated and eventually die. It's like a surprise! Only the surprise is your death and how quickly it happens."

"I shouldn't have asked."

After a check of the hazard meter on Clo's borrowed mech cuff—still stable—Ariadne only had eyes for the rock in front of her.

It was as though she held the warm honey of sunset on a summer's day in Tholos. She'd seen so many of those, through the little window in her workroom, wishing she could reach out and capture it, keep it close. She was mesmerized. By the gods, she'd never seen anything more beautiful.

Ariadne smiled smugly at Nyx. "See? Josephine is gorgeous."

"Does the ship's computer show any hazardous spikes?" Clo's voice sounded through the speakers. "Please tell me no. I don't want to hemorrhage and die."

Ariadne checked. "Nah, but it's still scanning the endospores that were just released. Stay behind the partition."

Ariadne shivered. Of course something so pretty would be dangerous. Wasn't that often the way of things? When Ariadne watched her vids, she remembered seeing explorations of a planet called Colchis. It had a flower called the Night Rose, which only bloomed once a year, when the moon was highest in the sky. It was considered to be the most beautiful in all of the Empire, and for those brief hours of its bloom, the poison on its petals killed any human who touched it within minutes.

Yes, beautiful things were always underestimated.

"So, what's the purpose of this?" Nyx asked, leaning closer, as if hypnotized by the subtly shifting colors. The inside of the rock was so vibrant it made fire opals look like cheap marbles in comparison.

"Maybe it's a gift?" Ariadne asked. "I mean, it's lovely enough. The Tholosians have a clear protective blocker they can use to paint these for jewelry. It costs a lot, but I've seen them do it with lustercite, which can kill people in its natural form. It's *so* sparkly." At Nyx's questioning look, Ariadne pressed her lips together. "On the vid-screens. I used to watch the holiday balls from the Temple."

Nyx stared at her for so long that Ariadne wondered if the other woman pitied her for such an admission. But in the end, Nyx just shook her head. "No, you're not turning it into a necklace. Too dangerous. And it looks flammable," Nyx said.

Ariadne opened her mouth but Nyx cut her off. "*No.* Absolutely not. We are not setting the hazardous rock on fire. Do you hear me?"

"Gods, you sound like a mother." Ariadne pretended to be annoyed, but really, she liked it. She'd never had a mother. Not a good one, anyway. "Let me run the analysis."

The analyzer ran composition through the Oracle's database, which stored details of every known and identified material in the galaxy. Ariadne herself had helped organize and maintain the database for Tholosian scientists exploring new planets for resources.

The analyzer beeped twice.

Ariadne frowned. "That's strange."

"What's strange?" Clo asked. "Oh, gods, am I going to die?"

Ariadne shushed her. "Nothing like that. Analysis has remnants of a record about *something*, but it's been almost completely wiped. The truncated entry shows that there are teeeeny tiny pockets that hold more endospores. But if those were identified and catalogued, that information was removed with the deleted log. The rest shows that this thing is extremely dense and hard. Very, very. You all saw how much the Mors struggled."

Nyx leaned in and gave a low whistle at the results. "Could they make it into a high-density blast?"

"That's a possibility."

"How possible?" Eris asked into the mic.

Ariadne gave it a thought. "Welllll, if—theoretically, of course—we were discussing another battle against the Evoli, I'd say that their armor has become extremely effective against Mors weaponry. And that—*theoretically*—this could puncture it." She put a finger up. "But, conversely, this brings me to my second thing: it could make some very, very pretty armor."

"Hmm," Eris said into the mic. "All right, put the damn rock into one of those canisters, get cleaned up, and meet us in the rec room down the hall."

Ariadne slid the glowing rock into the lead-lined canister and sealed it up tight.

She felt the loss of that sunlit glow. It had been that beautiful.

18.

Present day

"All clean." Ariadne breezed into the mess hall. "Josephine is back in her lead home."

"Good riddance," Clo muttered from where she stood at the cupboards. "You're not both sick, are you? No liquefied organs? No hemorrhaging? No bleeding from your eyes?" Her words were flippant, but underneath, Ariadne thought—hoped—that there was some genuine concern.

"I'm about to make you bleed from one of your eyes if you don't shut up." Nyx gestured to the plate Clo held. "What's that?"

"The Legate's rations," Clo said with a wicked grin. "No vat slop for us. Not immediately, anyway. Have a seat."

The room was filled with long, low gray tables, meant to be filled with soldiers, laughter, and jokes. Ariadne didn't like how big the ship was. She was used to small spaces. *Zelus* was meant for a hundred people instead of six, one of whom was responsible for the deaths of all on board.

Ariadne tried not to think about those deaths. She knew, though, that when she closed her eyes to sleep, she'd see them there. She wished she were strong like Nyx. She wondered if the other woman dreamed of everyone she had ever killed, if that impersonal way she handled the corpses of the soldiers and the Legate was all an act.

For Ariadne, she would always remember Nyx ordering her to close her eyes and cover her ears, because some things couldn't be unseen or unheard. But, still, Ariadne should have done more. She should have *helped*.

The doors to the mess hall creaked. Kyla entered, and Ariadne put on a bright smile. *Focus on here. Now.* Kyla, in real life, not filtered through codes and firewalls.

Kyla gave Ariadne a wan smile before approaching the larder. "Gods, everything is a mess." She nodded to Clo. "Serve me up some of that, would you? Is there any hooch in these cabinets?"

Clo fixed Kyla up a plate and handed it to her. "Legates aren't supposed to drink."

"If you don't think diplomats aren't occasionally drunk, raving bastards, you're more naive than I thought you were."

Eris looked over as Kyla grabbed her food and sat across from Ariadne. "What are they saying at Nova?"

"*Zelus's* official records said the ship and its crew were going to Paloma. The team at Nova is still trying to figure out if that's bullshit or a lead," Kyla said. "Nothing yet."

"And the truce?"

Ariadne took her own plate. She dipped a fork into the rich, red-brown sauce and brought it to her lips, savoring the flavor. The Oracle thought of food as nutrition and cared little for variety of flavor. Ariadne had drunk the same three meals, at the same time each day, all her life. Kykeon—a boring gruel. No seasoning. No flavor. Enough to survive but not to thrive. The Oracle preferred it because Ariadne could drink kykeon while she coded.

The first sweets she'd ever had were the ones Rhea had given her when they'd escaped. Ariadne had cried. And then later, she was sick. Rhea had held her in the dona chamber on the ship, soothing her as she shook, hand on the back of her neck. She was still introducing new food slowly over the four days they'd been on *Zelus*. Her jaw often cramped as the muscles became accustomed to chewing. She'd bitten her tongue more times than she cared to admit. The digestion tablets couldn't fully erase the discomfort and stomachaches.

But oh, the flavors. She had no idea what she was eating. But the chunks of meat had a firm texture, so different from the boring gloopy nutrient porridge she'd been raised on her whole life. Her tongue tingled with new sensations. There were little granules through the chunks, and more pieces of something a bit firmer and orange.

"Ariadne, are you listening?" Kyla asked.

Ariadne opened her eyes, startled. She shoved down her shame. Though the Oracle was more than aware of human physicality and understood the psychological advantages of food variety, Ariadne's meals were still kykeon ninety-five percent of the time. The Oracle would give her treats only if she'd truly proven herself.

The women here might know she'd been raised by the Oracle, but they had no idea—*no idea*—what that had been like. Even a kid growing up in the slums or on the poorest farm planet usually had some variety in their diet.

Let them wonder.

"Sorry," Ariadne muttered through a mouthful of food. "I'm listening."

Kyla stared at her pointedly before addressing the other women. "The Archon does want to make the truce with the Evoli official. There are rumors that Damocles is less keen, but he's falling into line."

There hadn't been any large-scale skirmishes with the Evoli since the Battle of the Garnet—the most devastating conflict in over fifty years. It was only after the Evoli Oversouls offered the Archon proof they were not involved in Discordia's death that he finally let up his military campaign against them, deciding it must have been the Novantae who were responsible for his daughter's crash.

Damocles had taken Discordia's place as general—the next Heir Apparent. But it was clear that the Archon had about as much regard for his son as most citizens in the Empire: a grudging acceptance of his claim to the throne.

Officially, Damocles had a right to sit on the dais. But Ariadne had read the newscasts, listened in on gossip in corners of the palace. Unofficially, even with the Oracle's programming, many questioned whether he was competent or even a fraction as capable as his sister. In whispers, of course. Everyone wondered if he'd be able to protect them from the Evoli once he took up the robe and double-bladed scythe.

Now, he might not have to.

"Of course, the news of this possible truce has not been well received by everyone in the Empire," Kyla added.

"No shit," Eris said. "The Oracle will have to rewrite One's programming. Even with control over citizens, completely reconfiguring their sentiments toward the Evoli is going to take some time. It might take a new generation of cohorts."

Tholosians were taught from birth to believe in conquest, in the superiority of their Empire. The Evoli were a threat that could not be tolerated, and the Tholosians had been at war with them for over five hundred years. Evoli were considered a risk to the Tholosian way of life. Demonized sorcerers. Majoi.

Ariadne had always wanted to meet one.

She'd read up on them in the Oracle's archives. Evoli had populated other planets in the solar system that contained their home planet Eve, but not as conquerors. They didn't crush other lifeforms—they shared resources.

Yet with Evoli abilities and technology, they had managed to defend themselves against the Tholosians. Evoli cloaking tech remained a mystery even to the Oracle; the Tholosian Empire could not even find Eve with its reconnaissance ships. They only knew the quadrant—just outside the Karis Galaxy—but each time they neared, their navigation failed and sent them into circles. Skirmishes and battles were confined to the planets on the outer edge of Evoli territory. The Evoli had retreated or been slaughtered but never colonized. Tholosian troops were more numerous, but the Evoli were nimble enough to outsmart them.

The Oracle always said it was the final civilization to be collected.

"I believe the rumors," Rhea said softly. "And I believe the Archon is sincere. After Charon's asteroid . . ." She shook her head. "Damocles had fierce fights with his father over how to feed the Empire once the food stores go dry. The Archon didn't want to risk the resources for another costly battle, but Damocles insisted conquering the Evolian planets was the only way our people could survive. The Archon controls the programming, but even the Oracle's powers can't flip a switch immediately in an Empire so sprawling. It's a risk, and one I suspect Damocles doesn't agree with. Discordia might have chosen differently, but we'll never know."

Ariadne tried to read everyone's emotions, something difficult for her at the best of times. Eris clenched her jaw and glanced away as if . . . irritated? Clo scowled. Rhea was resigned, perhaps. Nyx was Nyx.

"Rhea's probably right." Clo stabbed at her food. "You don't end five hundred years of hatred and war by signing a document and just expect everyone to go along with it. I might not have received the upload of the Oracle's bullshit straight into my brain every day, but we had our share of propaganda in the Snarl. More than half villainized the Evoli. *They are a threat to our civilization, our way of life*, remember? It's why even the rebels at Nova are still assholes to Elva and the other Evoli at headquarters."

Ariadne sat up straight. So did Rhea. There were Evoli in the resistance? She bit back all the questions she wanted to ask.

"And now we're without intel in the Temple," Kyla said, a flicker of regret in her features.

Ariadne felt some stirring of discomfort. She had staged this escape during a critical time, when her intel would have mattered most. She would have been in her pallet and its nest of pillows in the Temple, spying for Kyla, making sure Damocles really was on board with the treaty or only pretending.

"You said earlier that Damocles asked you to guard the cargo?" Kyla asked Nyx.

Nyx's back straightened. Ariadne knew she still struggled with the remnants of the Oracle's programming—the constant refrain that when your superior spoke, you came to attention. Nyx might not be under the Oracle's control anymore, but those old commands were still a part of her memories.

"Yep," Nyx said. "Along with two dozen other royal soldiers. And before you ask whether the Archon knew, he's been busy evaluating the damage on Charon, so my best guess is no."

Clo looked doubtful. "If Damocles were planning something behind his father's back, wouldn't the Oracle alert the Archon?"

"Oh." Ariadne breathed it softly, but everyone still turned to her. She ignored them for a moment, thinking back on her commands from the Oracle in recent months. Every. Single. One. "In the Temple," she finally said, "the Oracle and I have processed requests directly from

General Damocles for a while." She looked at the others helplessly. "I'm sorry; I was so distracted planning our escape without the Oracle's knowledge—which was not easy, I might add—that I didn't even notice right away that Damocles had taken over the Oracle's commands. I just . . ."

She bit her lip. It had been so hard. Rhea had no programming and Nyx had mostly broken through hers, but they'd had to slip through microscopic cracks in surveillance. Ariadne had to send bogus commands and hope—*hopeprayhope*—the Oracle didn't notice.

Obsolete. Forgetful. Inattentive.

One would have punished her over such a stupid mistake.

"Damocles has taken over the Oracle's commands from the Archon?" Kyla asked, gaze sharp. "How much?"

"Perhaps ten percent. Maybe more. I should have . . ." She trailed off.

"You were barely sleeping," Rhea said, clearly rattled, though her voice stayed gentle.

Didn't matter. It was a detail Ariadne should have caught.

Kyla was all business again. "Then we need to know more about this cargo so I have a solid answer on what it'll be used for. If Damocles is planning a coup, I want intel. Eris, there's an engineer on Macella who can be manipulated to give us more information on the shipment with the right push. We've used him before."

"Used?" Eris scowled. "Like sex used?"

Kyla pressed her lips together. "That's one way. He's also responded to patriotism, threats, and bribery. Choose a button and push it. It's your choice."

"Hmm." Eris considered her options.

"It won't be easy," Kyla continued. "We need to infiltrate the royal palace, find out whatever this rock is—"

"Josephine," Ariadne corrected helpfully. "She might be used to create a high-density blast or a pretty armor material."

Kyla pressed her lips together. "Fine. Assume that. We need to know what plot it's connected to. Gods help us if it's a fucking coup, because Damocles isn't exactly known for showing mercy."

Ariadne put the dishes in the cleaner, needing to stay busy. Kyla still hadn't said if the Novantae were actually going to let them stay, if they were going to have a new life out from under the shadow of the Empire. *Prove your usefulness. Prove your efficiency. Prove you're not just a waste of time and—*

Eris clicked her tongue against her teeth. "The palaces on Tholos, Macella, and Agora have spies, don't they? I helped—" At Kyla's guarded expression, Eris broke off. "What's that look? What haven't you told us?"

"We believe our operatives within the Three Sisters are dead," Kyla said shortly. "They've been going dark one by one for months. The most recent was just after this shipment."

Eris froze. "But how—"

"I don't know, Eris."

Ariadne flinched. She hated it when people yelled. The Oracle, for all of One's faults, never yelled. One was cold, with decisions often brutally practical. The Oracle had always stated outbursts were a weakness, yet another flaw within humans that clouded their ability to think, to make decisions.

They can't control themselves, Ariadne, the echo of the Oracle whispered in her mind. *What would they do to you, dear girl? You're so small, so frail. You can't program the weakness out of them, no matter how clever the code.*

A gentle touch on her arm. Rhea, of course, offering wordless comfort. Ariadne held on to her hand like a lifeline.

"Don't you dare snap at me, Kyla," Eris said, jaw tight. When Kyla opened her mouth, Eris interrupted. "And yes, I know that I am being deeply insubordinate. You and Sher sent me and Clo on a mission *knowing* your spies were likely being compromised and executed. That the same might have happened to us. And you didn't even bother to mention it."

Down the table, Clo crossed her arms and glared. "Now, that is a good point."

Kyla raised her chin. "ITI mission. You knew the risks and you both agreed. I didn't feel you needed to be aware of the other details."

"Bullshit."

Guilt flickered in Kyla's features, but she said nothing.

"I knew a spy in the Three Sisters," Rhea said, quietly. "Are they all dead?"

Kyla didn't need to say anything. Rhea's head fell. Nyx made the hand gesture to the God of Death and whispered a prayer.

"Juno," Rhea said, almost a moan.

Ariadne's gaze snapped up. Juno was one of the Archon's most favored courtesans. The Madam of the Pleasure Garden.

Ariadne had never met Juno, but she knew the Madam helped protect Rhea. If she had been discovered, she'd have been tortured. Unless she killed herself first. Ariadne wrapped her arms around herself.

Kyla heaved a sigh. "Look, Eris, Clo, feel free to be mad at me. But I am in the middle of a shitstorm and fresh out of spies. The records room on Macella is where the Archon keeps the most comprehensive logs on shipments, and we need to access it for information on *Zelus's* cargo and what they plan to do with it. Would any of you happen to know how we can get in?" Her gaze shifted from Nyx to Ariadne and Rhea.

Nyx laughed. "Yeah, I've been to Macella. Drank with a few of the recordkeepers at the palace there. Let me break it down for you. The way to Records is a maze. The Oracle uses shifting digital projections in the rooms so the way in never looks the same."

Ariadne plastered a falsely cheerful grin on her face. "I did help design those." *Prove your usefulness. Prove your efficiency.*

Nyx glared at her before continuing. "To say nothing of the heat sensors. If you trigger the lasers, the guards will be on your ass in two seconds flat."

"I can disable those," Ariadne whispered.

"—and if you approach the door," Nyx said, her voice rising, "and it scans you and if you don't have the correct height, weight, body type, and retinal scan of someone with clearance, it releases an airborne toxin that leads to your painful demise in under five seconds."

Ariadne winced. "I helped design that, too." *Prove your worth.*

Nyx side-eyed her. "And then you'd have to weave through laser grids, which are based on *Ariadne's* movements." She put up her hand when Ariadne opened her mouth to say something. "I'm done stroking your ego, kid. Let me finish. Say you find the intel you need and get out of Macella without being pierced with several lasers. The source of these rocks will likely be *another* secure location. If you destroy it, is there more? You have to find out. It's a great game, except we're all fucking losers. Good luck."

Kyla's eyes narrowed. Ariadne's nerves coiled in her stomach. She might not have seen Kyla's face before today, but from the communications when Ariadne sent intel, she knew the commander well enough to sense when she had a plan. Ariadne had a feeling she wouldn't like it. Kyla gave a slow, vicious smile.

Uh-oh, Ariadne thought.

"Congratulations," Kyla said, "all three of you have the job. You'll be joining Eris and Clo in infiltrating the palace on Macella."

Ariadne's mouth fell open. Rhea went pale. Only Nyx looked as inscrutable as ever.

The Oracle knew she had escaped by now. But she wouldn't suspect Ariadne would still remember how to move through some of the systems.

It had been years since she designed that grid. Ariadne's muscles twitched, but she still remembered just how to duck and flip, how the laser grid moved. Even if the Oracle changed the order and configuration, Ariadne's reflexes were sharp. It was a perfect puzzle. A game for a little girl who had no one to play with but death and an AI who claimed to love her but didn't know the meaning of the word.

Nyx gave something like a cough. "Sorry, I just had a horrible waking nightmare where you told us to infiltrate the Empire we just escaped from. Come again?"

Kyla kept that reptilian smile as she reached into her pocket and brought out three Pathos. Ariadne and her friends stared at those small, needle-like brain implants like they were weapons. "You'll be needing these."

Ariadne reached for them. Nyx smacked her hand aside. "Don't even think about it. We're not going. We only just broke free."

Rhea nodded. "We gave you more than enough to deserve being sent somewhere safe." Her voice was as polite as usual, but there was an edge to it. A blade hidden beneath the silk and finery. "That was our bargain. Information. Not this."

Kyla's smile disappeared, replaced with steely annoyance. "I don't recall bargaining with any of you. And I thought you wanted to help the resistance topple the Empire. You came to *us*. This is how you resist."

"It has to be a choice." Nyx glowered. "Otherwise, you use people just like the Empire does. We're nothing but tools."

Something flickered in Kyla's gaze. "If you complete this mission, you'll get your new identities. I'll send you somewhere safe. Call it what you want, but that's my offer."

"That's not an offer," Eris snapped. "And you know it."

Clo made some placating motion. "Aside from the issues Nyx pointed out, I've never even been near the Three Sisters. I've never had an Oracle implant—"

"We don't have a choice," Kyla snapped. "This cargo showed up just as the Archon declared a peace summit? Then we need to know if Damocles is planning to overthrow him, and *I* can't do that when my best fucking spies have been compromised." Her voice softened a fraction. "I am offering you three a choice; I never said it was a good one. I know it's a risk. You have to decide whether it's worth it."

Eris's face was back to stone. Ariadne was deadly curious. What had made Eris join the resistance? What had she fled on those cursed three planets?

"And if we decide to leave, we'll be caught at the nearest checkpoint," Nyx said flatly. "Great service you're offering here to refugees. And here I thought the Novantae were dedicated to ending tyranny and promoting peace and love or some bullshit."

Kyla's eyes flashed. "Do you want to know what happened to the peace-and-love movements? They didn't even put up a fight when they were caught, flayed alive, and left in front of the palace grounds as a deterrent. I make the difficult, ruthless choices so we can still fight. If you don't like it, no one is stopping you from leaving."

Nyx shifted, but Rhea put a restraining hand on her shoulder. "Don't. Not now." Rhea sucked in a breath. "All right. I'll take that offer."

Nyx turned to her. "*No.* We're not going back to the Empire."

"We have to," Rhea said, "if we want to start over somewhere else. If we really want to stop running. You know we do."

Nyx looked to Ariadne for help, but Ariadne already knew her answer. "I'll do it."

"I said no," Nyx said. "How could you even consider this after what the Oracle did to you?"

Ariadne's shoulders hunched. She'd told Nyx and Rhea some of what she'd gone through but not the worst of it. Never the worst of it.

Nyx was only getting started. "The Empire treated me like I was just a weapon to aim and fire," she said. "I wasn't any different from the Mors in my hand. You can't even begin to imagine how many people I killed. And Rhea"—she swung her head toward the other woman—"they treated you like you were property. They dressed you in all those gold trinkets and had you lay naked on top of the dinner table like you were a centerpiece. To the Tholosian royalty, we are *things*. Possessions. Dona."

"Nyx . . ." Rhea started, but the name caught in her throat.

Nyx breathed raggedly, her hands curled into fists. Ariadne had seen this in other soldiers who had managed to break through the Oracle's programming and then come to her to be re-coded. Mercenaries like Nyx were so used to channeling their anger into violence, or the Oracle would dampen it down deep, only to arise when they needed to kill. Nyx didn't know what to do with this flood of fury.

"If we go back," Nyx said. "If we are caught, they'll turn us into gerulae, if they keep us alive at all." Humans so rewritten by the Oracle's programming there was nothing left. Ariadne had helped craft the code.

Instinctively, Ariadne reached out to touch her, but Nyx jerked away. The younger girl almost recoiled from the heat of it. "If you and Rhea want to go on this mission, fine," Nyx said through her teeth. "But I'm not exchanging one set of chains for another."

Nyx strode from the room, posture military-taut.

When Rhea moved to go after her, Eris stopped her. "Kyla needs to brief you on the mission. Let me speak with Nyx."

Ariadne sniffed.

"You don't know her," Rhea said, frowning.

"You both know her too well. And neither of you have been soldiers."

Rhea nodded once, and Ariadne bit the inside of her cheek. Eris offered something resembling a reassuring smile and went after Nyx.

Ariadne sidled up next to Rhea and put her arms around her. It was still such a recent thing to have friends. Rhea's grip tightened, pressing her close.

Ariadne just wanted to feel safe for a few more minutes before she went back to the place worse than the darkest depths of Avern.

19.

NYX

Present day

Nyx was still breathing hard when Eris found her. She had sprinted across the whole of the ship to the training room, run the circuit in the gym several times. She was in a mood to punish her body.

"If you're here to get me to change my mind, don't bother," Nyx said.

Practice blades hung from the walls—long and short ones, some curved and some straight. Each different weapon was from a planet conquered by the Tholosian Empire; the military prided themselves on learning different battle techniques to improve their training and their brutality on the battlefield. Each instrument was heavier and blunter than what they'd use in real life, but still deadly.

In comparison, the rack of false Mors on the far wall were for newer recruits; they only left a faint red mark instead of a hole in skin. Easy for guiding soldiers so green that they hadn't seen an enemy corpse yet. This room had taken every aspect of training into consideration. There were shields, ropes, and punching bags. So many ways to play at the art of killing. The air smelled faintly of sweat, disinfectant, and chalk.

Nyx had already started wrapping her hands, wanting to punch that bag in the corner until she couldn't think any longer.

Eris leaned against the door frame. "I was hoping we could talk."

Nyx didn't look up. She tested the wraps, gave the bag a few light punches. They were good. "Not interested in talking."

"You want to fight, then?" Eris said calmly, picking up strips to wrap her own hands.

Nyx studied the other woman. She was so small that her head didn't even reach Nyx's shoulders. But it wasn't even just her height; it was her frame. Muscled and compact, yes, but so little that Nyx felt like a mountain next to a boulder.

"I'd break you," Nyx said dismissively. She was engineered to break people. Big men, small women.

"You sure about that?"

Nyx wasn't. She figured Eris was trained to move quick, strike hard, again and again. Tire out a larger opponent. Smaller soldiers were taught like that. Nyx had learned to expect it.

"Tell you what: if you win, we can do all the talking you want," Nyx said.

Eris raised an eyebrow. "And if you win?"

"You leave me the fuck alone."

Eris bared her teeth, a gesture too devious to be called a grin. "Deal."

Nyx waited for her to finish getting ready. They circled each other, slowly. Eris feinted first, a quick test jab. Too easy. Nyx barely had to move. She blocked the next punch.

"You're weak at misdirection." Nyx's breathing had slowed. She felt tethered in her body again. There was only the fight. Eyeing her opponent, finding their weak point, and hitting it.

"Am I?" Was Eris . . . *amused*?

What in the seven devils?

Eris tried a few more punches. She was good. Fast, focused. She was someone who fought dirty.

Nyx could fight dirtier. She darted forward, tripping Eris just enough to throw her off balance, then pushed. Eris staggered back, but her face didn't even register the pain. Did she even *feel* it? Eris caught herself and moved forward faster than Nyx expected, landing a hard hit on the soldier's forearm. Nyx's very bones seemed to shake.

"Not bad," Nyx said, holding back a wince. "Where did you train?"

Another quick duck, a double jab that Nyx just managed to block. "None of your damn business."

Eris spun into a high kick. Nyx ducked low, struck out and grazed

Eris's torso. Nyx prided herself on her prowess in hand-to-hand combat, but this woman was putting up a damn good fight.

Their pace increased. Punch after punch. Block after block. Nyx grabbed Eris's arm but she twisted away, leaving scratches on Nyx's still-tattooed forearm. Nyx didn't even feel it. She snarled, landing three good punches in a row. Eris absorbed the blows without a sound. Where in the fucking Avern had this woman trained? Why had Nyx never heard of her?

Didn't matter. Nyx had to be better. Eris tried to land a few of her own hits, but though she punched well for her size, they didn't hurt Nyx at all. The Oracle might not be in her mind anymore, but one of the effects of old programming still lingered: dulled nociceptors. Her ability to feel pain was minimized. It was one of the few good things about having an AI mess with her brain.

Then everything changed—it was as if a switch flipped in the other woman. Nyx went in for a hit and missed. Again and again and again. Nyx's speed had been lauded back on the training base, but Eris moved like smoke. Nyx would be certain she'd land a hit and strike nothing but air. Again. Air. Again. Air. Had Eris been *toying* with her?

Enough of this.

Nyx dodged another hit and lunged. She got a good hold on Eris and shoved her against the wall, dragging her up until her feet dangled six inches off the ground.

"Enough games," Nyx growled. "Yield."

Eris shook her head. She was breathing hard, but godsdamn it, she didn't even look like she was in pain. Who the seven devils *was* she?

"Yield!"

Eris's eyes narrowed and she smiled. *What—*

She threw her head back, then slammed her forehead into Nyx's nose. Cartilage cracked and blood wet Nyx's lips. *Bel's balls*, that shit hurt.

Nyx staggered back, spitting blood onto her shirt. Eris didn't even hesitate; she sensed an opening and took it, smashing her fist into Nyx's face.

Nyx fell to the floor. The breath left her lungs and she struggled for air. Eris straddled her, knees on Nyx's upper arms, pinning them to her side. Her forearm came down hard on Nyx's throat.

"Yield," Eris said, baring her teeth.

Nyx tried to let out a growl, but it only came out as a short gasp for breath. Eris's forearm dug into her throat.

"Damn it, Nyx," Eris snapped. "Yield before you pass out."

The small sound Nyx made might have been a laugh if it didn't sound so pathetic. She struggled to stay conscious as the black crept into the corners of her vision.

"I'm taking that as a yes," the other woman said. "Don't even think about hitting me again."

The forearm came away, and Eris rolled off her. Nyx sucked in precious air. She shook her head once, twice, and her vision mercifully began to clear. The headache was new and un-fucking-welcome.

Eris settled on the floor next to Nyx, brushing her hands on the front of her jumpsuit. "I won. Now spill."

"It doesn't count as a win if I didn't yield."

Eris let out a short laugh. "You wouldn't have yielded before I'd broken your windpipe and killed you, and you know that."

Smart ass.

Nyx dragged herself up into a seated position. "Fine." She focused on breathing in and out, forcing her heart rate back to normal. Her nose throbbed. She pressed the bottom of her shirt against it to staunch the blood.

"Your nose is broken," Eris volunteered.

"I'm aware." Nyx pushed the pain away. She'd get Ariadne or Rhea to help her patch it later, already dreading the way they'd fuss. Nyx slumped against one of the gray columns, the coolness nice against her sweat-slicked skin.

Eris stayed quiet, her elbows resting against her knees. The dark curls by her hairline were plastered to her skin. She said nothing, letting the silence stretch.

After three minutes, Nyx caved. "If you're not going to leave, talk. Ask. Whatever. Don't just sit there and leer at me."

"What, they didn't teach you silence technique during torture training?"

Nyx learned how to stay quiet under pressure or intense pain. Even prayers to the God of Death were to be made in thoughts alone, never spoken aloud. That was a weakness to be beaten out of you.

"Sorry," Eris said quietly. "I shouldn't have asked that."

"Were you a royal guard?" Nyx asked.

Eris's face was blank. Every bit as in control as when she was fighting. "Something like that."

Only another royal guard could have lasted longer than two seconds against Nyx, and only someone higher ranked would have beaten her. Whoever this small woman was, she had body mods. They were strictly controlled, highly regulated, and damn near impossible to replicate outside of palace personnel. With a few exceptions, they could only be added during infant incubation. So, this woman had to have been a top cohort in the militus class, engineered like Nyx was for special ops. A lot of cohorts came and went—experimental engineering didn't always take, so infant mortality among some groups were higher than others. Most soldiers didn't know much about other cohorts unless they were young and impressive enough to warrant notice. Like Nyx.

Nyx would have heard about someone who fought like this. A soldier that talented would have her face splashed across the vid-screens in the military camps to inspire others.

She probably changed her face, Nyx realized. Then who the Avern was she?

"If you stared at me any more intensely, I'd be on fire," Eris said, clearly amused.

"Trying to figure out who you were. Before."

"Does it matter?"

Nyx considered that. *Before* meant being under the Oracle's control, when killing came as naturally as breathing and eating—it was just what soldiers did. No thought to the matter until the day something interrupts that programming and you recall all the things you've done and think that maybe the God of Death isn't a God at all but a monster. Something worse than a devil. And you've only been feeding it.

"Maybe not," Nyx said. "But if you were military, you know what they did to me and what they forced me to do. What's the point in offering to erase my tattoos if you're asking me to go back to the Empire that put them there?"

Nyx unwound the bandages, letting them fall beside her. A few of her knuckles would bruise. She took out a heavy ring from her pocket.

She always wore two, except when she sparred, and instead of slipping it back on her fingers, she rolled it along her palm.

"I don't *want* you to, and I'm not asking you to go back as a soldier," Eris said, her eyes following the ring. "We can get you a shifter to hide your face. No one will recognize you, Nyx." At Nyx's silence, Eris loosed a breath. "Listen, I know what that ring means. I know that they give it to soldiers who survive to make it to the royal guard. And I know what's on the inside of it."

Eris held out her hand. Nyx placed the warm metal band in the middle of the other woman's palm. Nyx felt the weight of the simple, circular jewel—the cut blue stone that signified the highest honor among the royal guard, those who scored the best marks during training. The ones who earned the right to defend the Archon personally.

Then she tipped the heavy silver band to see the underside, and Nyx heard Eris's breath catch. The tally marks on the underside were so small, she'd need a magnifying glass to count them all. They stretched across the entire circumference of the band, leaving no space at all. Whoever set them into the metal was forced to continue the marks to the outside of the band, circling all the way around to the edges of the stone.

Each single line signified an execution Nyx made during combat missions while training. Each one was a mark of courage, a sacrifice made to appease the God of Death, a ravenous, demanding God.

There were more tallies on that ring than thorns tattooed on Nyx's skin. If the Archon wanted a mercenary to kill in secret—to assassinate high-ranking officials or spies—then a guard did not mark their skin with the proof of that death. They carved it into metal that circled a finger like a yoke.

"I see," Eris breathed.

Few had seen Nyx's ring this close. Rhea and Ariadne didn't know what it meant—wouldn't think to search for that secret message of even more kills than the tale of her skin told.

"They couldn't fit them all," Nyx almost whispered the confession. She took out the second ring.

Eris swallowed, plucking it gently from Nyx's scarred palm. This time, the tally marks took up half of the band. On the outside was etched *Hear me, O Death. I kill for Thee.*

"When I took these rings, I was sure," Nyx said. "I was so sure."

Eris didn't ask, simply waited.

"I'd trained my whole life, but I was eleven on my first mission. People don't suspect a child. I made my first kill, earned my first thorn. I'd believed everything they'd told us, all they'd coded into our DNA. I was so sure that our war was right and every planet in the universe ought to belong to us. I believed every species not our own deserved to die." Nyx took the rings back. "So, I can't atone for these. I can remove the tattoos, throw these rings into space, but it won't undo these deaths. Some of us don't deserve second chances."

"I'm not asking you to atone," Eris said. "I'm asking you for your help."

Nyx met her eyes. "Why?"

"Because I believe in second chances, even if you don't."

Nyx didn't look away.

It didn't matter how much she regretted what she'd done in the past, or how many people Nyx had killed, how much she knew she'd bathed her soul in blood. Undoing the Oracle's programming had been like cutting out a piece of herself. She still felt empty. She knew how messed-up that was. You didn't regret a damn thing when you had it programmed into your head that you shouldn't.

Eris remained silent, letting Nyx work through her thoughts. Nyx wondered if Eris had thought the same when she left. Was there a void where her heart should be, or did something else eventually take its place? Gods, she hoped so. And she hated that she hoped.

"All right," she whispered, her voice ragged. "All right, damn it."

Eris nodded. She rose, but Nyx's hand shot out and gripped her wrist hard. "Rhea and Ariadne are my responsibility. If anything happens to them . . ."

She didn't need to finish the sentence. Eris lowered her gaze to Nyx's fingers. "On my missions, their lives come before mine. Yours too."

"So, you're the captain, and if this ship is bound for a crash landing?"

"I'm throwing your ass on a bullet craft whether you like it or not."

Nyx's lips curved upward. This was different from Ariadne and Rhea. They were both good, heroic. And Nyx wasn't good. She killed too damn easily. But this woman? They shared a background. Eris was just as bad as Nyx, but she was trying to be better than her nature, and that changed everything.

They strode back to the command center in silence, but it was almost comfortable. When the doors opened, Rhea's eyebrows rose. "You changed your mind."

Nyx lifted a shoulder in a shrug.

Ariadne grinned. "So, you're coming?"

"Yeah. Looks like you're stuck with me, kid."

Rhea mouthed *thank you* to Eris. Nyx pretended not to see.

Ariadne started chattering. "I'll help you fit the Pathos. It's just a very, very small incision in your cerebrum, takes five minutes with a laser—"

"Great," Nyx says dryly. "So, I just got a chip out of my head and now you're putting another one in."

Her hand went to the back of her head where the scar was hidden beneath her hair. Since Ariadne couldn't leave the Temple, she'd hidden a bot in a flower delivery for Rhea in the Pleasure Garden. That little bot had acted as her hands as she performed the surgery through the vidscreen. Rhea had held Nyx's hand the whole time. *You're doing so well,* she would say. *Almost done.*

It took every ounce of effort Nyx had to keep from screaming.

"This one connects to the *cerebrum*, not the *cerebellum*," Ariadne told her. "It won't mess with your motor functions."

"Not sure I find that reassuring."

"You shouldn't," Clo said, spinning in the pilot's chair. "You'll have people chattering in your head. And you can turn it off at will, but Kyla will yell at you if you do."

Eris rolled her eyes. "Stop being so dramatic."

"It's not *dramatic* to prefer the deep silence of my own fluming thoughts."

Kyla passed around the Pathos. "Cloelia will deal with it. Her favorite pastime is bitching; her second favorite is complaining."

"And her third is threatening people with knives," Clo said.

"I thought you also liked fixing engines. Where does that rank?" Rhea asked with a friendly smile.

Clo opened her mouth, but Kyla interrupted. "I'm going to put in a call to Sher and give him an update," she said to Eris. "I'll head back to Nova to see if there's anything else on this alleged truce, or further rumors about Damocles. I'll send you all a full mission brief from there."

"You're probably sending us all to our deaths," Nyx muttered.

"You ought to talk to Eris about that," Kyla said. "She's used to me sending her to her death, and yet here she stands." To Eris and Clo: "I'll be in touch." With a last look at the women, Kyla headed back to the bridge toward the docking bay and her ship.

When the stomp of Kyla's boots faded, Clo rose from the pilot's chair. "Good. Now that she's gone, we can blast music and drink like pirates before we all die."

"There's no alcohol on this ship, remember?" Rhea interrupted. "The Legate saw it as a weakness."

"What he calls *weakness*, I call *liquid courage*."

Nyx rolled her eyes. "Can we at least begin discussing this suicide quest? Fit Ariadne's new chip into my brain?"

Ariadne held up the tiny rod and examined it proudly. "It's more beautiful than I imagined it would be. Did the engineers manage to improve the range? I sent over my newer design."

"Sher and Kyla have newer ones in testing," Clo said. "Ours should reach the whole planet, and if we're in orbit. If you somehow end up on the other side of the galaxy from us, we might have a problem."

"Oooh, that's impressive. We're like a team," Ariadne said, then smiled. "Can we have a team name?"

"No," Eris and Clo said at the same time.

Nyx sighed. "This is going to be the longest mission of my life, isn't it?"

"Enjoy the next ten hours," Eris said with a smirk. "Longest Mission Ever starts at moonrise."

Rhea, who had been staring out the window at the stars, turned to look at them all. "Then I want to enjoy what might be my last ten hours of freedom."

20.

Two years ago

Breathe in, breathe out, Rhea told herself.

Stare up, don't blink too often. Keep still. Keep silent.

She couldn't see them, but she could hear them. The clink of silverware as the soldiers ate. The murmur of conversation that she strained to follow, to file away in case she needed it. Footsteps, music. Laughter. She smelled the food, tantalizingly sweet.

Rhea was hungry, but she hadn't been allowed her dinner. Damocles had been too angry, had thrown the food onto the floor. Rhea should know better. Push him too far, question a little bit too hard, and he resorted to stunts like this.

A finger brushed the bare skin of her stomach. A Tholosian soldier picked up a sweet molded into the shape of a warship no bigger than a child's ear. She heard the wet, sucking noises as he chewed and swallowed. The noise was all around her. There was no escape. She wished she could close her eyes, but she had to keep them open, had to stare up at the brilliant reflections of the chandelier above that left dancing spots in her vision.

The soldiers were in a fine mood. The Tholosians had emerged the victors of the Battle of the Garnet. Many of their own had died, but gloriously, in battle. A tribute to all the Gods. More of the Evoli had fallen. Rhea had listened to Damocles tell her the details, relishing how they made her uncomfortable.

They're our enemy, Rhea dear, he'd said. *There's no use in caring for those who aren't ours.*

She let her mind drift away from the heightened emotions of those around her, away from the image of her naked body offered as a literal platter. She dreamed of escape, of retribution, of revenge.

"Nyx?" one of the soldiers asked. "You're not eating." Male. His words barely reached Rhea. She was imagining racing through corridors, jumping onto a ship, shooting out into the stars, and never looking back.

"This doesn't bother you?" came a low, almost gravelly voice. Rhea set the daydream aside, coming back to the polite, lavish nightmare.

She glanced to her right. A young soldier, probably no older than her, in full military regalia. Smooth brown skin covered with dark twining tattoos. So many thorns. So many deaths. Medals clustered the cloth over her left breast.

Nyx Arktos-33.

The Arktos cohort had yielded some of Tholos's deadliest soldiers. She was so good, they'd given her a first name. She'd earned a special commendation for her battle. Damocles himself had set that ribbon around her neck. She should be a bottle deep into the wine, arms thrown around her fellow soldiers. Yet instead, her back was straight, her plate empty, her wine glass still full.

Nyx looked at Rhea's exposed body not with pity, not with desire . . . it was an emotion Rhea couldn't place—and if there was one thing Rhea excelled at, it was reading others' moods.

Their eyes locked. Rhea had Nyx's attention, it seemed. And Nyx had Rhea's in turn.

"Why should anything bother me?" the male soldier asked. He was as merry as Nyx was somber. "Come on, Nyx. We're celebrating."

He reached over Rhea's body, the side of his hand grazing her nipple. Rhea blinked, slowly, desperately picturing that ship taking her into the stars. Far away from there.

The soldier took another delicacy from her flesh.

"For you," the soldier said to Nyx, with an elaborate bow. "For saving my ass out there on the battlefield."

"No, thanks," she said. "I'm good."

"Come on. Look, it's still warm from her skin."

Rhea counted the crystals above her.

"I said no." Nyx's voice was sharp, dimming the laughter around her. Silence grew longer.

"Suit yourself," he said, and popped the food into his mouth.

Nyx didn't stay long, but for the rest of her time there, she made sure Rhea could meet her eye, if she so chose. And she didn't eat one morsel of food.

Once Nyx left, Rhea went back to dreaming of escape.

But she started to realize that maybe, with the right kind of help, it might not be so impossible.

21.

Present day

The party was nothing like the celebrations Rhea had attended on Tholos. There were no champagne fountains, no golden plates filled with the best delicacies the galaxy had to offer.

It was only the *Zelus* canteen—gray walls, the air filled with the fading smell of grease from their meal. No decorations save for a few Tholosian flags Ariadne took great delight in ripping to strips and hanging from the ceiling in tattered bunting. But the view of darkness and pinpoints of stars was just as beautiful as the gray and amethyst mountains on Tholos. Rhea had never traveled through space, never left the capital of the Tholosian empire.

If she left the Pleasure Garden at all, it was usually to Damocles's bedroom.

Now she traveled for herself and the women who had helped her escape. Even if the tether of the Empire was still drawing them back.

On Tholos, Rhea had worn such finery to those parties. Dresses of gold cloth, her hair heavy with the weight of jewels and gold and silver filigree. She had brushed her eyelids with shimmery blue or bronze, painted her lips carmine, dusted her skin until it shone like white gold. She'd been surrounded by people in the highest echelons of Tholos, and every word, every movement, every blink of her eye had to be practiced and perfect. Parties were nothing more than performance, the prelude to the night where she became the entertainment.

On those nights, she had danced only for others. Never for herself.

Yet the only guests of this makeshift celebration were five women with blood on their hands. Rhea, Ariadne, and Nyx hadn't slept for close to two days, and they'd been running on little more than adrenaline and hope. They should be exhausted. They should be resting for their return, but none of them even spoke of sleeping.

After going over as many of the details of the mission as they could nail down before actually landing on Macella, everyone agreed to Rhea's suggestion that they celebrate in case this mission was their last.

Rhea clutched her drink to her chest. Clo had found a hidden bottle of alcohol in the Legate's quarters. Of course, the man who had set the rules had broken them himself. It was good, dark rum from Argos, and it burned going down. As much as Rhea wished to drink and drink—to forget her worries, to simply *forget*—she kept in control. Small sips. Watered down cocktails. Nothing more.

She never let herself drink too much—it lowered her defenses, and she always had to hold herself apart. The mask must never slip, not even there.

Rhea's eyes followed Clo as she went around, topping up people's drinks. She found the other woman fascinating. The shortness of her hair highlighted the almost fey tilt to her eyes, her high cheekbones and strong jaw. The small scars that nicked her long, thin fingers. The muscles beneath light brown skin. She had three little moles by her right eye, and Rhea found herself wanting to touch them with the tips of her fingers. It had been a long time since she'd found someone attractive, purely for their own sake. Purely for hers.

Clo looked up and their gazes collided. For a moment, Rhea thought the other woman would turn away, but Clo simply tilted her head as if coming to some decision. What was she thinking? Could she sense Rhea's attraction?

Rhea drank more rum, lips tingling. Clo followed the movement, staring intently. When Rhea smiled, the other woman blushed and finally looked away.

Rhea's smile widened.

"Turn up the music!" Ariadne crowed, banging on the table as if it were a drum.

Clo reached over and flipped up the volume.

Rhea didn't recognize the music—so much was banned from the Tholosian citizenry, except that which was deemed acceptable by the Archon. These would be old songs Ariadne had access to from the Oracle's history archives. Music from the Old World, and after, before the Empire became so powerful that it deemed its own art to be dangerous.

She wanted to laugh, to sing and raise her voice to the rafters. To scream with the knowledge that they had done it. They had finally escaped. After a year of planning, she was far from Damocles, from the Archon, from that horrible palace. She could listen to banned music. She could—

Until moonrise, she reminded herself. *Only until moonrise.*

Rhea's smile disappeared. For all that hard work, they were heading right back to the heart of the Empire.

Nyx glowered in the corner, the sides of her face taped with bandages from her latest tattoo-removal session. Her drink might be more rum than the berry mixer from the Tholosian gardens, a way to deal with the pain of removal. Ariadne was fussing with Nyx's curls, braiding them away from the bandages and twining them around her head. Ariadne was the only person who would be able to do that without losing an arm.

"Hold still," Ariadne was saying. "You're going to make me mess up."

"Can we take a break so I can down enough alcohol not to care?" Nyx said dryly. She caught Rhea's eye and made a face as if to say *This kid.*

Rhea smiled back. That kid had saved their lives.

Clo offered Eris a drink. Eris took it with a tentative nod of thanks. The two women still kept their distance from each other, despite the small peace offering. There was a history there. Rhea wondered what had happened to make things so tense. Whether it was recent or far in the past.

Ariadne finished with Nyx's hair and made her way to the control panel to change the music. Unfamiliar instruments, echoing vocals, a strong, steady beat.

"This is old," Eris said, her voice very low. A small smile touched her face. "I haven't heard it in a long time."

Rhea glanced around to see if anyone had caught Eris's comment, but no one else had. Music was so tightly controlled by the Archon. She must have been someone very important.

But who? What position?

Ariadne's twirl drew Rhea from her thoughts. "I love it!" The fabric of the girl's jacket billowed behind her. "I listened to all kinds of music back at the Temple, from the beginnings on the Old World to last year. I snuck a lot of vids and books, too. Even the censored ones. Especially the censored ones."

"The Oracle let you watch them?" Eris asked.

A shiver went through Rhea. That woman was so intense. Rhea wasn't sure what to make of Eris yet.

Ariadne just grinned, tongue between her teeth. "One didn't know." Ariadne pirouetted about in the center of the canteen. "This is the song I always put on when I was bored and finished my work ahead of schedule. I used to climb to the top of the Temple and dance in the rafters."

She pinwheeled her arms, spinning faster and faster. Her hair slid across her cheeks. Her smile was luminous. Rhea had never seen Ariadne so unburdened—so happy—as she twirled across the command center.

As she came closer to Rhea, Ariadne stopped and held out a hand. "Dance with me, Rhea!"

Rhea smiled. She used to dance in front of her clients, in front of important diplomats and soldiers. She rose in a smooth motion, twisting and sending her skirt twirling. She rose up on her toes—

No. She wasn't in the Pleasure Garden. There, the dancing had been so formal and regimented. Her slippers had been made specifically for dancing on her toes, with ribbons that snaked around her ankles. Her dresses were silk, slit high up the thigh to bare her legs to onlookers.

She had been expected to dance until they told her to stop.

Rhea halted, her chest heaving. She looked down at her feet—scarred, callused, some of the old blisters still peeling. She remembered her feet had bled through the silk of her slippers some nights, and she still had to dance.

Rhea shook her head, her eyes stinging. "I don't have any dance shoes."

Ariadne gently grasped her hands. "Neither do I. See?" She showed Rhea her small feet. No calluses. No injuries.

"I can't," Rhea breathed. "I don't know how."

"Let me show you," Ariadne said, cheeks dimpling. "I'm a great dancer."

Rhea could deny this girl nothing. So, she forced a smile and let Ariadne lead. At first, Rhea was awkward; her face burned with embarrassment. But there was no one to watch her critically, no one to notice her failure—or even care if they did. Ariadne spun them both slowly across the command center, their hands linked.

It was . . . it was lovely. Different. *She* could be different. Rhea could be as wild and untamed as she wanted. There were no predetermined steps, no judging eyes, no one she had to seduce.

Just her. Just this. Just her own body.

Ariadne whooped with glee. "See? Isn't this fun, Rhea?"

Yes. Yes, it was.

Laughing, Rhea unpinned her dark hair and shook it free. It fell down her back to her thighs—a sign of her health, her pampering. One day, she'd cut it all off, maybe buzz it like Clo's. When she finally felt free from the Empire. From everyone who thought they could control her. She would throw that hair into space and tattoo her body with something fierce and beautiful, and dance how she wanted.

So, she danced with the girl who had saved her life.

Ariadne's hands were so small. Together, they twisted and twirled. Rhea lifted the smaller girl into the air. She couldn't help but be graceful— it was a skill prized in the Pleasure Garden—but she admired how Ariadne jumped around, awkward and strange and all the more endearing for it.

As Rhea pirouetted, she found Clo watching her. Rhea felt emboldened. Who was this other woman? What was in her past? "Clo," she called, emboldened. "Dance."

Clo let out a nervous laugh and shook her head. "No way."

"Just one dance. Be my partner." Rhea gave the other woman her best pleading expression until Clo finally joined her.

Clo's first movements were stiff. Rhea had noticed her limp; the silver glint of the prosthetic visible in the gap between her shoe and trouser leg when she sat down at the command center. It didn't seem to slow her down, but Rhea could understand why it might make Clo self-conscious.

Okay, Rhea thought, *Slow. Let's go slow.*

How did others do this? How did they indicate interest?

She inched toward Clo, her hips swaying. When the other woman's eyes met hers and their hands touched, Rhea's breath caught in her throat. She could sense Clo's attraction, clear as a chime. The music grew louder, drowning out thought.

Ariadne had chosen the song well. That insistent, thumping bass echoed in Rhea's ribcage, in time with her heartbeat. She could feel the music in her bones. In that moment, the gray, stark canteen and ragged bunting were as perfect a setting as the marble-and-gold ballroom of the palace on Tholos. It was fast and wild, and Rhea's pulse hammered when she brushed her fingers against the other woman's wrists.

As the song ended, they stared at each other, breathing hard. They had yet to release each other's hands. *I want to know you*, Rhea thought. Could she say that? She didn't know the rules outside of the Pleasure Garden. How to behave. What to say.

What *not* to say.

Clo broke the spell first. She dropped Rhea's hands and cleared her throat. "You're a beautiful dancer."

Rhea hid her pleased smile by grabbing her rum from the table and taking a small sip. Her hands were still warm from Clo's touch. "Dancing is the first thing we learn in the Pleasure Garden. Later, when we're old enough, we perform at palace balls to seek new clients." She leaned in slightly, as if to betray a secret. "Our madam calls it 'advertising.'"

"Advertising," Clo echoed. "Is that what you were doing just now?" She didn't sound judgmental, simply curious.

Rhea wondered if Clo were trying to understand Rhea, too. Trying to learn more about her. New attraction was such a careful dance of its own, Rhea was learning. She didn't want to say something wrong.

"No," she said softly. "For once, this was just for fun. This was for me."

Clo followed Rhea's gaze down to her feet and flinched at the scars. "What was it like there? In the Pleasure Garden?"

What was it like? Rhea wasn't certain it had an easy answer—some parts she remembered fondly, others she didn't. But which parts of her life were so ingrained that she simply accepted them? Which parts only seemed less terrible because they paled in comparison to the worst?

Her life had been regimented, she could say. She could talk about how every movement she made had been part of her training—the way she walked, the way she stood, everything. Rhea glanced down at herself, how even now she'd slid aside the silk of her gown so the slit along the side bared her thigh. A peek for her onlooker, intended to seduce.

A hint of skin, the Madam would say, *sends a better message than nudity. They grow curious. They want more.*

Rhea dropped her dress so it covered her leg. For the first time in a long while, she was speechless. She hadn't even realized how she was standing; it was as natural as breathing. "I can't . . ." She swallowed. "I don't know how to answer that yet. I'm sorry."

"Hey. I shouldn't have asked." Clo reached for her. Her hand settled gently on Rhea's arm. "Don't apologize. You don't have to tell me anything you don't want to. My ma always said I was curious as a marsh cat and just as likely to put my paw in a bog."

Rhea smiled, charmed at the mental image. But it was strange. People always expected things from Rhea. She was so used to *giving*; she kept little for herself—only those secrets she couldn't tell Clo.

When she was a child, she always sought Madam's approval. She won it by being the best dancer, the most graceful. Later, when she was of age, it was the approval of her clients. Their contentment came first. *They* came first. And Damocles had been the most demanding of them all.

Rhea stepped back slightly. "Will you ask again? When I'm ready?"

"Aye," Clo said. "I can do that."

Rhea was quiet as another song switched on. What did she want *now*? To kiss Clo, yes. But not yet. She wanted to savor this—no expectations. No performing. An attraction that came without obligations. Slow.

"How about another dance?" Rhea asked.

Clo smiled and gently took Rhea's hands. It ended up being more than one dance. And Rhea loved every moment.

As the night wore on, they switched from the rum to water, knowing they all needed to be sharp the next day. Nyx and Eris went off to the officers' quarters to sleep. Ariadne curled up in the corner, bringing up old programs on her tablet. Before long, the tablet fell by her side, and she slept with her head in her hands.

Later, after Rhea had turned the music off and draped a jacket over Ariadne, she and Clo cleaned up and retreated to the observation room. There, they sat in deck chairs and watched the stars as the ship glided through space.

"Have you ever been to Macella?" Rhea asked Clo.

Clo swirled her water and leaned her head back to view the stars above them. "Nae. Never been anywhere near the Three Sisters. Have you?" At Rhea's amused look, Clo gave an embarrassed chuckle. "Been to Macella, I mean."

"No. I've never been outside of the palace grounds on Tholos. I hear the one on Macella is . . . very grand. Damocles talked about taking me there once he became Archon."

"How do you feel about having to go back?" She winced, as if realizing she'd asked another personal question like back in the command center. "Sorry. You don't have to answer that if you don't want."

She was sweet. Considerate. That was so rare in Rhea's life that it made her want to open up just a little.

"It's all right," she said. "Honestly . . . I'm terrified." Rhea had worked so hard to escape the first time. It had been a relief when they'd made it onto the ship, more so when they had successfully commandeered it. "I'm afraid of being trapped again."

Clo's eyes met hers, and Rhea thought she heard a catch in her breath. "You don't have to do it, you know. Kyla talks a big game, but she'd still give you all identities if you refused. She acts like a bermhole when she's worried."

Rhea gave a short laugh. "She's not wrong. The Novantae need us. As much as I wish that weren't the case, it is the hand we've been dealt." Her mouth twisted wryly. "At least Eris seems confident."

"She's good at pretending," Clo said, her face closing as she stared out at the stars. "Whatever front she puts up is for our benefit." Clo shifted, rubbing her false knee.

"Does it hurt?"

Clo glanced down at the metal peeking from the bottom of her trousers. "Sometimes. My prosthetic needs to be upgraded, but no idea where I can find one or how to pay for it. It rubs. But it's more my center of gravity is a little different. I can't trust my movements in the same way, but I can still do what I need."

"May I ask how you lost it?"

Clo's lips flattened. "Eris."

Rhea couldn't hide her shock. "I'm . . . Oh gods, I'm so sorry. I didn't mean to—"

Clo's laugh was dry, forced. "No, it's okay. It—" She shut her eyes and made some frustrated noise. "Fuck. I hate her so much for it, but it saved my godsdamned life." Clo sat up, scowling. "But *she's* the one who got us into trouble on the mission in the first place."

Rhea tried to keep her expression gentle. She didn't want to discourage Clo, didn't want to show any judgment. Part of her work in the Pleasure Garden had been listening. It had been the part she found the most rewarding. "Did she?"

"*Yes*. She—" Clo let out a breath and ran her hand across her buzzed hair. "No . . . that's a lie. It was me." Clo looked at Rhea. "Still don't like her, but I'm trying to let it go. Can't change it."

"None of us can change what's happened to us, but we can work on making things better."

Clo raised her glass. "Wrong thing to toast with, but cheers." They clinked their water glasses.

Clo's eyes lingered on Rhea's face. It would be so easy to lean forward, to close the distance and distract them both from what was to come. But was that truly what they needed? Or was Rhea defaulting to how she dealt with emotions in the Pleasure Garden? Sex as a weapon, as protection, as distraction. And sometimes, as comfort.

"Thank you," Rhea said. "For the dances."

"You're welcome." Clo chuckled to herself, and Rhea couldn't tell if it was in sadness or joy. Perhaps both. "I haven't danced like that since . . . gods, since I was a kid in the Snarl loitering outside the clubs."

Rhea didn't know anything about life on other planets, let alone in the slums, but that explained the hint of dialect lurking in Clo's swearing. Rhea had never met someone natural-born before. "You lived on Myndalia, then. One of my clients was an officer stationed there. I didn't know they had clubs."

"Practically one on every corner in the Snarl. Places where people would dance and take"—she shifted her gaze away and shrugged—"stuff. You know, to forget. It's easier to forget you're starving when you're too salted to give a shit. The Empire provides the drugs, passes 'em around like sweets. Keeps us natural-born dependent on the high, so we never resist. Just another tool of control."

Rhea's life in the Pleasure Garden—as vast as the garden was—had been a cage. The walls there were so high, so impossible to climb. Rhea would often stare up at the stars and wonder what it was like to travel, what it was like beyond those vast walls.

There were whole worlds. People like Clo. People from different lands, and she wanted to learn about it all.

"And you?" *Tell me about your strange slang. About the scars on your hands. About your life in the Snarl. The things you've seen. Tell me everything.* "Did you go to the clubs to forget too?"

"No. I just wanted to dance."

Gods, Clo was lovely. Not overtly beautiful, not like Eris. But she had a stubborn jaw and haunted eyes and Rhea wanted to make her smile and laugh and drive those ghosts away. Rhea curled her fingers into her palm so she didn't reach for Clo—as much as she wanted to.

Clo leaned back again and gazed up at the sky. "This is my favorite place in every ship," she said wistfully. "Other than the captain's chair, of course."

"I can see why." Rhea leaned back with a contented smile. "I've never been on a ship before this."

"Never?" Clo sounded astonished. "Not even in the palace hangar?"

"No. Damocles kept me within the walls of the Pleasure Garden. I never even left to visit the city. That's why I'm—" Rhea pressed her lips together. *That's why I'm afraid to go back.*

Clo must have understood her unspoken sentiment, for she nodded once. "If we survive this mission, I'll take you out in a bullet craft. They have wide windows and it makes you feel like you're outside among the stars."

"I'd like that."

"Good. It gives us something to look forward to." She glanced at the door. "I should probably get to bed."

The other woman started to stand, but Rhea's hand shot out and grasped her wrist. "Clo?"

"Yeah?"

"Will you . . ." Rhea swallowed, then spoke hesitantly. "Will you take me other places, too? Distant worlds? I'd like to see them."

Clo paused, her lips curving into a smile. "Sure, Rhea. I'll show you the whole galaxy, if you like."

Rhea smiled back. She loved that. She wanted to see everything.

After Clo left, Rhea burrowed into her chair and watched the stars. She let tears come freely, for come moonrise, she would once again be behind those high walls.

22.

Present day

Hold back your feelings, Eris. Don't let anyone see them.

She was on the bridge, her body tense as *Zelus* came ever closer to the Three Sisters. The bridge was much bigger than the one on *Asteria*. There were ten seats and stations. This ship was meant to be helmed by so many more soldiers—but the old *Zelus* crew were ghosts, their bodies floating out in the vastness of space.

Before they grew too close, the ship slowed. Eris brought up a closer view of Macella on the main screen.

Eris hated Macella.

After leaving the academy on Myndalia and surviving duels with all her siblings, Eris had been required to report to the Three Sisters. Each planet served as some testing ground for her father's torturous form of training.

The worst had taken place on Macella, the smallest of the Three Sisters. Like at the academy, Eris's rewards were food and sleep, and the punishment beaten into her by other soldiers while her father watched. She had learned on Macella that Mistress Heraia had only been preparing her for what was to come: her father's training.

The Archon was a brutal taskmaster. He was not kind. He did not tolerate weakness.

Worse: Eris hated how much she and Damocles had craved his

scant, often-withheld approval. She once went a full year without hearing her name on her father's tongue. He only spoke to her by name to indicate his pleasure. No compliments. No kind words. Just the right to be called something other than "girl." Damocles was her partner through all this torture. He could never get through a session without breaking.

Once, on the training grounds of the palace, beaten and half-starved, she'd heard the Archon call her *Discordia.* Eris hated how warm it made her feel.

Her father had never once spoken Damocles's name. He was always referred to as *boy.*

She shoved the memory away, focusing on the ship's slow approach.

The planet looked so welcoming, no doubt the very thing that had attracted humans to it almost a millennium before. It had been the first planet after Tholos to be terraformed for human habitation. The green and blue planet looked much like the Old World, or so the history texts said. The orbit was so similar to that planet's, they used nearly the same units for time. The first Archon kept the months and days of the week, named after other gods, other kings.

The main difference was that on Macella—like on so many of the conquered Tholosian planets—the buildings were decorated with bones.

Macella had once been home to four-legged creatures called the Olos, who had made the mistake of communicating with early humans via rough sounds and symbols drawn into the sand. That alone was not reason enough to slaughter them, but their food sources were. When the Archon believed the God of Death called for sacrifice, it was easiest to slaughter nonhumans. The Olos had served their purpose. It was only after Eris had betrayed her Empire that she started wondering what these various life forms would have been like. What the Empire had murdered for their ravenous God.

"Eris," Clo said, gently tapping her shoulder. "Kyla's on the line."

Keep it together. She couldn't afford to be pulled into her past, the centuries of conquest her family was responsible for. There would be time enough for guilt after this mission, before she was sent on her next suicide mission.

Eris reached over Clo to press the button that would put Kyla on speaker. "Hey, commander," Eris said. "Briefing?"

Kyla's dry laugh was slightly muted by the static. "I lost communication with Sher, so we are officially off-script. ITI mission, Eris. Big time."

"ITI?" Ariadne asked from her swivel chair next to Clo. It'd have once belonged to the head of security, now floating somewhere in the void between their current location and Myndalia.

"Impossible to Infiltrate," Clo clarified. "Apparently, Eris gets off on these."

<Shut up, Clo. You have no idea what gets me off,> Eris said through the Pathos. Clo laughed in response. "What am I doing, Kyla? Does it involve shoving Clo out the airlock?"

Kyla paused. "You're not going to like this. The engineer angle is a bust. I'm going to need you to be Zoe."

"No," Eris said immediately.

Ariadne and Clo mouthed, *Who is Zoe?*

"Eris." The commander's tone was a warning of its own: *Don't piss me off.* "I didn't call you to negotiate. I called you to give an order."

She didn't move a muscle. She could feel Clo's eyes on the back of her neck. "I've taken every order you've ever given me without question. And I'm telling you: come up with a different plan. Zoe is too dangerous for Damocles to know directly."

Hunting down Zoe Eirene-X-2 had been Eris's first assignment with the resistance. Eris had been desperate to throw herself into a mission—to prove her changed loyalties. The more dangerous, the better. Zoe was an arms dealer who had been of relatively low consequence until she'd provided innovative and destructive weapons for the Battle of the Garnet. The Tholosian military had used her weapons to slaughter thousands of Evoli until the Oversouls had managed to prove that Discordia's death had not been one of theirs.

Eris had a responsibility to go after Zoe; she was just as responsible for the deaths of Evoli as the woman who supplied the weapons. For months, Eris watched as the arms dealer had been catapulted to riches and secured more weapons contracts. It had also made her a prime target for the resistance, but no one had been able to get close to her.

Except Eris.

Eris killed Zoe—quick and too clean—and stole her identity.

After that, "Zoe" decided she was rich enough to semi-retire. Eris would make sure she was seen cavorting and spending riches on the pleasure planet of Revelries, or pulling odd jobs that wouldn't actually result in overt deaths. She was a handy cover, able to wriggle into both official and unofficial corners of the Empire. Damocles would recognize Zoe's name. The Archon's military commanders had purchased from the real one often enough.

But Eris had never played Zoe Eirene-X-2 near Damocles, much less spoken to him.

"I don't *have* anything else," Kyla snapped. "I have ten spies dead in the Three Sisters, and possibly dozens more have had their covers blown by the Oracle. Zoe is the only godsdamned identity that hasn't been compromised and might hold up to an inspection on Macella." She let out a frustrated breath. "Look. Just get on that planet. Meet with General Damocles. Sell him something. Get him to trust you. Sher and I need to know what the fuck is going on."

Eris swallowed. The last time Eris had seen Damocles, he'd had a spray of blood painted across his cheekbone. Eyes bright with triumph. The full monster out behind the mask.

"Sell him something," Eris repeated. "That something will have to be a *weapon*, Kyla. Zoe's an arms dealer."

"I know, Eris."

"That *something* will have to be a weapon impressive enough to justify a meeting. Enough to take her out of retirement. It's not something we can half-ass."

"*I know, Eris.*"

Eris let out a slow breath. She needed to make the commander understand. So she tried another tack. "Kyla, I can't . . ." Eris's fingernails dug into her palm. "I may not be able to keep my promise to you. As Zoe. Not for this mission."

The silence on the other end was so heavy. The real Zoe Eirene-X-2 had traded in death. Capitalized on it. Eris couldn't promise not to kill anyone when the woman she was playing was the type to watch a massacre with a smile on her face. *It's just business*, as Zoe would say.

Eris, at the end of it, would have to live with the guilt.

"I know that, too," Kyla said. "But I can't think of another way. If Ariadne's right and that cargo is intended to be used to make high-density blasts, then this is what we have to go in with. We give Damocles something he'll think he can use."

Eris squared her shoulders. *Do your job.* "Fine. I need more time, and specs aren't going to be good enough to earn a face-to-face meeting. With Zoe's reputation, he's going to want a prototype. Something he can test."

"We don't have time, Eris." Kyla made a frustrated noise. "Ariadne will help you with the design, and Clo's built weapons before. We need one quick."

Clo straightened. "Are you seriously asking me to make a *killing machine* for Damocles?"

"Clo—"

Ariadne cleared her throat. "I . . . may have something." At Eris and Clo's questioning look, she said, "The Oracle gave me a project—had a fancy code name and everything—but never saw the result. I designed a lot of weapons for fun."

For . . . fun. Good gods, this girl. Eris didn't know whether to be terrified of her or impressed. "Listen, your damned hobby isn't guaranteed to get us a response, Ariadne. All requests go through Maximus." As Zoe, Eris had previously interacted with Maximus, the royal weapons tester. "The man comes off as an idiot, but I can promise you, that's just an act. We need something really convincing."

Ariadne chewed her lip. "It's convincing. It's also risky, because hardly anyone will know about it. I mean"—she let out a high laugh—"Damocles might just kill you anyway. But. He really wanted this weapon. Like, really, *really*. Maybe even for this cargo."

Before Eris could ask about the details, Kyla interrupted: "We're fresh out of options, so just send the specs." Over the line, Eris swore she heard Kyla mutter something that sounded like *Fuck me, we're fucked.*

You don't say, Eris thought.

Ariadne loading the specs onto the main screen. The images that came up—the details attached to each one—chilled Eris. They couldn't hand this over to Damocles. If they did, they'd quash any progress the Novantae had made toward bringing down the Empire.

Clo's jaw dropped. "My gods," Clo said, voice soft with something like awe, then her face hardened in horror. "We can't let them have something that could do this. Absolutely not."

Ariadne nodded, her earlier excitement deflating. "I know. That's why I never showed the finished specs to the Oracle and kept faking dead-ends. As far as One knows, I was still working on it."

Eris settled in one of the chairs and ran a hand through her hair. "Something else, then," she said. "Preferably something that *won't* give the Empire the exact weapon it needs to beat every single one of its enemies into submission. Right, Kyla?" Kyla made a sound of agreement. Good. At least her commander was thinking clearly.

"Oh! Better news!" Ariadne said, brightening. "I *think* I can limit the number of times the weapon works before it breaks, and I'll make sure the Empire can't recreate it. Or I'll do my best, anyway."

Eris narrowed her eyes. "*You think? You'll do your best?*"

The small girl crossed her arms. "Yes. I will do my best. If you have a better idea, let's hear it."

"Eris." Kyla let out a breath that echoed through the bridge. "I don't like this either. But Ariadne's right. Unless anyone has something else?"

The silence lengthened. They all knew people might suffer as a result of what they were doing. But if they didn't act, how many more would?

Kyla swore softly. "What's the code word, Ariadne?"

"Project Harpy." Ariadne fiddled with the hem of her uniform. "We'll need a few supplies if we build it. I'll send the list over with the specs. Um." She wrung her hands. "I'll need Evoli DNA, too. For the weapon."

"Okay." Eris had never heard Kyla sound so tense. "I'll send an unmanned craft with the supplies and the DNA. It'll get there before you make it to the Three Sisters."

"Kyla?" Eris was exhausted and this mission hadn't even begun.
"Yeah?"

"You owe me." She turned off the transmission.

"So," Rhea said, coming through the door of the command center.

"How bad is it?" At everyone's stare, she shrugged. "Apologies for the eavesdropping. Occupational hazard."

"It's bad," Eris said tightly. She considered Rhea for a moment. "Did you pack any other gowns?"

Rhea hesitated, bemused. "Just one, if you can call it that. More would have been waiting for me at the Legate's residence."

"Fine. Cosmetics?"

Even more puzzled, Rhea said, "Some."

"Good. Get them for me." She tapped the button for the intercom, her voice booming across the ship: "Nyx, grab me one of your spare uniforms and pile it outside my door." Before leaving the command center, she looked at Ariadne and Clo. "Finish up that weapon. And for the love of the gods, don't let them replicate it."

Eris made a face as she picked up Rhea's dress. The fabric was soft as water and just as transparent.

The real Zoe Eirene-X-2 had been born into a merchant aedifex cohort, and at the time of her death had established influence well beyond the humble origins of her siblings. Eris had studied every detail about her. She was the same height and build as Eris, which made transitioning into Zoe so easy. All it took was a facial and hair shifter.

Zoe, both real and false, lacked the sophisticated air of someone who had grown up surrounded by politics and spent years learning the proper ways to walk, talk, and hold herself. Rather, she had put on a show of pretending to know these things—but there were just enough cracks in her performance to betray the falsehood.

Zoe's smile was a bit too easy. The clothes she wore were a mix of professional and too revealing. She spoke too fast, with a hint of overly practiced refinement. Despite having no practical combat experience, soldiers liked Zoe because she smoked and drank with the best of them. Eris had kept that aspect of Zoe's identity because it made them more willing to talk to her, to trust her.

Last time, Eris thought to herself. Then Eris would let Zoe's name join her body in the fires of Avern.

"Why me?" she muttered to herself as she held up Rhea's dress. Well, *dress* was too generous a word. It was glittery and didn't even include strategic covering.

Nyx's clothes were better. They were practical, fit for a soldier: slim-cut trousers, boots, heavy buttoned jacket. It included all of her buttons, honors she had earned in battle. Eris ran her fingers along them, recognizing each one. This, for winning a major victory. This, for playing a major role in strategy. So many more.

Eris dressed as if she were preparing for a battle. In a way, she was. She was doing something the others on this ship wouldn't be able to.

Eris tried to kill less than she used to, but she knew when to break her promise to Kyla and Sher. She was invaluable to the resistance for her previous life, but also because she did the horrible things no one else would.

She took the firewolf figurine out of her pocket and traced the smoothly carved lines of its face. "I can't take you with me on this one, Xander," she whispered. "I think you'd be disappointed in what I'll have to do."

With a sigh, she left the firewolf on the table.

When she walked out of her private quarters and back into the command center dressed as Zoe, a hush went through the room. Eris knew how she looked. She was showing just enough skin to make men ogle but not enough to make them uncomfortable. Beneath Rhea's sheer, shimmering dress, she wore the undershirt from Nyx's uniform. Because of their height difference, the undershirt served as a slip.

Using the shifter embedded in the roof of her mouth, Eris had transformed her face into Zoe. Her jaw was wider, her nose a little longer, and her eyes a bright blue. She looked like someone who had done her time in the battles of business and won.

Zoe was just another of Eris's many masks.

She kept her makeup subtle. A mere hint of shading around her eyes and glitter at her cheeks. To men, it communicated: *I care, but I'm not high-maintenance.*

Every choice she made exuded the ideal woman that men thought they wanted. No matter how successful Zoe was, she was still in a cage crafted by men. Eris sometimes wished she had never killed Zoe and taken her identity.

"Uh," Clo said, covering her face with her hands. "I feel very uncomfortable."

"She means you look beautiful!" Ariadne offered. "Very glittery. Like you might seduce someone but also stab them in the neck."

Clo scoffed. "Okay, that's pretty accurate."

Rhea lay a fingertip against her bottom lip. "The dress is bewitching, I know, but I'm glad I don't have to wear it." Her lips twisted, wryly. "I wasn't allowed to choose what to wear for the Legate. Sheer isn't really my color."

Clo went very pink.

<*You're imagining her in the dress now, aren't you?*> Eris didn't bother hiding her amusement.

Clo went even pinker.

"Is that my shirt?" Nyx squinted. "What did you do to it?"

Eris crossed her arms. "I pinned it. Now if you'll excuse me, I have to make a call." She strode over to the communications board and keyed in a number through to the palace switchboard on Myndalia. When the deep male voice picked up, Eris transformed into Zoe. "Maximus, darling, it's been an age!"

Clo looked appalled. <*Darling?*>

Eris flashed her the scythes out of view of the vid-screen—the universally rude symbol of a curved index and middle finger.

The man's voice went from formal to friendly. "Zoe, is that you?"

"Of course it's me, you handsome creature. How are you? How is the weather? Have you killed anyone recently?"

Every question was spoken at exhausting speed, but Maximus, the royal weapons tester, only laughed. "Not nearly enough these days. Hopefully, that truce doesn't go anywhere, or I might be out of a job."

Zoe's laugh was husky. "Well, darling, that's what I'm calling about. I saw the announcement on the vid-screen and of course I don't have a *personal opinion*, you know, because I'm not terribly learned at politics, but I thought it might be important to go into negotiations with some protection for the Archon. You never can trust those *dreadful* Evoli, am I right?"

Maximus made a sound of agreement. "That's what I always say. What do you have for me?"

"A beautiful weapon, you gorgeous man. My very best. But I need to show it to the general directly. I know that's not the normal protocol but, well . . ." She paused for dramatic effect. "It's to do with Project Harpy."

The man sucked in a breath. "How did you—"

"Never you mind, Maximus. You know I have my secrets." She tapped the side of her nose. "Put in a good word for me, then, won't you? You'd be the one to let the general know I've solved his problem. That might work out well for you."

Maximus was quiet on the other end. She could almost hear him thinking it through, weighing up the glory with the risk of death. "All right. I'll see what I can do. Give me a moment."

Maximus's line went out with a small beep, and Eris held her breath. Off-screen, Ariadne bit her knuckles, and the others were pale with nerves.

A few minutes later, the weapons tester spoke again. "General Damocles said he will speak with you during the palace ball tomorrow evening. I've put your invitation through to the Oracle." He gave them the code to pass through the gates and bypass the main security queue.

"You're a star, Maximus!" She made a kissing sound.

When the transmission ended, Eris dropped into a chair and put her head in her hands. "Kill me."

"Was the real Zoe like that?"

"Unfortunately, yes."

"Watching you be her is hilarious," Clo said. "I mean, this is probably going to get us killed, but I'm enjoying the flark out of it anyway."

"Shut up, Clo."

With a lopsided smirk, Clo angled the ship and began their descent. Many merchants used retrofitted Empire ships, sold off once the Empire no longer required them. Luckily, *Zelus* was a slightly older model—the entire fleet hadn't yet been replaced by new technology, so the ship wouldn't be too suspect. Ariadne sent out drones to paint over *Zelus*'s name and temporarily change it to *Euphemia* before entering the Three Sisters' checkpoint. Eris went up to the observation deck and paced, agitated.

Could she face her brother?

Would he see right through her?

"Eris?" Rhea's gentle voice came from the doorway. "Clo says to come. We've been given permission to enter the Three Sisters quadrant."

Had she been gone that long? It had only felt like minutes. "Good. I'll be there in a moment."

At the other woman's disappearing footfalls, Eris dropped her hand and stared out at the stars.

"Queen kills King," she whispered.

———

Zelus crossed into the Three Sisters territory.

Tholos, Agora, and Macella were three habitable planets in the same system that comprised the first Tholosian colonies. They remained the most populous parts of the Empire, the seat of its power. On their path to Macella, *Zelus* passed Mylos, the largest of the moons that orbited the Three Sisters. One half of its surface was a prison, packed with criminals awaiting their fates who could only look out their portholes down onto the world below. Once their cases were reviewed and their next planetary destination decided, they would be turned into gerulae. People whose entire existence was erased from their memory until they were reprogrammed to question nothing, choose nothing, and be nothing.

Eris wondered how many people in there were imprisoned for daring to run from the Empire. That would be the fate of the women on this ship if they were ever caught—that is, if they weren't executed outright.

Ariadne had fitted them all with metal shifters, stamped to the roof of their mouths. The clothes were raided from the ship's stores. Shifting clothes was only to be done in an emergency. The energy output would potentially be too noticeable.

Eris gave the other women a once-over. Part of the soldiers' training was to notice inconsistencies in people's clothes, behavior, accents, and demeanor. The smallest details could expose them.

Ariadne and Rhea were wearing smart, dark blue sheath dresses to fit their roles as an accountant and a personal assistant. Rhea would be staying behind on the ship, called out only if needed.

Eris had noticed Rhea's relief when she'd asked the other woman to remain aboard. It would be difficult to mask Rhea's behavior from the

Oracle. Ariadne was able to make their Pathos implants look like Oracle chips on the scan, but though Rhea might have changed her appearance, her graceful way of moving could never be concealed. She practically floated. It was too risky.

Nyx and Clo were decked out in dark bodyguard uniforms and looked equally pissed off about it.

By now, there would be projections of their images on every planet in the Empire, and the Oracle would be working to find them. Ariadne had finished programming their new features that morning. The effect from the shifters had to be enough to fool the scans but not so extreme that it roused suspicion.

Nyx's face was softer, more delicate. Her lips were fuller, her cheekbones more prominent, and her jaw more rounded. Ariadne, by contrast, had puffed up her own features. Clo kept her hair the same but widened her nose and thinned her lips.

Zelus was hailed through the shield around Macella by one of the satellite security points.

"Here we go," Clo said with a long exhale. "Say a prayer and hope we make it out alive, bermholes."

They set down in the landing zone outside of the palace. As *Zelus* settled on the platform, they all gathered to look out the window. The Macellan palace towered above them, a goliath peppered with the bones of the Olos. Eris had seen renderings of the reptilian creatures, and she had thought their multicolored scales were beautiful.

Those scales had been used to make palace arches that glistened in the Macellan sun. They framed a manufactured lake with robotic birds.

Despite how lovely and calming the palace appeared, it was a fortress. The Oracle scanned every person who entered and left, mapped their foot traffic, their features, and their behavior. Humans were creatures of habit, easy to predict. If their behavior was inconsistent with the Oracle's prediction, One flagged that person as suspicious. And One was never wrong.

Clo unbuckled herself from the flight chair and let out a breath. "We're going to die," she muttered to herself, standing.

Eris pushed her toward the door. "How about a little optimism?"

"I prefer realism. That way, I'm less disappointed."

"Neither of you are making me feel confident," Nyx said as they gathered near the door and waited for Rhea to lower the ramp from the comm center. "And I wasn't exactly enthused about this before."

"Clo is being dramatic. As always."

"We're walking into the main seat of our enemy," Clo said. "We're completely unarmed, hoping a thin mask obscuring our features, some phony papers, Ariadne's weapons plans, and Eris's role as some scantily clad arms dealer will see us through the day. Even if we do all this, we might not even find out where the cargo came from or why Kyla's spies are all dead."

Ariadne tilted her nose up. "The files will hold up. Your DNA will match your identities." She fiddled with some small square object in her hands. "We're going to be fine. I make great stuff and my specs are amazing because *I'm* amazing."

Kyla's unmanned craft had come in shortly before *Zelus* crossed into the Three Sisters. Aside from the weapon components Ariadne had asked for, Kyla included a few small gadgets to help with their mission. Among them was a device to aid Ariadne in hacking into the Oracle's DNA storage database to change Zoe's identity.

Fear spiked through Eris. Did Ariadne know Eris was Discordia? Or had Kyla somehow encrypted the information? She looked askance at the little girl, but she was still fiddling with the component. Eris had to hope Ariadne hadn't discovered her secret.

"Look, I don't doubt your skills—" Clo started.

"Great, because I really am excellent!" Ariadne grinned. "I only hope *you* are as good as you claim."

Nyx snorted.

"Focus," Eris said, holding her breath as the ramp hit the ground. "Just so we're clear: Nyx, you're going to remain with me while I convince Damocles to buy our weapon. Ari and Clo: steal a security badge and find out about the rock." Eris cut Ariadne off before she could interrupt. "I'm not calling it Josephine again; get over it. Here we go."

Because the Tholosians had no God of Life, Eris only had one option: Salutem, the God of Survival.

Eris prayed they all made it out of this alive.

23.

Five years ago

Discordia should have known that training under her father would be worse than with Mistress Heraia. Despite the sleepless nights, the battle simulations, and the combat training, life at the academy had been easier. Decisions had been simple. Even in field training, where Discordia had killed her first Evoli soldier at the age of ten, death was always in the heat of a fight. A split-second decision. A sacrifice made.

Easy.

The Archon demanded cold rationality. Not mercy, no. Never that. He wanted whoever survived as his Heir to be feared, to be adored, to be a successor proven worthy of his throne. When Discordia killed for him, it was hardly ever in battle, though she did fight. Often. She had impressed her father enough to be taken under his personal tutelage.

The Archon had picked his favorite, even as he played at impartiality. He wanted Discordia to survive. Eighteen were gone. Thirty-two to go if she left Damocles as her Spare.

Discordia's first major victory in the war against the Evoli came after a year under the Archon's harsh lessons. She led the Empire's soldiers into a bloody, fierce battle that won her father a resource-rich planet that would ease the strain of dwindling resources in their Empire. She was celebrated across the Tholosian Empire for it. Her icon was flown over thousands of skies, and her people rallied around her image.

For her father, though, it wasn't enough.

The Archon had watched Discordia closely to ensure she would never be weighed down by guilt or sentiment of any kind. If she was to be his executioner—his Servant of Death—for every crime committed against the Empire, Discordia would have to grow used to the scent of the dead, the sound a body made when it hit the ground. One shot to the head, out like a light. Another. Another.

"Line them up," her father commanded his soldiers.

They were on the battlefront with five Novan prisoners who had tried to warn the Evoli of the Tholosians' impending attack. These rebels had been caught infiltrating the military compound on Solaris. Every soldier there knew them, had befriended them. Had never suspected the truth.

The Archon wanted them all to watch the execution.

All five in a row, eyes on her. Her father wanted her to meet the gaze of every person she killed. Always a test.

"Go on, Discordia," her father said.

Discordia didn't hesitate. She raised her Mors and went down the line: One. Two. Three. Four. Five.

So easy.

The deed was done. The God of Death would smile upon her.

But as Discordia shoved her Mors in its holster, her eyes snagged on someone in the crowd.

Xander.

Why had the Archon not let Discordia know that her brother was there? Her father's gaze met hers and he nodded in satisfaction before striding back to his tent. No indication he was aware that his son was standing nearby.

Unless . . .

Discordia almost let out a bitter laugh. He didn't recognize his own. Didn't care. Xander hadn't impressed him enough to warrant notice, to be chosen for the Archon's personal tutelage. That Discordia had was both a gift and a curse.

Xander was taller than she remembered, every bit as muscled as Damocles. The similarity ended there. Where Damocles was fair-haired,

Xander's shone as dark and lustrous as polished volcanic rock. His skin was tanned. She recalled Damocles had tracked him to Vega but lost him after his ship had become overheated from the temperature of the scorching suns there.

Alone, Discordia reminded herself. Xander had always been alone. Had never chosen his second, and now it was too late.

Such an easy kill. Why would he risk coming here?

Discordia would have moved forward to call him out, but something in Xander's features puzzled her.

What's he doing?

He stared at the bodies of those rebels. The Archon's children were taught never to have sympathy for the dead. They were the agents of the God of Death. His chosen.

They killed; they sacrificed.

It was in their nature.

His grief was so stark that Discordia flinched. Mesmerized, she watched as her brother reached up to grasp his scythe necklace. Xander's lips moved in a silent prayer. A last rite.

No, they did not give this to traitors. They didn't *deserve*—

Xander's eyes snapped to hers; the sadness was gone, as if she had imagined it. But Discordia had seen. And it had sparked an emotion she hadn't felt since the night she'd killed her first sibling.

That, more than anything else, was why she had to kill him.

———

Discordia gathered her weapons: two blades, two Mors, and a small boot knife that she had yet to use. She hadn't been that desperate.

She had killed ten siblings to Damocles's eight. They were always trying to outdo each other. Most sibling pairs remained together for protection, but Discordia and Damocles were often apart.

They had their competition. Discordia would gift the God of Death with number eleven.

Xander's tent was alight when she came—he was no doubt expecting her. The duel declaration had to be vocally made, after all. Sneaking up on a sibling the way one would in battle was discouraged. Damocles had, of course, disregarded such rules.

Discordia always gave her victims chances. Earning a win was better than stealing one.

She flung back the thick canvas of the tent.

Yes, Xander had been waiting, sitting on his cot with a single lantern lit. His military uniform was folded beside him, and he wore the threadbare clothing of a thuban, a low-soldier. Someone undecorated and barely acknowledged. The Archon called them cannon fodder. Why was a son of the Archon wearing a thuban's uniform?

If he wants to live like cannon-fodder, then he should die like one. Damocles would sneer if he were there. Her brother came up with creative ways of murdering their siblings. He would choose something brutal.

Discordia's fingers closed around her holstered Mors. She would be quick. It was the closest thing to mercy she was capable of giving.

"Discordia," he said easily, resting an arm on his knee as he leaned back in his cot. "What took you so long?"

She frowned. Why wasn't he challenging her? He smiled as if sensing her thoughts, and it was a strange sort of defiance. He knew why she was there, what she had seen earlier, and perhaps he hoped to lower her guard. His open, relaxed hands held no weapons. How could she duel a man who didn't fight back?

Their gazes met. His eyes were disconcerting. How had she not noticed them before? They were gray, like the metal of a spaceship. Striking and pale and all too sharp.

"Stand up," she commanded, trying to gain some semblance of control. "Choose your weapon, Xander. I challenge you."

He stood and his tall frame towered over hers. "I think you've found me at something of a disadvantage."

"Bullshit."

They trained their whole lives for this. He had seen her earlier. He had all the time in the world to get his weapons ready—to make his choices. More than most of their siblings would have given him.

He held his bare hands out. "Empty."

"Then take one of mine," she snarled. She'd had enough of whatever game he was playing. "Mors or blades?"

He let out a breath, a short laugh. "Blades, then."

Discordia slid the blades out of the sheaths at her wrists and tossed him one. Xander caught it easily, holding it in front of him as they circled each other. *Finally*, Discordia thought, feigning left, then stepping into a lunge. He blocked her, twisting his body to avoid the tip of her blade. He fought better than the last time she'd seen him at the academy.

Battles removed all complications. All questions. Kill Xander. Forget him. Forget what she'd seen. What she'd felt.

Swipe. Discordia almost had him, but his forearm came down against hers. He'd made no move to attack her. Not once. Discordia smacked her palm against his cheek, an insult from their training days. A reprimand a prefect would give to a child. Xander let out a small hiss of breath.

"*Fight me*," Discordia snarled.

Xander's lips flattened. "Why?"

Why? "Because you're *supposed* to." She slapped him again. "Because this is what we were trained for."

"You don't need me to fight back, Discordia. You want to kill me?" He grasped her wrist, knelt down so he could hold her blade against his throat. "Then kill me."

"That's not how it works." He was supposed to fight for his life, die with honor. "You duel. *We* duel."

"What if I don't want to?" He asked. They were breathing hard. Discordia's knife broke the skin of Xander's throat and a small trickle of blood stained his shirt. "What if I don't want any of this?"

Kill him. Her father's voice was in her head, his constant refrain. It would be so easy, wouldn't it? *Slide in the blade. Don't ask him why. Don't ask any questions about back in the square, why he said his prayers over their enemies.*

She met Xander's eyes and flinched. So many emotions she could now name: weariness, guilt, grief, trauma.

Discordia swallowed hard. "Those men out in the square today. You knew them?"

Xander kept still. "No."

"But you grieved for them." Discordia didn't understand. He was like a puzzle she couldn't put together, an unwinnable game of zatrikion. "You gave them last rites."

"You don't need to know someone to grieve for them."

He said the words so gently. Had he seen her shame earlier? "We're not supposed to feel anything for anybody," she whispered. "It's a weakness."

"Is it?"

"*Yes.*"

Xander's gaze searched hers. "Then why haven't you killed me yet?"

Why hadn't she? *Why hadn't she?* What was he but some inconvenience, a corrugation in her otherwise smooth path to being her father's Heir? It angered her that he should show up in that crowd, force her to question things, stand here so still as if he were some willing sacrifice.

Fight me, she'd commanded him. She had already killed five people today who hadn't fought her back.

And it shamed her.

With a whispered curse, Discordia took her blade from his throat and backed away unsteadily, her hand finding his desk. A map of the Iona Galaxy was laid out there, topped with little figurines. The ophidian, the lavi, the firewolf—Old World animals whose DNA had been brought by the first generation ship to Tholos and reintroduced to certain terraformed planets. Every Old World animal was considered sacred, cherished.

Discordia picked up the firewolf, tracing her fingers across the wood. Were these pieces to Xander's puzzle? Figures on their metaphorical zatrikion board? Discordia felt like a child again, trying to understand how the world worked. Her role in it. Her purpose.

"You made this." Her words almost sounded like an accusation.

She heard him let out a breath as he approached. Discordia tensed—her fingers clutching her knife in one hand—but when Xander reached out, it was only to take the firewolf from her. "I made a lot of them back on Myndalia," Xander said, studying his work. "My prefect used to break my fingers over it. The nanites healed them overnight, but I always remembered the pain."

Discordia flinched. The Archon's children were not allowed any interests that might be perceived as weaknesses. As too soft. Such things were problems to be solved. Discordia had enjoyed drawing. The small pictures she created on her tablet were erased daily, lest Mistress Heraia discover them.

One day, the prefect had. Yes, Discordia had her fingers broken, too. She remembered that pain of bones knitting together too fast, how tender they were the next day in training. But unlike Xander, she had never disobeyed again. She had conformed.

"Why?" she asked in a low voice. "Why keep making them if you were punished?"

He must have seen her vulnerability. Her control fraying at the edges. He handed the firewolf back to her, closed her fingers around it. "Because when I made these, I could forget," Xander said softly.

"Forget what?"

"Everything," he told her. "Everything they did to us." When Discordia didn't respond, Xander nodded to the firewolf in her hands. "Keep it, if you like."

"I don't need it," she said flatly.

Xander gave her a slight smile. "Then bring it back the next time you try to kill me."

"I have to." Discordia needed him to understand. This was some fluke. Some moment of softness. She could not let it happen again. "I have to kill you, Xander."

His smile disappeared. "If you say so, Discordia."

She took the firewolf back to her tent. After putting out the lanterns, Discordia lay in the darkness with the firewolf pressed to her palm.

And for the first time in her life, she let herself forget.

24.

Present day

Zoe Eirene-X-2 strolled with the confidence of a woman at ease with her life and the way she manipulated people.

Eris walked between Ariadne and Nyx. The skirt of the sheer dress trailed behind her, thin fabric clinging to her legs. It felt powerful, as if she were wearing armor.

No one looking at her would ever guess she wore the face of a dead woman, and beneath that was another alias. No one would suspect that the whole galaxy could have been hers.

Clo brought up the rear as another assistant, the kind of person Zoe would bring along for effect. No one needed three personal assistants, but the arms dealer had a flair for the dramatic.

<Nobody speak unless you're spoken to,> Eris said through the Pathos. *<Let me handle everything. And do whatever I ask.>*

<Don't make me regret this,> Clo grumbled.

<Don't be an asshole,> Eris sang back.

<Assholes are warm and sensitive,> Clo returned. Eris fought down a startled laugh.

At the entrance of the palace, the guards scanned her fingerprints and pricked her thumb to run her genetic code through the Oracle's system. Eris forced herself to breathe evenly, to keep her heart rate steady.

Eris relaxed at the *beep* of the all clear. The guards bowed politely and ushered them inside.

The grand hall of the palace was comprised of millions of bones separated by the glittering blue lapis from the mines of Macella. The various decks ringed the edges, endless doors leading to offices, conference rooms, and secrets. Everything shone—the bones that had been painted a rich gold, the bright silver of the archways. All of the walls were etched in more scenes of conquering and victory of other planets. Over one hundred planets in eight hundred years, systematically emptied of indigenous life forms, no matter their sentience, and smoothed over to pave the way for humans and the regimented Tholosian way of life. The floor was made of burnished Tholosian marble, white with veins of black, silver, gold, and soft pink.

Another guard guided them through the open space. People bustled to and fro, everyone on a clear mission. The countless footsteps echoed through the grand hall. Eris held her head high, shoulders back—the same careless grace that Zoe Eirene-X-2 gave to everything.

Training alone kept Eris's hands from trembling, her face showing her true emotion: the desperate urge to run.

The doors to the ballroom opened, graceful violin music filtering out into the long, carpeted hallway, and Eris disappeared into her character. The way she walked held a hint of too much speed. And when she grasped the champagne flute off the plate in the steady hand of the wait staff, she drank without the same delicate sips Eris had been taught for years.

Eris spotted a familiar face from a past mission. Commander Ronan. Now, *there* was a man who would have access to the Oracle's record room.

<*Found your target,*> Eris sent Ariadne and Clo, surreptitiously tilting her head. <*Give me a moment to chat him up while you take his pass. Be careful.*>

"Commander Ronan!" Eris-as-Zoe boomed, smoothly inserting herself in a circle of the highest-ranking politicians. "It's so lovely to see you, and under such pleasant circumstances, too."

The tall commander turned and grinned. He had a square block of a face, large hands nicked with scars from battle and missing the pinky on his left hand. Jet-black hair with a hint of gray. "Zoe." He came forward and kissed each of her cheeks. Eris held back a cringe. "What the seven devils are you doing here, beautiful?"

The commander was someone she had known as Princess Discordia; she'd trained some of his soldiers herself. That familiarity with him had helped her gain his trust as Zoe, a somewhat gauche but invaluable friend and asset. Being a weapons dealer with a pretty face certainly helped.

Clo's gaze flickered to Eris and narrowed. Eris knew she was surprised—no doubt rightfully wondering why Zoe and a commander of the Tholosian Empire were on such familiar terms. Their delicate truce was still spiderweb-thin—and trust could be just as tenuous.

Focus, Eris told herself. She couldn't worry about Clo's suspicions.

"Oh, you know me," Eris said, playing up Zoe's Solarian accent. A reminder that despite her surroundings, Zoe was not a politician or royalty. She was a merchant. A dealer. Any Oracle programming in her cohort would stick to business. "I'm always on the job. The God of Death doesn't sleep in my line of work." Eris grinned.

Commander Ronan laughed and looked at Clo, Nyx, and Ariadne. "You have an entourage today."

Eris glanced over her shoulder at the other women. Clo was barely suppressing a scowl. "Oh, they're not important." Eris waved a dismissive hand. "Assistant, assistant, assistant."

"Are they gerulae?" the commander asked with interest.

Eris scoffed. "No, no. They'd be even more useless. They'd walk into walls or some such." Eris tilted her head at Clo. "Well? I believe my glass is empty."

Clo stared in bemusement at the half-full glass. With relish, Eris downed the glass in a single gulp, handing Clo the flute. Clo's lip twitched. "Right away, Negotiare," she said, body language respectful but her eyes glared a *flume you*.

"And you," Eris said to Nyx. "Cheese plate. Now."

Nyx set her jaw and followed Clo. Eris sighed. "It's so difficult to find useful servitor, you know. That's why I have three. In case one or two of them are useless at any given time."

<*You sound like a silthead,*> Clo said through the Pathos.

<Agreed,> chimed Nyx.

Ariadne made a small noise of agreement next to Eris. Short and fine-boned as she was, some might think her too young to be an assistant. It was unusual, but not uncommon, to take those from servant cohorts in as soon as they left training. It was easier to shape their programming around specific owners' needs at a young age. Most young servants were taken in by politicians and other high-ranking officials, a mark of their privilege. That Zoe had a servant so young was a wordless brag of accomplishment.

The commander smiled, with an attempt at charm. "Well, you've certainly convinced me to consider adding to my assistants."

Eris kept her own fake, warm smile. "Just as long as you don't poach mine, Commander."

Those in the circle laughed.

<Ariadne,> Eris sent on the Pathos. *<Go in for his pass now.>*

Back on *Zelus,* Ariadne had sworn to Eris that her fingers were as light as feathers and she'd be able to lift the badge. Eris sure as flames hoped the girl could deliver. It was easier to work alone. Fewer variables.

"I'd love to know what my commander finds to be so amusing." The voice came from behind Eris.

Her back stiffened. She reached and grasped Ariadne's wrist so tightly that the girl let out a short gasp of pain. *<Don't move.>*

She ignored Ariadne's look of confusion. It took every ounce of her effort to paste on that false Zoe smile as she turned to face her brother.

Three years had changed Damocles. The Heir Apparent had a pure, chiseled, engineered beauty. Blond, glossy hair, perfectly styled. Strong brows like wings. Piercing dark eyes, strong features, an expressive mouth. A body molded to strength and agility, filled out with age into a mountain of a man. Perfect. Cruel. His black military uniform was immaculate and pressed, the golden buttons gleaming in the chandelier light. Each one marked his high rank and stature. No one in the galaxy could match the ones he wore—except for Eris. Once.

The rage simmering in her belly burned hot when his gaze touched hers. She thought about how easy it would be to take out a hairpin and, with one thrust into his throat, end his life. Skin was so delicate.

Stop it. Don't compromise the mission. Do your godsdamn job.

Eris knew Damocles's weaknesses—and one of them was a soft spot for beautiful women. Despising herself, she curled her lips into a charming smile. *Don't throw up. Don't throw up.*

Thankfully, the Commander dropped into a deep, stiff bow. Eris followed with a curtsy, holding out the glimmering fabric of her skirt. "The Negotiare here was just telling us about her assistants," Commander Ronan said. "Have you met Zoe, General Damocles?"

<*Oh silt,*> Clo muttered. She must have seen him by Eris's side.

Eris tried not to let her expression waver. Back when she had been chosen by their father to be general, her brother had been brigadier, one step below her. Now he had taken her place. Her title.

Damocles's eyes shifted to hers. Cold, even when he smiled.

"I haven't had the pleasure, no," her brother said. His voice sounded deeper, rougher. "But I've heard enough about her to catch my attention."

Maximus had come through.

She laughed Zoe's sensual, throaty laugh, and reached out her hand, palm down. "Zoe Eirene-X-2," she said. "It's wonderful to finally meet you in person."

Eris didn't miss Damocles's perusal of her clingy dress. She wished she were wearing something shapeless. Like a long coat. Or a sack of some kind. With a bag over her head.

"One of the Eirene cohort," Damocles said, not yet moving to take her hand. "Not impressive genetic stock, that, even for a merchant aedifex class."

No one seemed surprised by his blunt observation. After all, everyone there placed importance on the cohorts people were born into, and her class barely registered in their glittering world, except as a means to acquire goods.

Eris kept Zoe's smile. "Yes, I'm afraid you'll find the vast majority of the Eirenes to be quite useless, General. Good only for selling scrap and whatever slop the servants eat. I aspire to provide goods with *actual* use for the Empire's expansion."

"How intriguing," Damocles said, gently taking her offered hand. "If you'll excuse me, Commander, I'm going to steal her." The commander bowed as Damocles led Eris away, with Ariadne trailing silently behind. Clo and Nyx paused halfway across the ballroom, one with the wine and one with the cheese plate.

Damocles led her to a quieter corner. "My weapons tester speaks very highly of you. He tells me, Negotiare, that you have a solution to a particular problem of mine."

"Please," Eris said with a laugh, "call me Zoe." If she knew one thing about her brother, it was that while he obsessed over tradition, he preferred women who were more straightforward. The real Zoe had been exactly his type. "I'm so glad I finally have the opportunity to meet you in person. I'm often so deep into research, I can never seem to come to such glittering events like these." She shrugged. "Nature of my business."

Clo and Nyx showed up with her wine and cheese. Eris didn't miss the way Clo edged away from Damocles and handed Eris the wine with her lips pursed. In contrast, Nyx remained rigid, her back straight. A soldier's stance.

She wasn't playing a soldier.

Eris couldn't risk one of them blowing their cover. Eris had to distract him. Now.

She handed her plate to Ariadne and waved off the other women. "For gods' sake," she said, a touch too loudly, "don't just stand there and gawk at me." She glanced at the Prince. "Unless you'd like them to fetch you wine. That's the only thing they're good for."

Eris had to hide her breath of relief when Damocles shook his head. "No need."

"It's better that way. They'd probably drop it on your feet," she said, waving them off. "Leave me be." Clo passed her an inscrutable look as she left with Nyx.

Damocles's lip quirked up in amusement. "Actually," the prince said slowly, "I've changed my mind. I believe I'll have that wine after all." Before Eris could signal the women to return, Damocles gestured with a nod. "Let's have a bit more privacy."

Eris tried to calm her breathing. It had been years since she'd been alone with her brother. Playing Zoe around other people was easy because none of them knew her well enough to see through the performance. Her brother did. Eris was going to have to be very, very careful.

She smiled, flashing her teeth. "Of course." To Ariadne: "Find the others, and for god's sake, try to look like you're enjoying yourself."

At that last statement, she sent through the Pathos: *<Clo and Ari, back to the plan. Get the badge. And be careful. Nyx, stay close in case I need you.>*

Damocles led Eris to one of the refreshment tables in a sparsely populated section of the ballroom. What few people were there drifted off, sensing the general's desire to converse uninterrupted.

"My weapons expert implied you were colleagues," he said, all smoothness. "I've heard your name but not the specifics of your work." Eris understood when she was being tested. Damocles would never admit to knowing what the real Zoe had done for the Battle of the Garnet. No, he wanted to get a sense of her first.

"We're colleagues of a sort." Eris sipped her wine as if she didn't mind the severity of his stare. "Though I'm semi-retired these days, my role is less public. I am in the business of designing and manufacturing certain items for individuals with need and a great deal of funds."

Nyx swore through the Pathos. *<I've seen him execute merchants for selling to the wrong individuals. I hope you know what you're doing.>*

<Yeah, 'cause if you don't, we're all dead,> Clo chimed in.

<I appreciate the vote of confidence,> Eris replied.

The prince's expression didn't change; it remained as cold and impassive as ever. "And yet you knew the name of a project that Maximus most assuredly didn't tell you about." A step closer. "So, who did?"

<Get out of there,> Nyx insisted.

<He's testing me,> Eris pushed back. *<Let me do my job.>*

Eris knew two things: Damocles often disagreed with their father, and he hated the Evoli. Rhea said he wasn't pleased about the truce. If anyone knew how the rocks were intended to be used and where they came from, Damocles did. She'd bet her life on it. Right now, he was measuring her, noting her loyalties.

Eris kept her smile. "Looking to kill someone, General?"

"Yes." His expression was cold. "I can't abide disloyalty."

"We're in agreement." Eris laughed low in her throat. "Fortunately for you, the person who told me is already dead. Felix Iasion-17." One of the burned Novan spies. It was risky to give the name of a dead spy, considering how he met his end, but Eris couldn't put anyone else at risk. Felix had been one of the lesser members of Maximus's cohort. Someone who should have been forgettable. "He was hoping to prove himself. I found the project . . . fascinating. I only wish Maximus had trusted me with the problem himself. I could have solved it for you months ago. It was interesting enough to come out of my partial retirement." She gave a dramatic sigh. "Turns out spending vast amounts of money becomes remarkably monotonous after a while. Who'd have thought?"

Damocles sipped his wine. "Maximus is loyal. The Oracle saw to it after that spy was found."

Her brother sounded casual, but Eris noted how tense he was. Yes, Damocles was alarmed by the knowledge of spies in his midst; he would have the Oracle tighten One's influence, run One's programming more vigilantly. He might have already done that before Ariadne left, during those commands she'd forgotten under stress. Eris would have to be careful, because he would not trust her easily.

She saw one opening: greed gleamed in his eyes. She had promised Damocles an answer to a problem even the Oracle couldn't solve.

"Maximus can vouch for me," Eris said lightly. "Let me desist with the coyness: I specialize in the design and sale of advanced weaponry, which puts me in contact with your testing facility from time to time. Quietly." Her lips curved into a smile. "Disloyalty to my clients, General, would be bad for business. I deal with it as efficiently as you."

He leaned closer. "You're one step away from a pirate."

"A little step." She tilted her head back to drink. Damocles's eyes caught on the column of her throat.

<You're pretending to be a pirate again?>, Clo said through the Pathos. *<And ugh, I can't believe you're flirting with your—>* She broke off. *<Ari, would you hurry up and copy that fluming pass? What are you doing?>*

<I'm hurrying,> came Ariadne's voice. *<I'd go faster if you'd stop*

glaring at me.> After another beat: *<It's done. I'm going to go slip it back in the commander's pocket. Eris, we'll meet you at the ship.>*

Thank the gods. Clo had come close to slipping, and their squabbling was distracting. She couldn't afford even the tiniest mistake.

"Hypothetically," the prince said smoothly, "if your clients included the Evoli or the Novantae, that would be treason. The punishment is execution."

"I believe what I just designed proves I want no affiliation with sorcerers or traitors. Alas, that means I'd lose such a charming descriptor just when I was considering an eye patch. But if I was a pirate"—she lowered her voice conspiratorially—"well, I should think it would be fitting I go out in a blaze of glory."

Prince Damocles's smile was small, and her hatred burned all the brighter. Eris wanted to rip off her Zoe disguise and smash her fist into his face. Wipe that smile off.

Breathe. Bury your feelings deep, just like Father taught you.

He shook his head. "I ought to be insulted at your informality."

She half-lowered her eyelids. "Well, are you?"

"I'm not certain yet."

With another rueful smile, he set his half-empty glass down on the table. "If you'll excuse me, I need to greet my other guests. You understand."

"Of course."

Eris tried not to let her disappointment show. She had been hoping to get some answers out of him. Flames, *anything*, really. Without another chance for discussion, this would be the end of Zoe's part in this mission. Kyla wasn't going to be happy.

The prince stepped back and said, "You will return tomorrow night. My guard will bring you through the east wing of the palace, away from the other guests. Bring along a prototype of the weapon you promised my engineer. Let's see if you've solved Project Harpy as you claim."

———

Back at the ship's command center, Eris felt like running again. From the looks on the faces of her compatriots, she wasn't alone.

"Honestly," Nyx said, standing near Clo as she started dropping mechanical parts on the work table, "I'm surprised General Damocles didn't decapitate you right there in the ballroom."

"Zoe has a certain ribald charm." Eris eyed the piles of metal and hoped Clo knew what the seven devils she was doing. If they didn't produce an impressive-enough weapon to show Damocles, he definitely *would* decapitate her.

"Charm?" Clo snorted. "You were a complete silthole." She sat back down at her work table, organizing the component pieces on the table that she'd taken from various Novan weaponry, plus the supplies Kyla's unmanned craft had delivered. "You better hope we can build this in time. Ari and I are saving your hummocks."

Ariadne sat next to her, wearing oversized goggles. "That bit should go there." She pointed.

"Do you think you can do this?" Eris asked Clo and Ariadne, gesturing to that pile of parts she couldn't identify. Her voice sounded even, calm—a far cry from how she felt.

"Build a never-before-seen weapon impressive enough that a war-mongering prince will begin trusting you enough to confide the intel Kyla needs? In a day?" Clo examined a piece, set it down. "Doubtful. I say we all get drunk again and enjoy our last hours."

Nyx made an impatient noise and gestured to the weapon in Clo's hands. "Better get to work, then. I didn't escape the Empire just to come back and die."

Eris felt a pang of guilt. If she died on this planet, at least it was during a mission doing something she believed in. These three were refugees. And they were still risking their lives when they should have been given a chance at a normal life.

She met Clo's gaze, and the other woman bowed over the firearm she was taking apart. "Do you want the good news or the bad news?" Clo asked them, her expression reluctant.

They all exchanged looks.

Nyx spoke first. "Why don't we start with the good before getting to the steaming pile of shit?"

"I'm pretty sure we can make this weapon. I'm also pretty sure I can make it *in time*."

Eris let out a breath of relief. "And the bad?"

"I don't have any guarantees Damocles's engineers won't figure out how to retrofit it and use it to kill a bunch of people. We ought to plant a convincing fake." When no one responded, she made a noise in the back of her throat. "We're talking about a theoretical genocide, people. Come on. Look a little more alarmed."

"Clo's right," Rhea said softly, looking at the specs. "I know Damocles. If you give him this, he won't use it to protect the Empire—he'll use it to destroy everyone else. This isn't the weapon of a leader; it's the weapon of a conqueror."

Ariadne chewed her lip. "I can make it basically disintegrate after five uses," she said. "Just needs a little bit of a solution . . . here."

Nyx didn't look convinced. "And if Damocles makes a full scan of it before he shoots it five times? And he updates it to the Oracle's database?"

"Maybe he won't?"

Clo set down the tools, rubbing her temples. "Nyx is right, Ariadne. If they crack this, we'll be responsible for more deaths than the Battle of the Garnet. A *hundred*fold."

They all went quiet, and the four women looked at Eris. She had to do this. She had to earn Damocles's trust. At this very moment, he was probably having his experts run a search on Zoe Eirene-X-2 to make sure her alias was legitimate. It would hold for now. But if she went there tomorrow with nothing, that alias wasn't going to save any of them.

Fuck. Someone had to make the hard decision here. Let the deaths be on her conscience, to keep company with all the others.

"I know the risk," Eris said quietly. "But a fake will only get us all killed, and then there will be nothing stopping Damocles from whatever he's planning. Ariadne, put everything you can into the failsafe. Just get it made."

25.

Present day

The weapon Clo and Ariadne created was the worst possible thing they could put in the hands of any person, let alone a Tholosian. Let alone Prince fucking Damocles.

While constructing the weapon from Ariadne's schematics, Clo had wished she were a little less skilled at this. Ariadne's specs were a decent guideline, but they weren't perfect—they were created by someone who had very clearly never held a weapon in her hands.

Clo was different. She had taken apart and put together so many different weapons back in the Snarl: old and new, retrofitted, experimental designs. Her knowledge had helped fill in those last gaps in Ariadne's schematics. Without those small differences, she still would have produced something impressive. But not one that made her think, upon its completion, that she had made a huge mistake.

What have I done?

It was too late to change the design back or come up with something else.

"Send the updated schematics to Kyla," Eris said to Ariadne. "If something goes wrong, we'll need the engineers at Nova to know what they're working with and give our side a fighting chance."

Ariadne nodded and sat next to Clo, the same guilt radiating off her small frame. She pinged in Kyla's details and sent off the design. The whole command center was quiet—every woman lost in her own thoughts.

"You don't have to come," Eris said as Clo checked over the weapon. "I know Damocles murdered your friend. If this is too much, you can stay on the ship with Rhea. The others and I can handle this."

Clo pressed her lips together. *Briggs.* She missed him so much that every year, on the anniversary of his death, she got completely sluiced just to forget.

"No," she said. "Anything goes wrong with the weapon, I need to be there to fix it. I made changes to Ariadne's design."

"Okay." Eris helped Clo settle the weapon into a suitcase, and they sealed it up tight. "Clo?" she said softly. "I'm sorry for this."

Clo blinked in surprise, then ducked her head. Eris was holding their creation, and she knew how it was going to be used. Yet more sacrifices to the God of Death. "So am I," Clo replied.

They arrived again at the palace, per Damocles's instructions. The guard led them to a grand conference room that curved around the north side of the compound, giving them a glimpse over the mountains. During the few days they'd spent on Macella, Clo had pondered this view as closely as she had Ariadne's weapon schematics. This time of day, mist began to coil along the ground. By the time they returned to their ship, it would be knee-height.

Macella was the most populated planet in the galaxy—even more so than Tholos. Aside from the courtesans in the Pleasure Garden, the Archon allowed only the upper echelons of the Empire to reside on that planet with him. Macella, in contrast, was home to even the aedifex and opifex classes. The buildings rising from the mist were not as precarious and tight as the slums on Myndalia, but they spread as far as the eye could see.

The Three Sisters had very little farming land aside from the two moons that orbited Macella and Tholos, so most had to be imported from other planets. It was a weakness the Empire was well aware of—if a bottleneck were ever created with supplies, the population of these three planets would grow hungry quickly, and it would weaken the rest of the Empire.

The situation with Charon was bad enough that it ought to have necessitated a move to another planet—perhaps even outside the galaxy—were it not for the second problem: Macella had the most drinkable fresh water of any planet in the Tholosian Empire, fed from the mountains.

Even the Evoli desired the freshwater resources of Macella, which was no doubt why they agreed to the truce in the first place. The Tholosians could not leave such a precious resource vulnerable.

Clo knew Kyla had mulled over the possibility of interrupting the supply lines—with Charon's resources all but gone, it would have been a decisive victory over the Empire—but the commander grappled with the morality of starving out civilians. It would make the resistance no better than their enemy. For now, all they could do was increase their numbers and prevent Imperial expansion as best they could.

With this weapon, Clo felt as if they were going against everything the Novantae had fought for.

Prince Damocles waited for them in the conference room. Through her Pathos, Clo heard Rhea swear; the other woman was watching the video feedback in the ship's command center from the eye implant Ariadne had received from Kyla with the supplies.

<You all right, Rhea?> Clo asked.

<I'll be fine,> Rhea said quietly. *<Focus on the task. Don't worry about me.>*

The women all bowed to Damocles. Clo gritted her teeth, tightening her grip on the weapon case. It was light, perfectly built for speed in battle. Another feature Clo knew she would come to regret.

"General." Eris fell back into Zoe's slightly twangy Solarian accent. "It's so good to see you again," she said. "I notice your guests are still here. Hosting another ball?"

"It's the same ball," Damocles said. "It lasts five nights."

"Five nights?" Eris rested a hand against the hollow of her throat. "I hope it's not driving you to madness."

"As you can see, my sanity remains intact."

"And here I am, making more demands of your time."

"I prefer discussing weaponry, I assure you."

"So do I. Must be the pirate in me," Eris said with a flirtatious smile.

Clo made the smallest sound in her throat, unwittingly drawing Damocles's attention. The moment their eyes met, Clo sucked in a breath and meekly stared at the floor, trying to tamp down the memories of that face staring at her down the barrel of a Mors. She'd been barely more than a child, and he'd shot at her.

Gods, how she hated him.

Eris stepped in front of her, trailing her fingertips along the edge of the conference table, where a game of zatrikion sat half-completed. Sher was fond of the circular board game and had taught Clo how to play when she came to live at Nova. She was never able to capture his queen.

"Were you in the middle of a game?" Eris asked with a half-smile.

"Not a recent one. My father leaves me a move to puzzle over whenever he visits," General Damocles said. "Do merchants play?"

Eris's hand dropped. "It's rare in the aedifex class, but yes. I sometimes have the opportunity in my line of work."

He motioned to one of the chairs. "Then sit. Play a round with me."

<Shit,> Eris sent through the Pathos.

<What is it?> Clo asked.

Eris settled across from Damocles and smoothed her skirts, then motioned to Ariadne, Clo, and Nyx to step back. Though she looked calm, Clo could sense her unease through the Pathos. At that moment, all their disguises seemed frail, as vulnerable as glass.

<Nothing,> Eris replied.

Clo wisely kept silent as Damocles saved the existing game in the board's mainframe before rearranging the pieces to their starting positions. He invited Eris to make the first move.

She did. Peasant forward. A pedestrian move, indicative of someone who hadn't played in a long time.

Damocles didn't mention anything as he shifted his own red piece. "Tell me about your weapon."

"I'll be honest," she said as they moved through the first battle. "This is a prototype. Your testing facility will no doubt perfect it before use."

"We have plenty of weapons. Why should I bother giving this one my time and attention? Especially if the war might come to an end?"

Clo tried not to flinch. She could make an entire list of the reasons he should give this one his attention, and all of them were monstrous. If he created high-density blasts from the cargo, this weapon would be unstoppable.

<*I hate this,*> she hissed through the Pathos.

<*Me too,*> Ariadne added.

<*You think I don't?*> Eris shot back.

"Wars will always need to be fought, General. Let's start with the basics," Eris said, "It can shoot faster than a Mors—"

Damocles sat back, bored. "It doesn't matter how fast it shoots, if it doesn't improve on the technology. I'm sure that line might have been enticing for my father during the Battle of the Garnet, but the Evoli already came up with the technology to block a Mors blast. If that's all . . ."

Eris pursed her lips, as if she hated what she was about to say. "It targets specific genetic sequences."

Now, *that* got his attention. "Go on."

"All you need is to input a genetic code, and the weapon can target any individual or group of people you'd like. It would work on any alien species—even Evoli, assuming that truce doesn't hold. Test it with a high-density blast and it'll shoot right through Evoli armor. Perhaps through a ship, if you used projectiles that were hard enough. I assume this was the answer to Project Harpy you sought." There it was; Eris had taken the risk and given him the bait. If the cargo was intended to be used as ammo, Damocles would want the weapon.

Clo's lips thinned at the use of the word *alien*. She knew Eris was playing a role, but the Evoli Clo met had been as human she was.

Damocles's expression didn't change, but his eyes gleamed. It terrified the silt out of her. "And yet you're showing it to me in the midst of a possible Evoli truce with the Oversouls." He'd taken three of Eris's pieces already.

"Are you telling me I'm out of a job?" Eris's voice was light, charming. Only the Pathos betrayed her unease. "You still have the Novantae gaining in numbers. Pretty soon, they won't just be a small pain in your ass but a military presence to contend with."

"I can handle the rebels. I'm wondering about your motivation."

"Money, General. As always." Eris stared at the board, considering her next move. "But here's what you ought to consider: a truce leaves open the possibility of a vulnerable military, and I don't trust the Evoli. Do you?" She captured two of his pieces in a single move.

<Be careful,> Nyx warned. *<You are skirting the line of insubordination.>*

"My father is committed to making this truce work," Damocles said.

"Long life to the Archon." She inclined her head for the blessing. "But that's not what I asked."

<Now you've crossed the line to actual insubordination. Are you trying to get us killed?>

Damocles paused and stared at Eris. "Crossing the Archon is treason."

"Yes. Except that *you*"—she knocked over one of his pieces and nabbed it—"are going to be the Archon. If you agreed with this truce, you wouldn't have asked to see me after I told you that I solved Project Harpy."

The general rested his elbows on his knees. "Very good, Negotiare."

"Zoe," Eris corrected with a smile. "And I have to be, in my line of work. Money is an excellent motivator."

He studied her for a moment, then nodded. "Have one of your assistants bring the weapon and follow me." The general stood and called back over his shoulder, "Have another bring the board. I'm still contemplating my next move."

Clo and Nyx followed closely behind Eris while Ariadne picked up the zatrikion board.

<Where is he taking us?> Clo asked.

<Where do you think?> Eris replied. *<The testing facility. There's a firing range.>*

Beside Clo, Nyx let out a breath. *<You had better be prepared for whatever it is he wants. He might not be as straight-up evil as his sister was, but this bastard is sneaky and ruthless.>* The soldier had her gaze fixed on the back of Prince Damocles's head, as if through pure force of will she could make it explode.

Clo saw Eris's jaw clench, but she said nothing. Clo nudged Nyx with an elbow. *<If he catches you glaring at him like you're about to commit murder, he's going to test it on you.>*

Nyx gave *her* a brief death glare, then forced her features to relax. *<You don't think he's done it before?>* came her bitter response. *<Even his citizens are nothing more than sacrifices.>*

They made their way through more lavish corridors, then through the painstakingly manicured grounds. Some of the flora there was from the Old World, carefully managed in greenhouses, and found nowhere else in the universe. They were kept as reverently as artifacts, a historical record of how far humanity had come: from a backwater speck of a planet light-years away from this place.

The capital of a vast empire that spanned galaxies.

The firing range on the palace grounds was used only for royalty or the highest military personnel. No one else was practicing. One of Damocles's guards took the case holding the weapon from Clo and opened the latches.

Prince Damocles took out the gun. Royal guards hovered nearby, hands on their own weapons. Another appeared at the end of the field, marching someone else out.

Eris, Nyx, Clo, and Ariadne all sucked in their breath.

An Evoli.

He was shirtless and in shackles. Like her fellow Novantae mechanic Elva, he looked almost Tholosian save for the specks of darker markings along his skin. Evoli were all natural-borns, like Clo and those in the slums. Clo knew from Elva that their markings were unique to the individual. This man had thicker splotches, but like Elva, they mainly bisected the body, curling around the face and down the limbs like freckled stripes.

Elva had told Clo a little about the Evoli Empire, whispered in the middle of the night they had spent together. She had come to the resistance after she'd lost faith in her own Empire. Something to do with her sister, was all she would say. She, like the Novantae, hoped for a future peace between their people. Elva claimed Tholosians and Evoli shared common ancestors, not all that many generations ago.

The Evoli were descended from early Tholosian colonies, but branched off after settling on what became their home, Eve—a glittering jewel of a planet on the edge of the Karis Galaxy. It was hard to reach—the distance between the Iona and Karis galaxies was protected by thick asteroid belts the Evoli were adept at navigating in their nimble ships. Eve, like so many others, had once housed other lifeforms that were killed off during raids. But the atmosphere required adaptation to live in, synthetic alterations to their DNA that eventually passed through the generations to their children and gave them extra abilities.

To the Tholosians, it made them less than human. Other.

Alien.

Clo had learned the truth behind the rumors. She wasn't afraid of Elva or the Evoli anymore, though she had been when she first left the Snarl. Rumors passed on both sides; Elva had told her the Evoli believed Tholosians to be emotionless. Monstrous.

Clo's mouth had twisted. *I mean, the Tholosians are pretty monstrous*, she'd said, before pulling the blanket over their heads, distracting them both.

The Evoli Empire could be just as single-minded and destructive as the Tholosians. Their lead Oversoul, the Ascendant, stated that the universe demanded no Tholosians could be allowed to live. They were a menace that would spread unchecked.

The Novantae had reached out, offering to partner with the Evoli officially, but had been rebuffed. To them, even the Novantae could not be trusted. They feared the Oracle still lurked in the deepest parts of their minds.

Clo was only afraid of any Empire that wanted to kill civilians for no more reason than false beliefs. Tholosians like Clo or Evoli like Elva weren't monsters or sorcerers; they were pawns.

This imprisoned Evoli was someone else caught up in this power play between two empires. Clo's fingernails bit into her palms as she stared at him. From this distance, if Clo ignored the markings and soft glow of his skin, he looked no different from the rest of them. Terrified, alone. Sweat broke out along his forehead. He met Clo's eyes, and she couldn't help but look away.

Coward. You fluming coward, she told herself.

Clo glanced over at Eris to find her expression unchanged. Unsurprised. How could she be so calm? <*You knew Damocles would do something like this, didn't you?*>

Eris's gaze flickered to Clo. <*Yes.*>

<*And you two?*> She asked the others. Nyx stood as stone-faced as Eris.

<*I suspected,*> Ariadne said quietly through the Pathos.

<*Gods,*> Clo said. <*We really are the fucking monsters.*>

Eris's response was two simple, devastating words: <*I'm sorry.*>

Sorry wasn't good enough. *Sorry* was meaningless. She was trying to keep it together in front of Damocles, pretend to be programmed and under control. If she were engineered, the Oracle would be blocking the adrenaline in Clo's body to keep her heart calm. Was this all worth another death? Kyla and Sher would have told her so. One death to save many. But Clo still thought the price was too high.

Doesn't matter. Show nothing.

Eris turned away from the prisoner and asked Damocles casually, "A live Evoli. How did you capture him?"

"This one is a spy," the general said. "The Oracle caught him trying to infiltrate one of our military facilities." Damocles hefted the weapon in his arms. "Now show me how to use this."

"It has a micro sequencer attached to analyze DNA," Eris explained. "You can either isolate the offshoot strands specific to Evoli, or the ones specific to *him*." She nodded to the Evoli man. "All you need is a sample—blood, hair, saliva. Whatever is easiest."

"I can use any sample of genetic material belonging to an Evoli and it won't hurt anyone else in this room?"

Eris nodded. "That's right, General."

Damocles snapped his fingers to his guards and gestured to the Evoli. The prisoner struggled as they pricked his skin for the blood sample. One of the guards returned and handed the tiny vial to the general. The general loaded it into the gun and the weapon charged up, ready.

Damocles finished examining the gun and swung it around, aiming it squarely at the center of Eris's head. "You said that it'll only hit this particular Evoli, correct? So, I could fire at you, right this instant, and the blast will swerve?"

"Yes," Eris said. "If multiple Evoli were in this room, it would choose the closest match to the targeted genetic sequence, down the line to the farthest if you kept shooting. And you can use various things as projectiles. Mors blasts, hard bullets, gases. It's highly programmable."

"And if they survive the projectile?"

Eris flashed her teeth. "Barring any obstructions, they are sensored to detect vulnerable places on the body. It's programmed to make the kill shot, General. No fuss."

Clo and Ariadne's creation would work. It was what Clo did: she fixed things and made them better. Only, this time, she had helped create a tool only monsters would be happy to wield.

Clo froze. She didn't know what to do. She couldn't just let him *kill*—

<Should I try a distraction?> Rhea's voice came through the Pathos. *<I could have Damocles called away.>*

<No,> Eris said. *<Stand down.>*

<But—>

<I said stand down.>

<Gods,> Clo said. *<You can't be serious. You promised Kyla, Eris. No killing unless—>*

<Unless absolutely necessary. I told Kyla I can't keep that vow as Zoe. Zoe is programmed, Clo. She doesn't have a choice.>

<Zoe might not have a choice, but you fucking do!>

Nyx shifted closer to Eris. *<Eris is right. Damocles will execute us if she doesn't do this, and we're all supposed to be programmed to feel nothing.>*

<I don't accept that,> Clo snarled.

<Listen to me,> Nyx said. *<That Evoli was dead the moment he was captured. What do you think Damocles will do to him if we stop this? I've seen what he does to people. I've experienced it first fucking hand. At least this way it'll be quick, almost a mercy. Pray to the God of Death if you need.>*

<I don't pray to your sick God,> Clo snapped. *<I've seen how much He takes. I'll pray to Soter if I have to.>*

Eris's voice was so quiet that Clo wondered if she were meant to hear it at all: *<Salvation is too close to mercy,>* she said. *<And we have no God of Mercy.>*

The prince fired at Eris. He'd used a bullet instead of a laser, and it exploded from the weapon with a *crack*, and then changed its course in midair and struck the Evoli.

The man didn't even scream. He crumpled to the ground, dead from a single blow to the head.

Damocles tossed the weapon to his guard. "Good work, Zoe. Send over the schematics and I'll have my engineers begin production. Maximus will negotiate your payment then."

He'd just killed a man, and it didn't even phase him. Clo averted her gaze from the dead Evoli. From the hole in the center of his forehead caused by a bullet from the weapon she'd made.

"If I might," Eris said sweetly, as if she hadn't just been shot at by her own fluming brother. "I'd like more time with the schematics. At the moment, it can only hold three samples at a time, and my own engineers may have a way to improve on that."

Damocles scowled. "You'll have eighteen days. The night before the truce ceremony. Whatever you have by then, it comes to use."

"Of course." Eris bowed.

Damocles studied the back of her exposed neck. "In the meantime, why don't you and your assistants enjoy the rest of the ball? Tomorrow is the last night."

Eris let out a small laugh. "Don't think I haven't noticed the irony of an arms dealer at a peace celebration."

"Here I thought you were a pirate."

"A pirate, then," she said with a charming smile that made Clo want to throttle her.

The general leaned in. "Then it's our secret."

Clo watched as the guards picked up the Evoli's body. General Damocles paid it no attention as he turned back to Ariadne, who was still holding the zatrikion board. She was staring wide-eyed at where the Evoli's body had been, at the small splatter of blood on the marble floor.

<*Don't look, kid,*> Clo heard Nyx tell Ariadne through the Pathos. She moved slightly in front of the young girl to block her view of the guards as they dragged the body out. <*You shouldn't have had to see this. I'm so damn sorry.*>

Damocles ignored Nyx, too. She was only a servitor. By the set of her jaw, she was struggling to keep her hatred in check. What memories haunted Nyx from this place?

The prince picked up a piece, and just when Clo thought he'd move it, he set it back down. "We'll finish the game some other time, Zoe." His smile was the smallest lift of his lips. "Until then, I'll think about my next move."

Clo didn't miss the flare of fear in Eris's eyes.

26.

One year ago

This was the longest Nyx had ever spent off the battlefield since she was eleven, training halfway across the Iona Galaxy. After the Battle of the Garnet, relations with the Evoli had cooled. No outright war—just machinations behind the scenes that Nyx had nothing to do with. There were no missions for her. She stayed in the beautiful, ornate palace on Tholos, her every need attended to.

She was so damn bored.

She'd been relegated to guarding Damocles. Everyone told her it was an honor to protect the next Archon of the galaxy.

But it ought to have been Discordia, they'd sigh if they were strong enough to voice anything close to dissidence. Beloved Discordia. Strong Discordia. The true Heir of the Archon.

Nyx had two minds. There was the soldier's mind, threaded through with the Oracle's touch. She would see him as her leader. The galaxy's protector. She'd yearn to please, to prove to him she was the best among his guard. If he gave her any sort of attention, endorphins and dopamine would flood through her, heady as any drug.

The soldier loved Damocles.

But sometimes, and more often over the last few months, other thoughts broke through. When Nyx saw Damocles, unfogged by the Oracle, her skin crawled. He tried to appear strong to others, as if he were the apex predator. But he reminded Nyx of nothing so much as the scavenger animals she'd seen over on Naxos. Blood-covered muzzles, unblinking purple eyes, glaring at you as if this was a kill they'd made rather than found.

She dampened these thoughts. They'd earn her nothing more than a swift knife across the throat.

Damocles loved having a decorated soldier outside of his doors. She was a predator turned pet, her claws dulled from lack of use.

Whenever he caught sight of Nyx outside his rooms, his eyes dragged across her from the tip of her head down to her toes. Every time he passed her, he found a way to brush against her arm. To lean in too close as he whispered his orders. Their skin was separated by armor and a glove, but it was still difficult for Nyx to keep that calm, stoic face, especially when his lips turned up in that knowing smile.

She didn't know why she could break through while others couldn't. In those stolen, clear moments, Nyx despised Damocles. She nursed her tiny ember of hatred, and she let it burn. Once, she had been so proud to serve. She couldn't pinpoint when that devotion had soured. Did anyone else around her feel it? Were they all pretending, or was their love still coded so deep it might as well be real?

The questions came to the forefront of her mind whenever she saw Damocles's favorite courtesan from the Pleasure Garden. Rhea Aglaea-7. Tall, willowy, every movement graceful as a dance. The long, curled dark hair, a scattering of darker freckles against her pale skin.

A year ago, those wide, green eyes had stared up at the chandelier as she had lain on a table. When she stared at Nyx before entering Damocles's chambers over the next few seasons, she didn't blink, didn't flinch from the tattoos on Nyx's face and all the slaughter represented.

Did you hate that night after the battle? Nyx had wanted to ask her that night and all the days since. *Being served up like a platter? Not having the choice to say no?*

Dangerous questions. Treasonous questions. Throughout each day, Nyx's loyalty waned. Like every soldier, every citizen, she listened to the Oracle's voice murmuring through the speakers in the barracks as they slept, the same words echoing the programming in Nyx's mind.

In the morning, she loved Tholos and its Heir anew.

Eleven months after that dinner where Nyx refused to dine on food still warm from the other woman's body, Rhea pressed a note into Nyx's hand as she left Damocles's room. Nyx startled at the touch, but her fingers closed over the paper. It stayed in her hand for the next five hours of her shift. It stayed in her pocket that evening, as she ate in the canteen with the other soldiers. Eventually, in the middle of the night, when the barracks were silent but for soft snoring, she crept to the bathroom and unfolded the note. Old paper, anachronistic, so nothing could be traced.

But the note was nonsense. A smattering of random letters. Nyx's anger flared—was this woman *mocking* her?

She kept the paper under her mattress. Every few nights, she took it out, puzzling over it. Wondering if it was some kind of code.

A few days later, when Nyx clearly hadn't turned Rhea in, the courtesan passed the mercenary another note.

The key to the cypher.

It was a page from an ancient book of fables. On the left was an ink drawing of a woman in a long black dress peppered with stars. Her hair curled around her face. The moon shone above her head like a crown. The woman seemed peaceful, serene. Nyx traced the illustration with a fingertip, hours before the dawn on Tholos. The page spoke of the Goddess—the Maiden, the Mother, the Crone. Nyx had never heard of a goddess, only of the gods.

Rhea had scribbled on the page in red ink. She'd circled the letters of the alphabet and added a number above. It took Nyx hours, but eventually, she decoded the message.

It was a time and a place. Rhea wanted to meet tomorrow.

Nyx didn't sleep for the rest of that night. What did she want? Would Nyx open the door to see Damocles, eyes bright with the knowledge that he'd caught a pretender in his midst? A disloyal soldier, fit for nothing but an honorless death, her cohort not even allowed to grieve her.

The next night, she went to the location: a room off of the Pleasure Garden with a discreet back entrance for those who didn't wish to announce their arrival and exit.

Inside was what Nyx expected, though she'd never visited a courtesan. Rich colors, a comfortable bed, soft lighting. Flowers, a fountain in the corner. In another was a cage, its door open. A small red bird rested on Rhea's finger, preening.

Nyx closed the door behind her.

"Am I being executed or not?" Nyx asked, not seeing the point in pleasantries.

The other woman looked like she was about to laugh. "*That's* what you thought? And you still came?" A pause. "I'm glad you read my notes."

"I burned them," Nyx said. She'd hated to watch that moon goddess go up in flames.

"That was wise." Rhea settled back against the pillows of the bed. The bird hopped to her shoulder.

"Is it real?" Nyx couldn't help but ask. She hadn't seen one like that, not in a color so vivid.

The little bird nuzzled Rhea's cheek. "No, but it's close enough."

"Are you sure it doesn't have a camera in it?" she asked.

The other woman's smile faded. "The Pleasure Gardens are the least surveilled part of the palace for obvious reasons. This room, in particular, was designed for discretion with Damocles."

"Don't care. Turn that thing off."

Rhea raised her eyebrows. "As you wish." With a last pet, she turned off the bird. Its head twisted, burrowing into its neck as though asleep. She set it back in its cage.

Nyx waited for Rhea to tell her why she was here.

"How long have you hated the Empire?" Rhea asked.

Nyx felt her neck stiffen. So far, she hadn't said anything treasonous. Was this the trap? To trick her into giving voice to her doubt, to admit that when she sacrificed to the God of Death, she felt a little more of her soul die each time.

"I'm loyal." Her voice didn't tremble.

"Are you?" Rhea said it almost mockingly. "I've watched you guard Damocles for months, and I'm not so sure."

No, Nyx couldn't have been so obvious. Damocles would have ended her by now. How did this woman know her secret, then?

Nyx narrowed her eyes. "What about you?"

She looked over at the empty place on the bed next to her. "Every time I'm next to Damocles, I think about how easy it would be to murder him in his sleep." A sigh. "But then they'd just make more Heirs, wouldn't they? The games would begin again, the new cohort just like the old. Nothing changes."

Nyx glanced around the room. "You shouldn't be saying any of this aloud. Seven devils, you shouldn't even be *thinking* it."

Rhea blinked. "You wouldn't turn me in. You'd worry they'd look closer at you."

"My programming, at least, is still intact." Nyx studied the courtesan, who even now, looked all too calm for treasonous talk. "Is yours fucking glitching, or what?"

A flicker in the other woman's gaze, one Nyx didn't understand. "I was bred to be a listener and advisor in this Garden," the woman said dismissively. "A few of us are not programmed or chipped. That's why they keep the walls so high and never let us leave."

Nyx had the distinct feeling that was either a lie or not the whole truth, but she barely knew this woman. They were not at any stage of trust.

"Then you're not Novantae," Nyx said, hating how her voice had dropped to a whisper.

"No. But I need to find them." She looked over at Nyx then. "I brought you here to ask for your help."

"*My* help?"

"Yes." She seemed so calm, so serene, but her fingers fiddled with the coverlet. "At the banquet all those months ago, you didn't eat from me. Why?"

Nyx pressed her lips together. "Wasn't hungry."

"Lie." The other woman's voice was soft, crafted in this garden to tell and keep secrets. "They kept you marching for hours in those streets, planet to planet. I know what you must have seen. Done. Now tell me the truth."

"This is what I was made for. I can't escape that." It wasn't an answer to Rhea's question.

Rhea stood, moved closer. "I think I have a way."

Nyx froze. Hope was dangerous. Hope could get her killed. "One doubt doesn't make me a traitor."

"You refused to see me as an object laid out for amusement and enjoyment. You're the only one that night who did."

Nyx sniffed, turning her head aside.

"The Oracle's programming is subtle. Everyone else ate those delicacies, even if deep down, something didn't feel right. But not you."

Nyx should have eaten that blasted sweet. If Rhea noticed, others might have as well.

"When else have you said no when others didn't?" Rhea asked, her voice soft.

"I pulled the trigger every time they asked me to."

"The Empire has made us all do things we don't want." She came closer. "Help me escape and we can both be free."

Nyx shut her eyes. She tried to imagine what her life would be like without orders, without assassinations.

She couldn't do it. She'd always known her future. Play the good soldier and when her body started aging and her reflexes slowed, she'd be replaced by a new cohort of younger, faster soldiers. She'd never have to go to battle again. That was the best Nyx could hope for.

Rhea reached for her. "Nyx—"

"No." Nyx put distance between them. "No. I don't care what you do. I won't tell anyone, but I'm not coming with you."

Rhea's face hardened. "How long are you going to keep pretending?"

Nyx didn't answer. She started to leave the room. "Good luck and try not to die."

As Nyx grasped the door handle, Rhea called out, "How many more times are you going to have to pull the trigger?"

The soldier left without replying. She figured they both knew the answer.

Too many.

————

Weeks passed, and Nyx remained stationed outside Damocles's door. She avoided Rhea's gaze every time the courtesan came calling.

Nyx didn't miss the finger-shaped bruises on Rhea's arms. Or how sometimes, when she was stationed to guard Damocles at dinner, the courtesan was again put on naked display, painted with gold and silver as if she were a piece of art. Nyx knew humiliation when she saw it. She didn't blame the other woman for plotting her escape or her revenge.

Stop it. He's your future Archon. He's your charge. You're supposed to protect him, not wish him dead. You're—

"Nyx!" The prince's voice sounded through the closed door. Nyx gritted her teeth as she stepped inside. Damocles was sitting at his grand gilt-and-mahogany desk. He gestured to the door. "Close it."

Nyx did as he asked and bowed stiffly. "How may I serve you, General?" She hovered near the exit, but he only beckoned her closer, taking a long sip from a glass of dark alcohol.

Nyx tried not to let her unease show as she edged farther into the room. She was rarely alone with Damocles. Not in there. In the hall, the way he'd let his hands linger on her uniform wasn't long enough to be improper, but not short enough to be considered impersonal. She reckoned he knew that, too.

Maps of the Perseus star system were spread across his desk, where young soldiers were trained in simulated battles. It had been years since Nyx had been there. The planets were frigid—deliberately so. A soldier's mettle was tested through exposure.

Damocles refilled his glass from the crystal decanter and sat back, his steely gaze meeting hers. His eyes were bloodshot. "Have you ever played zatrikion?"

Nyx frowned. "Sir?"

The prince stood, the chair scraping against the hardwood. "It was a favorite game of my sister's," he said, moving to the trunk on the far end of the room. He opened it and took out an ancient, battered board. "She and I played almost every day in my youth. Sometimes until the early hours of the morning, despite how tired we were." Damocles looked at her expectantly.

Nyx cleared her throat. "Yes. I played with the soldiers in my garrison."

Damocles set the board on the table. "Play a round with me."

Uneasily, Nyx shifted on her feet. "I ought to get back to my post—"

"I tell you whether or not to return to your post." Damocles gestured to the chair across from him, draining the glass and filling it again. She could smell the rum. "Now sit."

Nyx pursed her lips and, reluctantly, settled across from him. The general arranged the pieces, his movements calm, collected. Despite her growing unease, Nyx kept her expression even as he moved the first piece the board: the Priest.

He said nothing as Nyx slid her Peasant piece forward. He returned the move, taking her Peasant. Nyx had played this game both with other soldiers and her superiors during war. It kept her mind sharp and focused. Strategy was the first thing to go after the exhaustion of battle.

But Nyx did not play with Damocles the way she played with her peers. He was a prince, her superior, and he could command her execution for the smallest slight. And so she held back, letting him take another piece, and another, as she pretended to think her way through the game.

On his end of the table, the decanter level decreased. The scent of alcohol in the air made her stomach want to revolt.

Damocles slammed his fist against the table, jarring the pieces from their positions. "*Stop it.*" At Nyx's startled gaze, he reset the board. "You're holding back. Don't insult me."

"I'm not—"

"Yes. You are." His words might have been slightly slurred, but his gaze was hard as steel. "Move the pieces as you would if you were playing against a fellow soldier. That's an order."

Nyx exhaled and tried again. The game went on. And on. She began to fall into the role she did back in her garrison, advance and retreat, advance and retreat.

Damocles made rash decisions. Each piece taken drew a breath from him, as if it were an assent of his weakness. The decanter emptied. His tactics grew sloppier, to the point where Nyx could no longer pretend her choices were foolish. She had to move forward to win the game or he'd notice she'd held back.

Nyx took his King.

"Queen kills King," she said almost regretfully.

The general's gaze collided with hers. He was drunk, the whites of his eyes red. Nyx didn't even blink before his fist smashed into her face.

He hit her again. Again. She heard the bones of her face crack. "How did you do it?" He snarled. "How do you *always* win?"

"What—"

Damocles's fingers were around Nyx's throat. He squeezed hard, fingernails biting into her flesh. Uselessly, she grasped for his wrist to pry him off. She couldn't do anything to defend herself. He was her general, her future Archon. Hurting him was treasonous. As her vision faded around the edges, Nyx thought of Rhea and how she'd brushed off the courtesan's offer.

I should have taken it. I should have given myself hope.

"Tell me how you win, Discordia," Damocles said, breathless from hitting her. "*Tell me.*"

Nyx froze. "Not. Discordia," she managed between gasps.

Damocles released her. Nyx sucked in precious air, crawling away from him even as he backed toward his desk, breathing hard. He looked at her as if seeing her for the first time. Damocles stared down at his hands. His knuckles were bruised, blood beneath his fingernails.

"Get out," he said, his voice almost breaking around the words. When she didn't comply: "*Get the fuck out.*"

Nyx pushed to her feet and fled the room, taking up her post.

She barely got through her shift. The other soldiers looked like they wanted to ask about her bruised face, the scratches on her throat, but she betrayed nothing.

When she was released, she went to the Pleasure Garden and sought Rhea out. She shoved open the door to the courtesan's room, not even waiting for an invitation.

Rhea was at her vanity table, carefully applying makeup. "Nyx?" When she saw the swelling and bruises on Nyx's face, she drew in a breath. "My gods," she whispered. "What happened to you?"

"Doesn't matter. How do we do this?"

"You've changed your mind?"

Nyx nodded, one quick jerk. It pulled at the blood caking her temple.

"I have a friend who can help get us out," Rhea said.

"Who?"

"Someone even closer to the Archon than me."

It took Nyx a moment. "The madam of the Pleasure Garden would help you leave?"

"She knows she can't go, but she wants to see me fly."

Nyx let out a breath. *Fly.* Away from all of this. Before Damocles could finish what he started and get her punished. She'd be the one who suffered. She'd be the one the Oracle reprogrammed until One's influence was so impenetrable, Nyx would have no thoughts at all. And that's if she was lucky—the only other punishment would be execution delivered at the end of a Mors.

By then, it would be too late to escape.

"What do you have in mind?" Nyx asked.

Rhea held her palms out, her silk whispering in the quiet of the room. "I have years of ideas."

Nyx nodded and looked out the window to the glittering, lit trees of the Pleasure Garden. She let herself feel something like hope.

27.

Present day

Nyx didn't know how to comfort the other women.

They had all gone back to the ship in silence and returned their facial features to normal.

Once revealed, Eris just shook her head and went off to another part of the ship. Rhea seemed the most affected, having watched the Evoli's execution through Ariadne's eye camera. Sadness drenched every line of her body. Clo sat next to Rhea, offering her a steaming cup of tea. Rhea accepted it. She didn't drink but simply held the warmth in her hands for comfort.

Nyx rubbed her own arms, fingertips trailing the vanished swirls of her old tattoos. What happened to the Evoli wouldn't be marked on her skin, and yet Nyx felt like it should have been. She didn't understand why his death bothered her. It wasn't—

Realization struck deep. It was the first time Nyx had seen an Evoli executed since Ariadne had deprogrammed her. Now she could choose who to grieve, who to love, and who to hate. There was nothing to alter the patterns of her thoughts.

It was freeing. It was terrifying. What if she made the wrong choices? What if—

The bright light of the vid-screen jerked Nyx back into the room. Ariadne had drawn up her weapon schematics.

"I should never have made this," she said.

"You designed it," Clo said firmly. "I'm the one who made it."

"It doesn't make a differe—"

"Yes, it does," Clo snapped. "Those schematics were just a start. I'm the one who filled in the details and made the fluming thing work. I—" She looked at Rhea, who had shut her eyes hard. "I'm sorry. I'm so sorry to you all. You shouldn't have had to see it."

Clo slid closer to Rhea and hesitated before putting an arm around the other woman's shoulder. Ariadne shifted her chair closer, until her knees touched theirs.

Nyx didn't know what to do. She didn't *touch*. She didn't like physical affection, and she didn't know comforting words. She had seen too much death; it was so constant in her life that the sight of it was as common as food on her table. Anything—any word she might say— only sounded tactless, dismissive. *Get over it. You'll see more of it. Don't think of it. Push it out of your mind. Pray.*

Eris was right: there was no God of Mercy.

Except that since being free of the Oracle, Nyx had begun to think more often that death and sacrifice were just excuses for cruelty. Worshipping these gods—and having beliefs part of Tholosian programming—numbed citizens to the horror of it all. Some people shouldn't have to live with such daily brutality; they should have gods in their pantheon who weren't so harsh. That they could pray to for mercy, compassion, love—things that Nyx was just coming to understand that she had a choice to feel them.

People should have gods who didn't demand so much. Who didn't take so much.

But Nyx knew of no such deities. Only the cruel idols she had been taught.

Eris came to the door of the command center, watching the trio with a detached expression. But when her eyes met Nyx's, Nyx recognized her same longing and frustration. Wanting to be like those other women, knowing she never would be. They were born and bred differently, Eris and Nyx.

They were the God of Death's chosen.

Eris stepped forward and opened her mouth to speak, but instead retreated.

Nyx almost went after her, but then Rhea lifted her head from Clo's shoulder. "Let's focus on the mission, please. I need a distraction."

Thank the gods.

"Right," Clo said softly. "Me too. Ariadne, do you think you'll still be able to get into the Oracle's mainframe when we get to the ballroom?"

"Yeah," Ariadne said, straightening. "The commander's key will work for the identifier, and I know the access codes."

"How long before those codes are changed?"

"Every hour. But"—Ariadne tapped her temple—"I came up with the algorithm. The main problem is our identities. They might hold up for another check, but I haven't had time to weave backgrounds that hold up for closer inspection. They're not going to last through tomorrow night, if we're not careful."

Nyx let out a breath. "Damn."

"Can't you make time?" Clo asked.

Ariadne side-eyed her. "Sure, let me just pull it out of my hat. If I had a hat."

"I didn't mean that. I meant"—Clo waved a hand—"making our identities more secure."

"I can't do that in *hours*. Look, when I try to find out more about Josephine, the Oracle might put up defense codes to protect the information, but hopefully it'll take One a while. That's the best I can do."

Nyx raised an eyebrow. "A while?"

"Days," Ariadne said brightly. "Maybe weeks. I'm hoping for weeks before the military fleet tries to hunt us down and execute us."

"Kid, you're not helping."

"I'm hoping it's after we've completed the mission," Rhea said. She was still pale, and her voice shook. "With new identities, we can escape the execution. I want to move on with my life."

"And do what?" Clo asked.

Rhea considered. "In the Pleasure Garden, we learned a great deal about listening to people. I think I could help the Novantae with the trauma after war, the difficulties of leadership. And with deprogramming. Right, Nyx?" She gave Nyx a small smile.

"Holy shit. You helped Ariadne break Nyx?" Clo gave an impressed whistle.

"They didn't 'break' me," Nyx almost growled. "I wasn't broken."

Weren't you? her cruel inner voice whispered.

"Okay, *fixed* you, then. I'm just surprised. And impressed. You're meant to be"—she gestured wildly—"an amazing superkiller. No hesitation or fear."

Gods. As if Nyx needed a damn reminder that she had little will of her own before Rhea and Ariadne. She still had the sleep recordings repeat in her dreams even though she hadn't listened to one since leaving Tholos. Echoes of programming still slipped into her thoughts.

"Clo," Nyx said. "Do me a favor: stop talking before you wedge your foot so far down your own throat that you choke on it."

Clo tapped her lips. "Aye. Shutting up. Sorry."

Rhea put her hand on Clo's shoulder. "It's been a long day. You three get some rest before the ball tomorrow."

Nyx looked at her sharply. "What about you?"

"I'm going to make Eris such an incredible dress that no one will notice Ariadne leave. We need that intel on where the rocks came from, what they're for, and how Kyla's spy network was compromised. I'm not taking any chances, not with our future."

———

The next night, Nyx fit the small shifter device onto the roof of her mouth and put her false face back on for the ball. She hated the features Ariadne had given her, but understood why the girl had designed them in such a way.

Though she couldn't change Nyx's stature, she'd altered the shape of her face, nose, cheekbones, and lips to soften her expression into one less hawkish, less jaded. A closer look at her eyes would show Nyx's true personality, but if she kept her gaze cast downward, all people noticed was a tall woman who had been engineered to appear blandly pretty.

They had to move quickly tonight. If they didn't finish this part of their mission before their covers were blown, they had no future. It was that simple.

Still, Nyx was overly aware of how vulnerable they were, sitting in the loading bay. Security was so tight that it was impossible for her to relax as she, Clo, and Ariadne donned the gowns they had ordered on short notice from the palace's dressmaker.

Of all the things Novan funds should go to, Nyx thought wryly.

Rhea applied Nyx's makeup. "The last time I wore makeup," Nyx said while under Rhea's ministrations, "I was a guest at a ball on Macella."

"Yes." Rhea dabbed a touch of shadow across Nyx's lids. "I remember. The night that started everything."

Nyx swallowed.

"You look beautiful," Rhea said when Nyx didn't reply. "Even with this face. I can still tell it's you."

Nyx looked in the mirror and resisted the urge to curl her lip. "Are you coming tonight?"

"No." Rhea bowed her head. "I've faked too many smiles to do it again."

———

Nyx held her breath as they again went through security. They were surrounded by their enemies, people of influence in the Empire. The attendees at the royal festivities were considered the best examples of engineering the human race had to offer: most were military, but others were diplomats, governors, regional officers, magistrates, and other officials who kept each planet of the Empire functional for its citizens.

Each woman in Nyx's group had been taken and analyzed against the identities Ariadne created, and when the handheld machine beeped its approval, everyone's shoulders relaxed.

<Hard part done,> Eris said through the Pathos. <Good work, Ari.>

As before, no one had commented on the shifters in their mouths; over half the people there would be wearing the same to improve their features or be someone else for the night. Shifters could give their skin that extra glow, or make their eyes shine just that much brighter, their lips that much fuller. Shifters were as much for dramatic effect as the glittering ballroom dresses.

Though people took pride in the cohorts they were born into, shifters helped everyone at these celebrations show off for other genetic groups—for no one knew what was natural and what wasn't. Did the Pollux opifex cohort really produce those with eyes so blue? And that lone survivor of the Orphne militus cohort that fought in the Battle of the Garnet—had they all been so striking?

All performances. Nyx bit her lip so she didn't curl it in disgust. She had not missed the drama of ceremony.

Tonight, the ball was held in the upper levels of the palace, with grand views over the grounds and the skyscrapers rising into the mist. Impressive, and easier to protect from a security standpoint. All the palace watchtowers had a view of the ballroom, with sniper weapons trained and ready in case of attack. Far-off towers and farther-off mountains were hulking shapes in the gloaming. The setting sun tinged the mist rose gold.

As the double doors of the grand elevator opened, Nyx caught her breath. Her memory of this place after the Battle of the Garnet paled to seeing it again in person. The grand dome of the ceiling rose above them, painted deep indigo, the many conquered planets illustrated in gold foil. There were already one or two more than the last time Nyx had attended her tour.

Nyx froze as she spotted the familiar faces that belonged to members of her regiment. There was Alava Cordesian-13, one of the generals on Circe, her medals shining brightly on her chest. Near her was Conori Molkos-56, who had fought alongside Nyx in the trenches at the Garnet. She'd handed him her Mors to hold once, and trusted him to have her back. The Molkos cohort had nearly been wiped out in the battle, and yet Conori stayed with Nyx—a member of his regiment, yes, but not of his own cohort. She owed him her life.

Stop, Nyx told herself. *You can't think like that anymore.*

Trust on the battlefield didn't mean anything while soldiers were controlled by the Oracle. If Nyx were caught there tonight as a traitor who broke with the Empire and her coding, Conori would stand in the crowd, righteous as he watched her execution.

<*Nyx?*> Ariadne's voice was in her head. <*Are you all right?*>

She realized she had paused just outside the elevator; the other women were looking back at her with worry. Nyx shook her head. <*I'm fine.*>

<Are you sure?> Eris asked. *<Because you don't look fine.>*

<Let's just get this done,> Nyx said, catching up to them. *<You look ridiculous, Eris. Rhea made that dress?>*

<Out of parachutes. She called it a riot of color.> Eris sounded like she was praying for a swift death.

<More like a vomit of color.>

<I think she looks pretty,> Ariadne said. *<Like a cake with eyes!>*

<Thanks,> Eris said dryly. She swept her vomit-of-color dress out with her hand and led them farther into the ballroom.

The room was full of people resplendent in the latest fashion of their various planets. Women laced into corsets, the skirts of their gowns trailing behind them. Tholosians favored jewel tones—rich greens, blues, and reds—to match the heavy jewelry glittering at their throats, their ears, or in circlets across their brows.

Many wore wigs braided with ribbon, more jewels, or mechanical birds or butterflies, their wings fluttering softly as the women glided through the ballroom. The gowns were as much of a uniform as many of the men's military threads, medals shining at their chest, posture ramrod-straight beneath epaulettes.

Eris made sure to match. Her hair was somehow even more complicated than it'd been for the meeting with Prince Damocles yesterday. Deep purple braided silk, silver filigree set with gems. It looked heavy, like it pinched.

Nyx spotted others she knew, and self-consciously hunched her shoulders. It was difficult not to feel exposed, as if her lies were written upon her face.

Eris paused beside Nyx. *<Shit,>* she whispered. *<I didn't think he'd be here.>*

The other women followed her gaze and went equally still. The Archon sat on his throne, still as one of the marble statues ringing the room. Nyx's breath caught, and she forced herself to let it out slowly.

Even from there, his golden eyes blazed. His crown sat upon his brow, studded with precious stones from the worlds he had conquered in bloody battle, but the metal was the same Old World steel as the ancient palace on Tholos. The long, flowing robes of his office puddled on the floor. Dark blue velvet, a tapestry of his conquests stitched in gold and silver thread, just like the dome above him. Every aspect of his bearing a reminder that everything belonged to him. That he had the power to take anything he wanted. Their homes, their possessions, their lives.

The Archon's gaze traveled around the room, taking in his loyal subjects.

<*Change of plans?*> Nyx asked through the Pathos. <*His presence will tighten security.*>

<*No.*> Eris's eyes fixed on Damocles as he noticed her and left his father's side. <*No change.*>

"General." Eris dropped into a deep bow. As she rose, he took her hand, raising it to his lips.

<*I'll go with Ariadne, then,*> Nyx argued. <*If she runs into trouble . . .*>

<*Clo will go with her,*> Eris said firmly. <*This mission needs technical skill, not violence. You'll stay with me.*>

"Zoe," General Damocles said. "I'm glad to have someone here who doesn't infuriate me."

Eris smiled. "Is that what you say to all the ladies?"

"Only ones who give me things I like."

"Ahh, excellent answer." Eris edged closer. "Then as payment, you must show me around. I've never been up here before."

General Damocles offered her a small smile, and Nyx tried not to show her astonishment. He was usually so cold—unless, of course, he was furious. Then the prince was terrifying.

She had to hand it to Eris: she was damned good at her job.

"Deal," he replied, taking her hand in his. "I'll take you to the gardens."

Eris waved off Clo and Ariadne. "We don't need company." She narrowed her eyes at Nyx. "You. Trail behind in case we'd like a drink. But not too closely; I don't want to have to look at you."

Nyx gritted her teeth as Ariadne and Clo drifted to the edges of the ballroom, both taking a brief pit stop at the buffet table to nibble some treats and appear casual. Nyx sighed, wishing she could be the one doing the breaking and entering rather than the subterfuge.

Instead, she kept her head down and pretended to be a servitor.

28.

Present day

Clo's heart wouldn't stop hammering. She was convinced the guards would take one look at her and realize she was a threat. One shot of a Mors and then they'd incinerate her corpse, her ashes scattered to help fertilize the crops on one of the moons above her.

Ariadne was just as wary. She might meet her maker this evening, and the Oracle did not strike Clo as a creature who easily forgave betrayal.

Clo followed Ariadne's lead. They made their way to a quieter corner of the ballroom, as if heading toward the facilities. Ariadne took them a little farther along and then reached for Clo's arm. She put her hands on Clo's shoulders, as if they were having a slightly drunk but earnest heart-to-heart.

"This is a camera blind spot," she whispered. Clo could barely hear her over the music. "A small flaw in the building's security design, and a bad one since it's right in front of a cloak closet. I noticed it last year while watching the wintertide festival and never told the Oracle."

Ariadne took a quick glance around, made sure the coast was clear, and then took out the commander's copied pass from her small clutch. With the smuggled inorganic shifter cuff, she'd made it look like a thin notebook. She opened the door and ushered Clo inside, closing it behind them.

"Pretty sure the guards know about the flaw, but people have trysts in here and no one talks about it. Lucky for us." Ariadne's teeth gleamed white, visible even in the low light. The closet smelled of lingering chemicals and clean linen. "You sure your leg is ready for this next bit?" she asked.

"It rubs," Clo said, curt. "But I'll deal with the blisters tomorrow."

"I'm sorry. Was that rude?" Ariadne bit her lip. "Humans aren't as easy for me to interact with as machines. The same action won't work on the same two people in an expected response." The almost-robotic intonation of her voice was an eerie echo of the Oracle. Clo shivered.

"You're doing fine, kid." Clo forced her voice to soften.

"Your leg does hurt, though?"

Clo sighed. "Yes."

At first, it had throbbed all the time. Real pain and phantom pain hurt just the same. Eventually, her body grew used to the change.

"Okay. Right," Ariadne said. "Follow me."

Clo reached up, popped the hatch of the vent at the back of the closet, and gave the much-shorter Ariadne a boost before using a storage box to climb up herself. Her leg twinged, but it didn't slow her down. They shifted forward carefully to dull the echo of their movements. Within moments, they were covered in dust. Clo fought the urge to sneeze.

The air duct opened directly onto the elevator shaft. Ariadne sidled onto the support beam first. Clo leaned out.

"Don't look down," Ariadne warned.

Too late. "Silt," Clo breathed.

The shaft was the entire height of the building, lined with glimmering bones. She wasn't even sure she could see the bottom. Normally, she was fine with heights—she climbed around spaceships all the time and she'd been raised in the Snarl—but the drop there dizzied her.

Ariadne moved back along the ledge. "Come on, Clo," she urged. "We only have to go down two floors. The ball is enough of a distraction that we won't have people coming and going."

"And if the elevator appears . . ." Clo began.

Ariadne grinned, as if the thought delighted her. "We'll have to jump on the top of it so we're not squished. Easy."

Easy? Was she *flooded?* "And then we'll have to hope no one hears the thump, raises the alarm, and finds us on top of the damn elevator." Clo let out a breath and looked down again. "This is such a bad idea. Getting squashed by an elevator sounds like a terrible way to die."

"I mean, yes. It would be. But we'll be fine!" Ariadne said, falsely bright. "We just have to go along to the end there. There's even a service ladder. Ten minutes, tops." She started back along the ledge. Clo muttered a silent prayer and followed.

The ledge was barely wide enough for her feet, and she was wearing dress shoes borrowed from Nyx's stash—with flat soles, at least, but nothing like her grippy mechanic boots—and they were a size too big. She tried not to think about slipping, dangling from the narrow ledge, and losing her grip on the smooth metal. She tried not to think about those awful, few moments she'd have after she fell.

Ariadne reached the corner and descended the service ladder. Clo followed, making sure not to look down. The ladder was older and needed painting. Her hands were soon stained with rust. She gripped each rung as tightly as she could, moving slowly, surely.

Ariadne finished one level and started on the next. Clo steadied her breathing. Almost halfway there. Nearly done. With the first step of a series of dangerous tasks. She still couldn't believe they were actually trying to take down the Tholosians from the inside. It seemed a fool's errand. They were tiny gnats trying to take on a Procolian snow beast.

"I'm down," Ariadne called up softly.

Before Clo could answer, the shaft filled with an echoing metal shriek.

The elevator.

"Fuck!"

Clo clambered down the ladder faster. The one on the second level was in even-worse condition. The paint flecked off, making her hands slippery. She held on tighter and put her foot down on the next rung.

It slipped.

Clo's breath left her lungs in a rush. Her other foot lost purchase and she hung on by her hands. Ariadne was too far away to be of help. Clo kicked out. The clanking grew louder.

She managed to step onto the rungs again, and crawled down the ladder like a spithra bug. She had no time to check her grips. She could only move as fast as possible and hope her borrowed shoes didn't betray her again.

Clo reached the platform, and Ariadne grabbed her. They both pressed themselves flat against the wall as the elevator whooshed past. The wind buffeted them, and they closed their eyes tight. Within half a second, it was far above them.

"Fluming bogging fuck," Clo said, for good measure.

"Are you all right?" Ariadne asked.

"Just thankful I'm not greeting the gods face-to-face right now. Salutem, God of Survival, my heart." She took deep, ragged breaths and wiped her grimy hands on her dirtied top.

"Hopefully, that's as exciting as things get tonight," Ariadne said, pulling a small non-organic shifter cuff from her pocket. "Here."

"How'd you sneak that past the guards?" Clo asked.

"Wouldn't you like to know?" she answered with a grin.

Ariadne turned it on and gave them each a quick once-over. The dirt disappeared from their clothes, their faces, their hair. Their suits' creases smoothed, changing from private security to Tholosian guard uniforms. Underneath the illusion, Clo could still feel the dirt clogging her pores. She twisted around. All perfect, right down to the ID tags. It was risky, but it was easier to hide an energy signature than the amount of muck they were covered in.

"We don't have Mors," Ariadne said critically. "So don't brush against anyone." She'd created the illusion of a gun holster, but as it was flat against the fabric, it wouldn't hold up under the slightest hint of scrutiny. "Best I can do. Come on."

They left the shelter of the air duct and sneaked out of another storage closet. They were underground, in the depths of the palace. Labyrinths behind the walls. Clo wondered who else used them and for what purpose. They walked confidently, chins up, shoulders back, as if they had every right in the world to be there.

People, even guards, were not nearly as observant as they thought they were. Routine made people comfortable. Complacent. Even with the threat of Tholosian justice should they fail, it was easy to miss the little details. If someone walked confidently, looked the part, made eye contact, gave a little nod, then carried on with their business, few tended to question that assurance. It was easier for the guards to fall back into the routine programmed into their minds.

The command center only had one officer out front, with more on the neighboring hallways to come if he sounded the alarm. The hubris of depending on the Oracle for protection and surveillance would help Clo and Ariadne tonight.

Ariadne found the next blind spot, and they popped another hatch and boosted each other back up into the vents. They crawled farther through the dust, making toward a mainframe panel. Clo could barely fit, her shoulders brushing against the metal sides. The darkness closed in around her and Clo steadied a breath.

Forward, she told herself.

Ariadne opened the panel, fingers snaking into spirals and swirls on the small adjacent screen. She slotted in another small chip of her own design. Another feat of magic, slipping this past the guards.

"This isn't connecting properly," Ariadne whispered. "I'm more software than hardware. Can you help?"

She shimmied back. Their bodies had to press against each other to pass through the tight space. Clo could feel Ariadne's ribs. The Oracle might not have starved the girl, but Clo had heard enough about Ariadne's limited, dull diet to understand that eating had brought her no pleasure. Rage at how the girl had been treated burned hot and bright. Ariadne ate every chance she could, but Clo would be glad to see the former engineer healthy and happy.

Clo turned her attention to the chip. Something was interfering with the connection—the green light kept flickering on and off. Clo put her tongue between her teeth, dragging her chipped nails into the wire. Ariadne had warned her the electronics this deep in the building were older, less reliant on the Oracle's coding, and more prone to being finicky.

It only took Clo a few tries before it connected strongly enough that the green light glowed bright and steady. "Got it."

"Thanks," Ariadne whispered. "The cameras have recorded a loop for fifteen seconds, and it'll keep replaying on monitors." She fiddled for another few seconds. "I just turned off the weight and heat sensors in the hallways, but if the lasers trigger, I can deal with those."

They edged back to a vent just above the guard.

"Filters," Ariadne warned, and Clo took them from her pocket and shoved them up her nose as Ari did the same. They held their breaths just in case, mouths shut tight. Another tiny gadget emerged from Ariadne's pocket, and she tossed it down. The guard startled, then dropped to the ground as the sleeping gas took effect.

Clo looked at Ariadne in astonishment once the younger woman gave the all clear. "Are you *sure* you don't want to be a spy?" She took out the filters, wrinkling her nose at the itching.

Ariadne gave her a quick grin. "I have a knack for it, don't I?" She returned her attention to the vent. "Quickly."

Ariadne jumped down from the vent and landed without a sound. Clo followed more clunkily. They dragged the fallen soldier into that floor's supply closet. His heartbeat was steady.

"Now take his place," Ariadne told Clo.

"I look nothing like him," Clo whispered back.

Ariadne waved a dismissive hand. "They swap this post a lot. If anyone comes down here, tell them there's a security health check that will finish in one hour; cite code 11159. They'll leave in a panic. Got it?"

"11159. Got it."

"I'm going in. Remember what I told you."

"Good luck." Clo's heartbeat quickened.

"I don't need luck."

Ariadne keyed the code to the door and slipped inside.

29.

Ten months ago

Ariadne watched the two women through the red bird.

It was late at night up in the Temple, and the Oracle had finally let her rest. She was supposed to be asleep, but she couldn't look away from this. Better than any wall-screen vid—because it was real.

Ariadne never looked in the courtesan rooms. She was the only one in the Temple who could, other than the Oracle. Ariadne had no interest in watching *that*. Sex was something she didn't under-stand and didn't care to. She was more interested in closeness. Those casual touches of people who had a connection—friendship, love, anything. That was what she craved and yearned for up in her tiny garret.

Most people didn't know Ariadne existed. No one realized that the directives they heard in their minds used the voice of a real girl with her own hopes and dreams and wishes. As far as they knew, the per-sistent voice that whispered commands, repetitions, and instructions belonged to the Oracle.

The truth was: before Ariadne, the Oracle was an aphonic program whose commands had to be interpreted by an engineer in the Temple, who then ran the code through people's synapses.

The engineer before Ariadne had long suspected a human voice would help deepen Tholosian programming—that the Oracle would one day become indistinguishable from people's own thoughts.

It was Ariadne who had given One the ability to speak, and with it, lost one of the few things that had belonged to her alone.

Ariadne had never spoken directly to another human as herself. Never brushed her hand against anyone else's. When she slept at night, she wrapped her arms tight around her middle—an embrace that she pretended was comfort offered by someone else.

Loneliness had made Ariadne desperate.

In an effort to soothe One's despondent child, the Oracle had let Ariadne watch several wallscreen vids two years before—but Ariadne found ways around the Oracle's monitoring. Sometimes, when she was bored, she listened to others within the palace.

That was how she had found Rhea and Nyx.

The women had met many times. Different hours and days, but Ariadne watched them each time. They were good at covering their tracks, but the Oracle's logs would eventually begin to render a pattern. Human behavior was never as spontaneous as people assumed.

Ariadne erased every trace from the Oracle's records, but she didn't know how much longer she'd be able to cover for them. If they did something to bring the Oracle's attention, the women would never be able to escape Tholos.

She'd calculated their chances at finding freedom as less than two percent. And that was being generous.

But if Ariadne helped? Well, seven point five percent was still abysmal. But it was better.

Ariadne chewed her lip as she watched the bird's cameras on her small, contraband tablet. She needed to talk to them tonight, if she was ever going to do this. But they would be the first people she'd spoken to. She'd say the wrong thing. Her conversational skills were nothing but cobbled-together references from vids filmed in the last one hundred years. The odds that she'd make an ass of herself were high.

Nyx and Rhea were sitting together on the bed, sketching out possible escape routes. They'd narrowed down a list of ships, but they were hoping to stow away in the hold and escape when they landed on a planet like Myndalia or Tiryns for fueling.

"Here goes," Ariadne whispered before opening the comms of the bird. In its cage, the red bird awoke, ruffling its feathers.

Nyx and Rhea froze.

"Don't freak out," she said, her voice coming through the tiny speakers in the red bird. "But that plan won't work. You'll get scanned with a heat signature in the hold and they'll suck out all the oxygen."

"*Shit—*" Nyx jumped up from the bed, making for the hidden camera.

"Don't destroy the bird!" Ariadne said, frantic. "It's the only way I can contact you."

"Who—" She glared at the courtesan. "Rhea, you told me there was no camera in that stupid thing."

"As far as I knew, there wasn't!" Ari could hear the fear in Rhea's voice. That was an emotion Ariadne knew well.

"I've been watching you both for a month," Ariadne tried again. "In a totally non-creepy way, I promise. Well, I mean, mostly I just—"

"Get to the point," Nyx said through her teeth, "or I crush that bird under my boot."

This was not going as well as she'd hoped. "Look," she said, "if I was going to turn you in, I would have done it already. I want to help."

The women both paused. Nyx clearly still wanted to take the mechanical bird and dash it to the floor. Ariadne didn't blame her.

"Please," Ariadne tried again, sure she was messing this up. "Please listen to me. You're going to die if you keep on your current trajectory."

Nyx's hand inched toward her side. "Fine," the soldier said, her voice grim. "Talk."

Ariadne whooped, startling them. "Sorry," she said. "I'm new at this."

"Speaking through mechanical birds?" Rhea asked, voice mild.

"Speaking to people in general. As myself, I mean."

That took them aback. "The *point*," Nyx reminded her.

Ariadne stumbled over her words. "I'm Ariadne. My friends would call me Ari, if I had any friends. I always liked the thought of a nickname. I'm the Oracle's Engineer." Nyx's fingers clenched. "I've been raised by One," Ariadne added. "In the Temple."

"No one lives in the Temple," Rhea said, a tiny frown line between her brows. "It's forbidden."

Rhea was in full courtesan regalia, her eyes painted a shimmering purple, her lips wet with gloss. At the end of the meetings, Rhea would muss her hair, wipe off the gloss. Nyx once ripped the shoulder seam of Rhea's dress to add a little extra authenticity to people's perception of them as lovers. They'd laughed as they did it, almost like children. Ariadne had watched them bond, the trust growing between them.

She envied it.

"I'm the only one," Ariadne said quietly.

"Alone?" Rhea breathed.

"Yes." Ariadne pressed a hand to her chest to soothe the ache there. She was so tired of being alone. "Like One's previous Engineers, I was created by One's design, and will work in the Temple until I die. I'm One's fourth child. I've been with the Oracle since I was old enough to leave the Birthing Center."

Rhea and Nyx looked at each other in surprise. It was Rhea who spoke first, her voice soft. "What does the Oracle use you for?"

"Aside from enhancing the performance of One's AI, I'm the Oracle's hands and voice. I help with things One can't do." And with a swallow, Ariadne shed the childish, cheerful pitch she'd learned from the vids, all those little inflections that made her sound different from the way the Oracle made her. "Engines are engaged. Proceed to exit 153A-3 to exit Tholosian atmosphere."

"Gods below the seven levels," Nyx said. "You're the voice in my fucking head."

"Affirmative," Ariadne said, unable to switch out of the voice. At least the lack of inflection hid her fear.

"So, you've been hidden and trapped in the belly of the palace this whole time?" Rhea whispered.

"Affirmative."

"Gods," Rhea whispered. "How old are you?"

"Fifteen."

"I can't imagine what your life must have been like so far."

Ariadne coughed, forced herself to be bright again. "Oh, well, it mostly sucks. But that's why I'm so glad I found you. I don't want you to have all the oxygen sucked out of your lungs and then have your bodies thrown out the airlock. That seems a waste."

Nyx smirked. "That's . . . kind, kid. I guess."

"I'm not a kid," Ariadne protested. "My frontal lobe may still be developing until I reach full maturity, but I'm definitely not a child. The Oracle designed me to bypass the mental limitations of childhood."

"You said you wanted a nickname," Nyx pointed out.

Up in the Temple, Ariadne's body flushed with warmth. "Can I give you a nickname?" she asked. "Like . . . *Buttons*. I saw a vid with a fierce Old World animal called a *snowcat* and its name was Buttons. Can I call you Buttons?"

"No. Good gods, no."

Ariadne deflated. "Oh. Okay."

"Nothing personal," Nyx tried. She cleared her throat. "So, how do you suggest we get out of here without dying?"

Ariadne wrapped her arms around herself up in her garret, rocking side to side as her smile grew.

Nyx had said *we*.

———

It took every spare moment Ariadne had to claw back from the Oracle's endless work schedules. But even when she was crafting code, or recording her voice for the Oracle to blast through spaceships, buildings, people's very brains, she was always dreaming of escape.

They were a trio of different skills and knowledge subsets, and a triangle was the strongest shape. She was only sleeping a few hours a night, slurping down the kykeon the Oracle provided her. She grew even thinner, and she had little enough to spare before.

She made mistakes, and the Oracle punished her.

The months crawled by. Sometimes, in the deep of night, she looked up through the porthole of the garret at the stars and cried, certain she'd never be able to make it. Even if everything went to plan, the idea of finally leaving the Temple was terrifying. Rhea and Nyx hadn't even seen her.

What if they found her strange and repulsive?

What if she wasn't any good at being human?

The day finally came. They had done all they could. Rhea had some valuable information from the madam, Juno. Ariadne had hacked the registry of *Zelus*. She had massaged the Oracle programming on the soldiers aboard so they wouldn't think to question Damocles's favorite courtesan and one of his top mercenaries joining a complete unknown as dona aboard the vessel. She had programmed a way to cut *Zelus* off from the Oracle's main network once they boarded.

Rhea had spirited their costumes away, talked Nyx and Ariadne through how to carry themselves with confidence, how to speak, how to pretend to be something they were not.

Nyx had planned how they would kill everyone aboard once they hit space. Ariadne wasn't sure if she'd be able to do that. But she had a knife and a Mors from Nyx, just in case.

Once Ariadne left the Temple, they wouldn't have much time. Ariadne had tried to run a proxy of infrared readouts to fool the Oracle into sensing that she was still asleep in the garret, but it would not last long. Ariadne also had to hope that once the Oracle realized she was missing, One would be too protective of the secret that she'd used a human child at all to sound a palace-wide alarm. One would try to find One's daughter on One's own.

Ariadne knew she was no match for the Oracle. Eventually, One would find her. But Ariadne could help Rhea and Nyx escape, and she could have a taste of that freedom. It would have to be enough.

When Ariadne finally left the garret, Nyx and Rhea were waiting. The pity on their faces when they saw her scrawny frame made Ariadne ashamed. She hunched her slight shoulders. Rhea reached into her pocket and held out a small wrapped package.

"What's that?" Ariadne asked, almost suspicious.

"A sweet. You look half-starved."

She'd hadn't told them she'd never eaten food. Looks of pity, again.

"Here. Try it."

"We don't have time," Ariadne protested.

"Suck on it as we walk. Come on."

Ariadne unwrapped it with shaking fingers. Carefully, she put it on her tongue. Sensations she couldn't begin to describe filled her tingling taste buds. Her eyes widened, filled with tears.

Rhea slid her arms around her shoulders. "Let's go," she whispered. "We have a galaxy to explore."

The steps of their plan fell into place. Once on the ship, Ariadne slipped her code into the mainframe. They clutched hands as the ship took off from the ground, though Nyx only hooked her pinkie with Ariadne's. The last of the sweet melted in Ariadne's mouth as she watched the palace retreat into the distance as the craft rose into the sky and took them to the stars.

Ariadne would always associate the taste of chocolate with freedom.

30.

Present day

Ariadne stared down the long hallway of endless white tiles. The records room there was a copy of the command center in the Temple, which was deep in the ruins of the original generation ship brought from the Old World to Tholos with its first humans. Ariadne had helped design the security for this room, as the Oracle instructed her to do the things One could not. The things that required a small, undernourished body. Clever little hands. Her engineered, brilliant brain.

The Oracle and One's daughter had worked well in tandem. Ariadne still knew how One processed, where One focused attention and data. She knew how to move between the cracks.

Or she hoped so.

If the Oracle found Ariadne in this command center—just a single lesser temple of many outside of the main Temple on Tholos—she would never escape. She had to hope she could find the information for the other women first.

Ariadne moved on the balls of her feet. All was silent. Halfway down the path, the sensors triggered, the hallway filling with a buzzing hiss as the lasers snapped into being. Ariadne still had a deep scar on her leg from a past misstep. She could feel the heat of them against her skin. They moved almost lazily in their circular pattern, but they'd kill so easily. There were three different patterns, one for each of the Three Sisters.

If she'd triggered the program, Ariadne could only hope that her patch was still holding on the cameras and other sensors. She couldn't worry. She had two seconds to remember where in the pattern the lasers were before they sliced her into pieces. She let her mind go blank, reaching for muscle memory and rote memorization. A large puzzle she only needed to slot into.

She fell to the ground just as a laser went over her head, close enough she smelled the acrid burning of the tips of her hair. Her nose just had time to graze the polished tiles before she pushed up with her hands, flipping over another laser. She danced to the side, gave another little hop, and then did three backflips in quick succession. She was out of practice; her lungs hurt and her muscles were already shaking.

No time to think. She could only follow that pattern that'd been drilled into her more times than she could count. Up. Down. Left. Left. Half-twirl. Diagonal cartwheel. Right. Right.

Right.

She reached the other end of the hallway, her lungs working hard. She darted in to the main control panel, fingers already itching to manipulate the raw code.

She hoped Clo was holding up out in the hallway, but she couldn't spare more than a thought for the mechanic. The muscles in her back were so tight, she thought they'd break. She could feel One's presence behind the code. As long as she didn't trigger an anomaly, she should be able to slip in and out.

But had the Oracle already noticed that the sensors had triggered there? Would it drive One's attention away from training on countless planets, on the millions of cameras dotted through the Empire?

Ariadne's hands kept shaking.

Rhea was still helping her to unpack her childhood with the Oracle, but when would there be time for any of them to heal from their pasts? Ariadne was supposed to be living her new life by now, fixing odd things to get by on some quiet, faraway planet. Far from the Temple, far from the Oracle's tendrils. Not here in the depths of One's domain.

Her eyes scanned the information, all of it storing deep in her brain.

No time to make copies, no time to even think about what her eyes were seeing. She had it.

"Ismara," she whispered, scanning the text. "Ichor mines."

Josephine was a rock called ichor from the planet Ismara. Frustrated, Ariadne tried to read more, but the whirring of the mechanisms in the Oracle's mainframe stopped her. Though she had an eidetic memory, there was only so quickly she could scan the information in front of her. It would have to do.

She'd lingered long enough already.

She slid a small drive into the slot on one of the screens. The virus would enter the Oracle's interface as if it were a routine process to streamline code, and there it would sit until Ariadne needed to activate it.

From farther away, she thought as she quickly entered information into the report logs. *Way, way farther.*

If the Oracle did pay attention to the logs on the smallest of the Three Sisters, it should say that Minoa Katrakis-1, one of the chief engineers, came to check on shipment records. Ariadne made sure to look up other ships' manifests as well as *Zelus*'s, and Minoa had been assigned to work on that ship, as well. She was another small woman, though not as tiny as Ariadne.

She had to hope this desperate patchwork quilt held. Engineers would know how to pass through the maze, though Minoa would only work this one. If any heat came down on the engineer, it would be Ariadne's fault. She didn't want to risk another's life. She'd already caused so much death.

Now to find her way back. She was ready to dance.

"Goodbye, Oracle," Ariadne whispered.

She thought of the Oracle's cruelty. The long hours. What she'd had to do. But she remembered the stories the Oracle would tell her—those she deemed safe enough to tell a little girl. Fables and Old World lore, the offerings, the Named Things lined up in her room. A dried rosebud. Purple amethyst. The doll with the china face and yellow hair.

I love you, she thought.

———

Clo jumped a little when Ariadne opened the door.

"All right?" Clo asked.

"Done. Let's get out of here."

"What did you find?" Clo whispered as soon as they reached the claustrophobic air ducts again.

"Not now," Ariadne said. "First, we go back up the elevator shaft."

Clo let out a groan and a very soft "Silt."

Ariadne busied herself, turning off the shifters to save energy in case they needed them later. Once again, they looked grimy, and they only grew dirtier as they crawled back through the ducts.

"Right on time," she said as the elevator sped past them, blowing her hair back. Clo wiped her hands on her filthy clothes, and Ariadne did the same. Neither of them would slip again tonight.

After climbing up, they kept crawling. Ariadne's neck and shoulders burned, and memories of countless hours spent in the dark innards of ducts just like these haunted her. Sometimes, Ariadne would have to stop and close her eyes, mentally bringing up the map she'd studied. The Oracle was all around her, and even now, One could be turning One's gaze inward, sensing the anomaly.

Finally, they reached the edge of the building. Ariadne and Clo climbed out into the empty room.

Ariadne pointed at the small window. "We're out of the basement levels, so we jump out. If we time the drop, the hedge below should hide us from cameras. Then it's right back to the ship."

"How big is this jump, exactly?"

"Only a story."

"*Only?*"

Ariadne grinned. "You'll be fine."

"What if I crack my head open?"

"That would be bad. Try not landing on your head."

Clo scowled. "Thanks, that's fluming excellent advice."

Ariadne laughed, because it was that or sob. She took out the shifter and started going over their clothes again. "Damn it," she muttered.

"What?" Ariadne shook the shifter, but no luck. They both looked as dirt-streaked as before.

"Signal's jammed."

Or the Oracle has found us.

Clo exhaled hard through her nose. "So, now we have to jump out a window, hide behind a giant bush, and then walk into the loading bay and into our ship absolutely covered in dirt and hope no one will notice. Great. So great."

"Optimism, please!" Ariadne wished she had someone to reassure her. Someone to say everything would be okay.

Ariadne's breathing was quickening, fast and shallow. The panic rose up within her, threatening to overwhelm. The Temple. The tasteless gruel. The endless hours of work, her fingers twisting so many wires, typing so much code, that they almost bled. *The Oracle will hide you so deep in the Temple that no one will ever find you again. You'll be alone, forever and ever.*

"Ariadne." Clo's hands gripped her shoulders, hard. The pain helped bring Ariadne back. *"Ariadne.* Breathe slower. Sit."

Ariadne let her legs give out from under her.

"Lean forward, head between knees."

Ariadne complied. Clo rubbed her back while she forced her breaths to slow. Like Rhea did. It wasn't as good, but it was nice. "Are you okay?"

"Memories," Ariadne managed between breaths. "I'm afraid of going back. I'm afraid—"

"Shhh," Clo crooned. The hand on Ariadne's back made soothing circles. "Look at me."

Ariadne dragged her head up, her vision blurry with tears.

"You're never going back to Tholos. I swear on my life."

"I wish I could believe that."

"Then I'll believe it enough for the both of us." Clo gave her shoulder another squeeze before looking down at their disastrous jumpsuits. She paused, frowning. "I think I have an idea for how we can make it back to the ship. Once we get down, follow my lead."

Ariadne dug deep to find strength and banish her fears. She opened the window and climbed out onto the thin ledge on the building's facade. They had to hold on to the bones that made up the outer facade of the building. Ariadne tried not to think of how many murdered creatures it had taken to make this palace.

Just get down to the hedge. Keep going. Just a jump.

"Let's do this," Clo said. There was sweat at her temples, and her hands shook.

Here goes. She flung herself from the window, hoping Clo would follow.

Ariadne's stomach dipped, but falling through the air was almost freeing. Gravity pulled her down. Her legs took the impact on landing, the force reverberating through her body. She rolled out of the way for Clo. Would the other woman's false leg take the jump?

Clo landed hard and rolled twice. She let out a short hiss of pain, her hand going to the flesh above her prosthetic.

"Are you all right?" Ariadne asked.

"Fine," Clo ground out between clenched teeth.

Ariadne held out a hand to help Clo up. The other woman rose, favoring her good leg, and limped alongside Ariadne. They hid from view behind a hedge, narrowly missing discovery by a passing drone, its little beady camera eye swishing back and forth.

"That was closer than I'd like," Ariadne whispered after it sped away.

They crept back to the palace's loading bay and long-term storage of other visiting ships. Security was present but not as tight as back near the palace or at the Myndalian base.

Clo crouched down and picked up a handful of dark mud, smearing it on her already-filthy jumpsuit.

"What are you doing?" Ariadne whispered.

"Follow my lead, remember?" Clo started drawing designs on the muck on her face, hoping it was vaguely symmetrical. Almost like tattoos. Two winged scythes down her cheeks. A circle of a dark moon on her forehead. Ariadne caught on.

"We're pretending to be gerulae?" she asked.

Ariadne had helped create those ghosts in human form. She knew how deep the Oracle's programming went. She'd checked the code. Unlike an average Tholosian citizen, there was no way to break it and bring them back. There was nothing left.

It would never occur to someone raised in the Three Sisters to impersonate a gerulae. Nyx would have recoiled at the thought. Even Ariadne hesitated.

Clo's expression gentled. "Impersonating a husk is no worse than pretending to be guards. It'll get us back to the ship and that's all we need."

"Don't call them that," Ariadne said sharply.

She didn't like that casual slur, the implication they were too stupid to be human. They had been, once. She'd watched the humanity leak out of them. On some level, she'd been responsible.

"Sorry," Clo muttered, as if she hadn't realized what it meant.

Maybe she didn't. From Rhea, Ariadne knew that Clo had grown up on Myndalia.

Ariadne just nodded and let herself turn the idea over in her head. "It is a good plan, though."

Clo said nothing as she finished the last touches on their impromptu disguises. Clo dipped her fingertip in the mud and drew scythes on Ariadne's cheeks. A brand to the world that they were nothing more than biological machines.

They stood and made their way to the visitor ships' hangar. They held their faces down and turned away, subservient. They kept to the edges of the rooms, close to the walls. They needn't have worried: No one said a word to them. No one even glanced their way.

Mud-splattered, tired, and cold, they walked right up to their ship, slipped behind, and climbed into the small service hatch on the hull. Ariadne's stomach twisted as they crawled through their stolen ship.

Citizen or gerulae—they were all the same to the Empire. Expendable. Unfeeling.

Not even an echo of an echo.

31.

Rhea had never seen anyone die before.

When they had commandeered *Zelus*, Nyx had urged Rhea and Ariadne into an empty meeting room and slammed the door shut. That had been a kindness. She'd found blood spattered across her dress later, from walking down the corridors lined with masked corpses, but only seeing the aftermath had not stopped the horror from sinking in.

For once, she was glad the other women had left her behind. She never wanted them to see her like this: sitting in the ship's command center, staring at the wall, fighting back tears.

The Evoli had blue eyes. Dark hair. Pale skin.

He had been afraid. She could see it in his face. Now she'd never forget.

"I didn't know his name," she murmured, shutting her stinging eyes. "I didn't even know his godsdamned name."

She didn't use language like that. Her life had been comprised of poetry—soft words for reassurance, her voice never rising in anger. She could only think of that man as *the Evoli*. Other, according to the Tholosians. An enemy not worthy of a name. Did he have family? Friends? They would have no way to mourn him, no way of even knowing he was gone.

Gods. *Gods*. Her chest ached. Rhea knew the other women couldn't have stopped it—that his fate had been sealed with his capture—but it still hurt. That was what the Empire did: forced you to be complicit in the dehumanization of others.

They reduced you to same identifiers animals are given: a species name. *Orous zuinae*. Extinct. *Llidnian ixesuma*. Extinct.

That will be you in the end, if you're caught, Rhea thought. *No name. No one to care about you. Why would they? You're just an—*

"Stop it," Rhea told herself, digging her fingernails into the skin of her arms. "Stop it. *Stop it.*"

A soft *beep* emerged from the computers. She snapped her head up, her heart thudding hard against her ribs. Had a Tholosian guard sensed something was off with the ship's logs? Had their identities been compromised?

Rhea checked the controls, cursing her clumsy fingers. She'd rarely touched tablets or technology. In the Pleasure Garden, such things were considered distractions. Though Ariadne had taught her the basics, she was still slow to type.

She keyed in the command to find the source of the alarm.

Oh.

There was movement on the ship—a single signature on one of the lowest levels. And it was heading for the exit near the canteen.

"Seven devils," Rhea muttered, swearing yet again. She grabbed a Mors from Nyx's weapon pile.

Someone else was on the ship.

She threw on one of the Mors-proof jackets stored in the cockpit. A well-placed laser would still hurt, but at least it wouldn't slice her in half.

Rhea's breathing was ragged as she left the command center. She'd have to deal with this herself. She didn't want to be alone, but she couldn't call for backup when the others were in the middle of their missions.

You can do this, she told herself as she hurried quietly down the hall toward the canteen. The ship shuddered. The exit hatch was opening.

"Damn," she hissed, rounding the corner.

A man in a torn uniform was slipping out of the exit hatch. Who was he? How had he entered the ship in the first place without her or the ship's computers knowing?

Rhea slipped behind him as he slowly made his way down the ramp. He moved stiffly. Injured? Yes—a Mors blast must have glanced over his hip. The fabric was burned to his flesh. His skin at the back of his neck was yellow and covered in a sheen of sweat. He wouldn't be as strong or as fast. She had a better chance of taking him down.

The man turned.

Rhea froze.

It was the godsdamned *copilot.*

She had seen him when she boarded back on Tholos. He had caught her eye, then glanced away, as if she was nothing. Just a dona. But he had escaped onto *Asteria* days ago after Clo shot at him—or, at least, they *thought* he had. Rhea fixed her eyes on the injury at his hip. He hadn't escaped.

He'd been here the whole time.

The pilot pointed a Mors of his own at Rhea's head.

"Put your weapon down," he said, his voice rough.

"You first."

They stood at an impasse. Bruises hollowed his eyes, and sweat stained his pale, jaundiced skin. His hand was shaky, and his gaze was unfocused, eyelids heavy. Would he risk the shot?

No. He darted a glance to the open hatch, and she guessed what he was thinking: lock her in, escape.

The pilot went for the door.

Rhea lunged after him, but he was faster. The pilot scrambled out of the hatch and smacked his palm against the button to close it. Rhea leaped through, skidding down the ramp as the door slammed shut behind her.

"Shit," the pilot said, taking off in a limping run.

Rhea opened her mouth to yell after him, but they were in the hangar, with dozens of other ships around. There might be others resting in the crafts between journeys. There might be—

Two people came out from behind the crafts, moving slowly.

"*Hey!*" the pilot yelled, waving his hands. "Get me a fucking medic. Get the—"

Rhea lunged at the pilot, tackling him from behind. They both hit the ground. Rhea rolled hard against the concrete, letting out a soft grunt of pain.

His eyes met hers, and Rhea could see the rapid contraction of his irises. The Oracle programming was waking up. Any moment, One would fully activate and pump his system full of adrenaline. Even in his weakened state, he weighed twice more than Rhea.

He bucked against her as she tried to slide her hands down to his bare wrists . . .

The pilot shoved her off and stumbled into a run. "Hey!" he said to the people approaching. "You— Godsdamn it. Fucking *husks.*"

Rhea didn't even think. She scrambled up, darted for the gerulae's utility belt, and grabbed the first thing her hand touched. An oil canister.

She launched it at the pilot.

The canister slammed into the pilot's temple, and he went down with a muted cry. Rhea breathed hard, watching his body for any movement. None. Had he been at full strength, she wouldn't have stood a chance at knocking him out with one hit.

"Thank you," Rhea said, looking at the women next to her.

They stared expressionlessly down at the pilot, barely even blinking. The scythes on their cheeks seemed to absorb the harsh overhead hangar lighting.

While there had been servitor in the Pleasure Garden, the gerulae had been kept strictly on the other side of the walls. Attendants could answer queries, give polite responses that were just lively enough to show a facade of choice. Gerulae, Rhea knew, were different. Did they even know what was happening?

Rhea shook her head. No time for that.

"Can you help me?" she asked the gerulae. "I can't . . . I can't drag him alone."

They stared at Rhea wordlessly. Rhea reached out to take the first woman's hand. "Can you—"

A vast emptiness expanded inside Rhea. She couldn't hear thoughts, no, but this woman's emotions . . .

Nothingness. Dark. Bleak. An abyss, floating down down down down into the black can't scream can't speak nothing nothing nothing no—

Gasping, Rhea released the gerulae's hand. "Gods. *Gods*. I'm so—gods, I'm so sorry."

The women blinked at her, and Rhea could feel the echo of that chasm inside her. How dark and long it was. And she could do nothing to help them. *Nothing.*

Rhea shut her eyes, hating this. Hating everything the Empire had done. Hating how inept she felt because, right now, she couldn't do anything other than fix this one small problem: the pilot.

"Help me with him," she urged the gerulae firmly.

They only responded to commands. The Oracle would not let them act on anything that might be considered a choice.

The women grasped the pilot's hands and helped Rhea drag him back to the ship. Once they had him restrained in the command center, the gerulae returned to the ship they were servicing and kept scrubbing the metal clean. The Oracle had left them with nothing, just like that Evoli who had died. No names, no voice, nothing for themselves. Rhea wondered what crime they had committed to become this. It might have been nothing more than being too slow to bring Damocles his breakfast.

There's nothing you can do for them.

Rhea returned to the command center and looked over the pilot. He smelled of sour sweat and sickness, which meant his injury was bad. He'd been on the ship, hidden somewhere for days, with no medical attention.

Rhea ripped open the uniform around his wound, wrinkling her nose at the putrid smell. The others might consider it a waste, but Rhea found a med kit and rooted around in the box for supplies. Gauze, tape, disinfectant.

She held up a syringe. Thank the gods, a stress blocker. The Legate must have had this on hand in case the crew needed to briefly deactivate the Oracle's acute stress response during surgery. Rhea had injected Nyx with a dose while Ariadne remotely removed the chip from her cerebellum. Ariadne had excitedly told her how it worked.

Yes, a waste of supplies. But after the Evoli . . .

"I can't stand back and watch anyone else die," she told the pilot's unconscious face. "Not even you."

Rhea cleaned his wound, whispering a few words. Not a prayer—she'd left those gods and devils behind so long before. She'd never pray to any deity from the Avern again. No, she whispered something else, sent out into the quiet void of the universe.

It has to be better than this, she thought, as she bandaged the pilot's injury. *If we bring down the Empire, we have to make our lives worth more than this.*

With a sigh, she sat back and waited for him to wake. An hour later, his limbs began to twitch. Rhea readied herself, Nyx's Mors still clutched in her hand. She didn't know how to use it, exactly, but she figured she could embellish her skills.

The pilot opened his eyes. He tested the ropes as he met her gaze. The blank look that was a product of the Oracle's programming hadn't kicked in yet. Good. The blocker was working.

"Hello," she said with a smile. "I'm Rhea."

He shook his head as if to clear it, then winced. *"Avern.* What did you do to me?"

Rhea's expression turned apologetic. "Hit you with an oil canister."

"Unfuckingbelievable," he muttered. His muscles strained as he pulled at the ropes again.

"You're not going to get those off," Rhea said. She held up the syringe from the med kit. "After treating your wound, I injected you with a blocker that works on your sympathetic nervous system. It'll keep the Oracle in its background processing stage so One doesn't flood your system with adrenaline and cortisol while we talk."

His eyes narrowed.

"Are you hungry?" she asked. If he'd hidden in the vents for nearly a week, he'd be malnourished. "I can get you something to eat."

"Pass. For all I know, you'll poison it."

"If I wanted you dead, you would be." She rose and left him, grabbing the first thing she saw in the canteen: Ariadne's dessert bars. The girl was going to kill her when she found out.

When she returned to the command center, he looked more alert. She unwrapped the bar and held it to his mouth. "Eat."

"Told you I wasn't interested."

"You're starving."

"I'll live."

"Stop being stubborn," she said.

With a glare, he leaned forward and bit into the bar. He closed his eyes, as if to savor the taste, and kept eating.

"So, I take it you weren't in that ship we destroyed?" she asked. "Or *Asteria*?"

"Misdirection. I stayed behind to gather intel." He finished off the bar and leaned back, exhausted. "Stupid decision, really. Your friend shot me and it's worse than I thought."

Rhea frowned. His skin was pallid, his breathing too slow. When Rhea touched his forehead, his skin burned to the touch. "How long have you been like this?"

"Few days." He gestured to his midsection. Dried blood stained his jacket. "Wound's infected. Wasn't gonna live if I didn't make it off it the ship . . ." His voice was trailing off. He shut his eyes, shook his head hard, and started muttering Tholosian propaganda phrases: "Tholos is might. Victory is strength. Failure is weakness. The Scythe slices the soul. The Gods will have their sacrifice. I sacrifice myself to Tholos."

Seven devils. The Oracle might not be able to activate his acute stress response, but One's background processes were still active. Simple repetition to ensure constant compliance. One of Rhea's clients used to mumble phrases in his sleep.

"Hey." Rhea grabbed his jacket, shaking him. "*Pilot.*"

He still muttered under his breath, his eyes rolling up in his skull.

"No," Rhea whispered fiercely. "You're not going to die on me." Not after that Evoli. Not after what she'd seen.

When the pilot finally passed out again, Rhea checked his pulse every few minutes.

She was going to save him.

We have to be better.

32.

Five years ago

"On your feet."

The soft command jolted Discordia into awareness. How long had she spent in this room, sitting beside the murdered bodies of soldiers the Archon tasked her to fight? Yet another test, another demonstration he required from his favored child to keep his high regard.

Focus or die, he'd told her over the comms as he lowered the temperature in the training compound on Macella to conditions no one without body modifications could withstand. The soldiers had all been warm in their thermal uniforms while she fought them off in a thin jumpsuit—with no weapons.

Dimly, Discordia recalled water spraying from the ceiling's sprinklers as she'd dodged Mors blasts and hidden blades. The water had turned to ice on her skin, but still she'd fought. Her father was right: focus or die.

All she wanted was to survive.

The floor of the facility had iced over. The frost had burned at first, but then it only felt numb. Earlier, a movement had jarred Discordia from her frozen reverie, and she looked over to see one soldier still alive. His breath rattled.

His eyes were strange. Discordia frowned, scooting closer. His pupils were widening and contracting, widening and contracting. Discordia knew from her training that when the Oracle switched to foreground processing, the pupils dilated.

"Sergeant Gaius." Discordia said his name softly.

He sighed. "My head . . . so quiet."

Quiet?

The Oracle's voice, Discordia realized. He must not be hearing the subtle programming that indicated the Oracle was active, One's whisper in the head of every soldier that spoke of victory, conquest, and loyalty to the Empire. Was it the cold? Or something else?

He shut his eyes. Discordia had no time; he was dying.

"Does it hurt?" she asked him in a rough whisper. "Dying?"

"No," he breathed. She could barely hear Sergeant Gaius's voice, and had to inch closer to hear his last words. "I like the silence."

Discordia had unhooked her necklace and given every soldier last rites. But that had been so long ago. Had her father forgotten her?

She had no choice but to wait.

Her hand was stiff with blood when she slipped it into her pocket and felt the rough edges of Xander's firewolf. She'd flown to Macella after he'd given it to her, sought out her father. *I have doubts*, she wanted to tell the Archon when she arrived. *I felt guilt for killing people. Make it go away.*

She never got the words out. Her father had taken one look at her—perhaps he'd seen something in her face—and told her to get into the training room. "Don't disappoint me," he'd said before he locked her in.

Discordia didn't know how long she'd been in the room. Hours? Days?

"On your feet," the Archon said again, standing before her.

She hadn't heard him enter. He'd stepped in the blood of his soldiers and left boot prints on the floor. Did he care? Did he care about anything other than battle and conquest? These loyal soldiers had all died for a mere test.

Look up. Meet his eyes, she thought. *See for yourself.*

But when she did, Discordia found no answer. Her father's gaze was as frigid and inhospitable as the room he'd left her in.

Discordia had spent too long in the cold; her mind was not as sharp as it usually was. She was tired, and the guilt had settled cold and hard in her belly once more. That was the only explanation she had for why she said, "I thought about peace. I'm not fit to be your Heir."

Something in his expression faltered. In the end, he only reached out and lifted her chin. His fingers burned her cold skin. "On your feet, Discordia," he said once more, and released her. He left her.

Had the longing in his face been real, or was it only her imagination?

Discordia stood on shaking legs and closed her hand around the firewolf in her pocket. The sharp edges bit into her fingers as she stepped over Sergeant Gaius's corpse.

She wondered whether he'd be dead if the Oracle had given him a choice.

———

Urion, one of Discordia's brothers, was going to kill Xander.

Discordia had tracked Urion to Regulas, a moon in the outer quadrant of the Iona Galaxy where she knew Xander had gone. Xander had been reckless. He'd left an encrypted message that allowed her to track his whereabouts—a stupid decision, she'd thought. *Bring the firewolf back to me sometime*, he'd said. Why would he do that? Why would he make such a foolish choice just because she'd taken that carving? Didn't he know not to trust her?

More than once, Discordia had convinced herself to go after him.

Every time, she changed her mind.

Two brothers in the same place, she thought to herself, tracking Urion through the trees of the moon's thick northern forest. She'd put off killing Xander long enough. It was time to finally slit his throat and leave the firewolf behind. *Xander* was responsible for this doubt, this guilt. He had to die for it.

The scent of woodsmoke grew stronger as Discordia followed Urion—Xander's camp couldn't be far. As she edged through the trees, she watched her brother's movements for any indication that he was aware of her. He wasn't. When Discordia had seen Urion train, it was clear that he was unexceptional. Not weak or strong; an average candidate in a cutthroat competition. The fault, perhaps, had been with his prefect, a former member of the royal guard who had been too rash with his charge. Impatient for results, and for the prestige of having trained one of the surviving Heirs. Mistress Heraia had considered his teachings inadequate.

For Mistress Heraia's patience had been so endless that it, too, had been a form of torture. She had been the first to leave Discordia in desolate rooms with corpses for company.

Discordia crouched behind the bushes as Urion reached Xander's camp. Xander was there, sitting by the fire, as if awaiting such a fate. There was a formality to the way the royal cohort had been taught to duel; they approached each other as adversaries, yes, but there was a civility to it. Rules of straightforward approaches. The challenge had to be issued.

It was as formal as giving last rites.

Urion greeted Xander in the usual way: "I challenge you." No regret, no emotion. Only facts. "Choose your weapons."

Xander gave a short nod and rose. The brothers were of equal height, both had pale skin and dark hair. Discordia resembled neither of them; her and Damocles's features had been chosen differently, hair like spun gold to contrast their black-haired siblings. Where Urion lacked similarity in coloring, he matched Damocles in physicality. His body was large and muscled, whereas Xander's was more compact, athletic. Their strengths would be different.

"Hand-to-hand," Xander said.

Discordia reared back sharply. Was he insane? The entire point of the challenge was an acknowledgment of an opponent's strengths and weaknesses. It had been an opportunity for Xander to choose his best weapon—a blade. He had been good with blades, Discordia recalled. Urion outmatched him in hand-to-hand.

Even Urion seemed startled, but only said, "I accept."

Their fight began.

From the moment it started, Discordia knew Xander was going to lose. He was quick, yes, but Urion landed blows that made Xander double over with the force. Worse, it seemed he wasn't even trying.

Damn you, Xander, she thought. *Fight. Put up a fucking fight.*

But she could practically read his thoughts: what did it matter? Only two siblings would win, anyway. One was not going to be Xander. The other was not likely to be Urion. Why fight the inevitable? Why win now only to lose later?

Urion punched Xander so hard that he stumbled. Discordia winced, watching as her stronger brother slid an arm around Xander's throat and cut off his air supply.

Leave him, she told herself. Urion was doing her a favor. She wouldn't have to kill Xander; all she had to do was wait until her brother choked the life out of him.

Easy, she thought, as the guilt squeezed her chest. It felt like she was being choked, too. *So easy. Ea—*

Her hand found the firewolf in her pocket. Rough edges. Carved lovingly by Xander's hand, even after his fingers had been broken over and over and over again by his prefect to discourage it. He'd never carve anything that beautiful again.

He'd be dead.

Discordia's Mors was in her hand before she could think. She raised the weapon, aimed, and fired.

It was a killing blow straight into Urion's skull.

Xander heaved in a breath as he collapsed onto the ground. He looked up as she came out of the trees, and his eyes touched on her, on the Mors still gripped in her hand, then on their dead brother. A drop of blood slid down Urion's forehead.

"You didn't challenge him," Xander said hoarsely.

No, she hadn't. Discordia had broken the rules. She was a fucking fool for coming there. "And you didn't even put up a fight."

Xander shut his eyes and wiped the blood from an injury at his temple. The nanites in his system were healing his wounds already. In another hour, he'd be completely recovered. "Are you going to challenge me or not?" When she didn't answer, he just shook his head and took off his scythe necklace. "Then why did you even leave home?"

Home? Where was home? It wasn't back at the palace on Macella, where she had left the gerulae to their task of dragging her victims' corpses out of the training facility. Not back at the academy on Myndalia, either; nightmares forced her to recall every brutal session Mistress Heraia offered there. Neither of those places were safe. Nowhere in the galaxy was safe for her.

Discordia didn't have a home.

She gritted her teeth. *Stop it.* "I left because my tracker indicated Urion was coming here," she said a touch too sharply. "And you told me you'd be here."

"So, you executed him to save me."

A denial was on her lips. Save? She didn't *save* people. She was the God of Death's servant. She did not give life. "Did you want to lose to Urion?" she asked him.

Her brother went quiet. Some emotion worked through his features—a strange thing to witness that indecision. Survival felt like such a prominent aspect of their training that Discordia had mistaken it for intrinsicness. Something coded into their DNA.

"No," he said softly. His eyes met hers. "I want you to be the one to kill me."

Discordia did not expect such a statement to weigh so heavily on her. But it did. It hurt. Why did it hurt? Why did she care? "Another time, then," she said, taking off her own scythe necklace. "But don't get comfortable. You'll be next on my list."

Discordia ignored Xander's smile and settled next to him. Together, they said last rites over the body of their dead brother.

———

Xander was having a nightmare.

It had been careless of Discordia to accept his invitation to rest before taking her bullet craft back—but it had been even more reckless for him to fall asleep with her sharing his tent. She had set up her cot several feet away, and she kept her back pressed to the trunk he'd used for their dinner table. Carelessness was one thing; trust was fatal.

But Discordia had been weary after killing Urion. She had wanted to sit and rest.

Most of all, she didn't want to be alone. These days, she had thought too often of the freedom on Sergeant Gaius's face when he died.

Stop thinking about him. Rest.

When she shut her eyes, Xander gave another rough shout. He had tossed and turned for the last hour, his prefect's name uttered in some pleading litany. *No, no, no.*

"Weak," Discordia said to herself, rolling the word on her tongue. She played with the knife in her hand; she'd taken it out when she accepted his invitation to stay. She ought to cross his name off her list.

Still, she couldn't bring herself to move. One strategic strike of the knife, and she'd be all alone again, with no one but a father who used her as a weapon and another brother who loathed her as his competition. This one didn't. This one just wanted another day in this fucking galaxy. Discordia wondered at Xander. Perhaps she, too, slept restlessly. Perhaps some memories of her time at the academy floated to the surface then, negligently spilling over without her permission. No one had ever been in a position to let Discordia know.

The thought unsettled her.

She felt for her firewolf talisman. How ridiculous to draw comfort from a carving. How childish.

With a disgusted noise, Discordia slid her knife into her belt and stood. "Xander," Discordia called. "Wake up."

Her brother woke more quietly than he slept. He blinked and stared at her, as if he couldn't quite believe she was real. "You're still here."

"I'm leaving." She should have left hours earlier, when one of the other moons came over the horizon. She snatched the firewolf out of her clothes and held it out. "I only stayed to give you this."

Xander stared at the carving but made no move to take it. "Why?"

Discordia hated his questions, his probing eyes. Most of all, she hated that he made her doubt everything. "Why *what*?" she practically snarled.

"You could have given it to me earlier," he pointed out. "Or left it on your cot. You didn't have to stay."

She made some soft noise and looked away. How could she tell him that the unpleasant gnawing in her gut quieted when she saw him or when she felt the rough edges of his carving? That he had done her a kindness, and generosity was not a language she understood? It was as unfamiliar as the farthest reaches of the galaxy.

"You talk in your sleep," she told him. She had not meant the words to sound so accusing, but they did anyway.

Xander's lip lifted in a not-quite-smile. "Hear anything interesting?"

She did not answer his question. "We went through the same things, back at the academy. The grueling training, the long hours. I had my fingers broken for painting once. I had seen the gerulae mindlessly constructing a mural, and I marveled at the colors, the detailing. The Oracle had probably fed them the instructions and worked their hands. But I figured that if a husk could create something that beautiful, why couldn't I? I never picked up a brush again."

He didn't say anything right away. Rather, his gaze searched hers, as if trying to understand the sister who was his enemy. Perhaps he comprehended that he was there on borrowed time—time that she had bestowed. Because he asked, "Would you have wanted to?"

"I don't know." She slid her hands across the face of the wolf. "Every time I look at this, I wonder what life I might have lived if I had been given the choice. You would not be on my list. Because I wouldn't have one."

Xander sat up and rested his wrists on his knees. "I made that when I found out what happened to the firewolves. We revered them, put them in those murals you love so much. They thrived in the forests of Syrmia, a planet on the border of the old Tholosian kingdom—before we conquered the whole galaxy. And—"

"They died off," Discordia said flatly. "In climactic flooding after the firestorms of the first wars with the Evoli. I remember my history."

"Yes," Xander said. "Because what mattered was that the planet became ours. Nothing else. Every human in the Empire is like that firewolf. Including you and me." He nodded to the figurine. "You should keep it. Something to remember me by when you strike me off your list."

"Next time," she reminded him.

When Xander smiled at her again, Discordia knew her promise was false.

33.

Present day

Eris wanted off this planet. She'd spent hours that evening touring the ballroom with Damocles, dancing and drinking wine while Ariadne and Clo put themselves in danger and Nyx trailed behind her like a servant.

Her brother hadn't given her any more useful information. With their father in attendance, he wouldn't have risked discussing whatever he had planned for the Evoli and their truce—and it had to be *something*; otherwise, he wouldn't have shown such interest in Zoe's weapon.

I hate Zoe, Eris thought as she and Nyx made it safely back to the ship.

Her face hurt from Zoe's fake smiles and fake laughter, from pretending she didn't give a damn that her brother had murdered someone in front of her and that her team thought she was a soulless killer.

They're not friends, a small voice in the back of her mind reminded her. *They aren't here because they like you, especially Clo.*

Eris gritted her teeth as they closed the ship's hatch behind them. The storage bay was empty save for one lead-lined canister of the damn mystery rock Kyla had left behind for them, and a very filthy Clo and Ariadne. The duo must have arrived only shortly before; they were both wearing their natural faces, but Clo was still shaking mud off her boots.

Eris nodded to the pair. "Success?"

Clo shrugged. "Ariadne got intel, but I've had better nights. I need a nap."

"And a shower!" Ariadne added brightly.

"I can see that," Nyx said. The soldier discarded her servitor coat onto the floor like she couldn't wait to get rid of it. "You both look shitty. Why are your faces painted up like a couple of husks?"

"*Hey.*" Ariadne sounded offended as she swiped the markings off her cheeks. "Don't be mean."

"We were out of options," Clo said shortly. She gave Eris an assessing look. "All okay with Damocles?"

Eris understood Clo's unasked question: *how was it seeing your brother again, after all this time?* A part of her warmed at the concern, but she tried not to overthink Clo's intentions. If Eris botched this mission, they'd all be dead.

"He's still alive, unfortunately," she said, removing the shifter from the roof of her mouth. She relaxed as her face settled into its natural shape. Eris sighed. Gods, it felt good. "I'm going to my quarters. Don't bother me for three hours."

"What if there's a fire?" Ariadne asked. "Or another emergency?"

"Either handle it or let me die. I'm tired." Her bones were as heavy as her heart as she started for the doors. They opened before Eris reached for the button.

Rhea stood there. Her eyes were wide and panicked, her usual grace replaced by agitated jerking movements. Eris didn't know her well, but the other woman had kept a calm facade since she and Clo had first come aboard the ship.

"You all need to get to the bridge," Rhea told them, almost breathless. She must have run all the way from the command center.

"What is it?" Nyx asked.

Rhea just gestured with her hand. "With me. Now."

She led them to the command center. They all froze when they saw who was sitting in the oversized chair.

"Son of a bitch," Eris hissed.

The pilot was unconscious, his head lolling to the side. The women recoiled from the scent of him, a combination of body odor, chemicals, and things Eris didn't even want to contemplate since he'd been hiding somewhere on the ship for the better part of a godsdamn week.

"How the flark is he here?" Clo demanded. "He took my ship! There's *no way* he—" She stopped, coming to some realization. "He sent that ship out there unmanned. So we wouldn't look for him. That *bastard.*"

Rhea nodded. "He said he stayed behind for intel. Hoping for glory from the Empire for his trouble."

"So, he sent my ship down a wormhole for nothing? *That bastard!*"

"Clever asshole." Eris stepped closer to him. "Where was he hiding?"

"Found him trying the exit hatch near the canteen. My guess is he's been in the vents for days." Rhea gestured to his injury. "Clo shot him. His wound is infected and he's running a fever. I injected him with a hormone blocker to prevent the Oracle from triggering a stress response, so that's keeping him calm for now."

Eris scrutinized the intruder. His greasy blond hair covered his brow, and his beard was as filthy as his pale skin. He appeared to be from one of the colder planets, perhaps Lethe, where there was a large military outpost with its own Birthing Center. New cohorts of soldiers were grown there, built for brute strength. Most of this new lot tended to have fairer skin than the darker-skinned crops of DNA used in the warmer Three Sisters region of the galaxy. He certainly looked big enough to be Lethean.

As she decided what to do with him, something on his trousers caught her eye. Were those . . . "*Crumbs?*" She snapped her head to Rhea in disbelief. "You've been *feeding him?*"

Rhea crossed her arms. "What was I supposed to do? Let him starve? He could barely walk." At Eris's silence, Rhea's eyes narrowed. "If you're going to torture him, he'll need his strength, won't he?"

Damn. The woman had some cutting sarcasm.

Ariadne shoved through. "What did you give him? Because I smell . . ." The girl inspected closer. "Aw, you fed him the proto-bars! Those are my favorites!"

"Oh, enough of this." Nyx strode to the table and grabbed her Mors. She pointed the gun right at his head. "Eris?"

If Eris gave the command, Nyx would carry it out.

Eris met Clo's eyes, and the other woman shook her head slightly. Even with that small movement, Eris saw Clo's hesitation. They were thinking the same thing: what could they do with the pilot? They'd have to get him back to headquarters for deprogramming, and they didn't have time for that. They were in the middle of a mission. He was a liability.

"Do it," Eris said.

Nyx cocked the gun.

"*Wait.*" Rhea grasped the end of Nyx's Mors before it could fire. "I think we should speak to him and see if he knows anything about . . . uh, Josephine."

"Josephine has an official name, by the way. Ichor." Ariadne looked proud. "Means *blood of the gods*. Pretty fancy."

Nyx scowled at Ariadne before returning her attention to Rhea. "Pilots aren't paid to know what their cargo is, just to deliver it. He's dangerous."

Rhea was insistent. "He didn't reach out to anyone."

"Yet," Eris said quietly.

"Rhea, it's not for lack of trying." Ariadne had grabbed her tablet to draw up the communication logs. "His comms were damaged when he was injured. He tried to send several messages, but they were caught by my firewalls when I de-Oracled the ship." Ariadne opened one at random and read: "*Mayday. Injured and trapped aboard* Zelus. *Ship successfully commandeered by insurgents. Requesting aid.* He sent that one a few times, and then he called us *bitches* in this last one. I don't think he's nice."

"Of course he's not nice," Clo said. "He's brainwashed and controlled by the Oracle."

"I think he's pretty, though," Ariadne said. "In a gross, unwashed sort of way."

Nyx rolled her eyes. "You think everyone's pretty."

"Everyone has something pretty about them!"

While they nattered back and forth, Eris steeled herself, tilting the pilot's head up with the tip of her finger. Before his illness, the pilot must have been strong. Muscles still bulged at the shoulders of his filthy pilot's uniform. His features were sunken from dehydration and fever, but he still looked like so many other soldiers, except for the scarring on his neck. It only showed because the collar of his uniform was badly torn.

Eris leaned close, nose wrinkling slightly. "Interesting. He's heavily scarred here. I wonder what caused it."

As if at her words, the pilot groaned, head turning side to side. One eyelid, caked with gunk, cracked open as he looked at her blearily. "Am I dead?" he asked, groggy.

"You're awake!" Ariadne chimed from behind Eris. "Hi! Your messages were rude." She wiggled her fingers.

He shut his eyes hard. "Not dead, then. Godsdamn it."

"Afraid so," Eris said. "You look like shit."

"I feel like shit."

"Your humor is intact, at least." When he opened his eyes again, Eris let out a slow breath. Blue, as pale as the sky on Lethe. "I have some bad news: I think you're going to recover, pilot."

That blue gaze went hard, distant. "If you let that happen, I'll kill you. First chance I get. *In His name. Letum, God of Death, I kill for Thee.*"

"Five against one. I don't like your odds."

"The worse odds, the better." His voice was fainter, trembling.

Eris jerked back. That sounded like something she would say. Something drilled into their minds through blood and pain and training.

"If he mentions the God of Death one more time . . ." Nyx let out an irritated huff. "He's a liability. We'll never be able to break his programming."

"We broke yours," Rhea said softly.

"It was already fracturing on its own," Nyx countered. "It took weeks, and we don't have that kind of time."

"We have a duty to try." Rhea shook her head. "We can try to get more of the blockers to keep him calm."

"Or he can go out the airlock with all the rest," Nyx pointed out.

"Do I get a choice in this?" the pilot asked.

Eris raised an eyebrow. "You don't have a choice in anything. You're a programmed puppet."

"First of all," he said, "I'm not a puppet. Second of all—"

"Let me guess, you're not brainwashed?"

"Fuck you."

"Not interested."

"*Excuse me*," Clo said, snapping her fingers between Eris and the pilot. "I agree with Nyx that he's a liability."

"Of course you do." Eris's lip curled. "You don't believe people can ever change."

The edge in her voice made the room go silent. Clo's mouth moved, as if holding back the words. The curiosity from Rhea, Ariadne, and Nyx was so strong, it was as though Eris could taste it at the back of her throat.

"*Oookay*," Ariadne said, extra cheerful. "Hm. This is awkward. So, let's just clear something up first." She looked at the pilot. "Hey there, sir. Are you loyal to the Tholosians no matter what they do to you and the rest of the galaxy, and are you willing to die for that belief?"

His eyes glazed again. "*In His name*." Yet his body tensed, as if fighting the words. His back arched, mouth moving soundlessly.

And he fainted.

"That'll be a yes, then," Ariadne said.

Rhea put a hand to his head. "His fever is bad. Make a decision. Heal or kill?"

"My opinion remains the same," Nyx said. "He's everything that's wrong with the Empire. Did you see the way he looked at us? He wants to string us up and gut us one by one. He'd march into that palace, wearing our entrails as a scarf, all to get some stupid gold button for his jacket."

Rhea winced at that mental image. "That's his programming, Nyx."

"No shit. You could heal him and he'd still try to slit your throat the first chance he gets."

"True," Rhea said, ruefully. She looked down at his prone form. "But I feel like we've killed enough for a lifetime, don't you?"

"Before this is over with, more will end up dying," Clo muttered. At Rhea's expression, Clo sighed. "Directly or indirectly, this is going to result in death, Rhea. It might be better to turn off our conscience for a while. If only it were that easy." She gave a pointed glance at Eris. The barb landed.

"Ariadne," Eris focused on her. "You haven't given your opinion."

Ariadne blinked, sputtered. "I—" Her mouth snapped closed.

"That's an 'I have no idea,' then," Clo said.

Eris sighed and leaned over to open one of the pilot's eyelids. The pupil of those beautiful blues contracted. They weren't pulsing, so at least the hormone blocker Rhea injected him with was still working. Eris's instincts still said to kill him. Lessen the risks. Turn him into one more casualty of the Tholosian empire. Another broken promise to Kyla and Sher for the greater picture. But those instincts had been honed in the academy on Myndalia. The training grounds of Macella. The battlefields across the galaxy. This fevered, injured pilot had tried to break through the programming. It had been the barest glimmer, but Eris had seen it. She couldn't pretend she hadn't.

"I say we listen to Rhea and give him a chance."

Clo raised her eyebrows in surprise. Despite everything they'd been through, did she think Eris was still the person who killed first and asked forgiveness after?

Eris's fingernails dug into her palm. "Don't give me that look. You judged me for all the people I've killed, so don't be shocked I'm having some second thoughts."

Clo held up her hands. "I said bog all."

Nyx exhaled loudly through her nose. "Fine. He gets a shot. But first sign of trouble, we shove him out the airlock. Deal?"

Eris gave a short nod. "Give me a hand with him. We'll take him to the med center and take out his implant."

"I did that already," Rhea said. "Don't take me for an amateur."

Eris peered at the base of his skull. Sure enough, there was a tidy bandage, barely bloodstained.

"His programming is in too deep for removing it to make much of a difference, but it might give him a start. And make it harder for the Oracle to track us," Eris said. "How'd you learn to do this?"

"She was there when a surgical bot took out mine," Nyx said, shortly. "We taking him to the med bay or not?"

Eris put up her hands. "Fine. We'll get him patched and cleaned up." She raised half of the chair the pilot was tied to, and Nyx reluctantly took the other. They carried him off to one of the brigs. He was ridiculously heavy.

"Gods, he really stinks," Nyx muttered.

"Make sure Rhea doesn't feed him all my favorite foods!" Ariadne called after them.

———

After everyone had cleaned up and rested, the women met back at the bridge.

The pilot was still in the medical center on the deck below them, passed out but recovering. Eris had checked on him to see that Rhea had given him a tincture to bring down his fever and even bathed and shaved his face. Beneath the grime, he still looked ill, but Ariadne had been right. He wasn't ugly.

"Clo, Ariadne," Eris said. "Update me."

"Well, like I said, we found Josephine's real name, but I still like *Josephine* better. *Ichor* sounds so harsh. And we successfully hacked the Oracle's mainframe." Ariadne pumped her fist in the air.

"*You* successfully hacked the Oracle's mainframe," Clo said, "while I stood guard in mounting terror and also almost fell into an elevator shaft."

"We should probably run," Ariadne added. "Before the Oracle realizes I was here. One put up new blocks in One's system after I disappeared from Tholos, so it's only a matter of—"

Eris burst out of her chair. "Are you *kidding* me? Clo, start up the godsdamn ship."

"Unless you want to tip them off," Clo said, "we have to be approved for launch. I already put in the request, so sit down."

Eris reluctantly settled back into her chair. "How much time, Ariadne?"

"Not sure. The Oracle runs scans on One's programming every few weeks, so I'm hoping not until then."

"And the ichor?"

Ariadne let out a frustrated breath. "Whatever information I could find was encrypted, and it'd be too risky to copy it. I managed to skim a few documents One kept about storing the ichor. I couldn't see what it's being used for, or whether General Damocles is directly involved, but all the rocks came through a warehouse on Ismara."

"Anything on Kyla's murdered spies?"

Ariadne shrugged. "I didn't have time to look. I'd need to break the Oracle's encryption wall for that too. But!" She lifted a hand. "I snuck in a virus. The Oracle will know it's there if I access the information again, but in a pinch . . ."

Eris stared at her. "No wonder Kyla likes you."

The girl grinned. "I'm also very charming."

"She's so modest, too," Clo added with a sly smile from the pilot seat. "Flight approval has gone through. We're good to launch."

"Thank the gods." Eris rubbed her forehead. "Get us out of here."

Clo rolled back to the screens and prepped the ship to jump to Ismara. The ship whooshed to life and she started angling the craft out of the hangar before it abruptly powered down again with a short stutter of the engine. "Uh."

"Oh gods, what now?" Eris asked.

Clo shook her head and bashed at the controls, trying to get it to power up again. "Uhh. Ariadne? Help."

Ariadne leaned over Clo and typed something into the controls, then squinted at the screen. "Wait a minute. There's a lock on jumping. With a name of who gave the command . . . Cato. Who's Cato?"

The women all stared at each other. Then, as one: "The pilot."

34.

Present day

That *son of a bitch should have been killed the second he was recovered,* Nyx thought as she and the others stomped to the med center. She should have floated the pilot out into space her damn self.

"What the fuck kind of a name is *Cato* anyway?"

"It's Old World language," replied Ariadne, ever the encyclopedia.

"For what? *Asshole*?"

"Shrewd," Ariadne corrected, clicking away on her tablet as she pulled up the original *Zelus* manifest. "Cato Rigel-12. The Rigels were a militus cohort bred for intelligence."

"Then he's got a malfunction in his genetic engineering." Nyx followed closely behind Eris, hoping to get the command to put a Mors blast to his head.

"How did this happen?" Eris asked Rhea as they rounded a corner in the main hallway.

Eris's hands were balled into fists; she was probably frustrated because until they could get the ship up and running, they were stuck in Tholosian territory. Nyx didn't blame her. She wanted to get the fuck off this rock.

Rhea shook her head. "Maybe it was always a failsafe."

"Or he did it when you brought him into the command center," Eris said.

"I only left him alone for—"

"You don't need to explain yourself," Nyx snapped. "You were trying to help the bastard. As soon as he tells us how to fix this, I'm killing him."

Nyx flung open the door to the medical center. The pilot—Cato—didn't even show surprise when she seized him by the front of the shirt. "Get up."

"A little difficult when I'm tied to the bed," he retorted.

Eris undid his bindings from the posts and re-bound his hands together. Nyx hauled his ass out of the bed and half-carried, half-dragged him out of the room.

"Hey, careful with my wound," he protested as his feet skidded across the marble hallway of the ship. "Your friend just cleaned it."

"Careful? I ought to stick a knife in it just to watch you scream." Nyx flung open the door to another room and shoved him inside. "Get in there. Sit down or I'll send you straight to the darkest level of Avern."

The interrogation room was nearly sealed. The air ducts were too tiny to climb through. No escapes.

Eris, Ariadne, and Rhea followed behind; Clo had stayed in the command center to see if she could work around Cato's lock, but told them over the Pathos that it wasn't looking promising. The only way to unlock it was a code, and the cypher was this Tholosian brainwashed dickbag.

Eris stepped forward, but Nyx put up a hand. "Let me do this." It was what she was trained for. *Control*, Nyx told herself. *Control.* "You," she said to the pilot. "Talk."

Nyx knew how she sounded: wound tight, coiled with a promised violence itching to lash out. One wrong word, and she'd break the bones of his face to bash the information she needed out of him.

"Talk, huh?" His grin was slow. "About anything? Because I can chat for hours. It's one of my most infuriating qualities. Just ask your friend here." Cato glanced at Rhea.

"He ranted in Tholosian propaganda phrases the whole time I

cleaned him up," Rhea said, rolling her eyes. "He was out of it but it was still annoying."

"I'm wounded, literally and metaphorically. Here I thought you enjoyed the sound of my voice. And me without a shirt on. Or was it just my face? You touched it enough." He winked. "Thanks for the shave. I didn't much like the scruff."

Nyx studied him. Without the dirt and beard, he looked like a pretty boy, more fit for the Pleasure Gardens than military, but that sharp gaze was all soldier. She had no doubt that he had seen his share of ground battle. Faded burn scars smattered the neckline of his shirt.

"That one's quiet this time." Cato jerked his chin toward Eris. "I could have sworn she enjoyed swearing at me."

"Shut up," Nyx snarled.

Cato smirked. "I thought you wanted me to talk." He nodded to Eris. "I like her best. I'll talk to her."

Nyx balled up the front of his shirt and jerked his chair forward. "You'll talk to me."

"Nope."

"What'd you do to the ship?" Nyx asked, taking out her knife. The sharp edge glinted in the harsh overhead lights of the interrogation room. She pointed the blade toward his eye, touching with just the tip so he got the idea.

But he was a stubborn bastard. His slow grin was easy and he cocked his head at Rhea, away from the blade. "That pretty girl shouldn't have turned her back."

With a growl, Nyx tightened her grip on his shirt. "How do we fix it?"

"Oh, I don't know *that*—"

Nyx slashed the blade across the underside of his chin. It was a long cut but superficial. A perfectly controlled warning. Blood welled against his pale skin. Behind her, Rhea sucked in a breath.

"Try again, asshole." Nyx held the blade to his throat.

Cato didn't even drop his smile. "Cut me again. That tickled." At her glare, he lifted a shoulder. "Do you think this is worse than where I've been? I spent years flying in and out of hostile territory. This was supposed to be a cushy gig and now you've all fucked it up. I'll probably get executed with you."

"Don't care," Nyx said. She nicked his skin with the blade. "Tell me that cypher or I'll slice open your throat."

"Ah, but if you do that, you'll still be stuck right where you are, won't you?" He shook his head. "It was pretty ballsy of you to go to Macella. The general will eventually figure out you're traitors."

Her eyes narrowed. "At least you'd be dead." She slid the blade down his throat until she reached one of the scars. "Or maybe I'll add to this collection here." There. A flicker in his gaze. "You've got a lot of scars for a pretty boy, pilot."

His jaw tightened. "So do a lot of people."

<Keep digging,> Eris said through the Pathos.

Nyx almost smiled. "Rhea, you've seen him without a shirt. He just bragged about it. How far down do these scars go?"

Rhea ignored Cato's glare. "They cover almost his entire torso. Front and back."

"Front *and* back," Nyx repeated. "Wow. Now, that had to hurt." At his silence, Nyx almost smiled. "Come on, tell me about these scars, pilot. Couldn't have got them flying. You're from a military cohort. You get them on the field?"

His breathing grew ragged, and Nyx bet that if she put a finger on his pulse, it'd be quickening. "Fuck. You."

"And you were being so pleasant before," Nyx said. "I'll bet you got these scars in a battle. Some of the easiest soldiers to torture are pilots. My commander always said they were too damn soft. Caved easily. Screamed like children."

Cato shook his head, his chest heaving with his breaths. "*Shut up.*"

<His pupils are contracting,> Eris said. *<His programming is starting to kick in, Nyx. The blocker Rhea injected him with is wearing off.>*

<There's still time.>

"You want me to stop," Nyx said, drawing closer, "then give me the cypher. Otherwise, maybe I'll add to these scars. They don't look like they're from Mors."

<Nyx—>

"I said *shut the fuck up.*" Cato's head snapped back and his pupils contracted. The Oracle's coding was flooding his system with stress hormones. With a rough yell, he tore at the restraints and rocked his chair until he was on the floor. He slammed his head against the wall. "The God of Death, I kill for Thee. In Thy name I give my body." *Slam.* His forehead was bleeding. "In Thy name." *Slam.*

"Shit." Nyx tackled him, but he bucked against her. She held him fast, shoving him to the floor. She had her knee in the middle of his back. "Some help would be nice! Rhea, get another blocker from the med center!"

Rhea nodded. "On it."

"Ariadne." Eris's voice was calm behind Nyx. "Turn up the cooling system in here as high as it can go."

"But that's—" The girl bit her lip. "It'll kill you."

Eris didn't look concerned. "Just do it." Ariadne and Rhea left to do as she asked. It wasn't long before there was a noticeable dip in the temperature. "Keep holding him, Nyx."

The pilot thrashed against her, murmuring a litany of Tholosian phrases. If he weren't still weak from his injuries and restrained, Nyx would be a whole lot worse off.

"What's your plan?" Nyx asked Eris. The temperature kept dropping.

"Wait. Try to save him from killing himself." After a pause, she jerked her chin at Nyx. "How much were you made to endure in your training?"

Nyx's head snapped back, and she drove her knee harder into the pilot's back as he bucked again. "What the fuck kind of question is that?"

"Practical." Eris's breath was coming out in puffs of white. "It's going to get very cold very fast."

"I can handle it."

Eris didn't respond, just gestured to the pilot and said, "Flip him over. I need to see his pupils."

Nyx removed her knee and shoved him on his back. Cato growled low in his throat as he thrashed against her. *Wham.* His forehead struck hers. *Son of a bitch.*

"For Tholos," he was muttering. "For the Archon. For—"

Nyx slammed her fist into his face and held him down again. Her movements grew uncoordinated. The cold numbed her fingers, her nose. She shook her head to clear it, but she was starting to shiver. Her lungs burned.

Cato's litanies had progressed to low groans as tremors wracked his body. He could barely speak through chattering teeth.

"That's it," Eris murmured. She seemed unaffected by the cold. Who the fuck *was* this woman? "Only a little longer."

Nyx could barely breathe. "I c-c-can't—"

"I know." Eris nodded once. "He's stopped with the phrases. Look at his pupils. The Oracle's programming is returning to background processing."

Nyx forced a blink. Her vision wavered. When she focused, she could see Cato's pupils had slowed their contractions. He was still beneath her. She loosened her hold, huddling close to the wall. She brought her knees close to her body for warmth. How was Eris still functional?

"Cato," Eris said calmly.

He moaned. He was so cold his teeth were no longer chattering.

"Look at me." Eris crouched in front of Cato, resting her elbows on her knees. She stared at him until he finally met her gaze. "I can make it stop, Cato."

"Wh-wh—"

"I just need the cypher." Eris's voice had taken on a lilting, almost hypnotic quality. Or maybe that was the cold. Nyx thought she saw stars around the other woman. Fuck, Nyx was dizzy.

"No," Cato wheezed. "No."

"I can make you warm again. If you give me that cypher, I'll set you off on some quiet, safe planet with no memory of this. All of it wiped. I can help you forget where your scars came from."

"You're not— You can't—"

"I can. Wouldn't you like to forget what caused you pain, Cato? You could start over somewhere else. If you decide to leave, I promise I can do that for you."

Did she know how cruel it was to dangle that promise in front of him, or did she not care? She wouldn't keep it any more than Kyla had.

"Yes." Cato clutched at his clothes, gasping. "Y-y-y—"

"The cypher, Cato."

He gasped out a string of random numbers, barely managing to get each one out. Nyx was lightheaded, her entire body numb. She wanted this to stop. She could barely think, and her eyes felt so heavy.

"Did you get that, Ariadne?" Eris called.

"Got it!" Her voice crackled on the comms.

"Good. Turn the heat back up, please. Slowly."

Within a few moments, Nyx's body pricked with needles as the feeling returned. Like hers, Cato's breathing steadied.

"Rhea's here with the injection," Ariadne said over the comm.

Eris straightened and stared down at Cato. "Tell her to bring it here. Then we'll take Cato to the medical center for deprogramming."

Cato jerked back. "That wasn't in our deal." His voice was still weak, shaky.

Eris grinned. It was the first time Nyx had ever seen her smile when she wasn't playing Zoe, and it was terrifying.

"Oh, but it was," Eris said lightly, stepping closer to him. "I told you that if you *decide* to leave, we'll wipe your memory and let you go. For me, that means making your choice free of the Oracle's influence." When he looked too stunned to respond, Eris flashed her teeth again. "How about an incentive? You let Rhea and Ariadne deprogram you, and I won't consider dropping you off somewhere that makes the cold we just went through seem like a walk around the palace grounds."

Without waiting for a response, Eris left the interrogation room.

Cato was wide-eyed. "She is completely messed up."

"Yep," Nyx said.

"I don't know whether to be impressed or concerned."

"Both." Nyx took in deep, painful breaths. Her lungs hurt so godsdamn much.

Cato was still staring at the door. "Who the fuck is she?"

Nyx had no idea, but she wanted to find out.

35.

Present day

A few jumps from Macella, Eris tried to put a call to Nova headquarters. Ariadne watched as it beeped once and dropped. Eris tried again. And again.

Nothing.

"You've got to be kidding me," Clo said. "Everything is already marshed enough; what's one more issue to add to the list?"

"Focus on flying," Eris snapped. "It's probably just a sandstorm."

Ariadne trotted over. "Let me try. I might be able to boost the signal. Do you have coordinates?"

After working with Kyla in secret for all those years, Ariadne knew Nova's quadrant in the Iona Galaxy, but not the exact location. Her original plan after commandeering *Zelus* had been risky: set the navigation course and, once they were far enough from the heart of the Empire, hope Kyla would take a call from a Tholosian ship. Any contact and exchange of information back at the Temple would have been too dangerous. Ariadne hadn't wanted to chance the Oracle finding the resistance.

Eris reached past Ariadne and keyed in some numbers. "There."

Ariadne gave a low whistle. "Wow, that's really far." Nowhere near Ismara. On the outer reaches of the Iona Galaxy, just barely in the habitable zone of a G-type main-sequence star.

"No kidding." Eris gave a small smile. "It had to be as awful as Avern; otherwise, the Empire would be tracking it. I doubt they're aware anything that far out in Iona is livable."

"It barely is," Clo called out from the pilot's chair. "The dust storms are miserable and you don't know what hot is until you've been in that desert."

Ariadne frowned, ignoring Clo. Eris was right, the signal was bouncing off something. *Really bad dust storm* was an understatement. She tried again.

"I hope you're encrypting that," Clo added.

"What do I look like? An amateur?" Ariadne waved a dismissive hand and keyed in some code, her fingers moving rapidly across the keys. "Got it! Someone should be picking up any—"

"Yes?" Commander Sher answered, sounding distracted. His face appeared on the screen. He looked dusty and tired, his jumpsuit needed a good wash and press, but his eyes were still bright and sharp.

"*Finally*," Eris breathed, nudging Ariadne aside. "I've been trying to get through for ages. You having a dust storm?"

"Good guess," Sher said dryly. "Where's Alesca?"

Clo came over to wave at him on the screen.

"Look at you!" Sher grinned at her. "You haven't killed Eris and you're still alive. Well done."

"I deserve a fluming medal," Clo said. "Is Kyla there?"

"Yeah. She's dealing with damage to the eastern sector of headquarters. We're getting battered in this storm."

"Everyone all right?"

"Nothing we can't handle." Sher flicked a glance at Eris. "Report?"

Eris passed over the intel Ariadne had gathered from hacking the Oracle. *See?* Ariadne wanted to tell the commander. *You need me. You need me. I'm useful.*

"Ichor is obviously a weapon component, like we suspected," Eris said. "If Damocles used it in a blaster, it would go clear through Evoli armor. The records at Macella indicated the ichor was originally stored on Ismara, so we're following the trail to see if the outpost there has any logs that can give us an idea of what Damocles is up to."

On the other end, Ariadne heard a loud bang. Sher glanced to his left with a scowl. "Ismara's an interesting choice," he said, distractedly.

"Why?" Clo asked.

"There's nothing there." Sher returned his attention back to the screen. "The Tholosians mined everything they could, and the resources dried up years ago. It's a ghost planet by all accounts."

"Then no one would think to look there," Eris pointed out.

"Fair point." The banging continued, and Sher ran a hand through his hair. "Ping me when you get there. The Tholosian-Evoli truce talks are in three weeks, and if Damocles really is planning a coup, we need to know his plans. I'll fill Kyla in." They said their goodbyes and the signal cut out.

Eris sighed, rubbing tired eyes.

"He seems nice," Ariadne said.

Eris ignored that. "Onwards to Ismara, I guess," she said. "Clo, make sure you scan the planet for military craft before we hit the atmosphere. If there's extra security guarding the ichor, we'll need to be careful about touching down. Ariadne, you're in charge of the pilot. Wake him up and get him deprogrammed."

Ariadne wilted.

———

"I don't want to do this," Ariadne said as she watched Cato through the screen of the medical center. He was still unconscious from the anaesthesia Rhea had given him earlier. "Not after what we went through with Nyx."

I don't want it to be like Nyx, she thought, staring at his prone form. *Please don't let it be like Nyx.*

She'd hurt Nyx—so many, many times. All to get that tangled web of programming from her brain. Ariadne had hated every moment of it. Hated making decisions when all she wanted to do was soothe the other woman's pain.

"I wish you didn't have to, love," Rhea said, shoulder brushing hers. Despite her anxiety and nerves, Rhea's touch calmed Ariadne.

"I don't like hurting people."

"It's to save Cato," Rhea reminded her gently. "Like you saved Nyx."

Even Rhea's touch couldn't stop Ariadne from stiffening. "And if it kills him?" Rhea fell silent, and Ariadne let out a frustrated breath. "I don't know if he can even be deprogrammed. You remember how it was with Nyx. She'd already pushed the Oracle's influence to the surface, and the process still almost killed her." Ariadne shook her head. "He's not going to be easy."

"Could you forgive yourself if we didn't try?" Rhea asked Ariadne, voice low.

"No." *Never.*

"Then you know what we have to do."

Ariadne shut her eyes briefly, steeling herself. "Okay. Let's get this over with." She patted Rhea's lower back, where she'd stored Nyx's spare Mors since finding the pilot. "But leave that, please. I don't want him to view us as more of a threat than he already does."

"You can do this," Rhea said, setting the Mors on the counter. "And I'm here. I'll help."

Ariadne sighed, and they opened the door to the med center. She checked the monitor; Cato's vitals were all normal, his neuroimaging showing the routine patterns of dreaming. "Make sure his restraints are secure," Ariadne said. "I'm going to wake him up and prepare him for what's about to happen."

"He won't like it," Rhea said gently. "Not with Oracle in his head."

"I have to try."

They began the slow process of waking Cato up. Rhea gave him a reversal agent to counteract the effects of the anaesthesia, as well as another blocker to keep his adrenaline in check.

Cato muttered as he came out. Medical terms, snapped instructions for surgery. He requested a Mors blade, something that could cleanly cut through bone. Directions on holding the gauze in place to stanch bleeding. All of his statements were detailed enough that both Ariadne and Rhea looked at each other, baffled. Tholosian soldiers might receive rudimentary training in first aid, but usually they were bred for one main task. Fighting or flying, and usually dying.

He was a pilot, not a medic. Wasn't he?

Cato's face grimaced with pain, his hands pulling against the restraints as he muttered "stop, stop, stop" under his breath.

"Cato?" Ariadne whispered.

His eyes slowly opened, then shut hard at the light overhead. It took a few moments for him to gain his bearings, take in his restraints. Gods, he recovered fast. Ariadne had heard the Rigel cohort was an impressive feat of engineering. His gaze was sharp, no longer dulled from the anaesthesia.

"Ugh," Cato muttered. "What did you do to me?"

Ariadne tried to keep her face pleasant, but she was still getting used to expressions others saw regularly, and she thought she might be holding her eyes open too wide and not blinking enough. "Gave you a sedative while your Mors burn healed and your infection cleared," she said brightly. "You spoke in your sleep. A bunch of medical stuff. I thought you were a pilot."

His expression flickered. "Doesn't matter," he said. "How long have I been out?"

"A day and a bit. We're pretty far from Macella." *Thank the gods.* Ariadne's stomach was still unsettled from jumping, but Clo was coasting the ship and letting the engine rest before the next leg of their long journey to Ismara.

"Don't suppose you'll drop me off at the nearest outpost." At Ariadne's headshake, Cato made a face and tested his restraints again. "Look, your fucked up friend mentioned giving me a choice back there in the interrogation room. I *choose* to leave this ship, go to the nearest outpost, and—" He let out a breath and muttered, "and get raging drunk."

"But you don't choose," Ariadne reminded him. "Not really. You don't realize how deep the Oracle is in your brain." At his doubtful look, Ariadne leaned back and crossed her arms. "All right. You came in from debriefing after your last mission and before you were asked to fly to Myndalia, right?"

Cato looked a little wary. "Yeah, but it was routine."

"You slept in the palace overnight?"

"Yes." His voice was tighter.

"Plugged into your sleep cycling like usual?"

Silence.

Ariadne lifted her shoulders, then dropped the intonations. "The Oracle's influence is so subtle that you didn't even notice One's voice is my own." Even. Genial. Inhuman. "For the glory of Tholos. I give my life for Thee. I give my body for Thee. In the name of the God of Death, I kill for Thee. In Thy name."

His mouth fell open. Beside him, Rhea shifted uncomfortably—she didn't like when Ariadne used that monotone. None of them did. Ariadne had spent years being the Oracle's voice. Spent years hearing it give her orders. Her voice was not her own—not since she'd made the mistake of giving it to One.

"You're a convincing mimic," Cato said, clenching his jaw. "I see why the Novantae could use you."

"Not a mimic."

He made some noise, almost like a laugh. "Fine. Let's say I believe you. Why would a child be the Oracle's voice?"

"Flat intonation," Ariadne said, still using the voice. "One trained me in it. Doesn't sound little. Doesn't sound like a child. And if you call me either again, I'm going to electrocute your brain and leave you here in a vegetative state." She kept her Oracle voice to make the words all the more jarring.

She could tell it unsettled him. His shoulders were tense, his body straining. If it weren't for that blocker in his system, the Oracle would have completely overtaken him by now.

"No offense, you seem like a nice enough ch"—at her glare, he amended—"girl. But I don't trust you. How do I know *you're* not going to mess with my mind? Put some rebel bullshit up there?"

"How about I tell you a story?" she said, still in the Oracle's voice to unnerve him, as she leaned forward and gently placed electrodes on his forehead. "The co-commander of the Novantae and I got to talking when I fed her information. She told me she had known she was a woman since she was very young, but the Oracle kept trying to suppress those thoughts. One had assigned her male before birth, and programmed her to be hyper-masculine. The AI considers One's decisions to be infallible."

"The Oracle *is* infallible," Cato said flatly.

Ariadne leaned forward, dropping the Oracle's intonation. "No. Don't you see? The Oracle forces people into neat little boxes because One only understands order. But humans are messy. We are not binary; we don't exist in ones and zeroes. This or that. My friend was strong enough to keep pushing back—to recognize the Oracle was trying to change her very identity—but most don't. She became who she always knew she was after casting off the Oracle's chains."

He opened his mouth. Closed it. Shook his head sharply. "No. I already know who I am."

The machine beeped. Rhea frowned at a small spike in his vitals.

Ariadne tried a more soothing voice. "One will try to blunt your curiosity, but I'm guessing there's still something there that wants to be sure that's the case without the Oracle's programming. You're not a machine, Cato."

"No," he repeated, straining against his bonds. The machine behind him beeped once more. His pulse was spiking again.

Not good.

Rhea rested a hand on Cato's forearm as she searched the drawer behind her for the injection in case they needed to calm him again.

"It's all right," Ariadne said. "Your mind will be your own, Cato." She'd slipped back into the Oracle's tones, hoping it would calm him. "You'll be able to choose what life you want to lead."

He shook his head again. "Stop."

"Cato." Ariadne kept her voice low as his heart began to speed up. The machine's beeping was a jarring echo in the room. "Cato, keep calm."

He shook his head wildly, the electrodes stark against his reddening skin. "Stop it." He was breathing hard. "Stop it stop it *stop it.*"

Rhea inched closer, the injection in hand. "It's okay." She reached out to slide the needle into his arm. "I'm just going to—"

He jerked away, the chair shifting a few inches. His eyes bulged, veins appeared at his temple. "I'm not going to turn against my people," he snarled.

Before Ariadne could blink, Cato broke through his bonds, pulling the wires from his head. His hands were around her throat, squeezing,

squeezing. The Oracle was strong, even cut off from the larger server and the implant. Ariadne was no match for his berserker strength.

He slammed her into the floor.

"The Gods favor the strong," he said, tightening his fingers. Stars burst in Ariadne's vision as she struggled to breathe. "The Gods favor the strong. I am of Tholos, Tholos is me. We are Tholos. Letum, Bel, Rem, Salutem, Phobos, Algea, and Soter. Letum, God of Death, I offer myself to Thee. I willingly go to the Avern. For glory. For—"

Rhea leaped onto Cato's back to shove the needle into his arm, but he threw her off. The injection skidded across the floor and disappeared under the heavy cabinet. "Gods*damn it!*"

<Rhea . . . help . . . >

<Hold on, love.>

Cato was raving, lost to his programming. "Letum, Bel, Rem, Salutem, Phobos, Algea, and Soter. Letum, God of Death, I offer myself—"

Rhea clapped both of her hands over his cheeks and forced his head up. "*Cato!*" Her voice seemed to echo, as if from afar. "*Sleep!*"

The massive man dropped like a stone. His hands loosened around Ariadne's neck, but his bulk was on her slight frame. "Still . . . can't . . . breathe," Ariadne rasped.

Rhea started pulling Cato off of her, and the door opened. Nyx and Eris rushed in. "What the flames?" Eris demanded.

"Help me," Rhea urged.

Nyx and Eris grasped Cato under his arms, and all three of them managed to roll him off the smaller girl. Ariadne crawled to freedom and air, sucking deep breaths into her lungs. What had happened? Had Rhea . . .

Rhea caught her eye, gave an infinitesimal shake of her head. A plea.

Nyx snatched Ariadne by her arms. "Are you okay?" She stared at Ariadne's neck where the red welts were starting to form from Cato's grip. By tomorrow, they'd be bruises. "I'm going to kill that bastard."

"No," Ariadne managed. Her voice was hoarse. "He couldn't help himself. I doubt he'll even remember it."

"I don't give a *damn*—if we can't even keep him bound—"

"Ari's right, Nyx," Rhea said. "We can keep him sedated. Even the thought of him having a choice triggered some programming. I didn't realize it was embedded that deeply in some soldiers."

Eris grunted in affirmation. "When we do deprogramming at Nova, a lot of them don't survive the procedure."

Rhea shut her eyes and nodded. "Even Nyx's was . . . difficult."

"Difficult," Nyx said. "Nice word for it. Felt like being dragged through the fucking fires of Avern." She gestured to Cato's prone form. "Even just trying to cut the Oracle's programming makes you feel like someone is stabbing you through the skull. If he makes it, I'll be shocked."

"Nyx," Rhea chastised.

"What? Just being honest."

Soldier cohorts were programmed more intimately to one another. Taking away that connection would be difficult for anyone, but Ariadne suspected that Cato's coding was going to be different from what she'd seen before. He was from the Rigel cohort; like Nyx, they had been present at the Battle of the Garnet. The Oracle had been making upgrades to some in that group—especially ones who had shown signs of trauma from the battle.

He had medical training. His sleep mutterings had shown that clear enough. What had he done to get demoted to a cargo pilot?

Nyx still gripped Ariadne's arms, her fingers trembling. "Nyx," Ariadne whispered. "I'm okay."

Nyx jerked away. "Right. Good."

Ariadne opened her mouth but Eris spoke first. "How'd you knock him out, Rhea?" she asked. "I saw on the screens that the injection went under the cabinet."

A pause. "I think he must have short-circuited or something," Rhea said. She flickered her gaze briefly to Ariadne's. "He just . . . dropped."

Ariadne gave a nod despite her confusion. But Rhea wanted her to stay quiet, so she would. Whatever secret Rhea kept was her own to tell. Or hers to keep.

They injected Cato with another hormone blocker and gave him an additional sedative. "Get comfortable," Ariadne told the others as she hooked Cato up to the monitoring machine once more. "I'm going to map out a neuroimage of his programming. It'll take a while."

She started running diagnostics, squinting at her tablet. The room around her disappeared. She focused only on the code. The puzzle to be solved. She had no idea if anyone came in and out of the room, if the others spoke to her at all. She descended so completely into the abstract. It was easier than thinking about how she could so easily fry this man's brain.

She guessed Cato was around thirty. As a Rigel, he'd have been sent into the field at sixteen. Years of death in the far reaches of the galaxy, and he'd found a way to come back to the Three Sisters. That said to her that he didn't love the killing. That he wanted something more. Or, as she suspected, something had gone wrong.

Eventually, Ariadne looked up. Her eyes burned, her head throbbed from solving different equations and writing code in her head.

The others came to attention at Ariadne's exaggerated stretching. Cato was still unconscious, the wires emerging from his head like the coiled branches of a karya tree.

"Everything okay?" Rhea asked.

Ariadne nodded. "I just gave him a reversal agent. He'll be waking up in a few moments," she said, gently binding Cato's limbs once more. She'd left him untied during deprogramming, but Nyx and Eris held their weapons at the ready. Rhea kept one finger on the pilot's skin.

No injection. It had skidded somewhere.

Rhea had touched him while he was strangling Ariadne.

And Cato had dropped.

Ariadne studied Rhea. Her mind was still in problem-solving mode, her memory sharpening. Rumors she'd found floating through the palace tore at the edges of her awareness. She'd read reports of DNA mapping to an unnamed person in the palace. Diagnostics. The Oracle took the lead on that project. Ariadne had planned to find out who it was before she left the palace. She'd wanted to tell Kyla . . .

That subject could have knocked a soldier out cold with one touch.

Is that your secret? Ariadne wanted to ask. *Were you some experiment, made to be a weapon like Nyx?*

Rhea caught her glance and swallowed. As if Rhea had read her mind—*could she?*—she mouthed, *Later. Promise.*

Ariadne nodded, despite her unease. She was used to keeping secrets.

Cato groaned, his eyes opening. "You put me under again?" he asked, trying to sit up but stopped by the bonds.

"You tried to kill me," Ariadne said, turning on the bright charm. "I was tempted to electrocute you like I promised, but I showed great restraint."

"I appreciate that," Cato said, shaking off his grogginess. It seemed to take him a little longer this time to come to awareness.

When he did, his gaze fell to the marks on her neck. Ariadne heard his short intake of breath.

"Your stress response activated the Oracle," Ariadne explained. "I gave you a blocker and we removed your implant before we took off, but I figured we should talk before I start properly deprogramming." She tapped her tablet. "I've got your entire neuroprogramming mapped out right here. It's deep, but I think I can deactivate it."

He shook his head, looking sick. "No. It's my duty to house One, to move in tandem with my fellow soldiers."

Nyx rolled her eyes. "You're being used, you damn fool. We all were."

"Nyx is right," Eris said, her voice quiet. Cato's head swiveled to her, noticing her for the first time. "The Oracle's programming makes you believe that free will is a detriment."

"I know my history," Cato said. "Before the Oracle, the Archon was in constant danger of a coup, and any one of them would have shattered the Empire. The Oracle gives us all a collective purpose. I don't *want* free will."

Eris scoffed. "Oh, *please*. Yesterday in that interrogation room, you could have let the cold kill you before giving me those codes." Her voice was low as she quoted the Oracle's programming: *"Death before dishonor.* You had one small window of choice, and you didn't choose the Empire."

Cato had gone paler. Nyx, too, was stiff and unblinking. Months before, when Ariadne and Rhea had unpicked the last of her programming, there had been a close call. Nyx had almost been lost. Ariadne wondered if Nyx had fully forgiven the two of them for pulling her back from the brink.

"If you still want to be loyal to the Empire after Ariadne's procedure," Eris was saying, "that will be on you. But at least it'll be your choice."

Cato gazed at them all, helplessly. "Even if I wanted to, it's not possible."

Ariadne smiled. "Our escape on *Zelus* was impossible. We're all well acquainted with *impossible* by now."

A misstep. Anger flashed over Cato's face. "Yeah. You escaped by killing my crew. I remember."

Ariadne's smile faded. "We didn't *want* to."

Nyx's mouth twisted, as if to say, *Speak for yourself.* Mercifully, Cato didn't see.

"Regret doesn't bring them back." His hands bunched to fists. Nyx's hand moved back to her Mors.

Ariadne had cried for the crew every day since it happened. The soldier with red hair and a constellation of freckles who guarded their door. The soldier in charge of the storage hull, his sandy hair always sticking up at the back. The Legate hadn't been cruel, just uptight. Everyone on *Zelus* had been distant and cold, but who could those soldiers have been without the Oracle's programming? Perhaps they would have chosen not to be soldiers at all.

Now they'd never know.

"We would have avoided it if we could have. Gathered them in a pod and sent them out into the stars," Ariadne insisted. "But we couldn't. The Oracle's programming wouldn't let them surrender. If we wanted to escape, we couldn't leave a trail." She took a hitching breath. "There is no excuse. Murder is inexcusable. But desperate people will do anything for freedom."

"I'm not desperate," Cato snapped.

"You sure about that? You're still tempted," Rhea said. "Aren't you?"

Cato was quiet. He stared down at his bound hands with some inscrutable expression. Hands that, just hours ago, had nearly ended Ariadne's life without his awareness or choice. Ariadne wondered at his thoughts. Maybe he was trying to remember the moment those fingers had closed around her throat, when his actions had been decided not by his own judgment, but by those of a program coded into his brain since before infancy. Or maybe he was wondering what else had that program decided without his knowledge. What other memories were hidden from him.

Many, Ariadne wanted to tell him. She'd helped the Oracle program soldiers, after all. One suppressed inconvenient memories all the time.

Whatever path his thoughts had taken must have made up his mind. Cato nodded, once. "Yes. I'm tempted. Gods help me, but yes." He leaned back and closed his eyes.

He didn't move as Ariadne gave him another injection of sedative, and Rhea also gave him one last touch. His eyes fluttered shut.

Ariadne met Rhea's eyes again: *Later.*

"You go," Ariadne said to the others. "Let me do my work."

Rhea nodded. She was the first to leave, then Eris.

Nyx made no move. "I'm staying. I want to see what it's like."

"It won't be pretty," Ariadne warned. She stroked Cato's cheek. "Poor guy is about to go through that same nightmare you did."

"I know. That's why I want to stay." Nyx got comfortable in her chair, her hard grip on the armrest betraying her unease. Ariadne wished she was brave enough to give Nyx a hug.

Ariadne started running the code.

36.

CLO

Present day

Clo commanded the ship to jump again.

She'd let *Zelus* rest after the grueling pace she used to exit the Three Sisters quadrant, but anxiety still burned within her. It didn't matter how much distance she put between *Zelus* and the heart of the Empire, nowhere in the Iona Galaxy seemed far enough. Every time she considered pausing, she thought about that Evoli man back on Macella. She thought about Briggs. She thought about the weapon they'd given to Damocles and all the damage he could do if Ariadne's failsafe didn't work.

The stars had always felt safe to her. Space was vast; there were so many places Clo could hide.

Right then, the expanse of the galaxy felt like the sticky web of the Empire — and she was caught inside it.

The door opened behind Clo. "Go away," she called, focusing on plotting routes to Ismara. She turned with a scowl that disappeared when she saw who it was.

"All right," Rhea said, retreating a step. "I just wanted to ask how much longer we'd be jumping. Ariadne threw up a few times and I'm starting to get nauseated too."

Clo took her fingers from the controls. She'd forgotten that Ariadne and Rhea still weren't used to the hyperjumps of space travel. Clo was fine as long as they were in the abyss. It was only as she careened toward a surface, the hull of the bullet craft lighting up like a shooting star, that her stomach betrayed her. "That was the last one. Sorry."

Rhea paused, illuminated by the light streaming through the hallway. Her hair was braided around her head like a crown. She'd taken to swapping her dresses for flowing blouses, spare military trousers, and boots stolen from the dead of *Asteria*.

"I can leave you alone if you want," Rhea said, still hesitating at the door.

"No," Clo said. "Please stay."

They hadn't had time to speak alone since the night before they went to the Three Sisters. Clo had been too much of a dipwell to even say goodbye to Rhea before she crawled through the depths of the palace.

Their eyes met. Clo flushed and looked away.

"What's the pilot's prognosis?" Clo asked, clearing her throat and staring back out at the stars.

Rhea approached the command chair and leaned against the edge of the console. "Too early to say, but it looks like his programming goes deep. The Oracle's been upgrading."

"Always bound to be high on One's to-do list, right?" Clo asked, fiddling with the controls. "You need your soldiers loyal, especially for all those war crimes."

Rhea smelled like something floral and spiced, too exotic for Clo to recognize. In contrast, Clo was sure she smelled like engine grease, as usual. Awkwardness bloomed within her, pink as a blush.

Clo stretched back out along the pilot's chair, and this time, Rhea was the one who looked away shyly. Clo almost smiled.

Rhea cleared her throat. "You should eat something. You've been up here for hours."

"I can't stand the thought of more sawdust food."

Rhea sighed. "Me neither. So much red cheese flatbread that tastes nothing like cheese. All I want is a fresh piece of fruit. Especially a sweet, juicy papaya."

Clo's eyes lit up. "Ohh, yes. I ate a papaya for breakfast every time I could pinch one from the stalls."

Rhea's tilted her head. "I didn't think they had papayas in Kersh."

"Not in the Snarl," Clo said, clearing her throat. "The stalls were near the high-rises. Every morning, the servants would take the elevator down and gather meals for their masters. Sometimes, I was able to get past the guards." She shrugged. "Sometimes not."

Clo thought she heard Rhea suck in a breath. "Was it worth it? Just for fruit?"

"It was more to pretend, just for a moment, that I lived in those high-rises above the clouds. That was worth the beatings."

"I never thought about where those papayas came from. Who grew them, how they moved from tree to the breakfast table," Rhea said. She shifted to the copilot's seat, leaving a trail of sweet perfume. She was close enough to touch. "I rarely went hungry. I never had to steal. I was pampered."

"You were trapped too," Clo said gently. "We just had different cages, that's all." At least Clo had been able to leave her building, to see the sky. She'd found some fractured pieces of freedom down in the depths of the Snarl.

"I'm sorry, anyway."

"*Sorry*'s such a bullshit word, isn't it?" Clo adjusted the controls. "Says so much and bog-all at the same time. But aye, I'm sorry too." She looked over at Rhea. "Is there anything good you miss?"

Rhea considered that for a moment, a fingertip tracing her collarbone. "It's silly, but I miss lilies the most."

"Lilies?"

"Yes. I'd have fresh ones from the greenhouse delivered to my room every morning. The old ones gone before they even had a chance to wilt. A different color every day, but that same, sweet scent. No man ever sent me those. I asked the servants and they brought them. They weren't really mine, though—they belonged to Tholos. To Damocles. But I pretended they were." She stopped, as if embarrassed.

"Is that your perfume?" Clo asked. "Lilies?"

Rhea smiled. "Yes, but it's a pale, pale echo of the scent of fresh ones. What do you miss?"

Clo clicked her tongue against the back of her teeth. "There was this one machinery stall in the market closest to my mam's in the Snarl. It was different from the others. Woman who ran it kept everything so clean, the metal gleamed. Never stole from that stall. Saved my shale and bought what I needed, taking my time, picking up the little pieces, setting them down in their right place, just so. But it's not the owner I miss. It's those neat, perfect rows of clean metal, just begging to be picked up and made useful." Clo gave a laugh, a little forced. "Guess that's some obvious symbolism right there. That's what I do. Fix broken shit, ignore all the broken bits of my own life I left behind."

"Why did you leave Myndalia?" Rhea asked.

Clo shrugged. "Nae by choice, really. My mam—" Her throat closed. Clo had always thought the Snarled lung would get her mam in the end, but it was—

—soldiers. Mam shoving her in the closet, ignoring Clo's whispered protests. Harsh questions from soldiers, nasal accents so clipped compared to the rolling vowels of the Snarl. Her mother: placating. Friendly. Clo hunkered down in the dark. She wasn't a child, she wasnae going to hide—

The sizzle of Mors blasts. Soldiers rooting through their things, rummaging, grunting like animals. Mam down, chest heaving. Clo bursting from the closet. Holding hands over the wound in Mam's stomach. Useless. Useless hiding—

Open eyes. Glassy. Gone.

A night of vigil, the unmoving hand in Clo's growing colder.

—Clo closed her eyes, not wanting to remember, to feel.

Rhea reached out to touch her, but Clo inched back, arms wrapped tight around herself.

The next morning. Her mother wrapped up in an old blanket. Clo cradling mam like she was the child. Later, she'd woven through the slum on unsteady feet and tripped through the damp soil. Left the towering, cramped labyrinth behind for the open expanse of swamp. She'd found a twisted Nyssa tree, its long branches trailing in the water.

Deep enough.

Quiet enough.

She'd tied stones to the ropes around the body. Kissed the top of mam's head and let her sink, sink, down into the bog, to rest with the bones of others buried the same way.

Clo had said no words. There were none left.

A shaking breath brought her back. Rhea's hand lay on the cloth of Clo's sleeve.

"I'm sorry," Rhea whispered.

"Me too. After—after what happened—" Clo sniffed, wiping her nose with the back of her hand. "We'd helped Sher out of a tough spot a few months before. When he heard, he came back with a man named Briggs. They swore up and down they'd take care of me, that the resistance could use a mechanic like me." Clo gave a laugh. "I thought they were bogging mad. First, that they thought a scrap like me could be useful, but I told them the Novantae would no' barrage the Empire. Like trying tae move a boulder with a few drops of rain."

"Feels that way. What'd he say?"

"Some poetic shite about how drops of water could move mountains. Or it only takes one spark to catch a flame. Nonsense. Just giving a kid some comfort."

Rhea gave a half-smile. "He gave you wise words. It takes ages for water to move mountains, or for fire to catch on damp wood. It takes just as long to grieve someone we love." She rested her head in her hands. "What was it like?" Rhea asked. "Having a mother?"

Clo stiffened.

"You don't have to answer—" Rhea started.

"It's okay." She tried to think of an answer, letting the Snarl keep coloring her voice. "Ye took care of yer own, because no one else was gonnae. My mam held me at night. She sang me tae sleep. If scran grew too scarce, she gave me her own and told me she wasnae hungry, even though I knew she was. It's been years, but sometimes I'm so . . ." She tightened her jaw, stared at the controls.

"Angry?"

"Yes."

Their conversation lapsed into silence. Clo snuck a covert glance at Rhea.

Rhea met her eyes, as if she knew exactly what she was thinking. Clo coughed, put the ship on autopilot, and moved over to those wide, beautiful windows. She'd never been able to fly a ship big enough she could walk around the bridge with ease.

"You haven't forgotten what you told me before the mission on Macella, have you?" Rhea asked.

"If I didn't die, I'd show you the galaxy." Clo's grin was slow. "Yeah, I remember."

"Lo and behold, you made it."

"I did almost get hit by an elevator and I jumped off a damned building, but aye, still in one piece. More or less." She stood and beckoned with her fingers. "Come with me."

"Where?"

"Back to the observation deck. I want to keep my promise."

With a smile, Rhea followed Clo down the bridge and through the halls to the observation deck. Telling Rhea to wait, Clo shoved the chairs to the back and gestured for the other woman to stand in the middle of the room. At the control panel, she turned off the lights, flipped one last switch, and joined Rhea.

Rhea opened her mouth to speak. "Wh—"

"Shh." Clo tapped a finger to her lips. "Just watch."

A soft whirring echoed through the quiet room as the floor beneath them slowly, slowly faded away to become translucent glass. Clo had discovered many people didn't enjoy this feature to the spherical observation deck; another mechanic at Nova had said it gave him vertigo.

But Clo loved it. Above and below them, Clo and Rhea were surrounded by millions of bright stars and their solar systems as if they were dashed out in space, walking through the galaxy.

"My gods," Rhea breathed, taking a few steps forward. "I feel like I'm—like I'm—"

"Out among the stars," Clo finished.

Rhea craned her head back, twirling. "I used to look up at the sky behind the walls of the Pleasure Garden, and wish for this. I wanted it so much. More than anything." She laughed, and Clo warmed. She loved Rhea's laugh. "You've been to some of these planets, right? Which was your favorite?"

Clo approached Rhea, pointing to a light in the distance. "Do you see that light there, the one that looks bluer than the others? It's not a star, but a planet called Aegir. It's covered in oceans and sandy beaches, with the clearest water I've ever seen, that glitters like cut gemstones. My friend Briggs"—she pressed her lips together for a moment—"it was his favorite place in the galaxy, too. He always said he'd take me there one day. That never happened, so I asked Kyla to send me on assignment, and she did."

"It sounds wonderful," Rhea said with a sigh.

"Have you ever seen an ocean?" Clo asked. Rhea shook her head. "No? Well, then I'll show you that, too."

"Show me everything." Rhea pressed closer, her fingertips brushing against Clo's. "I want to see it all."

Clo bit her lip to keep from grinning like a fool. "I already promised you the whole Iona Galaxy, so I may have to upgrade that to *universe*. All the galaxies we know—maybe even those we don't."

Rhea's gaze dropped to Clo's mouth. They were so quiet, standing there surrounded by stars. Clo felt the brush of Rhea's fingertips against her palm again and drew in a breath. She wanted . . . she wanted Rhea.

Slow, Clo chastised herself. *She deserves slow.*

"Clo?"

"Yeah?"

"Do you . . . do you want to kiss me?" Rhea whispered.

Clo swallowed hard and let out a short laugh. "Am I that obvious?"

Rhea's smile was a sunrise. "I can guess."

"Can you? What am I feeling right now?"

"Good question." Rhea's fingertips skimmed the edges of her sleeves, and she shifted closer, her lips almost touching Clo's, but not quite. "Desire," she said. "Longing. Temptation. But you want to be careful. Because of what I went through. Who I was. Before."

"Yes." *No expectations.*

"Oh, Clo." Rhea pressed her hand to Clo's. "This is me giving you permission."

Clo's hands cupped Rhea's face. Her skin was even smoother than she'd imagined, or remembered. Clo brushed her lips against Rhea's cheek, so softly it barely touched. "Okay?" she breathed.

"Yes." That word seemed to catch in Rhea's throat.

Another soft kiss at the soft point where her throat met the square of her jaw, lingering slightly longer. "Okay?" This time Clo's voice trembled. Gods, she wanted. She *wanted*. More than anything.

"Clo, I swear to the gods, if you don't just *kiss me already*—"

Then Clo was kissing Rhea hard, and Rhea was kissing back. Her lips were petal-soft and parted so easily. Clo's tongue slipped into her mouth—hesitant, then confident. They touched, their hands exploring each other. A soft gasp lodged in Rhea's throat, then a sound of assent, a murmured *yes, yes, yes* that made Clo kiss her harder. She pressed Rhea's body against the clear window, and it felt as if they were alone on that spaceship. Alone in the whole universe.

The stars streamed by as they moved through the galaxy, and Clo's new favorite scent was lilies.

37.

Three years ago

"It's colder than a snowman's balls today," Briggs grunted, rubbing his hands together. "Hand me my gloves, Clo Alesca."

Briggs leaned forward, peering at the innards of the engine of Sher's ship. He was still a mountain of a man, massive and burly, with jet black hair and equally dark eyes. But Briggs was all hard exterior and soft interior.

Sher rolled his eyes. His ship had come in last night. Sher needed it detailed from a close clip with a Tholosian warcraft. "Not that cold," he said.

"Don't pretend with me, boy. You might be a commander, but I've been on this fucking planet since you earned the title," Briggs said.

Laughing, Clo handed Briggs his gloves. He leaned his hip against the craft, put them on. "Sher, you'll have to tell Kyla *Asteria* ain't space-worthy for another few days. I'm tired and my own balls are gonna freeze off if I try to push this any faster. You'll have to bunk with me and Clo."

Clo shivered in her massive parka. She'd been sent to Briggs's hangar in Jurran for pissing Kyla off, basically. So, she'd had a little trouble adjusting to the chain of command. So, one of her fellow recruits had bogged her off. So, she'd left him stranded for two days in the desert. He had water! It wasn't *her* fault he was a complete marsh-for-brains.

She figured Kyla'd give her a scolding, tell her to apologize and stop calling people by Snarl insults.

But no. Kyla sent Clo to this frozen silthole to learn "character" as she helped Briggs smuggle ships to the resistance. If she didn't freeze first.

The weather on most of Jurran was as cold as Novantae was scorching: it could kill people within minutes. The hangar was warm enough to keep them alive but not comfortable. At night, Clo curled up with her knees to her chest, wearing all her winter clothes.

"So *my* balls can freeze off?" Sher asked, bringing her back.

"Why not your fingers?" Clo asked, rolling her eyes. Men were so fluming dramatic. "Or your nose?"

"Can't speak for the commander here, but my face ain't my pride and joy. And my fingers are fine. So's my—"

"Nah, don't finish that sentence," Clo said, making a face. "Gross."

Briggs snorted, taking off the gloves and settled his hands on the cold engine again. Clo winced. As frigid as it was, they couldn't wear gloves while working with the delicate parts of the Tholosian engine. "Because I need 'em both. Right, Commander?" He settled the digital panel back into place for the navigation system.

"I'd rather all my body parts remain attached," Sher said, deadpan.

Clo snorted.

"One day, I'll have a lady who'd definitely mind." Briggs hunched over a part of the engine.

"Huh. Would have to be a desperate berm of a lass," Clo said.

Briggs threw a glove at Clo. "I got more charm than the commander here. You don't even know."

"Aye, and I'm Princess Discordia, preening about in my robe during the coronation." She straightened and gave a mocking royal wave.

Briggs gave a whistle. "She's feeling feisty today. Must be all that angst and teen hormones."

Clo flashed him the two bent fingers of the scythe and he stuck his tongue out at her in reply. A screeching beep from the command stopped them short. Sher went still, and a flash of fear crossed Briggs's features.

"Commander, get in my office and stay hidden," Briggs said, all traces of humor gone from his voice. "Clo, I need a cover for the ship."

Sher moved quickly but Clo remained frozen.

"Now, Alesca!"

She sprinted to the utility closet, grabbing a tarp. The thing was heavy as she dragged it to the ship. Briggs was at the deck, working the controls, his skin pale beneath the dark stubble. Covering their tracks. The tarp covered the ship, the surface changing to meld with the hangar behind. As long as someone didn't touch it, they'd never know it was there.

Another beep. Whoever was arriving had been cleared for landing. "Fuck," Briggs muttered.

"Who is it?" Clo asked. "What's goin' on?"

He jerked his head toward his office. "Get behind the desk with Sher, sweet. It's all right."

Sweet? Briggs was more likely to insult someone than use a pet name. The last time he'd called her *sweet* had been during one of the coldest nights of Clo's stay on Jurran. Her teeth had chattered so loudly that Briggs had given her one of his blankets, still warm from his body. "Here you go, sweet," he'd said before darting back to his bunk. "Don't die on me. I need those hands for the engines."

"Clo," Briggs said, bringing her back. "Go."

Clo didn't want to hide. The last time she'd hidden, she'd regretted it. But she did what he asked. The office was dark, but Clo knew her way around. She settled with Sher behind Briggs's massive desk in his darkened office, peeking over the table so she could just see Briggs through the office window. He fiddled with the controls until the roof overhead opened with a shuddering screech.

"Sher?" Clo breathed. "What is it?"

"Nothing good," he said, gesturing.

Clo looked over and watched as a ship slowed, then hovered over the launch pad to land. It wasn't massive, but what it lacked in size it made up for with capability. It was *Cetus*, an M class Tholosian ship still in the experimental stages. She'd only seen one once before, but she knew the weapons systems were top-of-the-line.

But the only people who would have access to these were high up in the military. Much higher in rank than anyone who ever passed through this frozen silthole to refuel.

"*Fuck*," Clo muttered.

Sher nodded. "Exactly."

The hatch opened. A young man strode down the ramp. She barely noticed the other Tholosian soldiers behind him. Her gaze was riveted on the color of his uniform, the sheer number of gold buttons that lined the tops of his shoulders.

It was Prince Damocles, Brigadier to the military and second in line to the Tholosian throne.

Damocles looked every inch the Heir Apparent. The Royal Spare. From his flawlessly brushed-back blond hair to the pressed lines of his coat, his entire appearance was immaculate. His eyes shone metallic gold.

Four guards flanked him. They were all nearly identical, grown from the same cohort. Their Mors glinted in their hands.

A shiver ran down Clo's spine. Beside her, Sher shifted, his hand on his own Mors. Clo couldn't tell if he touched the weapon out of instinct or if he was readying for a fight. Perhaps both.

Briggs bowed stiffly, and his face flickered with pain from his old back injury. "Brigadier Damocles, sir," he said. It sounded respectful to anyone else, but Clo heard the hint of unrestrained hatred. "Sirius Alcore-G5, at your service."

Sirius was the name Briggs used on official Tholosian records; Clo's own name was listed as Lyra. Both were intended to come from unremarkable genetic stock, large aedifex cohorts that were bred for labor. Nothing that would raise questions when Tholosian military crafts came in and out for service.

Damocles took in the empty hangar. "Where are your attendants?"

"Gave my attendant the day off, Brigadier. May I ask to what we owe this illustrious visit?"

Damocles studied the hangar. Clo ducked down when his eyes swept the door of the dark office. "We chased a resistance spy several days ago. His damaged craft was tracked by the Oracle as far as this galaxy quadrant before it went dark, which can only mean he landed on one of these backwater shitholes." Damocles strolled around, lingering his fingers against some of the ship parts set out on the tables. "I understand that an older Impusa such as the one he'd stolen requires special parts only a hangar like this would have on hand." His gaze flickered to Briggs. "Seen anything like that?"

Clo heard the soft click of Sher nudging the safety off his Mors.

Briggs didn't hesitate. "Can't say I have, Brigadier. The only ships in and outta here the last several days are supply crafts or military ships touching down for repairs and fuel. More movement than usual in the hangars out this way, on account of storm preparation. Keeps us busy."

Damocles tapped the worktable. "And yet so many parts."

Briggs's face remained inscrutable. "Some storms last a few months, Brigadier. A man needs to have a way to pass the time."

"Mm." Damocles's mouth twisted. "Call your attendant back. I want my ship serviced, and it's a two-person job."

Brigg's head tilted forward in resignation, and he pretended to put the call through on his comm. *<Go round the side and come in the main entrance,>* he sent through the Pathos.

<What about Sher?>

<Alesca, there ain't shit around for miles, and he'll die out there in the cold. He's not going anywhere right now.>

"Stay here," Clo breathed to Sher.

At least she didn't have to hide. She snuck out the side entrance and drew in a sharp breath, wincing at how her lungs burned in the cold. An hour out there, even in her parka, and she'd freeze.

Clo shoved the door open. Warm air made the skin of her cheeks burn, and for that she was grateful. She was about to be face-to-face with the Royal Spare, and the color in her face would hide an angry flush. Damocles had likely grown up above her on Myndalia, looking down on the Snarl, an ugly blemish on an otherwise beautiful view. He would have had no pity for those in the slums. He would have felt nothing for them at all.

She made her way across the hangar, tracking snow across the floor.

"Brigadier," Briggs said, "this is my assistant, Lyra Nekkar-Z1. She's responsible for many of your ships running in top shape."

And your enemies' ships, Clo thought with an inward smile.

She bowed, with no idea whether the form was correct or not. Avern, she hated showing this muskeg the back of her neck. "It's an honor, Brigadier."

He ignored her. "I want you both finished by moonrise. In the meantime, show me your logs. I want to see every ship that's come and gone."

Damocles's demeanor never changed, his expression a perfect, emotionless mask. Clo noted the way his eyes took in the boots in the corner, the blankets, the coveralls, and skidded right over the tarp that kept Sher's ship hidden from view.

"Of course," Briggs said smoothly.

He handed a tablet over to Damocles with a short bow. Clo admired how steady Briggs's hand was, his easy confidence shot through with the right amount of deference. Her own heart felt as if it were going to beat out of her chest.

As Damocles scrolled through the logs, his guards watched closely while Briggs and Clo started on the repairs. As they worked with numb fingers, Clo's nerves grew. The logs always looked like rubbish to her, nothing but time stamps. Hundreds of spacecrafts coming in and out, their models, the work required, and whether they were destined to be disposed of or launched into space.

Clo looked over at Briggs, catching the pinch of his frown. He glanced up, smoothing his expression with a small, reassuring smile.

She wasn't fooled.

What had Briggs put into those logs? How had he hid the Novantae coming and going, making off with Tholosian supplies? Clo wanted to curse herself for not asking, for taking such little interest in the details of how their operation worked. All she'd wanted to do was build and repair ships.

And if anything happened today, the consequence for Clo's incuriosity could be execution.

Clo tried to focus on her task. They got the ship fueled and checked over the engine. If it hadn't been piloted by Damocles himself, it would have been a joy to see such a new ship up close. She might have lingered a bit longer on that engine, puzzled over its parts and how it worked. But she couldn't allow herself to be distracted, not with Damocles and those soldiers so close by. She hated being watched.

Briggs patted the side of the hull. "And she's star-ready again."

Damocles looked up from the tablet. "Finished?"

"It wasn't too big a job. We're happy to help, Brigadier," Briggs said.

He seemed to be holding his breath. "Is there anything else you require?"

Seeing him so diffident made Clo uneasy. No dirty jokes, his head bowed.

He was afraid.

"For the ship, no," Damocles said. "You're shockingly thorough for a gene pool created in this disgusting backwater."

"Thank you, Brigadier, I—"

"Pity there's a discrepancy in these logs." Damocles's gaze was so sharp that Clo felt it like a blade to the chest. "You checked every inch of my ship so carefully, and yet made such small, seemingly careless mistakes in your entries."

Briggs went still. She saw his hand inch under his parka for his belt.

Clo thought quickly.

"Oh, no," she said, clicking her tongue. "Is there? That would be my fault. I get numbers mixed up sometimes." She spoke in a perfect Imperial accent and gave her best vacant smile. Why not play stupid? Damocles already thought her to be part of a backwater gene pool. "I'm sorry; I'll do better next time, Brigadier."

Damocles's lip curled in disgust. "I see this one is exactly what I'd expect of low genetic stock."

Briggs gently nudged Clo aside. "She means well, Brigadier, but—"

Damocles raised a silencing hand. "I'm not interested. Sort out your logs and don't let this fucking fool near the records again." He signaled to his guards. "Get ready for lift. I'm tired of this planet."

Clo held a sigh of relief as Damocles strode back to the ship.

Just before he reached the ramp, he paused, eyes glancing over to where Sher's ship lay hidden beneath the tarp. Clo bit her lip to keep from swearing. She'd missed the smallest corner—a curve of a wheel was visible. From their angle, it almost looked like a spare part discarded on the floor.

Almost.

Fool.

"Brigadier Damocles," she said, too brightly, "is there anything—"

"You two put on a good act," he said, striding over to the ship, pulling off the tarp to reveal *Asteria*. The metal nose of the ship gleamed in the harsh overhead light. "Shoot them."

The soldiers pointed their weapons, but Briggs was faster. He had his Mors in hand. One shot, one soldier down. The other trained his weapon on Clo and fired. Briggs's massive body slammed into Clo's to shove her out of the way.

"Briggs!" Clo's cry echoed through the hangar as she felt his body jerk. Warm blood slid across her palms as she pressed her hands to his side.

Morsfire echoed through the hangar as Sher rushed out of Briggs's office. He returned fire, ducking his way over to Clo and Briggs. He took one look at the older man and swore.

From the way Briggs was looking up at them, eyes glazed over in pain, he didn't expect to survive.

Flood that.

Clo reacted without thinking. She grabbed the Mors from Briggs and shot at one of the guards and Prince Damocles. Damocles's face dropped in surprise as he darted out of the way. The Oracle's programming would have prevented her from firing on Tholosian soldiers, and especially the Spare. But she was like Briggs—born, not engineered, the Oracle never in their heads.

Clo and Sher helped Briggs to *Asteria*, the craft shielding them from Mors shots.

"Leave me," Briggs gasped. "Leave me."

"We're not doing that. You had better not die on me, you old son of a marsh cat. Sher, cover me."

Sher opened fire once more, creating just enough of a distraction for her to haul Briggs the rest of the way into the ship. As the guards took cover, Sher scrambled after Clo and hurled himself into the craft.

Clo slammed the button to bring up the ramp and seal off the ship. Blasts sparked off the metal body from the hangar. Any moment, Damocles and that soldier would be in their spacecraft—

"I know this ship better than you," Sher said as Clo took over the captain's chair.

"I've worked on this damn ship from top to bottom," she said, flipping switches to turn the engines on, "and you're a shite pilot. Strap Briggs in."

Sher locked the older man into the copilot's chair. Briggs could barely keep his eyes open. His skin was pale. "Hold on, Briggs," Sher said. "We're getting you out."

"Told you both," Briggs said, sounding hoarse. "*Asteria* ain't ready to fly yet."

"She can fly," Clo snapped. "She might not be able to outrun that monster of a ship he's got, but I'm a better pilot."

Briggs passed out.

Sher sat in the passenger chair behind her. "I hope you know what you're doing, Alesca."

"You and me both."

Clo eased the gears by her side forward. When the spacecraft was up in the air, she slammed the side lever forward and the craft jetted up. This was going to be bad. Even if Damocles managed to get his own aircraft up and running, he would still end up calling—

She let out a foul curse when she saw the military spacecraft coming toward her as she exited Jurran's atmosphere. She couldn't outrun them. *Asteria* was a beaten old military junker that Sher had brought to her and Briggs with serious damage, and they hadn't even finished repairs.

"You don't have any speed-drive capabilities," Sher reminded her.

"I know that," she snarled. "We're just going to have to outsmart them." She flipped the switches for the ship's program mainframe. "Find me the nearest planet within an asteroid field," she told the ship.

"Are you fucking *kidding me*?" Sher leaned forward. "Alesca, you failed this simulation run on Nova."

"I got farther than anyone else, including you!"

Three options came up on the computer. The best one was a tiny dot of a planet, so small she barely noticed it at first. Perfect. She increased her speed toward the asteroid belt, as fast as the ship could go. Behind her she could see the blinking dots of a dozen other ships.

They fired. The ship shuddered, its cobbled pieces groaning with the effort to maintain speed as she dodged projectiles. The oxygen was holding up, but barely. Clo expertly wove through the lines of their fire—until she wasn't so lucky.

A torpedo slammed into the back of the ship. Clo jerked forward in her seat, the rough cloth of the belt biting into her shoulder. "Silt."

"Hull breach sustained," the computer intoned. "Sealing off."

"Alesca," Sher's warning voice came from behind her.

Before Clo could even dodge again, another torpedo smashed into the ship. Around her, metal shuddered.

"Wing breach sustained," the stupid godsdamned computer added. *"Alesca!"*

"Yeah," Clo said. "I get it. Flume off."

A groan from Briggs. "Listen to the commander and stop getting hit, Alesca."

"D'ye want to pilot this damn ship?" She gunned the engine toward the asteroid field. "I'll hand it over. Ye can hold your guts in while ye fly."

She swallowed a sob. *Please don't die, Briggs.*

He didn't respond. She hoped he'd passed out again. All she could do was dodge the flying torpedoes that were locked in to her ship's course. She couldn't let the ship itself do the work. It was all her, and it took more focus than she had. Her friend was bleeding and dying next to her.

The asteroid field was in view. "Hold on," she told Sher.

She jammed the lever for the thrusters forward, sending the ship hurtling through the asteroid belt. She was completely surrounded by dust, debris, and rocks. The remains of old ships that hadn't made it hovered as Clo eased through the maze of rock.

Clo wanted to pretend that this was all a dream and she was back safe in her cot on Jurran, huddled beneath a mountain of blankets. She wanted to hear Briggs tell her to get up and start her godsdamned chores.

His weak voice sounded beside her. "Driving like a fucking Proclian."

"Proclians drive better," muttered Sher.

Clo gritted her teeth as when another Tholosian missile hit the back of the ship. "Damage at ten percent," the computer monotoned. At least they'd changed it from the Oracle's voice.

Clo's hands were white knuckled around the navigator. "I'm saving yer ungrateful lentic arses."

Another missile. Another. The ship grazed past an asteroid that nicked the side of the ship. *Damage sustained: 15, 30, 40.*

"You won't be able to do shit once damage gets past seventy," Briggs muttered. "Thought you were a better pilot than this, kid."

She kept an eye on the computers as she went through the asteroid belt and almost cried with relief when the blinking dot of a nearby planet showed up on the screen. The computer scanned it.

"Fortuna," the Novan computer intoned. "Mostly water-based. Planet terraformed in the year—"

"Can I land on it?" Clo snapped at the computer.

"Sending landing coordinates," the computer responded.

Clo's entire body strained as another missile skimmed the ship. If it sustained any more damage, they'd all die in this asteroid belt, another ghost ship left behind to decay with the others. Three more deaths to add to the empire's billions.

"We're gonna make it," she said to Briggs and Sher, desperation the only thing allowing her to keep focus. "We're gonna make it."

Briggs's hand was limp over the bullet wound. His skin was so pale. "Alesca," he said. Clo flinched at the slight tremor in his voice. "You're a good kid."

"Briggs." Clo heard the concern in Sher's voice. "Don't—"

"And you're a damn fine commander." Briggs's voice was beginning to slur.

"Shut it," Clo said, as the ship crossed to the end of the asteroid belt. God, they were so close. Almost there. "Shut it, Briggs. Don't blare at us like yer already sunk."

Clo couldn't think about Briggs. If she did, they would never survive. "I'm going to have to crash the ship," she told Sher. When he opened his mouth to argue, she said, "We need something big enough to draw their attention while we escape, okay? This is all we have."

Sher gave a decisive nod.

Clo jammed the steering forward, and she and Sher unclipped their belts. They rose unsteadily to their feet and held on to the ceiling strap as the ship zoomed down, down, down.

One chance. That's all they had to make it. They grabbed two parachute packs from the hold and put them on.

Briggs was still as Sher and Clo dragged his heavy, muscled ass out of the seat and slid the strap of the parachute around him.

"Alesca," Sher said. Then, more softly: "Clo."

"Don't say it," she snapped. "Don't fucking say it."

She pulled the levers to open the emergency hatch. Her stomach dropped as she stared down at the ground below her, coming ever closer. If they waited much longer, they'd never get the parachute open in time.

"Now or never," she whispered. "I've got you, Briggs."

Briggs didn't answer.

Clo shut her eyes and flung them both out of the ship. As the air rushed around them, she clasped Briggs hard to her, her body trembling with fear. Distantly, she heard the ship skimming across the water to crash into the sand of the shallows. It didn't explode, at least, but the ship would probably need to be scrapped for parts and rebuilt.

Clo pulled the string to open her parachute. The same camouflage she'd tried to hide the ship with back on Jurran. She was jerked toward the sky as fabric billowed up above her. The air was still for the few minutes she glided toward the surface, with Sher in his own parachute beside her.

It was quiet. Peaceful. She spotted a clearing between the canopy of trees and glided with Sher to the ground. Her landing wasn't graceful. It was a hard jolt up her legs as she fell into the grass, Briggs landing heavily into her side. The weight of his body stole her breath. They were on the edge of a forest, next to a sandy beach. The waters of the sea lapped the sand, the sky above a dark purple-gray. The air smelled of salt and brine. Closer to home than the desert or the frozen rock she'd just left.

"Briggs." She pushed against him, but he flopped into the ground, unmoving. Eyes still shut. "Briggs?"

"Alesca." Sher's voice was quiet again as he unclasped his own chute and kneeled beside her. "Alesca, I'm s—"

"Don't say it." She shook her head. "Please don't say it."

Footsteps drew their attention.

A group of women stood at the edge of the forest, staring at them warily. Clo doubted they had many visitors out this way on their small island, least of all ones who fell from the sky.

The whir of Tholosian ships entering the planet's atmosphere sounded overhead, drawn to the smoking ruins of the ship.

Clo turned to the women. "Help," she said, in every language she knew. "Please."

An older woman stepped forward. She was tall and lithe, with lines across her face that told of a life long-lived but far from over.

She seemed wary of Sher but kneeled next to Briggs, pressing her fingertips to his pulse. She spoke a dialect of Imperial. Then she shook her head.

"No," Clo whispered back. "He's not. He's—"

"We have to go, Alesca," Sher told her gently.

The woman pointed upward and spoke again, her voice urgent. A warning.

If Clo didn't leave Briggs there, she would die too.

Leaving him was one of the hardest things she'd ever done.

Late that night, when the Tholosians had left them for dead, Clo sneaked back down to the beach. She tried to carry Briggs to the water, but he was so heavy. Too heavy. Three of the women whose names she still didn't know had followed, emerging from the trees like ghosts. Wordlessly, they helped her drag Briggs to the shore.

Clo pushed him gently into the sea, letting the waves take him, like the dark green waters of Myndalia had taken her mother. One of the women murmured something like a prayer.

He sank, down into the dark, and a piece of Clo went with him.

38.

Present day

Clo scanned the planet Ismara again, hoping the details *Zelus*'s mainframe gave her would come up differently.

The screen beeped, and Clo scrolled through the details.

Nothing out of the ordinary. No extra military craft.

Two and a half weeks until the Tholosian-Evoli truce, and they still had no idea what the Empire had hidden on Ismara, why they had gone through such complicated measures to make sure no one knew ichor existed or how the rock would be weaponized.

"Fucking bog-all," Clo told the others as she flicked her finger across the screen.

The other women were seated behind her in the command center, watching the slow approach to Ismara. Rhea and Ariadne seemed entranced by the sight, and Clo was once again reminded that neither had left their respective cages on Tholos. The entire galaxy was so new to them, that it made Clo reevaluate everything she saw.

Ismara wasn't far off the path Clo took to run supplies to Nova. From space, the abandoned planet was a smear of blue and purple, much smaller than the Sisters, Myndalia, or Sennett. They passed through the two moons, readying to enter the atmosphere.

Ismara was still a beautiful planet, in parts, but *Zelus*'s scan claimed much of it had been destroyed by mining. It had been abandoned for nearly a century, and pockets of growth were only now returning. One day, Tholosians would drain this planet to the dregs again. That was the way of the Empire: find planets that were resource-rich, eliminate all intelligent life that might be a threat, use up everything the planet had to offer for the Empire's vast citizenry, and then abandon it until it was ready to plunder anew.

Rinse, repeat.

"We don't know that yet," Ariadne replied, peering over Clo's shoulder as she slowly navigated the ship. "The ichor is down there; I'm sure of it." She gestured to the computers. "The scan is detecting the same endospores that we found on Josephine, so we'll take some suits and helmets."

Zelus glided birdlike through the air as they made their way to the main barracks. "Should someone stay behind with the pilot?"

Eris looked annoyed at the reminder of his existence. "He's locked up in the medical center, cuffed to a bed, and unlikely to do anything strenuous for a few days."

Nyx's laugh was dry. The soldier looked like she hadn't done much sleeping herself. "Understatement. He looks like shit; definitely feels like shit. Deprogramming is rough."

Clo suppressed a shudder. The sleeping quarters were on the same level as the med center. Even three rooms away, Clo had heard Cato's screams as the machine detangled programming from natural brain synapse. Rhea had told her that putting a soldier under general anaesthesia during deprogramming was impossible; they had to remain conscious during the whole procedure.

Eris read the planet report. "With the soldiers they had guarding *Zelus*'s cargo, I'm surprised there's no increase in security," she murmured.

Clo tapped the screen for a better look. "Maybe they don't want to risk tipping off the Evoli?"

Eris didn't look convinced. "Maybe. It doesn't look like there's anywhere near the coordinates Ariadne found to land a craft this size. We'll have to use the shuttle."

"And contact Sher once we land," Clo reminded her. "We really need him to send an unmanned craft with supplies."

"Cato needs more blockers," Ariadne added brightly. "Keeps him calmer during deprogramming."

Eris scowled. "You'd think this ship made for one hundred people would have more of the damn things."

"The Tholosians aren't in the practice of deprogramming or having regular accidents and surgery," Ariadne pointed out.

Eris made an irritated noise. "Clo, get the shuttle ready. Everyone, change into your suits."

The shuttle was a tight squeeze and Ariadne ended up perching on Nyx's knee. Clo brought the craft down near the Ismara warehouse on the southwest hemisphere. They fell toward the ground, the atmosphere whooshing over the craft.

The shuttle burst through the clouds. Clo's stomach roiled again. Not as bad as Myndalia but she still swallowed the sharp taste of bile.

Most habitable planets in the Tholosian empire were like Myndalia. Dry or swampy, with habitable sections few and far between, and thus overcrowded. Temperate planets like the Three Sisters, with large continents, were rare and valuable.

On Ismara, the ground was nothing but hard rock covered in shallow water and topped with a thick, unforgiving mist. Large lily pads provided some nutrition and compost for fuel, but nothing larger could take root down below. Ismara was unique in that natural islands floated several hundred feet above ground level. Some flat, some with rolling hills or even small mountains. Clo had no idea how it all worked. Magnetic fields? Magic? All the same to her. The universe kept its mysteries.

"It's so beautiful," Rhea said, voice filled with wonder as Clo maneuvered the craft around a small floating forest, even if half of the trees had been burned away to clear space for miners. A few saplings sprouted from the singed soil. The other woman had her hands pressed to the glass as she stared at the sight below.

Clo let her smile show this time. "Told you I'd show you the universe, didn't I?"

Rhea blushed.

Nyx rolled her eyes. "I hate to interrupt your romantic moment here, but how do we find the warehouse if it's literally floating over the surface?"

"The coordinates Ariadne got when she hacked the Oracle are pretty precise," Clo said, glancing at the screen. "These islands don't seem to move quickly enough to make a difference."

Ariadne fiddled with some of the controls, much to Clo's annoyance. She was the bogging pilot here. "There's no other use for this planet than hiding something. Here, go this way."

She showed Clo a map on the screen and locked on to the location.

Clo followed the signal. They were all silent as they passed over floating islands. Some had buildings already falling to ruin, crumbling in the moist atmosphere. The paths and roads were overgrown, foliage reclaiming the dark ribbons.

The abandoned buildings were unsettling, a ghost town. Even Rhea seemed more subdued. This place already felt haunted and they hadn't even set foot on land yet.

"Why did everyone leave?" Clo asked Ariadne.

"The records are unclear. When I ran the search through the Oracle's files, they said mining was unsustainable." Ariadne tapped a few buttons on her tablet, frowning. "It looks like the biggest mine was going to be at the ground level. The rock is hard, but they were developing machinery to do the job. Lots of raw material was completely untapped, but they just . . . stopped. They left everything."

A shiver ran through Clo. Something felt off. People didn't just abandon valuable materials like that, not without good reason. They were programmed to do the job, no questions asked. And no one had come to finish the job.

"How many people are we talking about?"

"At its height? Not many. Maybe thirty thousand."

They set down and the ship landed with a soft *whoosh*. Clo's breathing grew ragged, and yet again, she lost the contents of her stomach— this time in a vomit bag Ariadne had helpfully provided for landing. From the sounds of the retching in the bullet craft, she wasn't the only one.

"Should have aimed for your boots again," Clo told an unaffected Eris, who smirked. "Got any breath neutralizers?"

Eris passed them to Clo and the others, who all swallowed gratefully. Leaning back in her captain's chair, Clo took the tablet from Ariadne and pinged Sher. After a muted beep, his face appeared. Clo wished she could reach through the screen and give Sher a hug. He would smell like sand and metal and home.

She missed Nova—she even missed the blasted *heat*. She missed tinkering with engines and swapping jokes with Elva. She missed sending the craft off on their missions. She was ready to go home and leave the adventuring to others for a while.

"Hey, Alesca," Sher said. "I've missed that angry mug."

It was night on Nova. His dark green eyes looked black in the low light of his office. He had a room in the barracks, but he spent most nights working until he fell asleep on a cot set up in the corner. Even half a galaxy away, his eyes could see into the very core of a person.

"Shut up, marsh-hole," she said.

"Ah, there's that beautiful Snarl poetry." He grinned. "You made good time. I wasn't expecting your call this early. Where are the others?"

Tilting the tablet, Clo showed him Eris, Rhea, Nyx, and Ariadne— who gave Sher an enthusiastic wave. Eris nodded once in greeting.

"Well done on Macella, all of you," Sher said. "Any problems, Eris?"

Clo wasn't sure if Eris had mentioned the pilot to Sher. Clo didn't know how to broach the subject. *By the way, we're conducting an unauthorized experiment and trying to break through a potential new strain of deprogramming. The subject nearly throttled one of us to death, but otherwise, it's pure gleyed, promise.*

"Not yet, but something feels off." Eris gestured to the trees in view of their ship's window. "If they're hiding a bunch of precious ichor cargo, there should be security like what we saw on *Zelus* before we commandeered it. Anyone here would have approached the ship by now."

Ariadne nodded. "The Oracle's files mentioned security around the building but nothing else. On all official documents, Ismara is declared completely uninhabitable, so that seems to be keeping people away. We should be fine, but we still ought to wear the same basic protection I wore when I looked at Josephine."

Sher looked confused. "Josephine?"

"Josephine is ichor, that endospore-studded rock that's probably a high-density blaster in a weapon of mass destruction," Ariadne said with a serene smile.

"Right." Sher rubbed his hand against the back of his neck. Dust painted his collar ochre and the bags under his eyes were larger.

"How are things back at base?" Clo asked. "Dust storms letting up?"

A twist of his mouth. "Most of the food and water is contaminated. Our communication is shit, tech at headquarters is glitching, and everyone is exhausted trying to keep things in order. Our engineers are looking at setting up biodomes for the long term, but we can't begin recovery efforts until the weather lets up."

"I guess now is a bad time to ask you to approve an unmanned craft to send us supplies? We need medical stuff. Still fine on food." The ship had only been outfitted with enough food to get to Myndalia, but meal packets for one hundred people for two weeks would keep the five of them—ugh, the six of them—pretty for months to come.

"Anyone hurt?"

Ariadne opened her mouth, but Clo shot her a look and she snapped it closed. Telling the co-commander of the resistance that they had an injured Tholosian pilot aboard while on a mission of this importance would only complicate things. The last thing they needed was to be reassigned. "Not yet."

Sher nodded. "Send me a list."

They said their goodbyes to Sher. Ariadne double-checked everyone's suits and helmets, then they all departed the bullet craft.

"This way," Ariadne said. The girl's tablet had a blinking dot to indicate the coordinates she'd found back on Macella.

Clo's skin prickled in alarm as they progressed. *Not even wind in the trees,* she thought. No animals rustling through the thickets. The coordinates led the group to a warehouse. The warehouse—the entire island, really—was completely still. Flat shelves of red mushrooms lined the bottoms of the trunks of trees and rocks of what might have been rough ichor in its natural habitat.

Clo rubbed her arms. Rhea reached out to take her hand, squeezing gently. Despite the thick material of their gloves, the gesture brought Clo comfort. A warm sense of home and belonging. She flashed Rhea a grateful smile and the other woman returned it.

Soon, the only sound between them was Ariadne's rapid tapping as she used the tablet to hack the building's security. It was no match for Ariadne. Within a few minutes, she whooped in delight. "I'm in!"

The warehouse door gaped open with a metallic creak. There were no heat signatures on Ariadne's scanner, but Tholosian soldiers had ways to cloak themselves if they wished to avoid detection. Clo, Eris, and Nyx pulled out their Mors, keeping the weapons raised as they crept into the dimly lit warehouse. The skylights along the ceiling let in just enough light to see inside.

But there was nothing there. It was completely empty except for the dust motes dancing in the dim light that filtered through the shatter-proof, barred windows and crops of mold in the damp corners.

Nyx lowered her Mors and ran a hand through her hair. "Great. Nothing. A false trail."

"No," Ariadne said, annoyed. "The intel on the Oracle's database was good. The ichor had been here as recently as last week. They must have just moved it. I don't like this."

Nyx glowered harder. "Maybe they knew we were coming."

"No, they didn't," Ariadne shot back. "I was careful. Even if they moved the ichor, there should still be records somewhere. Manifests."

Silence descended on the dusty warehouse, shafts of weak sunlight filtering through the gloom. Next to Clo, Rhea shivered. She looked uneasy, her face pale.

"You okay?" Clo asked her.

"I feel nauseated. I—" Rhea paused and tilted her head, as if listening. "Check for false walls. I don't think this place is empty." At Clo's confused expression, Rhea folded her arms over her stomach. "I heard . . . I felt . . . I just . . ." She trailed off, pausing by the far wall. "Nyx. This wall. There's something here."

The soldier strode over and rapped on the wall. Hollow. Nyx ran her hands along the seams of cool concrete until she found the hidden latch.

A doorway, stairs descending underground.

A slight glimmer on the ground caught Clo's eye. Before she could bend down, Nyx investigated it. She picked up a tiny morsel of ichor in her gloved hand, its iridescence as brilliant as it'd been on the ship. She held it close to the glass of her helmet before setting the shard of ichor down.

Wordlessly, they went down into the black.

39.

PRINCESS DISCORDIA

Three years ago

Only three children from the royal cohort remained alive: Discordia, Xander, and Damocles.

When there are two of my children still living, I will make my final decision, the Archon had said to Discordia, taking her chin in a firm grip. *But I have a feeling I'll be hanging the coronation cloak in your suite on Macella.*

Discordia tried not to show surprise at his favoritism. If Damocles had heard their father's words, he'd plot her assassination on principle.

Why? she had asked the Archon.

She wanted to know what her father still saw in her. She craved words that would chase away the doubts that plagued her after Xander had given her that unassuming little carving she carried in her pocket even though she should toss it into flames to send it straight to Avern.

Her father only released her chin and said, *Because you know better than to disappoint me.*

Upon returning to Macella, Discordia went to the hall in a quiet corner of the palace where the coronation cloak hung behind the glass. It had been displayed since the Archon himself had worn it centuries earlier. Light from the two moons almost turned the glittering gold material and the grand furred collar of one of the Tholosian's first conquests silver. The display case had careful temperature and technology so the fabric, fur, and metal would remain intact and pristine. If her father was right, she'd wear it, hold the ceremonial scythe stored in the Archon's chambers, and the people of the Empire would all bow before her.

Discordia should feel glad. Relieved. Her father was confident she'd be declared the Heir, and she was going to rule the galaxy in his name. The first woman to do so. But the doubts remained. She and Xander had dared imagine other lives they might have lived. Things they thought about in secret, that they could tell no one else.

And the only thing she'd have to do to earn it was kill one more person.

Xander or Damocles.

She had made the decision to ally herself with Damocles—but it had been the choice of a girl who cared only for enough strength in an ally to guarantee survival. There was too much softness in Xander. She remembered the way he'd rest after training with his prefect: seated on the bench, head against the great glass wall that overlooked the clouds of Myndalia, his eyes shut and his expression weary.

That sort of vulnerability should have gotten him killed years earlier.

She was the reason Xander was still alive. She had chosen to kill her other brothers before they could catch him. She had warned Xander if Damocles had started tracking him, and—despite seeing Xander dozens of times over the years—she always failed to put a Mors blast in his brain.

She wasn't ready to lose him.

Knowing it was a risky, foolish thing to do, Discordia disabled the alarm and picked the lock. Her computer skills stretched that far, just.

"Thank you, Mistress Heraia," she muttered as she opened the glass so she could slide her fingertips along the material of the cloak. Did she really want to wear it? Or had she been engineered to desire power? But no, she wasn't like the other citizens of the Empire, programmed to know what to think or how to feel. The answer didn't come easily.

Discordia drew in a shaking breath and unhooked the cloak from its hanger to slide it over her shoulders. She would take this moment for herself, even if the Archon never ended up giving it to her. If she couldn't earn it.

The weight of it bent her spine. The crown would be just as heavy. She shouldn't linger. If anyone caught her—

"It suits you."

Discordia sucked in a breath at Xander's voice. She hadn't heard him come in. The only person who could sneak up on her. He leaned against the heavy wooden door of the hall, holding a small box in his hands.

"You can't be here," she whispered. "If Damocles realizes you're on Macella—"

Xander laughed. Discordia marveled at the sound, how easy he made it seem. Laughter had been beaten out of them at that training school in Myndalia.

This was for her. Just for her.

"I sent a false trail away from the Three Sisters," he said. "Damocles has a tendency of running off without thinking." He took in the cloak on her shoulders. "I wanted to see it too. You ought to—" He pressed his lips together.

"I ought to . . ." she asked as he came closer.

Xander shook his head. "Teach Damocles to be less impulsive. When you cross me off your list."

An ache went through her at his words. If she were practical, she would have reached for a weapon the moment he walked through that door. Finished it. Become the Heir, once and for all.

Eris was beginning to understand that feelings were not practical.

During their meetings over the years, Xander had never tried to pretend his life consisted of anything more than borrowed time. Any other brother might have taken advantage of this, tried to press for Discordia to betray Damocles. But Xander accepted his fate; all he'd asked for was more time.

And she had given it to him. She wanted to give him more.

"Don't talk like that," she said.

Xander's expression softened. "Discordia—"

"Please."

She had never uttered that word her entire life. *Please* was too close to begging, an admission of some deficiency. No wonder her father warned her about feelings. No wonder he taught her never to show emotion, to tamp it down inside her where it could be caged and tamed and hidden.

Discordia wanted Xander to live. She wanted him to live more than she wanted to rule an empire.

Dangerous thoughts—destructive and reckless and weak. Thoughts that she would have killed her other brothers for, because the God of Death was their patron, their lord, their deity, and He did not tolerate such failing.

Xander froze. For a moment, Discordia felt embarrassed. Damocles would have mocked her for the plea, challenged her. Their father would have tortured her at such a disappointment. Rethought his decision to make her Heir.

Xander only let out a breath. "I have something for you."

Discordia tilted her head, her hand resting against the fur trim of the cloak. She knew she should take it off, but she was compelled to bear the heavy weight of it a moment longer. "Another gift?"

"Something like that." Xander placed the box in her palms. "Here."

Discordia lifted the lid and her breath caught. Nestled in velvet was an antique gun, an old limited edition RX Blaster. Avern, they did not make guns like this anymore; Mors weapons were all utilitarian designs, made to look the same. This? Oh, it was a beauty. The barrel was long and filigreed, and it curved into a beautiful pearled handle.

"Where did you find it?" she asked.

He only smiled in answer. "You'll have to buy more blasters, but I thought you'd be up for the challenge of learning a new weapon." As if nervous at her silence, Xander cleared his throat. "I remember from Myndalia that you liked experimenting."

That made her look up. "You watched me from the observation deck."

"We all did," Xander admitted. "I doubt a single one of our brothers would have turned you down for an ally. Our one surviving sister." His gaze shifted.

"What?"

His eyes met hers. "I saw you and Damocles the night you both challenged Adrian and Xerxes. You showed compassion."

Discordia still remembered Xerxes bleeding out on the floor of the gymnasium, his expression pleading. The way Damocles thought his father's attention was more important than his brother's suffering. They had all been taught to work for the Archon's satisfaction above all else. Not her first kill, but her first of many kin.

Discordia remained silent. Xander took the weapon from her and placed it back in the box, its lid still open. "Our other brothers would have let Damocles wait, no matter how long Xerxes suffered. You were different."

Discordia brushed her fingers against the cold metal of the gun, snug in its box. "I've killed every time Father asked me to."

"You haven't killed me."

She shouldn't feel grief for the living or the dead, but she did every time she thought about Xander and her gift of borrowed time.

Discordia swallowed. She had so many questions. She could only bring herself to ask one: "Why didn't you run from me?"

His gaze held hers. "I took the chance that you'd be different from our brothers. From Damocles."

She turned away from him, the damn cloak so heavy. It was all too heavy. The price too high. Xander knew what she was capable of before him, before this. The person she was still capable of being.

"I've slaughtered so many people," she said, her voice ragged. "I'm exactly the same as Damocles."

"Discordia—"

"No." She shook her head. "This gun isn't a gift, is it? It's a request." At his silence, she let out a dry laugh. "You told me once that all you wanted was a few more years. Are you so eager to die?"

Xander shut his eyes briefly.

Discordia slammed the box's lid down and shoved it toward him. "Take this back and get the fuck out of here. I'm not shooting you today. I'll cross your name off my list next time."

"Discordia."

"Get out."

"*Discordia.*" He gripped her shoulders through the coronation cloak, forcing her to look at him. "Listen to me. I want it to be my choice. When and who and by what method. I want you to be the one to say last rites over me. I want it to be your voice that guides me into Avern."

This was the price she'd pay for her feelings. Attachments made a ruler easily distracted, manipulated, and vulnerable. He knew that as well as she did.

"Why are you asking me this?" she whispered. "Why now?"

His expression was gentle. "You've delayed striking my name off your list for so long. It was always *next time*. I'm the last name you've got." Xander's thumb brushed the fur collar of the cloak. "It's time for you to wear this, *soror.*"

Soror. She blanched at the old word for sister. It fell out of favor when children were grown rather than born. When they no longer had parents or siblings, only castes and cohorts.

It was cruel, using this word while asking her to end his life.

"What if I don't want it anymore?" The question was a barb in her throat. "What if I don't want to wear this horrible cloak and pretend that it represents something I still believe in? Damocles is more suited to it than me."

He hissed out a frustrated breath. "Don't you dare say that when you know it isn't true. Damocles isn't fit to rule over an empty field."

"Fine." Discordia ripped off the cloak and shoved it into his hands. "You, then. You be the next Archon."

Xander studied the cloak. His fingers played along the fur collar. She'd have to put it back soon, before she risked damaging it.

"I am not fit to rule any more than Damocles is," Xander said. "I'm better at hiding than fighting. I'm not a leader. Even my prefect knew that."

"And what makes you so certain that *I* am?"

He sighed. "Every time you've doubted yourself it's because you felt obligated to rule the way Father has. Change the damn Empire, Discordia. Make it yours. Make it better."

"I don't know how."

Xander shook out the cloak and placed it once more on her shoulders, hooking the collar into place. "Do you want our people to fear you or love you?"

"Fear me." She gave her father's response. The words she had learned since she was in the cradle and the recordings of his voice whispered into her ear of power and conquest. *Let them fear you.*

Xander's brief smile was so sad. "Are you so sure?"

Don't feel. Don't feel. The chant caught fire in her mind, but it was mere background buzzing, a litany that meant nothing in comparison to the confident, no-nonsense way he buttoned the front of the cloak. As if he considered it to be hers already.

"If you were," he continued, "you would have sliced that blade across my throat the first time we spoke." A quick, larger smile. "You wouldn't have taken my firewolf, much less kept it."

Discordia didn't know who she was. With her father, she felt compelled to be someone he would be proud of. It was a child's fantasy with him, the need to boast of her skills, to prove something to him. Just so she saw that small glint of satisfaction in his eye that came when she had mastered another test, shown herself to be in control. Unbreakable.

But it was a lie. When she was with Xander, Discordia allowed herself to think beyond a cloak, a crown, an empire. She couldn't forget the face of every person she had ever personally killed. Her brothers, rebels, Evoli, prisoners, soldiers, civilians in the wrong place, the wrong time. People who loved and feared her. Before she allowed herself to know Xander, killing was as routine as sleeping.

Now? It felt wrong to sacrifice so many. To worship a god, the devil who was never sated. But she knew no other path.

Discordia slid her hand into her pocket and grasped the firewolf, running her finger over the carved grooves already growing shiny from the oils in her fingertips. It had become a talisman. A memento of the first moment she went against expectations by letting him live.

"What if you don't have to die?" Discordia asked.

Xander's smile faded. "What?"

"What if I chose you instead of Damocles?" At his hesitation, she grasped his arm. "You said yourself that he's not fit to lead. Damocles is too impulsive. He can't think clearly."

"I also just said that *I'm* not fit to lead, Discordia."

"Then be my second. My Brigadier, my Spare. We can take Damocles out while he's too distracted with the conflict at the Garnet."

Her father wanted to conquer a newly discovered planet in a nearby solar system that tests determined had excellent soil composition: another potential source of food for their expanding empire. One the

Evoli Oversouls were just as interested in making theirs, and the conflict had killed too many soldiers as it was. Discordia knew it was only a matter of time before her father had her direct more forces away from the planet and engage the Evoli in more familiar territory. Until then, Damocles thought to prove himself to the Archon by coming and going from the frontlines.

"Discordia . . ."

"Do you want to die?" she asked him. "Do you want me to take this gun and shoot you today and say last rites? Strike your name off my list? Do you want Damocles to be the one who stands second in line to the throne?"

He exhaled, long and slow, then shook his head.

"Then help me, *frater.*" She saw his surprise at her use of the old word for brother. "You said to change the Empire and make it mine. I say we make it ours. I can't do this on my own. We can make it better."

By killing Damocles.

40.

Present day

They descended into an old mining tunnel.

A few glimmers of ichor threaded through the black rock like rivers of opal, and while Eris admired its beauty, she reminded herself of the danger. Rhea had heard something down there, and they didn't know how stable this tunnel was.

Eris strained to listen for any indication that they weren't alone. She heard nothing more than the echo of their steps and the cadence of four other breaths crackling through the comm devices in their helmets, one more ragged than the others.

Rhea.

Concerned, Eris glanced back to see Rhea stumble, only just managing to hold herself up by the handrail. Through the helmet, Eris could see Rhea's dark hair stuck to her temples, beads of sweat dotting her forehead.

"Rhea?" Eris said. "Are you all right?"

"Something the matter?" Nyx's voice echoed through the shaft. The soldier was leading the way, the light from Ariadne's tablet held aloft.

Rhea steadied herself once more. "I'm fine. Probably still shaky from transport sickness. Bullet crafts are unpleasant."

Eris didn't believe her. Rhea's expression went blank when Eris studied her closely, but her shoulders remained slightly hunched. Her body swayed. She held up a hand, eyes pleading. A clear *Don't ask. Not right now.*

Eris nodded once and continued down the passage. Who was she to demand someone's secrets? She still kept her own.

As they descended farther into the earth, the air grew musty and cold. The tunnel bent, and Nyx's light showed a gray door with a panel to the right. A slim shaft of light filtered from the bottom of the door, catching on the glittering colors of the surrounding ichor.

Nyx handed Ariadne the tablet and raised her Mors. Eris did the same and eased her body in front of Ariadne and Clo. If someone came out shooting, she would not have the others go in first. They weren't soldiers trained for a potential ambush.

Ariadne went to work on the panel, tapping a few commands into her tablet. Within a few minutes, the door slid open.

Nyx and Eris met gazes. Nyx tapped her finger once to the side of her helmet just over her ear, then to the glass by her eye, and gestured to the other women. Eris understood why Nyx didn't say anything over the Pathos: she would go in first, and if anything happened to her, Eris would lead everyone out. She'd sacrifice herself and stay behind.

Eris bristled at the idea, but Nyx made the motion again. A clear indication to stick with her plan. Before Eris could silently argue further, Nyx pushed open the door and went in, Mors at the ready.

And froze just a single step inside, a choked gasp wrenched from her throat.

"Nyx?" Eris shoved the door wide and went in. "What—" She made some strangled noise at the sight before her.

Not all of the miners had left Ismara.

Behind her, a retch echoed through the clinically bright room. Eris couldn't tear her eyes away from what she saw in that medical wing, hidden away for a damn good reason.

In the middle of the room was a quarantine enclosure—no, that was too generous.

It was an airtight glass prison.

And in that cell were dozens of corpses.

Gods of Avern. These people had been executed, and not recently. Their skin was gray, puckered, stretched tight and making its slow way to bone. About thirty in all, with most wearing the rough clothes of their trade. There were a few minor Tholosian soldiers. Their skin was pale and waxy, partially preserved only due to the temperature in the room. Decay had begun to set in.

"Who did this?" Clo asked softly. "And why? Why would they . . ."

Rhea came up beside her, gesturing to a closed door just off the main cell. "In there," she whispered. "Open it, Ari."

Ariadne gave Rhea an unreadable look before hacking the door's lock. When the bolt released, Eris took the lead and pushed open the door.

Another prison, smaller.

The three men in the glass cell wore the gleaming buttons of Tholosian officers. Eris counted them, taking in the symbols branded into the metal, each one symbolizing rank. The colors had faded, but these were undoubtedly a commanding officer and two juniors. She couldn't see the two other names stitched to their breasts, but the commander's read *Talley*.

Avern, Commander Talley even had a symbol of valor on the jacket of his uniform—the two infinity symbols for the God of Death. He'd probably retired to this godsforsaken outpost after the Battle of the Garnet. It was an easy position for an aging officer, away from violence and brutality.

At least, it was *supposed* to be.

Eris hung back as Nyx approached the glass. The men were as gaunt as the corpses in the other room, their skin nearly as gray. The three sprawled against the glass, dark liquid caked at their ears and the corners of their mouths. The ducts of their eyes darkened with red-black tears.

The commander opened his eyes.

Nyx gave a startled cry and jerked back, smacking so hard into the ichor wall of the cave that Eris worried she'd damaged her helmet. Eris stepped forward, alarmed, when she noticed the small tear in the arm of Nyx's suit. The other woman quickly patched it from a kit in her belt pouch.

<*Nyx, you okay?*> Eris kept her focus on the commander.

<*Yeah. Fine. The suit's good. He just startled the shit out of me.*>

Commander Talley blinked at the brightness, the whites of his eyes turned black. He was alive. *Gods of Avern, he's fucking alive.*

What about the other two? They looked dead—seven devils, the commander had looked dead until the moment he opened his eyes. He was trying weakly to lift his head. How was he still moving? He had a cluster of small dark lesions at his temples, wattles at the base of his jowls.

Nyx hurried to the cell door, but the commander spoke. "No," he croaked. "Don't open. Might be dangerous."

Nyx paused. Eris's fear spiked.

"Keep it sealed," he managed. "Safe . . . safer."

Eris looked at Ariadne. "You said the pilot rattled off medical expertise during deprogramming, right?" Ariadne nodded. "Good. Then maybe he's useful. Take the shuttle back to *Zelus* and tell him to bring the med kit and an extra decontamination suit from the lab." Eris gestured to where Rhea stood in the corner of the room, barely supporting herself on the medical table. "And take Rhea with you outside. Get her some air."

Ariadne seemed uncertain as she wrapped a supporting arm around Rhea's waist. "Okay, but I don't know if Cato can walk yet. Deprogramming—"

"Then tell him to crawl," Eris snapped.

The girl hurried away as quickly as she could with Rhea.

Eris returned her attention to the commander and crouched near the glass. "We're getting someone who can go in there to see you, all right?"

Commander Talley only drew in a shaky breath and took in their protective suits. He spent a moment studying Eris; she fought to remain expressionless. She doubted she succeeded.

"You're not . . . with them?" he whispered.

"Who?" Eris asked.

"The . . . Empire."

Eris managed to keep from showing surprise, but only just. "No. We're not."

The commander gave a shaky sigh of relief. That was proof enough of how close to death he was, that the Oracle was no longer in control of his thoughts or feelings. One had simply gone into background processing, One's tendrils loosening as the brain began to die.

Eris pressed her gloved hands to the glass. "What did they do to you?"

Talley's head lolled to the side. The blackness near his eyes cracked, sending a new tear of red-black down the grayed skin of his withered cheek. Eris hadn't wanted to admit it to anyone, but sending for Cato had not been to examine this man alive—there was no saving the commander. No, they needed to examine his corpse.

And another part of her had wanted Ariadne and Rhea out of this room. Away from the bodies, the death, and the dying. Some people shouldn't have to see such things. Eris wished she hadn't.

"Check . . . the logs," he said. "In my office . . . the barracks."

"I will," she told him. "I'll make the Empire pay for this, commander. I promise."

His nod was so slight she might have missed it had she not been watching. "They'll be back," he murmured, shutting his eyes. His voice was so faint, Eris could barely hear it. "For . . . rest of the ichor. You should . . . leave. Don't let them . . . find you."

"We'll do that," Eris said. "Thank you, Commander."

They all remained silent, waiting for Ariadne and Cato to come. Eris didn't want to voice her concerns to Nyx or Clo aloud—that they had come mere moments before the commander was to give his last breath. Eris slipped a hand into the pocket of her suit and grasped her scythe pendant.

Talley began to cough, red blood trickling from his mouth. He tilted his head to the side, sucking in a rattling breath.

The other hand went into her pocket where she kept Xander's carved firewolf. She felt the grooves of the firewolf's muzzle.

Xander, she thought, watching the commander's chest go still. *I'm failing.*

"Eris?" Ariadne's voice was hesitant at the doorway. "I've brought—"

"Gods of Avern," Cato murmured, limping into the room.

Clo pointed to the commander. "Get in there and help him. He's still alive."

"He's not." Eris straightened. She was gripping her scythe hard in her glove. "He's gone."

Nyx swore softly.

Eris unhooked her necklace, bent her head and whispered last rites. Nyx and Cato joined in. Clo and Ariadne stayed silent but bowed their necks in respect.

Hold it together, she told herself.

When she had trained to be her father's Heir, Eris used to imagine a space inside her chest. An empty chasm that was deep and endlessly dark. If she ever became overwhelmed—if she ever *felt* too much— she'd picture that space filling up and up and up, like the banks of a forest stream in the rain.

And when it became too much, she'd empty it. Empty herself. All those emotions would drain out of her, leaving that hole in her chest barren and dark once more. It used to come easily, but near the end, it was like the more that chasm filled, the more emptying it was like trying to drain a whole ocean.

She wondered if it'd ever be easy again. If it'd stop hurting so much.

The firewolf in her pocket reminded her that it probably never would.

Eris finished her prayer and returned her necklace to her pocket. She gave the firewolf one last squeeze and turned to the others. "He said there were documents in the barracks that would explain what happened. I saw the buildings just past the warehouse. Before examining the"—Eris took a breath—"the bodies. We ought to know what we're dealing with."

Without another word, she strode out of the glimmering tunnel— past those glass prison cells-turned-tombs—and hurried up to the surface. The others were only too eager to follow. Outside, she caught her ragged breath.

Rhea watched her from where she had been resting against a tree. "Eris. Is everything all right?"

"The commander is dead," Eris said, and Rhea blanched. Eris cursed her tactlessness, but she couldn't offer soft words. No comfort. She was not made for these things.

Hold it together. Eris left Rhea, striding toward the barracks. She didn't care if the others followed. *You can't fall apart now.*

Eris's boots were silent across the moist soil. The temperature had dropped since they landed, even if she couldn't feel it through her suit. If she hadn't left Tholos—if she had remained the general—she wouldn't have let them all die. Maybe they'd still be alive. Maybe—

Stop. A maybe solves nothing. A maybe changes nothing. Do your damn job.

The barracks were threaded with the dark red mushrooms and mold that snaked their way up the black timber of the officers' quarters. In the thin afternoon light cast between the clouds of the overcast sky, it looked like the building was bleeding.

Eris swallowed hard and turned the rusted handle of the door, pushing her way inside.

The interior was wet and colder. The automatic lights flickered on, lazily, casting the room in a hazy, yellow glow. It was a bare room, only consisting of a single desk with a small cot off to the side. Nothing appeared touched or rifled through. It was a small relic on this dead planet. It had the damp, musty scent of disuse, dust gathering across the surfaces of the few pieces of furniture. How long had Talley been down in the glass box?

Eris walked over to the desk, her eyes skimming the stacks of paperwork, the little trinkets of Talley's life. She picked up the small digipad in the corner of the desk that had stuck on a single vid file of a woman, also in uniform, standing outside the barracks with her head tipped back and a smile on her face, her hair ruffling in the breeze.

The caption read: *Octavia on our first Ismaran anniversary.*

Eris's chest tightened, eyes stinging with unexpected tears. It took her a few tries with her gloves, but she managed to load the digipad. They were built to keep power for hundreds of years, a digital library that would last for three generations at least. Maybe more.

A creak made her glance up. The others had come inside but hesitated at the doorway. Their features were all stricken. As much as Eris wanted to spare them knowledge of whatever awful information they would find in Talley's logs, they all deserved to know the truth.

"Ariadne," she said, voice low. "Project the logs so everyone can see them, please."

The girl nodded and navigated the files. A miniature hologram of the man they had just watched die loaded. Hale and healthy, barely a trace of the shadow he would become.

Gods. He'd recorded this less than three Tholos moons before. Turned from a proud, loyal, muscled Tholosian officer to a desiccated husk of a man, who had just died choking on his own black blood.

Four logs, dated just before the mines were reported as shut down. Eris clicked on the first one. The miniature version of Talley-I-32, paced the desk and spoke, as if he had returned from the dead:

Data log: 89 days ago:

<Comm. Arctus Talley-I-32:> The miners are making good progress. Extraction is difficult. Toxin levels in the caves are increasing as drilling progresses. We have introduced new tools to assist with their work— larger drills that run hotter. The sparks have injured several workers. Request additional protective gear, including respirators.

<Sen. Comm. Felix Rhys-X-49:> Supplies incoming, but continue work until then. Your usual quota of ichor by the end of the moon is expected.

<Comm. Arctus Talley-I-32:> Understood. In His name.

<Sen Comm. Felix Rhys-X-49:> For the glory of Tholos.

Ariadne pressed her lips together. She tapped the next file, from just a few weeks later:

Data log: 71 days ago:

<Comm. Arctus Talley-I-32:> Respirators have arrived, but despite this, the miners continue to sicken. Please see the attached file for a catalog of symptoms. Dr. Octavia Byze-M-71 is attending them, but so far, they are not responding to treatment. It does not appear to be contagious but acts like atmospheric poisoning. This is new—over the last five years I've been on this planet, I've never seen anything like this. Ten dead, and the medic center is filling up fast. Your command, sir?

<Comm. Arctus Talley-I-32:> Senior Commander, what are our next steps?

<Comm. Arctus Talley-I-32:> Sir?

<Comm. Arctus Talley-I-32:> Any time now. Sir.

Ariadne clicked open the med file for a miner. Chloe Marinos-C-1. Age: 39 Tholos years. Notes filled out by Dr. Octavia Byze-M-71.

First day: Patient experienced nausea and vomiting two days ago.

Pulse 96 beats per minute—elevated from last recorded 58. Breathing heavy, labored. Eyes puffy. Skin sloughing on palms. Buildup of dark red liquid at corner of eyes and ear canals, and genitals. Swelling of lymph nodes in the neck and under the armpits, which were lanced. Medications ineffective.

Third day: No improvement. Physical health deterioration. Continued leaking of darkened blood from nose, mouth, gums, rectum, eyes, ears. Patient sleeping up to eighteen hours a day.

Fifth day: Patient's teeth loosened in mouth. This isn't the most medical description, but they were like chalk. She keeps spitting them into the bowl at her bedside. She keeps trying to speak to me, but I can't make out her words, and she doesn't know how to write. I'm making her comfortable.

Seventh day: Patient deceased.

With a small sound, Ariadne hesitated before clicking the next name, but Eris nodded for her to continue. Nikolas Lasko-J-14. Age: 19 Tholos years. Patient deceased after five days in the med clinic, same symptoms but more progressed by the time he was admitted.

Beside Eris, Clo was gasping as Ariadne pulled up the next name and the next name and the next. Each case file was virtually the same, but the longest anyone managed to hold out was fifteen days.

Fifteen days.

More names—gods, thousands of them. Tens of thousands. Eventually just names and time of death, no notes. Every miner on Ismara.

Ariadne loaded Talley's last log. He was noticeably thinner, and he coughed wetly.

<Comm. Arctus Talley-I-32:> No one will see this. The soldiers have come, and they're not letting any survivors leave. They're running tests on ichor. Something we did during extraction released the illness. So far, it seems to lodge in patient's respiratory systems. Not contagious, but Octavia worried about possible mutation. She made the mistake of putting that in one of her files. I saw them shoot her. Kicked her into a mass grave like she was so much rubbish.

None of us will make it off this rock. But I have nowhere to go. Not now.

We're all a fucking experiment. They're taking most of the ichor off planet—don't know where—but they'll come back for the rest. They'll put me down in the mine before they go. We'll have some automated meals, me and two of my cohort. We've lasted longer than the others. They want to see how much longer it will take. I suppose the Oracle will take notes as we die.

May the God of Death punish everyone who took this off-planet.

Cato stared at the projection in disbelief. "This isn't possible." He ran a hand through his hair. "Look, they wouldn't do something like this. I've seen any number of plagues and illnesses, and quarantine is common even if it doesn't seem contagious. But the Empire wouldn't just *leave* them here."

Nyx's laugh was dry. "So, what, we hallucinated those bodies down there? Wake the fuck up, pilot. The Empire doesn't care about *you* any more than they cared about the people on this planet. We're all expendable."

"Nyx," Eris chastised. Like Nyx, Cato reminded Eris too much of what she had been like before becoming so close to Xander. Blindly following orders. Believing everything she had ever been told. She didn't even have the Oracle as an excuse—it was brainwashing, pure and simple. "I'm going to tell you something you won't want to hear, Cato." She nodded to the projection, paused on Talley's gaunt frame. "This is what it looks like when you don't have programming to tell you what to feel and how to think. When they don't make you forget. You have nothing to explain away your emotions, or tell you that the Empire's reasoning is infallible. Every battlefield you ever saw had some atrocity covered up in your mind. Perhaps you've seen them in nightmares."

A flicker of shock showed in his features. "No." He shook his head once. "*No.* Those aren't real."

Like a child, Eris thought, *learning the world for the first time.* The Oracle kept everyone naive.

"I wish they weren't," Eris said. "But these people are real, and they were left here to die. You're not dreaming this."

Cato shut his mouth.

Ariadne cleared her throat. "It looks like there are references to other experiments, too," she said, voice so small. "I can find the files, but it's risky. If the Oracle activates, One could run a search on our location and find us." Ariadne swallowed. "I could take the digipad back to the ship—"

"No," Eris said. "The Oracle has trackers on these pads. One will know the second it leaves the atmosphere. Either we take the information now, or you waste time disabling it. Choose."

"Okay. Save me the work," Ariadne said. Her fingers sped across the tablet, fast as lightning. She went still as she found another list and projected the information in front of everyone.

The girl clicked the first file, labeled VESTA REPORT. Eris went numb as she read the first few lines: *Ichor administered. Average survival rate: 10 days. Longest survival rate: 12 days. Shortest survival rate: 8 days. Total casualties: 5,673.*

Clo's breath hitched and Rhea reached out to grasp her hand.

Ariadne selected the next file. CERCYON REPORT. *Ichor administered. Average survival rate: 9 days. Longest survival rate: 10 days. Shortest survival rate: 8 days. Total casualties: 10,422.*

Close to half a dozen worlds. All of them on the outer fringes of the Iona galaxy. Small backwater planets and moons colonized by the Tholosian Empire that were rarely visited because either they were resourceless, they had restricted access, or their colonies never grew beyond the few people randomly assigned at birth to live there. They were places no one would miss.

And since the asteroid hit Charon and took out the Empire's most productive food source, they were a drain on the Empire.

Too many mouths to feed.

Ariadne scrolled down to the last one, and Clo let out a choked whisper. "I know that one. *I know that one.*"

She seized the digipad from Ariadne and her hand trembled as she clicked on the words FORTUNA REPORT. The projection flashed. Clo pressed a hand to her mouth to muffle her sob. Tears filled her eyes and the digipad dropped to the floor with a clatter.

"Gods," she breathed. "*Oh, gods.*"

Eris's heart slammed against her ribs as she read the words projected in front of them all.

FORTUNA REPORT: *Ichor administered. Average survival rate: 3 days.*

Longest survival rate: 5 days. Shortest survival rate: 2 hours 22 seconds. Casualties: 15,341. Complete extermination.

Clo snapped her head up and looked at Eris. "This is all your fluming fault."

Rhea sucked in a breath. "Clo—"

"Don't," Clo never tore her eyes away from Eris. "None of you understand what she did. What she's responsible for."

Eris tried to keep her features even, composed. "Stop it, Clo."

"The people on Fortuna saved me and Sher. And the Empire killed them like they were nothing." She slammed her hand on the commander's desk. "This mission doesn't erase the things you did. It doesn't make you any fucking different."

The stares of everyone in the room burned. Eris had known the others would learn her secret eventually, but she had wanted just a bit longer before they resented her. Hated her.

Like Clo had. Their delicate shell of new friendship was cracked. Had she hated Eris all along?

"Clo," Rhea whispered. "What are you talking about?"

"Ask *her*," Clo snarled.

Eris's hand went into her pocket. She felt for the firewolf, her talisman. "I never said I was different," she said, ignoring Rhea's question.

"No, I guess you didn't." Clo laughed bitterly. "You never even told me why you really left the Empire. Someone you cared about? Silting *lies*—"

"*That wasn't a lie.*" Eris flinched at the hoarse, broken note of her words. Clo's mouth snapped shut. "What happened with him—" Eris broke off. The firewolf felt like it burned in her palm. "The Empire takes everything from us, Clo. You know that more than anyone."

"It gave you more than anyone else and you still ran like a godsdamn coward. You could have changed everything. You could have fought."

You could have made it better, a small, inner voice accused. *Like you promised Xander.*

"Yes," Eris whispered. "I ran. I was grieving and didn't know what else to do, and I regret it. Is that what you want me to say? *I regret it.* But I'm fighting the only way I know how."

Clo backed away, almost bumping into Ariadne. "I don't want you to say anything. I don't want anything from you. You've already done enough."

Clo stomped out the door, her limp more pronounced.

Eris stood in the center of the dead man's office, as lost as she'd been three years ago after Xander's death, Clo's words echoing in her ears. The projection still displayed the thousands of dead on a planet that could have been hers if she had only kept her promise to Xander. All of those people would be alive.

A godsdamned coward.

When Eris glanced at Ariadne, the girl stared back with a flicker of fear. *And you don't even know the whole truth,* Eris thought. *You'd be so much more afraid if you did.* Eris had tried so hard to atone for her former life. No matter what she did, it would never be enough. It didn't matter.

Eris felt a hand on her sleeve. Rhea. The other woman still looked unwell, unsteady on her feet. "Give her a bit of time to calm," Rhea said. "But let's do it back on the ship and wait for the supplies there. This place is poison."

Eris nodded. "Thank you." Her hand brushed against Rhea's as she moved for the door. "Let's—"

Rhea gasped. Her eyes went wide, pupils dilating.

The overhead lights flickered.

"Rhea?" Eris shook her. "*Rhea!*"

The other woman seized Eris's hands in a grip that was shockingly strong. Rhea's gaze bore into Eris's. "You have so much blood on your hands, Eris. You hurt so much." Then she shut her eyes briefly, exhaustion plain in her features. "I can feel your grief. Ever since we came here, I can feel everything. I can't . . ."

"Rhea, what are you talking about?" Ariadne asked. She edged forward, but Rhea held up a hand, urging her back. Ariadne shot Eris a look of fear. "We need to get her out of here *now*. I think the ichor on this planet is enhancing her—"

Rhea fell to her knees and screamed.

41.

The scream echoed through every atom of Rhea's being.

She'd felt wrong as soon as she'd stepped onto the planet. Dread had furled deep in her gut. Each step was like moving through sand, her entire body leaden and heavy. A ringing had filled her ears, as if she were plunged underwater.

Once they went into the mines, the buzzing grew worse—reverberating in her mind. It was the ichor in the walls—pulsing, pulsing, pulsing, like a heartbeat. It was different from how it'd been on *Zelus*. The rock there had been dampened, half asleep.

Here, on this planet, it felt alive.

Rhea was aware of Clo shouting her name. "What's wrong with her? Eris, what the flames did you *do*?"

Clo reached for her, but Rhea twisted from her grip. It was too much, even with the thick material of the jumpsuit between them. She was nothing but an exposed nerve, vibrating with every one of their emotions.

Guilt. Fear. Anger. Dark, cloying. Thick enough to choke on.

Hold it, she told herself. *Don't let them see your face. Don't let them see your face.*

Rhea panted, her gloved hands digging into the floor. Gods, her hands burned—her whole *body* burned. The effort to keep herself hidden hurt.

"*Rhea!*" Clo's desperate call came again.

Rhea looked up, and lost control. Her illusion dropped.

A release of pressure was like a coiled spring. She knew exactly what they saw; through the helmet, they could see her face or her neck: the shimmering skin, pale with dotted swirls like fractals. Glimmering in the low light, almost glowing.

Just like an Evoli.

"Oh, Rhea," Ariadne breathed.

The girl had worked out Rhea's secret and kept it to herself. Sweet Ariadne. Her aura tasted like spun sugar in the back of Rhea's throat. All glittering bright colors to hide the darkness of her upbringing.

The others moved closer, but Rhea stumbled back. No, she couldn't stand their stares, the way they all *felt.* She had never seen emotions in such vivid colors before landing on this infernal planet, and now they were all focused intently on *her.* On her skin, which burned as bright as someone from the Evoli Empire. Their feelings stabbed at her like blades to the gut: Cato's purple wariness. Nyx's startled orange. And Eris . . . no, she couldn't sense Eris anymore. That made her pause. Damocles and the Archon had been the only ones she couldn't read unless she was touching them.

"Rhea," Clo whispered. Clo drew Rhea's attention away from Eris. The other woman was staring at her, eyes wide. "Ariadne, what's happening to her face?"

Clo was afraid. Her fear emanated in jagged lines, bright blue. Afraid for Rhea, or afraid *of* her? Rhea couldn't tell. *It doesn't matter. It's too late. The damage is done.*

Rhea doubled over, wanting to be sick.

"*Ariadne,*" Clo snapped. "You have those files. Is Rhea sick like the others from the ichor?"

"Use your damn eyes, Clo," Eris said impatiently. She gave Rhea a hard stare. "We have members of Evoli resistance back at Nova. She's clearly Evoli."

No, not that. You would be blessed if you were Evoli. You're the opposite, a small inner voice told her.

Clo's gaze felt heavy. Too much. All their emotions crawled across Rhea's skin like insects. She kept pushing and pushing and pushing it all away—protecting herself from the jagged edges of their judgment—and everyone in the barracks physically backed away from her.

She was controlling them, offering no choice but to feel and to do as she commanded.

Rhea curled into a ball, covering her face with her hands.

"Rhea?" Ariadne. Her soft steps tiptoed closer.

Back! Rhea thought, as loud as she could. Before, she'd only been able to moderately influence emotions. Had they heard her thoughts or just the wild surge of fear, rage, and revulsion she felt for herself?

Ariadne retreated, stumbling in her haste. Dust rose from the floor of the barracks, glimmering gold in the shafts of sunlight. Everything seemed suspended: sound, movement, time. Rhea's whole body was hyper alert, her skin tingling.

It was this place: this toxic planet filled with rock that felt alive. She wanted to go back to the ship, watch the stars with Clo, pretend everything was normal.

Someone else tried to approach, but Rhea threw her hands up, palm out. *Leave. Get out!*

Unable to resist the influence of her abilities, the others wordlessly left the barracks—except Eris. Eris remained by the door, her expression shuttered. A part of Rhea wanted to touch the other woman, learn more of her secrets. How could she—

No. She wouldn't try to force Eris out with the others. If she used her abilities at all, it was for comfort, to make things easier back in the Pleasure Garden. To smooth minor day-to-day interactions. But she had to be careful. Push too hard, and she had the power to influence their thoughts, decisions, movements. It made her no better than the Oracle—just someone else to control them. Steal their choices.

She'd just proven it.

"The ichor is enhancing your abilities?" Eris asked, her voice strangely flat.

Rhea nodded. "I can't . . . I can't control myself." At Eris's silence, Rhea asked, "How are you still in here?"

"Trained against Evoli mind techniques. I have more skill than most." Eris let out a small breath and glanced out the window. "Get it together. They're worried."

Rhea sensed the others outside. Their fear battered her like phantom fists on the grimy windows. They would have so many questions—and they deserved her honesty. Rhea bit the inside of her cheek. She should put her illusion back first, make things easier. But when she tried, she lost control again. Did the ichor interfere? Was she still too afraid? Or did she, deep down, finally stop wanting to hide?

She squeezed her eyes shut. *Think of calm, cool green. Think of lilies. Think of the open expanse of stars with Clo on the observation deck. You still have a whole universe to explore with her.*

Rhea's breath slowed. She bowed her head until her helmet pressed to the ground. She was too exhausted even to draw the illusion over her skin again. Too drained to force the others to stay outside while she tried.

The door to the barracks squeaked open.

Rhea cringed deeper into the shadows as the others entered.

"Rhea," Clo said, her hands up as she approached. Her expression was soft, understanding. "You're fine, Rhea. It's okay."

Clo gave her the courage to come out of those shadows. Rhea rose. Her hands remained by her side, gloved hands balled into fists, as she moved from the dim corner of the barracks into a patch of sunlight. She raised her head, until they all saw her face once more.

No one said a word. Rhea didn't look away. She was aware of what they saw. Her features were the same. In every way, she appeared just as she had before, aside from her skin almost glowing from within and the telltale spiral freckles.

"So," Clo said, voice low. "You're Evoli? Were you a spy on Tholos?"

"No. Not exactly." Rhea doubled over again. "I need air."

Clo nodded and gently grasped Rhea's arm. "Lean on me. You can barely stand."

Everyone moved aside as Clo helped her out the door. She could taste their emotions on her tongue—especially Cato's. His was like a blade sliced through her skin. Hatred. His or implanted? Nyx, as if sensing the pilot's emotions, tightened her hold on him.

Rhea felt better outside the barracks. Losing the ability to hide her skin was terrifying. Her illusion had held up in sleep, during a fight, during sex—nothing had ever shaken it loose except for a conscious decision to show herself.

And now the others knew. If only the rumors about Evoli abilities weren't lies, propaganda made up to sow fear in the Empire. Then she could make them forget what they had seen.

You have to face them. They deserve the truth.

Ariadne hurried out of the barracks after them and took Rhea's other side. "Let me help." Together, Clo and Ariadne helped her to the shuttlecraft. "The others will come around," Ariadne murmured to Rhea. "You'll see."

Rhea thought of Clo. Would she be repulsed? And what about the others? Rhea understood a lifetime of suspicion and Tholosian programming was not so easy to unlearn, even if the Oracle was no longer active in the minds of anyone there. One left echoes. Nationalism cultivated prejudice. Everyone here was fighting against their own upbringing, Rhea included.

Eris was the first to leave the barracks, and the one who stopped closest to Rhea.

Clo edged in front of Rhea. A protective stance. "Keep that blaster in your holster, Eris."

"It's staying," Eris said. "I'm not going to shoot someone for being Evoli, Clo."

"You would have once," Clo muttered.

As Nyx and Cato came outside, a wave of nausea hit Rhea. Cato's emotions were sharp and curved as thorns. His hands were still bound in front of him.

Clo slid an arm around Rhea's waist, pulling her close. "We need to get you on that shuttle," Clo murmured.

"Not yet. Please. I need a moment for my stomach to settle."

Rhea pressed her helmet to Clo's shoulder as the other woman rocked her. She wished she could take the suit off, touch Clo's skin. Press her lips to the other woman's and forget everything. It was a strange reversal—usually Rhea was the one to offer comfort to others. To soothe their fears and worries so they could leave the Pleasure Garden and go back to their roles in the unyielding machine of the Empire.

"You're not angry? Or afraid?" Rhea asked.

Rhea had held on to this secret for so long. So few had known about her abilities. The Archon. Damocles. Juno. The Oracle. Ariadne, only recently. Damocles had loved to use her skills as a tool for pleasure for himself. As a weapon against her. The Oracle couldn't command or program Rhea, so Damocles had kept her hidden, locked deep in the Pleasure Garden.

His caged bird, unable to fly.

Clo's arms tightened around her. "Angry? Gods, no. Surprised? Aye. But I'll get over it. We have Evoli working with us back at Nova."

"I'm not Evoli," Rhea said, gently pulling away. "I'm not Evoli," she repeated to the others, this time more strongly.

"You look like a fucking Evoli to me," Cato muttered.

Nyx and Eris turned to glare at the same time, but it was Eris who said, "You'd do well to remember that Rhea is the one who begged for your life. I almost had Nyx put a Mors blast through your skull."

"And I wanted to comply," Nyx added.

Cato pressed his lips together and glanced at Rhea. His emotions faded slightly, uncertain.

Eris nodded to Rhea. "Go on. Tell us."

Rhea took a deep breath, tried to form the words. There, in the bright sunshine, on a floating island above the rocky surface of Ismara, her secrets fell free. "I look Evoli, but I wasn't lying when I said I've never left Tholos. I was engineered in a Tholosian lab—part of a very small, experimental cohort personally overseen by the Archon. His goal was to hack Evoli DNA, access their abilities, and use it to weaken them." Rhea shifted away from Clo. "They made multiple attempts at mixing our DNA with the Evoli. The Archon's engineers still don't understand how I'm the only one who survived."

"So, you're a spy?" Cato asked with a dry laugh. "And I'm the one tied up."

Nyx glared at him. "You're about to be the one with a broken nose if you don't shut up and let her finish."

Rhea shifted uncomfortably. "He's not exactly wrong. I was created for the purpose of one day infiltrating the palace of the Evoli Oversouls. The intel I could gather as someone perceptive to their empathic abilities would have been invaluable; the Archon hasn't been able to get anyone into that palace because it's too easy for them to detect a Tholosian mind."

Cato stared at her in disbelief. "That goes against everything the Empire believes. I would have expected them to kill you on principle. They would never have allowed you to live."

Nyx moved as if to hit him, but Cato held up his hands. Though the worst of the programming was gone, he still had a lifetime of being told the Evoli were evil, something to be destroyed for the good of the Empire.

Cato's face contracted with some emotion, the sheen in his eyes breaking for an instant. He looked at Rhea like he actually saw her. Unfogged by the Oracle. His shoulders hunched as he pulled against his bonds.

Rhea shook off Clo's comforting touch. "They let me live because I was engineered to help destroy the Evoli," Rhea said to Cato. Her voice barely wavered. "That's the only reason."

"It makes sense from a military standpoint," Eris said. Her voice was soft, but the expression on her face was tight. Rhea wished she could touch her again to catch a glimpse of her feelings. "Create someone loyal from birth, who can't be compromised. But you were never programmed by the Oracle."

"I couldn't be. They learned from an earlier testing group that Evoli abilities are incompatible with programming."

"Unless they've had a brain injury," Eris said softly, her expression inscrutable. "But for the most part, yes."

Rhea frowned. Now, more than ever, she wondered about who Eris was before she became a member of the resistance. How did she know so much about the Evoli? How did she withstand Rhea's abilities?

"But you affect emotions," Nyx said, drawing Rhea from her thoughts. "It's how you helped Ariadne deprogram me." Nyx's face was implacable, but Rhea felt the other woman's unease. "And you can control people. Why didn't you just escape Tholos on your own? Why did you need us?"

"The Archon and Damocles are mostly immune to me." Rhea bit her lip. She decided not to bring up Eris, despite her questions. "And influencing more than one person at a time takes too much concentration. I usually have to be touching them. The amount of ichor here seems to be making the difference—I'm not usually so . . ."

Out of control, she almost said.

Rhea kept her walls up, trying to keep their emotions separate from hers. Her heart hammered. Keeping the illusion was like having a layer of dried paint on at all times. She felt strangely free.

"I guessed who you were," Ariadne admitted. "When you knocked Cato out with your abilities. The Oracle had files on the Evoli DNA experiments and mentioned one living child, but she was always referred to as *TBDAM-43425.*"

"Wait a minute, when she knocked me out with *what*?" Cato asked.

"You were going to kill Ariadne," Rhea said. "There are still bruises on her neck, Cato."

Cato quieted, his expression flickering with shame. But his unease remained. Rhea couldn't read thoughts, not exactly, but she'd guess he was wondering if there was much difference between Rhea and the Oracle. If Rhea wanted, she could make Cato throttle someone against his will, too. But only one at a time. There was an Empire of difference between her and the machine, she wanted to say.

Rhea kept looking out at the hills, away from the others' scrutiny. The view was so peaceful, marred by the ichor threading through the floating island beneath her feet. Wind rustled through the trees as it swept down onto the floating island. Rhea wished she didn't have her helmet on; it would make breathing so much easier. She was still nauseated, and her body trembled.

Nyx frowned. "What does *TBDAM* stand for? That's not the usual cohort naming system."

"No, it's not," Rhea said quietly. "It means—" She bit her lip.

Ariadne finished for her: "It means To Be Destroyed After Mission."

They all fell quiet.

Clo hissed in a breath and pulled Rhea close. "Salt," she swore. "I hate them. *I hate them.*"

"We should go," Eris said, businesslike once more. "Sher's supply ship will be here within the hour. Commander Talley"—she paused, cleared her throat—"he said the Tholosians would return for the rest of the ichor. We need to leave this quadrant before that happens."

"Oh!" Ariadne brought a hand to her mouth. "Oh, oh, oh, *oh, damn.*"

"Nyx," Eris said, "you speak fluent Ariadne, right?"

"Yep. Means she's just thought of something shitty. What is it, kid?"

Ariadne's hands started moving as fast as her mouth. "It's just that the ichor made the miners sick, *and* was used to kill a bunch of people in experiments on other planets, *and* Rhea being around it also made her drop her illusion. So . . ."

Rhea went cold. "The truce," she said. "Thousands of people will be attending to celebrate the supposed end of the war. Evoli spies would be exposed if the ichor works on them like it did on me. The Oversouls will be there. The *Ascendant* will be there."

"The truce is a godsdamned lie," Clo confirmed. "The rock isn't just a projectile; it's going to spread the disease and kill everyone in the palace."

"Not just the palace, Clo." Eris's fingers curled into fists. "Think bigger. If Damocles starts a pandemic, it'll be everyone on Laguna. And we just gave him the weapon to do it."

42.

Present day

Nyx hated the silence.

She was beginning to realize how much she appreciated the camaraderie of the women around her. They hadn't been a team for very long, but she had grown used to a ship full of chatter and bantering, of Ariadne's music and Rhea's dancing, and Clo and Eris's verbal sparring. This, she realized, was what it was like to be around people free of the Oracle: their bond wasn't something programmed or forced. It was chosen.

But choice made it tenuous and fragile.

Clo and Eris were avoiding each other. Whatever history was between them went deeper than Nyx had suspected—something that made them both grieve. Rhea had kept to her rooms and hid from the others and their emotions.

Partly your fault, Nyx thought to herself as she and Eris unpacked the supply cache Sher had sent in silence.

Ariadne and Rhea had picked apart Nyx's programming, but like Cato, Nyx still heard a litany of the Oracle's voice in her mind, reflections of old commands hardwired into her brain since birth. Undoing a lifetime of Evoli prejudice wasn't easy. She couldn't hide those emotions. And Rhea had heard and felt all of them.

Nyx scratched absently at the shallow cut along her shoulder where she'd stumbled in the Ismaran cave. It was like some small, universal rebuke for the pain she'd caused Rhea. A reminder of what her friend had gone through.

Eris looked up from unloading the food, weapons, spare disguises, and uniforms. She seemed exhausted. None of them had slept since leaving Ismara. "You should get Cato to look at that. Put some healing ointment on it."

"I'm not going to waste our medical supplies on a scratch." Nyx shook her head as she stacked the bags of food. "I'm concerned about Rhea, Eris. She felt my emotions toward the Evoli back on Ismara."

The other woman let out a breath. "You can't help the echoes of your programming, Nyx."

"Maybe not. But it's *Rhea*."

"Listen to me," Eris said. "If you still had the Oracle in your mind, you would have held a Mors to her head. Being deprogrammed doesn't mean you erase what the Oracle said and did to you; it means you can make the choice not to pull out the gun. Rhea knows that."

The echo of a sharp cry down the hall made them pause. Cato. Another deprogramming session.

Nyx's deprogramming had taken place in Rhea's room in the Pleasure Garden, where anyone might have heard such agonized cries. Rhea would turn music on. She'd touch Nyx's skin—which Nyx now recognized as the other woman using her abilities—and even that couldn't dull the pain entirely. Lasering the thorns from her flesh had been nothing in comparison.

Ariadne had broken Nyx down into little pieces and built her back up into something different. Eris was right: once the Oracle had left her thoughts, answers weren't easy anymore. They weren't commands that repeated through your thoughts until you were certain—*absolutely certain*—that every action was for the glory of Tholos. Those old orders were just memories to be ignored.

Her mind, now her own, was sometimes too quiet.

"I wouldn't have even questioned what we saw back on Ismara, would I?" she asked Eris, afraid of the answer. *Needing* the answer.

"No." Eris's voice was surprisingly gentle. "You wouldn't have."

Nyx couldn't stop thinking of those skeletal faces, the withered, flaking skin and twisted fingers, reaching out for help none of them could give. An entire planet thrown away. Not a large planet, or populous, but its purpose was clear: it was an experiment. The beginning of something larger. The soldiers who left them there weren't just following orders—they were programmed to think their actions served the glory of the Empire.

Another of Cato's screams echoed down the hall.

Eris wordlessly hefted a bag of food onto her shoulder. "I'm going to take these to the canteen. Tell the others we're having a meeting in an hour."

"Eris?" The other woman paused at the door. "How was Rhea able to control everyone but you back on Ismara?"

Eris didn't look at her, but Nyx saw the tension in her shoulders. In the end, the other woman only released a soft breath. "Get some rest, Nyx. You'll need it."

———

They all gathered in the command center.

Eris stood in the middle of the room, with the others congregated in a rough semicircle around her. Clo stood the farthest away, her scowl fixed firmly on Eris. Eris's expression was carefully composed as she gazed back, but Nyx noticed her fingernails dig into her palms.

What are you both hiding? Nyx thought.

The secret floated over those two like a specter, and Nyx sensed her unspoken question wouldn't be answered. That chafed. Their lives were in each other's godsdamn hands, and the tension made these walls unbearably claustrophobic. What if the group ran into danger again? Secrets like this could be fatal.

And Clo clearly didn't trust Eris—not entirely.

"After what we saw on Ismara, I've come to a difficult decision," Eris said, her voice ringing clearly across the command center. "We're going to continue this mission without the resources at Nova. That shipment we just received from Sher will be our last. Starting now, we go dark."

"That's salted." Clo took a step forward. "We only have eleven days until the truce ceremony on Laguna, Eris. The Tholosians are going to slaughter thousands of people, and we still have no way in. We don't even know how Damocles is planning to smuggle ichor into the ceremony." She shook her head sharply. "No, we need to get Nova on this. We need backup. We need help."

Eris grimaced. "I think Nova might be compromised."

Clo froze. "*What?*"

"Think about it." Eris spread her arms wide. "All our undercover operatives have been exposed, a lot of them caught and executed before they managed to escape. The last spy ceased communication *just* after she sent information that *Zelus* had left Tholos with the shipment of the ichor. So, either the Oracle has somehow gotten into our systems or someone at Nova is feeding the Tholosians our intelligence. But I'd bet my life on it not being safe." She let out a long breath. "Right now, Sher and Kyla are the only ones who know about our mission and that we're getting close to a plan involving a coup. It has to stay that way. The second we involve the rest of Nova, we risk losing the element of surprise. We need to keep this to ourselves. The co-commanders agree with me."

Clo glanced around, her teeth worrying her lip. "Unless we've accidentally indicated we know already. We accessed the Oracle's files on Ismara."

Ariadne's eyes went wide and her hands flapped. "You think I messed up?"

"You didn't mess up," Nyx interjected. "For gods' sake, Clo, don't just throw around accusations like that. Ariadne isn't an amateur."

"I *know* that. I'm not throwing around—"

"*Stop.*" Rhea's command echoed across the command center. "I sensed Ariadne's emotions on Ismara. She was confident, and I trust her."

Everyone went quiet at the reminder. Nyx looked away, hoping Rhea didn't see the flash of shame in her features, and hoping that she couldn't feel it now that she wasn't surrounded by the ichor. Rhea endured Nyx's lingering programming, all that prejudice commanded from birth. How could she even stand to be in this room with her?

I'm sorry, Nyx wanted to say. *I'm so sorry.*

"Okay," Clo said, drifting closer to Rhea and taking her hand. "I'm sure you're right."

Rhea went still at Clo's touch. Rhea's face shifted to a frown and she gave Eris a hard look. *You have so much blood on your hands*, Rhea had told Eris back at the barracks.

Nyx's hands curled into fists. *And so do you, Nyx. Don't be a hypocrite.*

The reminder made Nyx scowl. "You two." Nyx gestured between Clo and Eris. "Can you get over whatever the fuck you're fighting about, please?"

"Not that simple," Clo said. She shot Eris a look that burned. "I need to know one thing: will you kill him? If it comes to that? I'm not trusting you with a mission that has no oversight from Kyla or Sher until I have your answer."

Who? Nyx frowned, catching equally baffled looks from Ariadne, Rhea, and Cato. Something to do with Eris's past in the Tholosian military?

"Yes." Eris didn't hesitate. A soldier's ruthless response.

"Fine, then," Clo said, sounding not remotely fucking *fine*. "We do this without Nova."

Eris nodded once. She turned to Cato. "Update me on the body. Anything we should know?"

Cato had gone back into the mine's medical center and retrieved Commander Talley's body in an airtight body bag. It had been brought on board, quarantined in one of the unused crew quarters that Ariadne had turned into a makeshift lab. With the air vents sealed off, Cato examined the body in a full suit after resting from his deprogramming session. Nyx had heard Eris snapping orders at him through the comms.

After a few tense hours, he joined the others waiting in the command center for news. The scent of disinfectant still clung to him.

Cato let out a slow breath and scratched his cheek. "A few observations," he said. "The endospore found in the ichor is pretty impressive from a biological-warfare standpoint. When I opened Commander Talley up, deterioration had spread to his lungs—a result of breathing in the spores. Frankly, I'm shocked he lived long enough to speak to you."

"And they experimented on how to transmit this illness more quickly on those other planets," Ariadne added. "I showed Cato the files, and we came up with a theory." She nodded at him, encouraging.

"If the ichor were ground up and pressurized into a gas, the endospores would cover large areas very quickly. It'd kill a lot of people very fast." Though Cato's voice remained steady, Nyx caught the flicker of anger in his features. He was at the part of his deprogramming where he found it difficult to hide his emotions. The Oracle wasn't there to numb them, wasn't there to run the code that told him this was all for the glory of Tholos. The haze of coded loyalty was gone.

Get used to it, soldier, Nyx thought. Having choices wasn't easy.

"Great," Clo muttered.

"Oh, it gets worse," Cato said. "Ariadne and I think—*think*—that the version of ichor the Tholosians experimented with in the labs can be spread by close contact rather than a one-off illness caught through the lungs. They're engineering a godsdamn plague."

Eris made some soft noise. "So, if Damocles wanted to conquer an Evoli planet . . ."

"They'd be fucked. He'd have it within hours."

Nyx swore softly. There were a million Evoli on Laguna, and more would be arriving for that truce ceremony—thousands of Tholosian citizens among them. All they had to do was release a gas and watch the chaos.

And if it got back to the Karis Galaxy—and the Evoli home planet, Eve—Damocles would end up killing them within weeks. Every Evoli eradicated. Their planets empty and ripe for the taking. The Tholosians' food problems solved and a new galaxy to claim for their own.

Just another Tholosian conquest.

Clo looked ill. She squeezed Rhea's hand. "But there will be Tholosians there, too, won't there? Would it spread to them just the same? Even Damocles?"

Rhea lowered her lashes. "The first thing Damocles would have done is to develop an antidote for himself and the most important people there. Avern, maybe he even invited some higher ups to Laguna as a tidy way to assassinate them. As for the others?" She sighed. "He would have weighed his options, called them sacrifices to build a better Empire. The God of Death takes before He gives."

Nyx recalled her games of zatrikion with Damocles. Nothing mattered to him more than power and winning. The lives of any Tholosian citizens caught in the balance would be worth the price. After all, the God of Death did not discriminate. Evoli or Tholosian, souls were souls. They all weighed the same.

"Damocles is already expecting Zoe to return with improved specs for Clo's weapon," Eris said. She shook her head and gave a soft swear. "I'll try and charm more information out of him and come up with an excuse to take the weapon back for testing. Then we'll see if there's a way to neutralize the ichor."

"If you're right about a leak within the Novantae," Rhea said, "then Damocles will be more careful. He may not give up information about the ichor if he suspects someone is onto his plan."

"Another Impossible to Infiltrate job." Eris locked eyes with Clo. "My favorite. Cato, can you isolate the compound? Find out how it's different to the original spores?"

Cato hesitated. "Not exactly my expertise, but I can try. No promises."

Ariadne grinned. "Cato, look at you! You're like a pilot medical expert badass!"

The pilot's expression went vague. "Yeah. Except that I don't know where one of those things came from."

"The Oracle tampers with memories sometimes. Or maybe you have a glitch in programming that gives you medical knowledge! I could open your skull up to—"

"No." Cato put his hands up. "Absolutely not."

Nyx's lip lifted. "What? You afraid she'd cut open that big head and find a rodent in a spinning wheel instead of a brain?"

Cato glared.

Ariadne, ignoring this, considered Cato. "Since you've chosen our side you can be on our team now. We still need a team name." She tapped her lower lip with a finger. "It'll come to me."

The pilot ran a hand through his hair. "Look, I'm still fighting against this voice in my head that says I ought to turn you all in. But I can't pretend I didn't see that shit back on Ismara." He gestured to the door. "By all accounts, that Tholosian commander I just dissected was loyal. They still left him there to die."

I get it, Nyx wanted to say. She wanted to tell him about the times she pulled the trigger and she wasn't sure the Tholosian on the other end deserved it. But she never questioned. She followed orders. Played the good soldier. The Oracle's voice in her head made it so simple to block out the questions and the doubts.

Then she'd met Rhea, and she saw the other woman's bruises, and she couldn't pretend anymore.

Rhea approached the pilot and held out her hands. Though her skin had lost the Evoli-like fractals revealed on Ismara, Cato still flinched away. "May I?"

Cato let out a dry laugh. "Don't trust me?"

"You just admitted you were still tempted to turn us in, and your hands are no longer tied," Rhea pointed out. "This is a precaution. It's not personal."

After a hesitation, Cato gave a small nod. Rhea placed her hands on his stubbled cheeks and closed her eyes.

Cato flinched.

Rhea's fingers pressed firmly to his skin. "I know. I know this freaks you out," she said. "You don't have to be ashamed, Cato. You're making a choice to help now. That matters." Rhea released him and stepped back. "We all have pasts in the Empire we're atoning for."

Nyx still couldn't help but feel shame too. All of them had to admit the ways in which they were complicit. Programming or not, they participated. They helped. They were small but important parts of the Empire. There was no forgetting. No forgiving.

"I don't want to atone," Nyx said, surprising herself. "I want to destroy the Empire."

Clo's hands closed into fists. "Yes."

The others nodded.

"Then we do it together," Eris said, gazing at each of them in turn. "Planet by planet. We burn the Empire down."

43.

Present day

Eris hoped this was the last time she ever had to become Zoe. It would be a relief to finally put the arms merchant to rest for good. She hated looking at the shifter mask she wore, the carefully braided hairstyle, the clothes that were meant to draw attention.

The loose, airy dress that showed more skin than she was comfortable putting on display. Everything Zoe wore was for show: gold shimmer glistened across her eyelids, contrasting with deep black lipstick; her few makeshift weapons: the little jeweled rings on her fingers, sharp enough to do damage, a hair stick plated in gold that could puncture a vulnerable throat.

Eris stared at the thin metal tips of her rings and imagined ramming one into her brother's eye.

No. She had to keep him alive for information.

For now.

Zoe was a role she had taken over when she had less of a conscience, an extension of General Discordia without the expectations and the rules that had governed her behavior as Heir to the Archon. It had been easier when she let her anger and grief for Xander consume her—it had still been so raw, so new.

Being cold, heartless Zoe Eirene-X-2 didn't come easily anymore.

One final time, she told herself.

Eris turned her back on the mirror. Her gaze landed on Xander's small firewolf carving—the only thing on the table beside her bunk. She ran her fingers over the small figure.

"I'm doing my best, Xander," she whispered. "I wish you were here with me."

But she couldn't even bring her talisman with her. Zoe's clothes wouldn't allow it. No fucking pockets.

With a sigh, Eris returned the firewolf to the table and left for the command center. Clo didn't speak as Eris took her seat in the copilot's chair. The silence from the other woman reminded her of those days after their last mission, when their relationship had fractured as irreparably as Clo's leg.

Eris had hidden so much from Clo. She wondered how different their last mission would have gone if she had been upfront about who she was. Maybe it would have changed nothing.

Maybe it would have changed everything.

"The person I lost . . . his name was Xander," Eris said, not returning Clo's look. She took a deep breath before continuing. "He was one of my brothers, but he was different from the rest. Kinder, more compassionate. The way he died . . ." She couldn't finish. "You asked me if I'd be willing to kill Damocles, and I want you to know: if I get the chance to put a blast through his head, I'm taking it."

Clo nodded once. They went past the Three Sisters's checkpoint and waited in the queue for clearance into the royal palace's airspace.

"Be careful," Clo said finally, gazing down at Macella as they waited for security clearance. "*Zelus* is getting indications that the Oracle's security on Tholosian planets has increased in preparation for the truce ceremony."

"You're concerned about me?"

Clo pressed her lips together.

Eris almost smiled. She'd take that as a *yes*.

Rhea entered the command center and approached the captain's chair. "Are you sure you don't want me to come along instead of Ariadne?" she asked Eris. "I can keep the soldiers calmer and more acquiescent."

Ariadne and Nyx, back in their servitor disguises, were the only ones accompanying her. They had to do this fast, without complications. Fewer people were less of a risk.

Eris shook her head. "I don't want to risk Damocles recognizing your abilities."

"It's just that Ari's nervous," Rhea confided in a whisper. "With the Oracle on high alert . . ."

"I need Ariadne there *because* the Oracle is on high alert. She's the only one who can get around One's security mechanisms."

Clo's eyebrows went up. "You sound like you're expecting trouble."

"I'm always expecting trouble. That's what makes me good at my job." She glanced at the monitors. "They're giving you permission to land."

Clo followed the air lanes down to the same hangar they'd gone through before. She wisely made sure to dock near the exit. It was busier this time, with merchants and suppliers ferrying supplies for the peace talks. All was the bustle of gerulae and mechanics scurrying along the ships like worker ants. Cogs in the greater machine.

Eris tried to stay focused as they followed the security guards up to the palace, Ariadne and Nyx flanking. Eris stared at the soldiers. They would obey no matter how abhorrent their orders. If Damocles told them to shoot all three women in the head, they wouldn't hesitate.

For the glory of Tholos, they believed.

Even though she'd been there recently, it still felt strange for Eris to breathe in the air of a planet she had once considered home. It was impossible to describe, yet it was so familiar, she'd recognize it anywhere. It was fresher, greener than the stifling-hot air of Nova. Sometimes, she missed the gentle scent: the trees swaying in the wind, the cool air coming off the distant sea. Nova demanded too much. It wasn't for the weak. And sometimes, in her quiet moments working with the resistance, she pretended she was right back here: in the palace square, breathing in the scent of sea salt.

That grand palace rising above them, made up of the bones of creatures her forefathers had slaughtered, was a symbol of everything this Empire stood for. Everything they worshiped. Letum, Bel, Rem, Salutem, Phobos, Algea, and Soter. Death, War, Honor, Survival, Fear,

Agony, and Salvation. The glory of the Empire and sacrificing to their gods were all that mattered. She couldn't let herself forget.

"Negotiare?" The guard's voice made Eris jump. She hadn't realized she'd stopped.

Ariadne's voice sounded through the Pathos: <*Is something wrong?*>

<*No.*> Eris straightened her shoulders as she followed the guard once more. <*I'm just distracted.*>

<*Better get undistracted,*> Nyx muttered. <*I worked my ass off not to die here.*>

Eris was surprised when the guard led her to the private wing of the palace. The compound had changed so little since she had left. The same shining floors with no speck of dirt. The walls carved with scenes of their many conquests, offerings to the Gods of Death and War. The views from the portholes and the particular tinge of purple entered the overhead lights this time of day, to better complement the coming twilight. How could she still miss a place so horrible, that had caused so much pain?

She risked a short prayer to Letum herself, for despite everything, Death was her patron. Her fingers automatically went to her throat but found only the delicate gold chain of something Zoe would wear, rather than her scythes.

The gods would not help her there.

The guards posted outside Damocles's room snapped to attention as she approached. "General Damocles is expecting her," Eris's escort said.

The one to her left spoke in a rough, firm voice. "Just her, then." He gestured to Nyx and Ariadne. "These two can wait in the Star Rise Room."

Eris had expected this. With the tightened security, no unnecessary detail came in or out of these rooms.

"Of course," Eris said pleasantly. She took the case with the schematics from Nyx. "Don't annoy the nice guards, ladies."

<*Be careful,*> Ariadne said.

As Ariadne and Nyx were escorted away, the doors slid open.

Damocles sat at a table laden with food. Eris sucked in a breath at the sight of it all, but she schooled her features into polite interest.

There were so many delicacies she hadn't been able to eat since she'd fled this planet. Piles of sugar pears glistening in the soft light. The long, thin tendrils of the Mussuma fruit cut into perfect rounds, its violet flesh begging to be eaten. There was no rehydrated protein in sight. Fresh meat, creamy cheese, skewered meats, freshly baked bread. All foods that would go into rationing now that their resources on Charon were devastated.

Unless, of course, Tholosians were able to access the Evoli planets—by either truce or death.

Eris couldn't afford to make a mistake.

The room itself was similar to her old quarters. Gigantic bed with a canopy of the royal arms. A chandelier of twisting, shifting holographic lights mirroring the colors of the sunset outside. Smooth walls and floors softened with rugs of living, russet-colored grass. Everything was tasteful, expensive. Completely devoid of Damocles's actual preferences and personality. Eris doubted he spent much time there at all, except to sleep.

"General," Eris said. "How lovely to see you again. And in a much quieter setting."

Damocles stood and Eris bowed as etiquette demanded. It smarted to bare the back of her neck to him. If she hadn't abandoned her true rank, he would have had to bow to *her*. She could almost feel that ghost next to her—the person she would have been if she hadn't left it all behind.

Her brother studied her. "You look dressed for a ball, Zoe. I should have mentioned I preferred for us to meet in private."

Eris knew he had done that on purpose. To unnerve her, throw her off balance. It was a show of power—nothing more, nothing less. "General, I think you'll find I'm *always* slightly overdressed," she said with a laugh. "I'm an arms dealer with expensive tastes. I like to be the fanciest woman in the room if I can." She threw him a smile and turned to the large windows. "I see you didn't exaggerate your description of this view the last time we met. I don't know how you manage to get anything done with a sight like that."

How long since she had seen a sunset on Macella? The whole world looked blue, purple, and orange. The mists lay over the ground, the skyscrapers and mountains peeking above and touching the sun as it dipped toward the horizon. Above, the two moons of Macella glimmered, half-full. The bright twinkling planets of Tholos and the smaller Agora, the other two Sisters, were visible in the sky. She hadn't realized she could feel homesickness standing right at the heart of her old home.

"Easy," he said, coming up behind her. "I'm usually on Tholos, and I don't work in here. It's too much of a distraction."

"Smart man."

"*I like to be the smartest man in the room,*" he said, mimicking Zoe's accent.

He was too confident, and she needed him more unnerved. He was impulsive when he was emotional; he tended to reveal too much.

"Humble, too," she said smoothly. "One would never have thought you originally the—" When his expression hardened, Eris stopped talking. "I'm sorry. I didn't mean—"

"You can say it. I didn't earn my title, not by skill. My sister did. I was only the Spare."

There we go. Still bitter. He couldn't escape the echo of being second-best.

"General," she said, sounding regretful. "I'm—"

"Stop talking," he interrupted. "Sit. Eat."

Damocles had always had mercurial moods; his favors came and went on a whim. She needed him upset enough to be desperate to prove himself at the reminder of his sister. Not angry at Zoe for doing the reminding.

So, Eris did the only thing she could do. She shut up and settled in the chair across from him, trying to slow her hammering heart.

Everything tasted even better than she remembered. She forced herself to keep her table manners, but she wanted to scarf the food down. How she'd missed Tholosian soups, silky smooth against her tongue. The feel of tearing into properly cooked meat with a rich sauce. Spreading melting sage butter onto still-warm bread. It was almost too much. She was grateful for the med cuffs that matched Zoe's outfit. As long as she held the first bite in her mouth for a few seconds, she'd know whether or not it was poisoned.

Damocles watched her, his face betraying nothing until she finished. "I apologize for my earlier rudeness, Zoe."

Eris almost let out a sigh of relief. The pendulum had swung back. Progress. "It's all right, General. My thoughtless comment deserved that response."

"Then why don't we make up by finishing our game of zatrikion?"

Eris paused, trying to keep her expression steady. Playing with him last time had disarmed her more than she was willing to admit.

The last thing she wanted was that board between them again, but there was no refusing. She forced a smile. "Of course. I'd be delighted."

Damocles motioned to the guard, who went into the other room and returned with the elaborately carved zatrikion board. Eris kept quiet as Damocles set the board as it had been the last time they played, and they both resumed the game.

"So, you've brought the improved schematics with you," Damocles said, shifting a piece. "I'll have my engineers reproduce the design and send you payment."

Eris stole one of his pieces. "Aren't you going to look at them? Test the weapon?"

She needed him to bring it out—if not to come up with an excuse to take it back under the guise of more improvements required.

He raised an eyebrow. "Do I need to?"

"You have four royal guards stationed at your door"—another piece was hers—"a legion out the front, and you've sent my assistants to another room. So, either you enjoy the presence of military and think my employees are as useless as I do, or you've increased security."

Damocles sat back, a small smile playing on his lips. "Very astute, Zoe."

"Pirates know a thing or two about security, General. I just thought you might like to verify my work."

He made a move and took one of her pieces, but she was still winning. "I have every confidence your new schematics are more impressive than your prototype. You wouldn't want to disappoint me, would you?"

Eris tried to stay calm. He was confiding in her; that was the important part. "Never," she said lightly. She took a breath and risked it: "I take it you don't trust the Evoli to remain peaceful."

Damocles watched as she made another move on the zatrikion board. "What would you say if I signed the truce and didn't honor it?"

And there it was. *Damocles, you're still so easy,* Eris thought.

"I'm a mere merchant, General. My opinion matters little." When his expression made clear that he expected her opinion regardless, Eris gave an answer that made her sick to her stomach: "If my weapons killed every last Evoli, I'd lose no sleep. For the glory of Tholos, and *you* as its future Archon. My loyalty is to you."

Eris hated saying it. Zoe, both the dead one and Eris's alias, would not have cared. She hated this part she had to play in degrading people from another Empire, and she hated how convincing it sounded. Because Eris had been taught her entire life that their lives didn't matter, that the Evoli were necessary sacrifices to keep the God of Death sated.

But Eris also knew that her brother's self-worth came from loyalty, from being seen as deserving of his place. The flare of satisfaction in his eyes was proof.

"And if they were the Evoli Oversouls?"

"I would be the first to congratulate you on your new conquest," Eris replied.

So, it wasn't just a coup. Rhea had guessed right: he planned to assassinate the Oversouls. The weapon could fire blasts but also disperse gas projectiles. It'd work with pressurized ichor. The weapon wasn't large. It would be easy enough to hide. He still had three, maybe four shots left before Ariadne's failsafe kicked in.

Eris anticipated Damocles's next moves the way she would in the game before them: he only needed an excuse to go to Laguna, get close enough to target one person—perhaps the Oversoul, or even just a straggler celebrating the truce. Hit them from afar. It might not even hurt. That poor Evoli would stagger into another, perhaps a bystander looking to help. Diseases spread so easily that way. No one would know that all it took was one projectile in a weapon.

Damocles's gaze flickered up to hers as he stole another one of her pieces. "Have you ever seen copies of the restricted Old World books in the Ancient Library?" At her confused expression, he explained.

"Before my grandfather perfected the Oracle's programming influence on all Tholosian citizens, some of the ancient texts were digitally copied and smuggled out of that library on data storage units. Literary pirates," he added, leaning in as if to tell a secret. "There's a reward for every copy found, of course, but a few of those texts still remain in circulation. I suspect they were acquired by the Novantae to inspire their pathetic little band of rebels."

He was right, of course. Kyla acquired every book she could find on those rare old data units. Literature had been restricted since the second Archon spread the Tholosian Empire far beyond that which his father had acquired, and that emperor ruled ruthlessly. Information was carefully controlled, and literature became relegated to a single library and accessed only by those approved by the royal family. The Archon's thinking was that if you controlled what people read, you could control their ideas.

After the Oracle was designed, and One's program was downloaded into the brains of every lower citizen of the Empire, there was little need for such a heavy ruling hand. Only a few were born with the natural resistance to buck programming—those like Kyla and Sher, and every child born with the potential to become the next Archon—but a vast majority of citizens would never, ever pick up a book to read it.

Because the Oracle had programmed them so it would never occur to them that they could.

Eris laughed, as if the idea of reading was ridiculous to her. "Of course not," she told him. Then, she quoted the Oracle's programming: "'There is no purpose to be found in books that cannot otherwise be discovered in the role you were born to fulfill.' I was born in a merchant's cohort, General. Weapons are a passion the God of Death has given me."

Though there was no outward sign of it, she almost felt as if her answer had disappointed him. He moved his zatrikion figure—the Commandant—and took one of her pieces. They were tied. His skill *had* improved.

Angry with herself for being distracted, Eris nabbed her Soldier piece and took one of his. Damocles didn't appear the least bit bothered.

"Well, allow me to tell you a story from one of those books," he said, considering his next move. "It was an Old World religious text, revered by a faction of our early ancestors before the First Plague came to Tholos and wiped out nearly every family except the Archon's. This fable had a parallel, you see. It was about a man named Leonis who was very close to his God, and he alone could see the corruption and violence that had overtaken his people. Leonis's God instructed him to build a ship, in which those he cared for would be spared from his deity's inevitable wrath. Leonis and his family left that planet; their God set fire to the world He created. Leonis's family alone were given a new planet— our Old World. They became God's new children, our first ancestors."

Eris stared at Damocles, trying not to let her alarm show as he shared that tale with a gleam of pleasure in his eyes. What was he doing? She tried to decipher his meaning, his next move, but it was like a puzzle missing pieces. She cleared her throat. "That's an interesting story. I—"

"I'm not planning a battle. Think of this as me picking my chosen. I am burning everything to ash to re-forge the Tholosian Empire anew." His eyes met hers as he moved his final piece across the board and knocked over her queen. "*King kills Queen*, Discordia."

Adrenaline sang through her veins. <*Nyx, get Ariadne out of here.*>

<*But what—*>

<*Damocles knows who I am. Go!*>

<*What the fuck do you mean he knows who you are?*>

"Discordia?" Eris gave him a bemused look. Beneath the table, her hands gripped the chair to force herself to remain seated. Damocles's soldiers were still by the door; she wasn't getting out of there without a fight. "General, as flattering as that is, I'm—"

"Enough games," Damocles snapped. "There are a dozen guards stationed outside that door, and more ready to kill your friends. You lose, Discordia."

Not yet. She didn't lose until the God of Death took her to Avern.

"How did you know?" The words sounded calmer than she felt. How could she be so stupid?

Ariadne's voice sounded in her head: <*We're not leaving you.*>

<*I said get the fuck out of here. Nyx, my brother has soldiers headed your way. Kill whoever you have to.*>

<Wait a godsdamned minute,> Nyx said in shock. *<Your* what?>
<Nyx, just go!>

Damocles rose slowly, his expression even, almost bored. "Oh, I've known since before our first little meeting."

Before? But how could . . . Her gaze fell to the game board, the pieces scattered. Of course. Of *course*. If Nova was compromised . . . "You killed the Novan spies. But you kept my Zoe identity intact, didn't you?"

"The important spies, yes. Enough to ensure they'd assign you to investigate as Zoe. I figured you'd have to bring me an impressive toy to maintain your cover, but that weapon?" He let out an awed breath. "A pleasant bonus that you solved Project Harpy for me. It really is magnificent."

Eris stepped back to keep her distance from him.

"Now, your new friends were a surprise," he said, circling her. "Nyx, Rhea, and the little one. They might have escaped if they hadn't met up with you. I think I'll take Rhea back after I punish her. She's mine, after all."

Eris felt sick. "You let us infiltrate the palace and find those files on Ismara, didn't you?"

His eyes gleamed, as if he were proud of this, proud of outsmarting her in this competition they'd had since childhood. "Come on, Discordia." He clicked his tongue. "You didn't really think you all got this far without me letting you? Without the Oracle being tipped off?" Eris tried to hold back her flinch, but he saw it. "Oh, you did. That's cute."

Eris went still with dread as the trill of alarms sounded through the palace. Ariadne and Nyx were on the run. Could they make it?

<Eris?> Clo's voice. *<What the flume is going on?>*

<Start the engine, Clo. Nyx and Ariadne are coming to you. Get out of here.>

"Where did you get your information?" Eris asked her brother. Was the Oracle just that deep? Had One infiltrated Novantae's systems? Or was there someone in Nova giving him information?

"Not important," Damocles said with a wave of his hand. "What's important is that I have you, I have your weapon, and I have your intent to ignore the truce and slaughter the Evoli on record. Everything that happens now can be traced back to you and the Novantae."

<Eris!> Clo again.

<Leave me here, Clo. I'm not going to let any of you die for me.>

<No. We can't just—>

<Damn it, Clo, for once in your life, just listen to me!>

Eris dove for an antique vase. She grasped the handle, swung, and slammed it into Damocles's face. His guards rushed her, their Mors raised. Eris dodged one blast. Two. She punched a guard in the jaw. Bones cracked beneath her fist, his nose gushed blood. The other launched himself at her, but she lashed out with her ring—one quick swipe across the neck. Dead, bleeding out on the floor.

Damocles was up. He swiped the blood from his face. "You're still quick."

"You're still slow. Might as well call your other guards in and give me a real challenge."

"They know I want this for myself. Test me, Discordia."

Eris and Damocles went for each other, blocking and punching and kicking. Eris had forgotten what it was like to fight against someone in the royal cohort. All the Archon's children had been built for speed, for strength, for the damage their bodies could take. They crashed into furniture, breaking and splintering wood. Eris threw her brother into the table, and that glorious display of food toppled to the floor. Eris shattered a glass bottle and swiped at him. Damocles dodged, smacking her hard in the face with a metal tray.

Stars exploded in Eris's vision. Warm blood trickled from her nose. The ringing in her ears only made the palace alarms seem to blare louder. What were Ariadne and Nyx doing? Would they survive?

Focus. Get up, get up!

"It's better this way, sister." Damocles hit her. Again and again, until Eris's knees buckled. "I'll be a great Archon when Father dies."

He kicked her in the stomach. Eris's breath left in a *whoosh* and she spat blood on the floor. Her sight was blurry as she crawled away from him. Weaponless. That stupid dress let glass cut her legs, the palms of her hands.

Get. Up.

His booted toe caught her under her chin. Eris heard the snap of her jaw dislocating. Pain made her vision go black around the edges.

To someone else, Damocles snapped, "Find out what the fuck is going on out there." Retreating footsteps.

Ariadne. Nyx.

Clo's voice, echoing in her mind. *<Eris? We're going to come for you, all right? Just stay alive. We're coming.>*

As the darkness closed in, she felt Damocles's fingers lift her face. "I hope they tell stories about us, hundreds of years in the future." Then a whisper in her ear: "I'm going to be the hero in all of them, Discordia. And you'll be the villain."

44.

Present day

The soldiers crashed through the door.

Nyx grasped Ariadne roughly by the arm and shoved her onto the floor. She leaped onto one of the soldiers guarding them, slamming her fist into his face as she stole his Mors.

Morsfire blared in the small room as Nyx shot the soldiers in quick succession. *Bang! Bang! Bang!* Three dead. One blast each to the head.

Ariadne remained frozen on the floor. Nyx was so fast. *So* fast. Ariadne couldn't move. The echoes of Mors blasts rattled in her mind and it was too much *bang bang bang bang*—

"Get up." Nyx's grip was gentler as she dragged Ariadne to her feet. With a hand on either side of her face, she forced Ariadne to look at her. "I need you to keep moving. When I say get behind me, you get behind me. When I say run, you run. Understand?"

The alarms clamored through the palace. Ariadne flinched. So much noise, too much noise, too much *too much.* She wanted to scream. At any moment, the royal guards would be there to arrest them. Nyx would be executed. Ariadne would be taken back to the Temple.

Ariadne froze. They were going to be trapped. She was going to be under the Oracle's eye again, and this time, she'd never make it out. This time—

"Ariadne." Nyx shook her shoulders. "Do you understand?" Ariadne nodded jerkily. Nyx shoved her forward. "Then let's go."

Nyx opened the door and peeked out. All clear.

<What's the plan?> Clo sounded alert but not surprised.

Ariadne would have frozen again if not for Nyx propelling her forward. Clo *knew*. She knew that Eris was Princess Discordia this whole time. The fight on Ismara—

<If we survive this, you and me will have a talk about secrets.> Nyx's thoughts were so cold, Ariadne shivered. *<Ariadne and I are going to make our way to the hangar. Load up and clear us a path, because we'll have company.>*

<What about Eris?>

Nyx's hold on Ariadne tightened. *<She told us to get out, so that's what we're doing.>*

Ariadne was shocked, but Nyx sounded *furious*. As a soldier, Ariadne knew Nyx hated surprises and hated secrets among her friends. Ariadne felt the same: If plan A fell through, then plans B, C, D, through Z shouldn't come with finding out one of your colleagues was a dead princess who was once more brutal than her own brother. Contingency plans were difficult enough; they were downright impossible with lies.

<I should have seen,> Ariadne thought as Nyx dragged her out of the room. *<I should have guessed.>*

<Kid, I'm going to need you to do me a favor and focus on not dying. We can deal with Eris's bullshit later. Got it?>

Out in the hallway, the alarms were almost deafening. Soldiers rounded the corner from the main stairwell and opened fire. Nyx shoved Ariadne behind her and kicked a hallway table over for cover. Delicate vases shattered to the floor around them. Ariadne cringed. Too loud. Too messy. She couldn't *think*.

"Eighteen soldiers," Nyx said to Ariadne. "Count my blasts."

"W— Why?"

"Keeps me motivated."

No. Nyx was trying to keep Ariadne distracted. Ariadne felt a surge of gratitude.

Nyx whirled, steadied her gun against the table edge, and fired off at a rapid pace. *One. Two. Three.* Ariadne counted the blasts, focusing on the numbers, the feel of the words formed by lips and tongue.

Four. Five. Six. Seven.

Numbers made sense. Numbers were easy. She didn't have to focus on anything but saying them.

Eight. Nine—

Nyx pushed Ariadne to the ground and covered her with her body as return Morsfire battered the table. Glass from shattered vases cut into Ariadne's legs, but she couldn't focus on that. Any moment, the Oracle would be deploying another line of defense. One couldn't risk Nyx taking out too many royal guards.

This wouldn't work. What would? Think. Think. *Think*! She shook her head as if she could rattle a plan loose. She pressed her fingers to the rug, focusing on textures. This was fine. Focus. *Focus.*

Yes.

Nyx opened fire again as Ariadne counted, her voice firmer this time. *Ten. Eleven. Twelve.*

Texture. Renewed focus. The Oracle would be filling the command...

Ariadne scrabbled at her pockets, shoving two tiny filters up her nose. She'd brought a bunch—just in case—because she knew what Oracle could do. What One's protocol was when things grew too messy. Ariadne grabbed for Nyx.

"What—"

"Just trust me!"

With a soft swear, Nyx holstered her Mors and shoved the filters in. They both clamped their mouths shut.

Not a moment later, the alarms cut off. Ariadne heard the hiss of gas from the overhead dispensers, and a thick haze blanketed the hallway. Down the hall, the surviving soldiers dropped hard to the floor, unconscious but alive. The stuff was strong enough to fell a Lacustrian sea monster.

Quiet. Noise gone. The silence was like an embrace.

Nyx moved her fingers in an indication to go. They crept quickly down the hallway. When Nyx went to move the way they came with Eris, Ariadne held her back and shook her head. *<One will be sending*

the rest of the Royal Guard that way. We're going to have to go another route.>

<So, how are we getting out, kid?>

<Give me a second.> Why couldn't she think now that it was quiet? Logic had been her comfort in the face of chaos.

Soldiers in gas masks hurried in formation through the thick mist of the hallway. Shouts echoed around her.

They broke into Morsfire.

Nyx grabbed Ariadne. *<Run!>*

They kept low, sprinting down the hallway as blasts dotted the walls around them. Was Ariadne feeling light-headed? She hoped the filters were holding.

Numbers. Counting. *One,* she thought fiercely, her lips forming the word. *Two. Three. Four. Five—*

<Nyx! Go right!> The map of the palace emerged from Ariadne's tangled thoughts. Yes. This was the way.

Nyx spun Ariadne into a wall a moment before a shot sizzled the wall where her head had been. Then they were running again, their breath a roar in the quiet hallway.

<Clo, where the fuck are you?> Nyx returned fire behind her.

<Still at the hangar. They've closed up the hatch and I'm playing whack-a-silthole with a bunch of security and this ship's Mors weaponry.>

They rounded another corner, leaping over servants unconscious from the gas. *<Stop wasting the godsdamn ammo and fly the ship to the south side of the hangar. It shares a wall with a wing of the palace.>*

<Uhhh. And then?>

<Blast your way inside,> Nyx snapped, as if the answer were obvious.

<What?> Ariadne asked in shock at the same time Clo asked, *<Excuse me?>*

<Break. Down. The. Godsdamn. Wall. Clo.>

<I heard you.> A pause. *<This is bogging marshbrained. I can't believe I'm going to do this.>*

Up ahead, a door opened, and royal guards burst through. Nyx and Ariadne ducked down and Nyx shot at them in a hail of Morsfire that forced them to retreat. Ariadne felt powerless, dragged along by Nyx, keeping close. She was useless. She couldn't think her way out of this. If more guards came, they'd be trapped.

The ones coming up from the rear were gaining on them. The Oracle was around them. In the walls. How long until One saw through Ariadne's flimsy disguise? Ariadne wanted to cry, to scream—anything but this helpless cowering.

<Get out of the way of the wall!> came Clo's mental shout. <Get out of the way of the wall! Out of the way, out of the way—>

Nyx tackled Ariadne behind a cabinet just before their ship exploded through the wall. Ariadne covered her ears at the screech of metal, the crash of furniture and debris around them, and the yelling of soldiers as *Zelus* mercilessly barreled into the once-pristine palace hallway. Clo mowed down the soldiers who had been chasing them, leaving an empty hallway and a big, gaping hole to the inside of the hangar.

Before, they were traitors. Now they were *palace-destroying traitors*.

The latch to *Zelus*'s cockpit swung open. Rhea appeared, gesturing them inside. "Hurry."

Ariadne was trembling so badly that Nyx practically carried her into the ship. The door swung shut behind them.

Clo was sitting in the pilot's seat, her hand in a death grip around the joystick. "Got out of the way, I see."

Nyx brushed dust off her uniform. "That was an entrance," she said.

Clo laughed. "Well, we're about to make one flame of an exit. Strap in."

Cato was sitting in the copilot's chair. He returned their shocked look mildly. "Pray she doesn't kill us."

Ariadne collapsed into her seat and buckled the belt as tight as it would go. She said a small prayer as she clung to the armrests. Nyx managed it all with a lot more composure.

Alarms blared even louder than before, screeching through the entire compound and in the streets of the Macellan capital. Ariadne shut her eyes. *Shit.*

"Tertiary protocol," Cato said. "Oh, we are *fucked*."

"Be quiet, Cato," Clo snapped. "Everyone strapped in? Good." Clo shoved the stick forward and *Zelus* jolted upward. "Hold on, dipwells."

Was she really going to . . . ? Oh gods, she was.

Zelus burst through the roof of the palace, destroying the entire east wing of the royal compound. Around them, the metal wings of the ship screeched through remnants of the palace, bones, wood, brick, and gold tumbling into the gardens below. With a rev of the engines, the ship jolted through the air.

"Clo." Nyx clutched the armrests of the seat. "I said break down the wall, not break down the *whole godsdamn palace.*"

"I'll take your advice into account next time. Shut up and let me fly."

Unmanned Tholosian military ships launched from Macellan hangars all over the city—One's tertiary protocol in case of foreign invaders. In the wait for more soldiers to arrive, the Oracle sent up ships to attack and quell a possible invasion before it started, and to keep loss of life to a minimum. They were already getting into attack formation in the skies. Never mind the citizens below. No time for them to evacuate. A sacrifice for the greater whole.

They'd be programmed to feel it was their honor to die.

Do something, Ari, she told herself. *There's an answer here. Concentrate. Focus on your numbers, on your counting. One, two, three, fourfivesixseven—*

"Fly through the city streets to evade," Ariadne breathlessly ordered, slipping her hand inside her jumpsuit to grab her tablet.

"The ship's too big," Cato argued. *Zelus* was meant for a hundred crew. "Maybe if we had something smaller . . ."

"Don't remind me," Clo said with a glare. "You're the one who blasted *Asteria* into the aether." She sped the ship up. Not fast enough.

"We don't have time for this," Ariadne snapped. "Find the widest streets!"

"Are you sluiced?" Clo's panicked shout echoed through the command center as she evaded projectiles from the attacking Tholosian ships. "They're streets, not asteroid fields, Ari!"

Ariadne's fingers flew over the tablet as she pulled up the schematics for the tertiary-protocol ships on Macella. "I'm going to try to hack into the ships' mainframe to turn off the Oracle the way I did for *Zelus* when I escaped with Nyx and Rhea. Since it's remote, it won't be for long, but it should give us enough time to run."

"How long?"

Ariadne paused briefly to consider. "Thirty seconds."

"One minute," Clo insisted.

"Forty-five *at most*," Ariadne argued.

"Oh, for fuck's sake," Clo muttered, thrusting the throttle forward. She took a breath as the ship sliced through the air toward the towering tenements of the city. "Say a prayer, marshholes."

Clo dodged more projectiles and swooped through the streets of the capital. Outside the palace's walled compound, the roads were more winding.

"Left, Clo," Ariadne commanded. "Go left!"

Ariadne may not have left the Temple when she lived on Tholos, but she had memorized these streets and many others from the Three Sisters. She had watched vids from every angle she could, desperate for any exposure to the outside world. She saw, in real life, the gleaming cobblestone streets that were filled to the brim with markets and stalls full of fresh produce, baked goods, and glimmering fabrics imported from other planets in the Empire. Macella was a planet for the wealthy, and only the best foods, spices, and garments were shared among its people. She knew from the surveillance that the people had few worries there. Little fear of danger.

"Go through the markets, Clo."

Ariadne's fingers flew across the tablet as she accessed all those vids she had watched—they would help her now, just like they did then.

With a swipe of her finger, she paused the live feed and turned every camera inward to face the bricks of a building. One's dependence on surveillance gave Ariadne the advantage here.

For right this moment, the Oracle was blind—and if One was blind, then One was distracted.

Those in the markets screamed and fled as *Zelus* barreled through their pristine streets, ripping into the upper layers of the market stalls. Tholosian ships came in behind them. Their shots struck *Zelus*'s protective shield. *Bang! Bang! Bang!*

"Projectiles detected," the ship intoned.

"*You think?*" Clo snarled. "Hurry up, Ari."

Ariadne ignored the panicked looks of her crew as she dove into the remote system. She had one chance to do this before the Oracle fixed surveillance, adapted to the invasion, and put up new protections. Worse, One would know it was Ariadne—her signature was too obvious; no one else had knowledge of the schematics for tertiary protocol ships. One would know—

There it was. One had fixed surveillance and was implementing counterattack sequences as Ariadne dug into the code. Her breathing quickened as a *clang!* echoed through the command center and the ship shuddered.

"Damage sustained," the ship's computer said.

"Stop stating the obvious," Clo shouted. "Ari? Update!"

The tablet's screen flickered as One attempted to shut Ariadne out of the system. But Ariadne had helped build this; this system was as much hers as it was the Oracle's. She cut around the code, putting up blocks to slow down the Oracle's processes.

"Daughter," One intoned. So quietly that Ariadne wondered if she had heard the voice at all.

"Stop it," Ariadne whispered as more images flashed.

Her favorite programs. Her collections. Her room. One showed her these things even as One fought against Ariadne's code, trying to distract her with memories of the Temple. Her prison. That lonely place where the only company she'd had was an AI that left trinkets as if that made up for her cloistered childhood.

"Stop," Ariadne said again, trying to work through the chaos around her. Another projectile hit the ship. More damage.

She couldn't do this. She was a failure. The Oracle was always going to win. Her shoulders slumped, fingers pausing. Why try? She wanted to curl up, close her eyes, and block out the world. Wait for the end. The Oracle would likely kill her and grow a new Ariadne from her cells. A better daughter. More compliant.

A burst of blue calmness. Rhea's hand was on her shoulder. Her voice drawing her from the storm. "Come on. Finish it. You can do this."

That touch was enough to give Ariadne a final burst of strength. She shoved through the images the Oracle had put up, laid down the code—

Another jolt through the ship almost knocked her down.

—and with a final keystroke, finished her attack.

The onslaught stopped. She'd overtaken their navigation systems. Behind them, most of the Tholosian ships crashed into agricultural fields outside the city. There would still be deaths, but at least she'd diverted them from buildings and market stalls, which would have meant higher body counts. That would not matter to those still in the line of fire. She'd still helped cause that. *Her fault. Her fault.* Plumes of smoke and ash rose to the sky around *Zelus* as it sliced through another narrow city street. *Don't think. Don't think.*

"Pull up," Ariadne ordered. "Pull up *now* and prepare the ship for a jump!"

With a whoop of relief, Clo shoved the throttle back and the ship tore through the sky up and up toward the stars. She entered the command for the jump, her face focused in grim determination. The ship shook as it prepared to barrel and leap into space.

Rhea's hand settled on Ariadne's other shoulder. Ariadne heard the other woman's voice in her ear: "Well done, petal."

Ariadne closed her eyes and sat back as the ship carried them to safety.

Don't think.

45.

Present day

The ship sliced through space, a speck in the darkness. The endless void of black surrounded them.

Clo kept her head up. *Eyes on the darkness, hands on the controls.*

Her crew stood around her, the quiet in the command center almost unbearable. Ariadne's black skin was beaded with sweat. She was trembling and her eyes were closed, her lips forming numbers in a silent count. Rhea kept her hand on Clo's shoulder, a presence meant to comfort but that only succeeded in making Clo feel numb. Nyx was impassive as ever, as if she hadn't just shot dozens of royal guards to escape Macella—her old comrades. Cato was silent in the corner, looking down at his hands.

They'd left Eris behind.

There had been the perfect opportunity for Eris to betray them all, if she'd considered the possibility. But instead, she had urged them to save themselves, and Clo was fluming *pissed*. Eris was meant to be selfish, not selfless.

Clo had accused Eris of not caring.

She'd accused Eris of being no different than Damocles.

Gods, the shame ate at Clo. She'd left Eris behind. *She'd left her behind.*

"What do we do?" Ariadne asked, perched in one of the command center chairs, her knees drawn up to her chest.

"Simple," Nyx said. "We move forward and we don't look back."

"We just left her there," Ariadne said, her voice small.

"So what? She asked us to." Nyx clenched her jaw at Ariadne's shocked expression. "Don't look at me like that. Eris was the one who sacrificed herself. So, we don't have Princess fucking Discordia on our ship anymore. Excuse me for not getting emotional. She'd be the first to tell me to cut our losses."

Clo shot to her feet. "That's *enough*."

"Oh, it's nowhere near enough, Clo. You knew this whole damn time who she was and didn't tell any of us."

Rhea released Clo's shoulder. "Stop it, Nyx. That wasn't Clo's secret to tell. Eris saved you back there, and you want to abandon her?"

Nyx shrugged. "Maybe she wanted to be caught. Maybe she can convince Damocles to step aside, take up her place, and stop the assassination from within. Which isn't exactly a bad idea."

"She would have told us," Ariadne insisted.

"Would she?" Cato asked from the co-pilot chair, with a pointed look to Clo. He shrugged. "I'd have kept it to myself. She's the one who's worried that Nova's compromised."

Clo's lips thinned. "She's not you, marsh-hole. She trusts us."

"No. She's just a trained general who earned her place as Heir to the Archon with blood." Cato ran a hand through his hair. "I like Eris, or I thought I did, but she's not exactly someone I'd bet on to choose emotion over practicality."

"Look," Clo said with a sigh. "A week ago, I would have agreed. Now? No. She would have told us. She would have given us *that* much." When Cato opened his mouth to argue, Clo cut him off. "Oh, enough of this. Ari, can you communicate with her? See if she's still alive, at least?"

Ariadne shook her head. "If he hasn't removed her Pathos already, she's well out of range."

Clo focused on the command deck. The stars outside the wide glass began to blur. Clo shifted her leg, the prosthetic rubbing against her skin. The last time Eris had done what she thought was best, Clo had lost a piece of herself. She waited for the anger to emerge and crawl across her skin, but it didn't. After holding that rage for so long, she understood that it wasn't directed at Eris for making that practical, ruthless decision to save Clo's life by amputating a leg.

No, that fury had been over a loss of trust. Over the lies.

But Eris hadn't lied to her. She'd saved Clo's life—twice. Clo wasn't about to abandon her.

"Then we operate on the assumption that she's alive," Clo said. "We go after her, and we complete this damn mission. We save the people on Laguna."

"Why?" Cato asked, crossing his arms.

"What the fuck do you mean, *why*?" Clo curled her hands into fists. "Is your programming still stuck? Or are you that heartless by choice? Let me know right now so I can shove your ass out the airlock."

Cato glanced at Nyx, and even she looked uncertain. Clo couldn't fluming believe this.

"Nyx?" Rhea's voice was soft. "You think we shouldn't. I can feel it."

Shame flashed in Nyx's features. "The Oracle's programming would tell me that the Evoli deserve this. That their Empire is as brutal as ours."

"Well, let me cut through that bullshit right now," Clo snapped. "We have Evoli members of the resistance. They had to come to us because the Tholosians are doing everything they can to steal their resources and starve their people. So, you can judge their priests if you want for being brutal to survive, but don't stand there and tell me that thousands of their citizens deserve to die. Thousands of *our* citizens too. This will be a massacre on both sides and Damocles doesn't give a damn who dies."

For the first time since Clo had met the soldier, Nyx looked taken aback. Frayed at the edges. Even Cato had the decency to seem guilty. Clo was trying to understand what they were going through—the lingering programming in their thoughts, the effort it took to fight against it. But they couldn't afford one iota of doubt. Not now.

"I understand," Nyx said, gentler. "But without Eris, we don't have leadership. Laguna is going to be surrounded by security—both Tholosian *and* Evoli. Infiltrating a planet with that level of protection isn't going to be easy."

"It's impossible," Cato agreed. "And how do we know Damocles will take Eris to Laguna for the ceremony? He could have already killed her."

Rhea shook her head. "I know him, gods help me. Damocles has always resented the fact that she earned her place and he didn't. He'll want to make her suffer for it publicly, and she'd be the perfect person to set up for the fallout of any assassinations. She'll be there. He'll make it look like she released the ichor and planned a genocide."

Ariadne curled herself up even smaller. The soft light of the cockpit fell on all of them, making their expressions look grimmer. "I don't think I can challenge the Oracle again."

Clo didn't know exactly what Ariadne had gone through during her childhood, but she recognized that fear that haunted the younger girl's face.

"The Oracle's influence isn't as strong on Laguna," Rhea told Ariadne, her voice gentle. "It's an Evoli planet."

"That doesn't mean One won't be there," Ariadne whispered. "The Oracle will be on the ships. In their minds. And I don't . . . I don't think I'm strong enough to fight."

Rhea drifted closer, resting her hand on the girl's shoulder. "You are. We *all* are. If we were the type to crumble, we never would have risked leaving Tholos to begin with."

"We made it out to *leave*," Ariadne said, uncurling and moving away from Rhea. "We didn't run away to keep going back into trouble. We did it. We helped the resistance. I want to help Eris, I do, but I also want a life."

"None of us want this." Clo spread her arms. "The gods know I'd rather be anywhere but here, but if we allow the Tholosians to assassinate the Evoli leaders, the Empire will grow completely unchecked. It'll be worse than it is now."

"Then we should just tell them," Nyx said. "That's less risk for us."

Cato let out a dry laugh. "I appreciate the thought of *less of a risk*, but unless one of you ladies has any way of contacting the Evoli Oversouls in the few short hours we have before the ceremony, that's not exactly an option."

"You're right," Clo said. "It has to be us."

Nyx snorted. "Five of us? Shit odds. And that's me being generous."

"Seven if we include Kyla and Sher. We may not be able to trust the rest of Nova, but without Eris, we have to bring them in on this." At everyone's silence, Clo let out a long breath. "Listen, this is what we're faced with. I wish we weren't, but we have to save the people on Laguna and we save Eris. We owe her." Rhea nodded, but Nyx still looked doubtful. Clo scowled. "If it were Rhea or Ariadne, wouldn't you do whatever it took to save them?"

"I would," Nyx said. "You know that I would."

"Then we're going for Eris. She bogs me off, but she's one of *ours*. Not theirs. She would do the same for any of us."

Nyx shut her eyes and nodded. "Fuck, but you're right."

"Me too," said Cato. He shook his head and gave a rueful smile. "Gods help me, but I would. After Ismara, I can't go back to the way I was before." There was no trace of cockiness, no uncertainty.

Ariadne nodded. "Okay," she murmured. She let out a rough, shaking breath. "Okay. Count me in."

"Good," Clo said. "First, we figure out how to get past the Laguna checkpoints. Then we infiltrate the ceremony, get our stubborn fluming princess, and stop a genocide." Her face split into a sly smile. "Easy."

She returned to the captain's chair, put her hands back on the controls, and moved the ship faster through the endless expanse of space.

46.

Present day

Damocles had bound Eris's hands so tightly that she couldn't even wiggle her fingers.

She watched her brother give commands in the same sharp way she remembered from when they were children. He sounded like their father, though she suspected that was for her benefit more than anything. When he rolled his shoulders back and glanced at her, it was in the way someone might seek approval. They had fallen into that role for so long, it came naturally—even after three years. Even with her captive.

"Get the medic," Damocles told his soldier. "Tell him to bring his mod kit."

The soldier left and Eris leaned back in her chair. She wouldn't let her unease show; this had been a game her father played once. Damocles would have learned it from him. How much torture could his children take?

Eris had always taken the most.

"You don't need the cuffs so tight," Eris said. "It's not like I can go anywhere."

Her brother sat across from her, crossing his long legs. "You're clever enough to find a way around that."

"I'm not armed."

"I'm not stupid."

Eris raked him with a gaze. "That's debatable."

She didn't even blink before he smacked her across the face. The blow rocked her chair back, but the toe of his military boot stopped her from falling. When she rocked forward, Damocles had her chin in his grip, a hard press of his thumb and forefinger.

"Who do you think our father would be more disappointed by? His second-choice son or his traitor daughter?" His voice was low, almost a growl.

There. She could use that. "Traitor or not, he'd prefer me. He always has."

This time, he snarled with anger when he struck her. His general's ring sliced into Eris's lip and she didn't even wince in pain. She just smiled and licked the blood from her lip. "Still so emotional," she mocked. "Father will think that makes you weak. I can't imagine his disappointment when you became general."

Damocles gripped the front of her shirt and pulled her roughly to him. "He told me none of this was meant to be mine. You were always better, always stronger. And when everyone thought you had died, even our own people looked at me like I was a disappointment. Despite the Oracle's programming. I hadn't earned it. The Empire was given to me."

"And you never faltered," Eris sneered. "You never questioned what you were given. It was a whole lie built on bones and slaughter. We killed our brothers for him."

His face flickered. She remembered the angry boy. She had picked up the pieces, helped him become a man. He wouldn't have even come close to being the Spare, if not for her.

And he knew it.

"Everything would have been mine either way," he said, voice low. "If I had told them all you were willing to give it up for that *weakling*."

"Xander," Eris said, her voice steady. "His name was Xander. My *frater*."

"*Brother?*" He said the word like the shape of it on his tongue was revolting. "Your weakness. Even now, your icons hang on every planet in the Empire and they all think you died in battle, a hero. They don't realize what a coward you are." His lip curled. "I'll show them something different before the end. I'll force our father to choose between us, and the entire Empire will despise you."

Eris's stomach coiled in dread. "Before the end?" She sounded calm. But if he could hear the beat of her heart, he would know she lied.

"Father's time is over," Damocles said. His lips curled in a sneer. "Do you know he mourned you? He'd spend hours kneeling in front of your icons in silence. Now he's growing soft. Maybe it was your death that started it. Making noises with those disgusting creatures about *peace*. Fucking lies. The Empire's resources are drying up. We have the chance to take the Evoli planets, use them for our own, and he chose the easy way because he's a coward too. It goes against our gods, Discordia. We don't share. The galaxy is ours. And he's no longer fit to rule it."

Eris held back a flinch. Even if her father cared about her in his own way, it was destructive. Toxic. The Archon had chipped away pieces of her humanity, thinking that it had made her stronger, but it only made her cruel. If she had stayed by his side, she would have been a callous leader. Worse than her forebears. Worse, probably, than Damocles.

If she had stayed, perhaps she would have agreed with her brother.

It was Xander who had truly cared for her. His affection had not come with pain.

The squeak of wheels on the floor signaled the arrival of the medic. Soldiers were all the same, even those trained in the medical field: same closely cropped hair, the broad shoulders and muscular stature from training and muscle growth supplements. Eyes blank and smooth and hard as river stones.

The cart he'd brought held various instruments that gave Eris pause. Scalpels, body mod kits, drugs. Zoe's features were long gone. She stared at a digital impression of her old face. Discordia, not Eris. Gold eyes instead of blue. Blonde hair instead of black. She'd permanently modified her features after what had happened to Clo on Sennett, she'd known there was no going back. No half measures. She had to become Eris once and for all.

In her old life, Discordia had looked delicate and fine-boned as an Old World bird in the royal aviary. Avern, she looked young. No matter how steely her gaze, there was a sweetness about her face that always managed to fool people into thinking she was compassionate and soft.

They never believed her to be capable of execution until the moment her blade kissed their throats.

She was the Servant of Death. They should have known.

Eris tore her gaze away from the cart and looked at her brother. "You don't have to do this," she whispered.

Damocles moved closer and lifted his hand; his fingertips grazed her cheek. "They'll see Discordia. Your face when Father chooses me. They'll all realize the Servant of Death is a traitor. That war left you a broken remnant of an Heir Apparent." His hand fell away and his face hardened.

He ordered the medic to begin. "The scan showed an object embedded in her cerebrum—must be a tracker. Remove it."

Eris tugged against her restraints, but they held strong. Damocles moved to sit, slow and unhurried. "You can be better than him. You can rule without destruction. Without fear and threat and pain. Don't—"

Damocles paused, giving her a narrowed, assessing gaze. "One last thing," he said to the medic. "When you're finished with her face, take that scalpel and cut out her tongue." Damocles met Eris's eyes. "And don't give her any anesthesia."

Then he stepped back and sat in his chair to watch.

The medic picked up the scalpel, and Eris never gave Damocles the satisfaction of a scream.

47.

Three years ago

Discordia hadn't heard from her brothers in weeks.

Damocles had gone dark before Xander—uncharacteristic of him with only one brother remaining. Xander, who was a better tracker than Discordia, had left to find Damocles's whereabouts. He had promised Discordia he'd leave the killing to her.

You were supposed to send me word, Xander, Discordia thought. *Where in the seven devils are you?*

She tried to focus on her duties, the tedious job of making sure her people were cared for, prosperous, fed well enough, housed decently. Above all, the Archon wanted citizens to become familiar with the last three potential Heirs, the final children in line to be the next Archon. Or the first Archontissa. The Oracle's programming was deeply rooted in nationalist sentiment, in a love of their Imperial family. Their faces blared across the galaxies. Discordia paraded herself as her father's daughter; the likeliest Heir to the throne, by all accounts; beautiful and capable and a hope for the future of the Tholosian Empire.

For a time, her father had let Discordia take the reins of the Empire in all but title. His way of telling citizens that he was confident that of the three children he had left alive, she would be the one to take his place.

Discordia began to make plans for that day. For phasing out the

Oracle. For giving each planet more independence. For giving people choices. She'd have to do it slowly. Carefully. Perhaps, by the time she aged into her role, they would no longer need another Archon, another Heir. The Imperial throne would simply become obsolete—the way old technology did after it had outlived its usefulness.

For now, such thoughts were treasonous. So, she played the dutiful daughter, and the Empire thrived under Discordia's watchful eye. She visited the planets of agricultural workers so they knew her face, her voice, her plans, her commitment. She was heard by those in the galaxy who needed her and worshiped her father and required every assurance that when he died, she would preserve his legacy.

Each thing she did was to distract herself from the fact that her brothers were missing.

She smiled (they were missing). She gave speeches (they were missing). She assured citizens (they were missing). She was her father's daughter.

Discordia would lie in her bed at night, traveling from one destination to another, and hold on to Xander's firewolf. If he were dead, Damocles would have celebrated. If Xander had tracked down Damocles, he would have sent word.

She pressed the firewolf into her palm. *Where are you, Xander? Has Damocles found you? Or did you decide to find him?*

The worry ate at her, until—*finally, finally*—three months after her brothers had gone silent, she received a missive through her inferiors with location coordinates.

I await your word.

Their code, his and hers. Discordia would go to some coordinates under some pretense of it being an order.

This time, it meant he found Damocles.

Had Xander killed him? Or was he waiting for her to finish the job?

She took the single-passenger aircraft and keyed in the coordinates. She suspected Damocles was still alive. Xander was not like her. He couldn't bear the weight of killing. It would be an albatross, heavy on his mind.

Another nightmare to add to Xander's fitful sleep.

The building was quiet when she arrived. It was some old factory on a moon called Pollux—where munitions and other military necessities used to be made before the moon's resources dried up. Xander always directed her somewhere there was little chance of discovery: outposts on backwater planets, abandoned buildings that were no longer useful to the Empire, or his camp set up in a place that was difficult to track.

Discordia pushed the metal door open and stepped into the dark interior. Something immediately felt wrong; Xander always came to greet her.

But as Discordia reached for her Mors, a voice behind her spoke. "Discordia."

She wheeled around, swallowing the gasp in her throat. Damocles stood in the light of the double moons streaming through a broken window, his face hard. Behind him, Xander was bound to a chair, his lips sealed with the gel they used to muffle the screams of their prisoners.

Discordia wanted to dart forward and untie Xander and count his injuries. Each cut on his face would be a small promise: a stab of a blade for each one, a whisper of a threat. Every bruise would have been a finger lopped off, a torture made worse. Discordia had never vowed revenge—such a thing was meant to be above the Archon's Heir. It hadn't stopped Damocles.

She had killed so many of her siblings, but she wanted to make Damocles's death painful. She wanted him to suffer like Xerxes had.

"You caught Xander before I did," she said, straightening. She closed her expression, pulled her shoulders back, and gave him the arrogant tilt of her chin she had perfected on Myndalia.

Damocles shrugged. "I couldn't risk him running again. Thought you might like to join me in finishing him."

"Why is he gagged?"

"His pleas grew dull." He lifted a hand and roughly wiped the silencing gel from Xander's lips. "There. Hello, brother." At Xander's silence, Damocles threw Discordia a look. "Not even a greeting. This one's rude, Discordia. We ought to make him pay for that."

She slipped her hand behind her. The Mors was too obvious; he'd notice her draw and dodge it fast. One of her blades had to distract him first, just long enough to put a Mors blast through his brain. "You never wanted my help killing our brothers before."

"This one is different, though, isn't he?" Those words were charged. Did he know? Damocles flashed a small smile. "Our last. It should be a celebration, shouldn't it? We survived the culling, Discordia."

Discordia eased her hand beneath her jacket and touched the hilt of her blade. "I'm not in a celebratory mood."

"No?" He slid his thumb along his own blade. "That's a pity. I saved him for you. You're going to be my future Archontissa, after all. We all know how this game finishes, who Father prefers." His tone was bitter poison. "Think of this as my first offering."

Discordia didn't dare look at Xander. If she did, she'd falter. Then her chance to save Xander would be gone.

"I won't kill him while he's bound," she said, as if disappointed in him. "Don't deny me a challenge, Damocles. Especially as a first offering."

"Of course." He waved a hand in Xander's direction. "You're free to untie him."

Thank the gods. Discordia kept her steps measured so he wouldn't see her eagerness.

The flicker of gratitude in Xander's gaze almost undid her. *It's all right, frater,* she wanted to say. *I've got you.*

"Tell me one thing first." Damocles's voice cut across the dark room, quick as a whip. Jarring enough that she paused. "Did you really choose this coward over *me*, Discordia?"

Betray nothing.

Discordia straightened, the way any general might when faced with insubordination. "I don't know what you're talking about."

"No?" His laugh was brittle. "So, he wasn't seen speaking to you on Macella? He didn't send you word to meet him here?"

She raised her eyebrows, ignoring the tremor that went through her. Had someone caught them on the cameras in the cloak room she was sure she'd disabled? He sounded mildly interested, but she could hear the edge to his words. Damocles was not capable of keeping his anger reined in for long. He had never been taught to make peace, and her attempts at teaching him strategy had been a source of frustration for years.

But as a priest to the God of Death? He played that role to perfection.

"Weighing my options is practical, Damocles," she said, cool and composed. "That doesn't mean I chose him as my second."

The lie came so easily that Xander went still.

Damocles's laugh was low, like when he managed to make her bleed in the middle of sparring. "Weighing your options," he repeated. His blade shook. "Weighing your options."

Discordia grasped her knife. *"Damocles—"*

She flung the blade, but he dodged it. The clang of metal echoed in the old factory. Damocles's snarl sent a chill through her: "I'm your only *fucking* option. I always have been."

He shoved his blade into Xander's side.

Discordia lunged, her Mors raised, but Damocles smacked it out of her hand. It skittered across the concrete and disappeared into the shadows. She grappled with him. The bloody blade in his hand came down hard, but she knocked it away. Her fist slammed into his face. Again. She heard the satisfying crack of cartilage breaking under her fist. *Good.* Again. Aga—

"Soror."

The strangled whisper made her stop. With a rough noise, Discordia shoved herself off Damocles and knelt beside Xander. His blood was everywhere, pooling around his body. She didn't know where to put her hands. She didn't know—

"Soror," he whispered. "It's all right."

"Shut up," she choked out. "Don't move, *frater*. Just don't—"

His breath grew shallower. "I wish I could have seen you."

"When?" Her voice shook.

"Wearing that cloak as you took your crown." He gasped again. "You'll make the Empire better. I know you will."

"Not without you." She pressed her hands to his wound, and he flinched. Where Damocles stabbed him . . . oh gods, he was going to die slowly. She looked up as her other brother rose to his feet, recovering from her beating. If she'd hurt him any less, would he have stabbed her in the back? "Damn you, Damocles. *Damn you.* Finish him."

Damocles wiped the blood from his face, swaying on his feet. "You stole my first. I'll give you my last. *General.*"

She might have lunged for him again if not for Xander's soft voice. "*Soror,*" he whispered, taking her hand. "You promised. Take me to the Avern, Discordia."

She shook her head wildly. "No. I could still save you, I—"

"You already did," he told her, sliding her blade from its wrist sheath and pressing it into her palm. "You gave me years. Time to cross out my name, Discordia."

The hilt of the blade seemed to burn, but she closed her fingers around it. "I love you, *frater,*" she said.

He tried to say the words back. It would have been the first time anyone had.

She sank her blade into his throat.

And then he was gone.

Discordia pressed a palm to her mouth as the first sob tore through her throat, rough, unintended. Her vision wavered. This ache in her chest, this awful feeling of incompleteness and desolation was grief and oh gods, it hurt. It hurt so much.

"Discordia." Her brother's harsh voice echoed. Damocles stared at her in astonishment and, then, disgust. "Get up. Wipe your face."

Discordia stood, but she didn't wipe away her tears. They were marks of her humanity. Reminders of Xander. Of what she'd lost.

"Get out," she said through her teeth. "You don't get to be here while I say last rites."

"You're not suited to rule—"

"I don't want it!" The words burst from her throat in a roar that broke at the last word. When Damocles only stared at her in shock, she repeated them, lower: "I don't want it. I don't want to be this. Not without . . . not . . ."

Not without Xander.

"*Feelings,*" he spat in disgust. "You would have killed our other brothers for this. You told me that it was a weakness. And then you did this."

"Then kill me." Her hands fisted at her sides. "Do it, you fucking coward."

Damocles's expression went as unemotional as her own when she tried her best. "No," he decided. "Take your crown. You don't have what it takes to rule. Father will see it. I'll prove what's mine." He gave a soft sound of disgust as he looked down at Xander. *No. That's not him anymore.* "Say your last rites, Discordia. When you go to father's palace on Tholos for the coronation, I expect you to be in control of yourself."

He left her there alone.

Discordia knelt beside Xander and did as she promised: she said the last rites that guided him into the Avern. When she was finished, and her voice was hoarse from prayer, Discordia began plotting her escape.

Her revenge.

She was going to make the Empire burn.

48.

Present day

Rhea watched Clo angle *Zelus* out into open space, preparing for another jump. They'd come up with a plan to land on Laguna.

Rhea hated it. It wasn't as elegant as they'd hoped, nor was it easy, but after two solid days of Ariadne trawling through the guest list for the ceremony and plotting likely security scenarios, this was the best chance they had.

Unlawful docking on a Tholosian craft.

Kidnapping.

Identity theft.

And that was just to *start*.

Rhea figured they had already committed at least fifty crimes that were punishable by execution, so what were a few more to add to the list?

She distracted herself by flipping through the Tholosian-approved channels on the vid-screen, searching for any news of their escape on Macella. Nothing. It was as if it hadn't occurred at all. "There's no mention of what happened to the palace on any of these stations," she told Clo. "They're only covering the Archon's speeches about the truce."

"I'm telling you," Clo said, easing the thrusters down to recover from the jump, "Damocles is keeping it quiet. The Archon would drop that fancy parade tour and delay the truce ceremony in a heartbeat if he found out his palace was destroyed by a Tholosian ship stolen by the resistance."

Rhea and Clo were the only two on the bridge. Ariadne was running updates on the ship's computer, making sure all was running smoothly after their mad dash through the labyrinthine streets on Macella. Nyx was with Cato, continuing the last rounds of his deprogramming regime.

Sher and Kyla had called them earlier to help cement the bones of their paltry plan on the most encrypted channel Ariadne could muster. The commanders had agreed to come, leaving a few of their subordinates in charge to oversee operations. With the truce ceremony so close, no one questioned why two Novan leaders would need to go dark for a few days. The rest of the Nova crew were distracted by dust storms, gritty and thick on the surface of their hidden planet. It was all hands on deck to keep the resistance colony powered.

"Then it confirms Damocles is plotting a coup against the Archon," Rhea murmured, shutting off the vid-screens. "And that he controls the Oracle. One would have alerted his father otherwise."

The light from the command buttons played across Clo's face and the buzz of her hair, the tiny scars on the backs of her fingers from countless hours taking apart engines and putting them back together again. Those hands had stolen to be able to eat, held weapons, caressed Rhea's face. Rhea found herself wanting to trace every scar with her own soft fingertips, bring them to her lips, and kiss away the remembered ghosts of pain.

"Do you think this is going to work?" Clo asked, her voice tight as her fingers danced along the controls.

"I don't know," Rhea said. "If Ariadne can block off the comms like she says, then there's a chance. I just don't like that I'm going to have to feel it all."

Clo's hand came off the control, hesitantly reaching for Rhea. Rhea closed the distance and laced her fingers through Clo's. She felt the warmth flow from the other woman and her cheeks warmed in response; Clo felt so . . . *alive*. Unfettered.

"They'll nae like it, but we have to do this for Eris and all those people on Laguna. It's only temporary."

Rhea nodded.

A message from Sher came through the comms. He'd be in their quadrant in an hour and Kyla in three. Clo sent a message back to him, telling him they were an hour and a half away from their target.

<You know what to do if I can't get there in time,> he sent back. <I trust you.>

"Wish I had the same faith," Clo muttered. "Without Eris here, I'm so 'fraid of sluicing this up." She let out a dry laugh. "Can't believe I'm saying that, after all the shite I gave her."

Rhea squeezed her hand.

Zelus picked up speed, weaving through the sky. Clo looked most at home there in the pilot's seat, eyes on the darkness of space, hands moving in that perfect dance. Rhea watched her and knew fighting was not Clo's true calling. Not war. She liked things to work, to fit. To come alive.

Clo's true calling was to fix what was broken.

Rhea rested her hands on Clo's shoulders. The other woman's muscles tensed, then relaxed. Rhea leaned forward and pressed her lips lightly to the back of the other woman's neck. She shivered.

In Clo's ear, Rhea whispered, "Place your faith in me, Clo."

Just before they entered the dark expanse of space, to break apart and come back together again, Clo turned her head and placed a soft kiss on Rhea's lips.

———

Clo hid *Zelus* behind the asteroids as the others joined her and Rhea on the bridge.

Their target was on the way. *Lysicrates*, an embassy ship from Philana, a war-proud planet that raised millions of soldiers for the Tholosian Empire. The ten delegates would be welcomed with open arms to the ball. Arriving with four fewer people than expected would raise questions, but they had their story ready. Ariadne had collected a dossier of information on each diplomat. Kyla and Sher would decide everyone's roles, and which four would be the missing delegates.

"Seven devils, I hope this works," Clo said.

"It will." Nyx's eyes were bright as she gazed out of the window, a hunter about to pounce. "We can't think in terms of failure. We can only hope for victory."

How Tholosian, Rhea wanted to say, but wisely remained silent.

"I'll go, if you need me," Cato said from his perch at the back of the bridge. All heads turned toward him. He no longer wore his uniform, but he stood as stiff and straight as any soldier.

"I'm not convinced you're ready," Nyx said. "Not that we don't appreciate the offer."

With Eris gone and this a military mission, Nyx had taken over command. Rhea had expected Clo to bristle at this, but she hadn't. Clo was more worried about Eris than she let on.

"What's a little identity kidnapping between friends?" He gave Rhea a grin, as if he didn't care, but Rhea felt his nervousness. "You need all of us for this. There are ten delegates and at least ten soldiers guarding them. So, unless you want to put yourself at more risk, take my help."

Rhea had seen so much change in him. Though Cato was working on building himself back up, he no longer recited Tholosian propaganda in his sleep. His military haircut was growing out, shaggy around the ears. He'd been regaining the muscle sapped by his wounds and fever. Rhea had seen this man sob and cry out for death as the Oracle programming dug its tendrils in deeper before the hold finally broke. She didn't know what sort of man he'd be now. Rhea doubted he did either.

"All right," Nyx said. "But stay close. I'll find you a weapon."

Rhea felt a bit of Nyx's pride beneath those words, a warm blue glow. Cato had risen to the challenge. Rhea realized that Nyx saw him as an ally—someone else who had been a soldier and gone through the agony of deprogramming. A kindred spirit.

"Remember," Rhea told the two soldiers. "No deaths."

"What about maiming?" Nyx asked. "Because maiming seems highly likely."

"No maiming unless you *really* can't help it. And even then, only a little maiming," Ariadne admonished, firm despite their fourteen inch height difference.

Rhea almost laughed, until she remembered that Ariadne had seen so much violence in recent days.

Nyx checked the various weapons, then passed Cato a gun and a belt knife. He took them solemnly.

"Five minutes," Clo warned them.

Rhea was nervous; Clo and Ariadne were remaining behind on *Zelus*, which meant she'd be left alone with two people familiar with military missions. Rhea felt like the odd person out, even if she trusted Nyx to lead.

"Right," Nyx said. "Ari, start blocking *Lysicrates*'s comms—they're in range if needed?"

"Just barely." Ariadne's brow furrowed as she concentrated. The rest of the group stayed silent as Ariadne worked her magic. When she finished, she sat back with a small nod.

"Nyx," Clo called. "Let's do this."

Nyx took up station next to Clo, ready to fire *Zelus*'s weapons. The unsuspecting *Lysicrates* came into view. A sleek ship, weaving through the debris of the asteroid belt with ease. The computers ran a scan and returned with a detailed blueprint of the Tholosian craft overlaid with the heat signatures of the crew.

"Twenty souls on board," Clo said.

Rhea held her breath. There was no turning back.

Nyx tapped the options on the screen. "Shuttles are good to go. Kid, will you be able to open the doors to their loading docks if they don't comply?"

"Not even a challenge," Ariadne replied, rolling her shoulders. Sometimes, the girl amazed Rhea. Few others in the galaxy would be able to do what she just did, and she treated it like it was no more difficult than making a cup of coffee in the canteen. "Nyx, I'm about to put you on over their comm system. You remember the codes, right?"

Nyx nodded once, and Ariadne gave her an encouraging wave when she made the connection.

"Attention, *Lysicrates*," Nyx sent to their ship. "This is Commander Hypathia Arktos-2. I'm going to need you to stand down for an emergency. Who am I speaking to?"

"Legate Cognos Philan-49." A deep voice. Firm, authoritative. Ready to fight or die for his honor if need be. "What's the problem, Commander?"

"Emergency code 06933. We've got a busted jump, little food, a glitching navigation system, and we're running out of fuel. Just a bit of a fucked-up situation here, sir."

The legate let out a laugh, and Rhea figured some form of emergency like this must have been common enough. After a short delay came the "Affirmative, Commander. But we have had nothing through our ship's Oracle to verify."

"Less chance of interception by Novan rebels. We had a run-in three jumps back that I've got to report to the general. If you prepare for us on the bridge, we'll brief you."

A long pause. "I don't have any record of Novan run-ins. Did you not report to the Oracle?"

"Our comms are busted for long-range transmissions. We were hoping to use yours."

Rhea hissed in a breath.

"Of course, Commander. In Tholos's name."

"He knows, or suspects," Rhea said. The ship was too far away for her abilities to work, but she was well-trained in spotting lies on the faces of men.

"Oh, we're so burned," Ariadne said as soon as the call dropped. "They're trying to send a distress signal. I can block it for now—"

"Fire," Nyx said, not wasting time.

Clo and Nyx hit *Lysicrates* with electromagnetic pulses at the same time. The other ship shuddered. The crew tried to return fire, but Ariadne had locked onto their system remotely. She was already opening their outer hatches to the loading docks.

"They're trying to get around the comms block," Ariadne warned.

"On it," Clo said, and she and Nyx fired again.

The *Lysicrates* shuddered again, drifting in open space. Clo maneuvered *Zelus* closer, trapping *Lysicrates* with a tractor beam. It was over so fast, Rhea's mind was still catching up. They'd all moved together so seamlessly. Ariadne on comms and systems, Nyx and Clo firing in tandem like two hemispheres of the same mind.

"And that's how you do it," Nyx said, satisfied.

The crew of *Zelus* strapped on their weapons and armor and made their way to the shuttle. Rhea's nerves fluttered. Ariadne would stay on

Zelus, but she had given them sleep canisters—a gentler form of what the Oracle had used on Macella—and their group were all fitted with filters. Even if the soldiers were knocked out, there'd be remnants of their emotions floating through the ship like dust motes—the moment their pride turned to fear and shame.

It might not work in time. And if any were still awake, she'd have to influence them into surrendering. Tholosians didn't give up easily. *Death before dishonor* was a refrain programmed by the Oracle, words etched into the core of their beings.

The thought of influencing them still made her recoil. She'd tried to do it on *Zelus*, the night of the mutiny. But at the first Morsfire, the first bloodshed, she'd lost it. The sight of Nyx taking the soldiers out one by one—no pause, no hesitation—had frozen her thoughts. The pain and death had driven her to her knees. By the time she'd recovered, they were all dead, their blank faces burned into her memory. Nyx's face had been nearly as still, locking away her guilt.

Rhea drew a shaking breath. This time, she'd be stronger. This time, she'd save them.

The ship was close, caught in *Zelus*'s beam but not fully docked. They slipped through the space, and Ariadne opened *Lysicrates*' bay remotely. Their shuttle slunk in and landed. A parasite. An invader.

Rhea pulled her coat around her, cold despite the climate-controlled bay. *Lysicrates* was much smaller than *Zelus*, and she felt closed in, claustrophobic.

Nyx leaned toward Rhea. "Breathe. You can do this."

"Right," she said. It was not her first battle, and it would not be their last. But she couldn't stop the dread that coiled in her stomach. *Breathe. Just breathe.*

Cato and Nyx tossed the canisters into the air ducts. It would only take a few minutes for the sleeping solution to worm its way through the ship.

Nyx gestured for them to move forward.

They made their way through the corridors. Everything was stark. Too clean, too perfect. The hallways were metal, polished, the dim light from above making the chrome almost glow.

The Philanians lived far enough from the Three Sisters that their culture had shifted, but their loyalty remained unshakable, thanks to the Oracle. They prided themselves on two principles: take only what they need; use only what they must. They lived in small, spare quarters, trained long hours, and ate simple food.

Rhea sometimes wondered what they truly thought of the Empire's ostentatious displays of wealth and excess. The delegates were on their way to a lavish feast, with more food than the hundreds of guests could hope to eat. Dresses, robes, and suits that cost eye-watering amounts of money, woven and sewn by people who ate as simply as the Philanians but only because they could not afford anything richer. An evening of shining lights, beautiful courtesans, the full display of the Empire.

They were loyal, but their beliefs were at odds with the Empire's principles. In the past, that would have been enough to plant the seeds of doubt that grew and flourished into a rebellion. Now, even if they harbored hints of resentment, their emotions would inevitably be tamped down by the Oracle.

<Ariadne,> Nyx asked. *<Where are the delegates and the soldiers?>*

<In the bridge, as instructed.>

<Are they moving?>

<Hard to tell.>

Rhea followed behind the others. Nyx and Cato strode ahead with their Mors at the ready. Rhea felt defenseless in comparison. She drew her abilities around her like a cloak, knowing that the fractals would be shimmering at her skin. She fought the instinct to hide them—the effort wasn't worth it.

Nyx was calm, focused, her fear so dampened she likely didn't realize it was still there, hiding beneath the surface. Cato's fear was acute, no longer massaged away by the Oracle. The closer they came to the bridge, the more agitated Rhea felt. Metal sometimes weakened her abilities, if the walls were thick enough.

The doors slid open, and Rhea prepared herself for twenty Mors trained on their heads. For gunfire and screaming and blood. For a repeat of *Zelus*.

Silence.

Twenty soldiers and delegates, sprawled on the ground. Sleeping like the dead. Rhea knelt down, pressed her fingers to the closest man's neck. This would be the legate. He'd receive a gentler fate than the legate of *Zelus*. That death she hadn't mourned.

The man's heart beat slow and steady. He dreamed of someone he loved. Murky, strange, drugged, but the strength of emotion still shone through, clear as a clarion call.

Cato stared down at them, his face rippling with the emotions that washed over Rhea's skin. He'd have known Philanians in the forces. In the features of those sleeping were the echoes of his friends. Soldiers who might have saved his life in battle. They wore their Tholosian uniforms. Cato had so recently worn his own with pride. He'd moved against his own in a way he couldn't explain away. He had already chosen his side on Ismara, but this cemented it.

Nyx made her way around the bridge. "All out like newgrowns still wet from the vat," she confirmed.

Rhea let out a breath, expanded her abilities. The gas wasn't meant to work for long. As Nyx, Cato, and Rhea gathered up the handful of delegates and twenty soldiers, snapping their wrists together with cuffs and loading them into the shuttle, Rhea kept them calm. Kept their dreams sweet.

They programmed the shuttle to jump them far from their location, far from their home planet, even farther from Laguna. Ariadne scrambled their comms but left them more than enough food to last them for a few days. She put the cuff keys in one of the women's hands. They'd wake up groggy, and it'd take them some time to debug the comms.

Enough time, she hoped.

"Thank you," Rhea said as she gathered the DNA samples for their shifters. "We'll use your faces well."

With luck, they'd save a galaxy.

———

Rhea wandered through the corridors of *Zelus*. It was their last night on this stolen ship that now felt like home. Their last night before Laguna. She didn't know what would happen tomorrow, and this uncertainty had plagued her dreams when she had tried to sleep earlier. When she shut her eyes, she saw the face of that Evoli man back on

Macella who had been killed by Damocles, the faces of all the dead back on Ismara, the dead men on this very ship.

It all felt like a preview of what was to come if her team failed.

Rhea sought out Clo, not wanting to be alone. Wanting one night of quiet before they risked everything again. Clo was in the observation deck, just as Rhea suspected, suspended against glass in a sphere of stars. Rhea would remember this place when they left *Zelus*. She'd miss it most.

"Can't sleep?" Clo asked as Rhea settled into the soft chair beside her.

The dim lights of the stars caressed Clo's face, softening the harsh lines. Rhea wordlessly reached up and traced the three moles at the corner of Clo's left eye. A small constellation. Clo shivered beneath her touch.

"Nothing like almost-certain death to ruin a night's sleep," Rhea said. She smiled and leaned forward, as if to tell a secret. "It makes a woman think about her place in the universe."

Clo sighed, wrapping an arm around her. "Don't joke about that."

"About what?"

"Dying. You haven't even seen an ocean up close yet. We've still got a universe to explore."

Rhea smiled and rested her head on Clo's shoulder, wanting to burrow herself in the other woman's warmth. She smelled of ardmint gum. After a few moments, Rhea tilted her head up, and Clo bent to meet her.

Their kiss was gentle, barely a brush of lips. Rhea's tongue flicked along Clo's lower lip, until Clo opened her mouth. Their kiss deepened. Thoughts fled, and Rhea focused on the taste, the smell, the feel of Clo.

Everything.

She wanted to memorize this moment. She wanted to forget about tomorrow. She wanted to stop time.

Here, now, this was what mattered: Rhea's fingertips moving along the strong muscles of Clo's back, exploring the coiled lines of her body; her hands moving down, down, down to the dip of Clo's waist; the other woman's movements echoing her in a mirror image.

Tonight. Tonight mattered.

Rhea dipped her head and ran her tongue along the line of Clo's jaw, flickering at the soft flesh where her neck met the bottom of her ear, feeling the pulse point there quickening. Clo groaned low in her throat. Her fingertips left burning trails along Rhea's jawline, down the column of her neck, along her collarbone.

More. More, more, more.

Rhea drew back. With a conscious decision, she dropped her illusion. Clo watched as the markings appeared on Rhea's skin, unfurling like moonlight across the slopes of a landscape. The pale cream almost glowed against Clo's golden bronze.

"You are so beautiful," Clo whispered, and then there were no more words as she traced the marks upon Rhea's neck with her lips.

Rhea's skin grew brighter, a torch lit from within. Clo's arousal fed Rhea's own, and this dual desire was almost too much to bear. Rhea pressed Clo against the unbreakable glass that separated them from the vast abyss of space. The other woman's legs fell open, and Rhea settled between them. Their torsos pressed together, their hip bones fitting against each other.

Rhea kissed Clo again, taking her time, unrushed. Her hands traced Clo's sternum, the underside of one breast, lower, lower.

Clo's hand caught hers. "Are you sure?"

Rhea pulled back at the unexpected question. But Clo's expression was somber, her eyes seeking. Rhea wasn't certain. A part of her wanted to wait, wanted that patience she had never been given before Clo. And the other part reminded her that she might die tomorrow in Laguna. And they'd never have this chance again.

Rhea let out a breath and settled her cheek against Clo's chest. "I said . . . that eventually I could tell you what it was like for me. In the Pleasure Garden."

Clo's heart thudded beneath Rhea's cheek. "Yes."

"Ask me," Rhea whispered.

Clo caressed Rhea's shoulder, the calluses on the tips of her fingers rough against Rhea's skin. A reassuring touch. "I'm asking."

"It was a nightmare that pretended to be a dream," she said, gazing out at the firmament of stars as she listened to the steady thump of Clo's heart. "It was cruelty always wrapped in courtesy and kindness. Yet there was connection there. My fellow flowers in the Pleasure Garden and I took bits of freedom for ourselves. Sometimes, it was with clients who were looking for their own escape. But it never lasted. Honey always turned bitter. And we endured, and we hated, and we didn't let ourselves hope. Because hope would crush us even more. So, we gave our pretty smiles. We danced for them. We did everything they wanted, and asked for nothing in return. We let ourselves disappear."

Clo's fingertips traced small circles along the small of her back. Rhea closed her eyes, letting herself revel in the feeling.

"We don't have to go any further than this," Clo said. "What do you want, Rhea? Tell me, and I'll give you as much or as little as you need."

"I don't want to disappear," Rhea whispered. She sat up again, shifted from Clo's lap. "Undress me. I want you to see me."

After only the barest hesitation, the mechanic's clever hands removed Rhea's clothes with utter care until they were piled on the glass at their feet. Then Clo returned her hands to her lap and simply looked. She drank Rhea in like nectar. Rhea felt her desire, but it was softened now. Tinged with wonder and awe.

No one had seen Rhea like this—not even when she'd been put on display. Their eyes had slid over her. In the Garden, she'd often felt like a means to an end. And they had never seen her as she truly was. Not like this. Every marking was truth written on her skin.

And she no longer had to hide.

"Let me see you," Rhea whispered.

Clo undid her shirt, button by button. Rhea took in every inch of skin as it was unveiled. Her vest fluttered to the floor, and she wore nothing to support her breasts. More scars spidered from her right shoulder, down her bicep and forearm.

"I fell in the Snarl," Clo said, as Rhea traced the marks.

She twisted, the muscles moving beneath the wings of her scapula, showing her ribs and the lines and dents of newer scars, only just fading to white. "Shrapnel, from the mission on Sennett. With Eris."

Clo shed the rest of her clothes, revealing a smattering of small scars that turned deeper and led to where puckered skin met the hard metal of her prosthetic. Gods, she was beautiful. Strong. She had endured so much before she met Rhea; the geography of her scars was proof of that.

Clo returned Rhea's appraisal with one of her own. They stayed like that in silence. Not touching. Only looking, memorizing every detail. Taking each other in.

Clo asked her for nothing. Expected nothing.

After a while, they donned their clothes once more. Clo grabbed bedding from one of the rooms and arranged them on the floor, a soft nest of blankets and pillows under the stars. Clo fit herself against Rhea's back, slid an arm around her waist, and pressed a gentle kiss to Rhea's neck. Surrounded by the warmth and comfort of Clo's body, Rhea's eyelids grew heavy.

As she fell asleep, she prayed to all the gods that this would not be her last night with Clo under these stars.

49.

Present

The two co-commanders of the Novantae had arrived.

Nyx stood at attention when they entered the bridge, her instinct to give a Tholosian salute to her superiors. When she realized where she was, she froze, hand in the air.

Kyla offered a small smile, as if to say, *I know the feeling.* "At ease," she said, grasping Nyx's hand. "It's nice to see you alive. Good work on Macella."

"Bit of a shitty exit in the end, but I always did hate that palace."

Kyla looked confused. "Wait, what?"

Behind Kyla, Clo shook her head rapidly and cut her fingers against her throat. *Oh, right.* Rhea had mentioned that the Tholosians were keeping news about the destroyed palace a secret. If the Evoli caught word about an attack, it might potentially undermine their peace cere-mony. "Uh, nothing. Never mind." She turned to Sher and grasped his hand. "Sir. Pleasure to meet you off screen."

"Likewise." Sher glanced at Clo, who smiled back sheepishly. "Don't give me that look, Alesca. You failed to report you had a Tholosian pilot aboard, and Kyla had to talk me down from handing you your ass. Take me to him."

The co-commanders of the resistance interrogated Cato for a couple of hours. Nyx didn't envy him that; answering questions after a round of deprogramming was like having metal nailed into your skull. And they couldn't leave him on the ship on Laguna, not when they needed all the help they could get.

After, they clustered in the command center, where Ariadne was hard at work readying the shifters for their new faces. She had already spent hours putting together a plan based on the layout of the palace on Laguna. Nyx had to hand it to her: that kid knew how to multitask like nobody else. At sixteen, Nyx had barely been able to plan which trousers to wear in the morning—and they'd all been the same damn trousers.

Ariadne pulled up the blueprints for the Laguna palace and projected the three-dimensional image in front of them. The palace was so vast that it took up most of the space in the center of the room.

"How did you get these?" Sher asked, visibly impressed.

Ariadne gave a dry laugh. "That was the easy part," she said. "The Evoli sent them to Tholosian officials so they could coordinate security. Both empires will work together to scan and search any ship that comes into port, and they'll flag anything that looks suspicious. So, if Damocles has the ichor and the weapon prototype with his entourage, they'll be hidden somewhere the scans won't pick up."

"I don't know about the blaster, but the ichor will be in a sealed container," Cato said, his focus on the ship manifests Ariadne had up on the computer screens. "Probably disguised as something every ship would need but in a quantity that's not suspicious."

"Food tins?" Nyx suggested. "They're sealed."

Cato shook his head. "Maybe, or fuel tanks. I'd put my scratch down on that, myself. But there would be thousands to look through. It'd be impossible to pin it down."

Everyone deflated a bit at that.

Rhea came forward, her hands clasped in front of her. "I can't help with the ships or security, but I'm an expert on Damocles. He loves being the center of attention." She nodded at the projection. "His plan will be very public, likely during the truce signing. If I know him as well as I think I do, he'll have an ichor antidote for his team—and Eris, too. He'll want her to be alive for the fallout after he leaves Laguna. It'll be easy for him to frame her for the slaughter."

"Then we can't let him leave," Nyx protested. "He'll take Eris with him."

Rhea nodded. "Yes, probably. Keeping her as a prisoner would give him better control over the political narrative later. He can paint himself the grand victor."

Nyx studied the digital image of the palace. The compound was massive, practically its own little village. There were over fifteen hundred rooms, according to the blueprints. Nyx felt a moment of doubt. There were only seven of them—and one of their own had already been captured. They'd failed once.

"Then we need a distraction," Nyx murmured.

"Exactly," Kyla said. "Something to throw off his plan, smuggle out Eris, and take attention away from all the pomp. Cloelia, that'll be our job."

"I ken that look." Clo gave a knowing grin. "What are you thinking?"

Kyla casually opened the pocket of her utility belt and pulled out a small metal orb. "I'm thinking we give them a show."

Clo's smile vanished and she made a face. "No. No, no, *no*. The last time we used smoke bombs in the simulation session—"

"I know. You were picking pink sparkles out of your hair for months. But sometimes, simplest is best." Kyla shrugged. "They're pretty, distracting, and will work just long enough for the others to make their move."

"That salted glitter was why I re-buzzed my hair," Clo muttered. At Kyla's eyeroll, she added, "Dinnae give me that look. You're going to make me crawl through more vents, aren't you?"

"And I'll come with you." Kyla pointed to the walled square that made up the palace gardens. "I know a bit about Laguna from our intel, and the carrion lilies on the grounds apparently have a bloom so large, you can sit inside them, but their pollen causes allergic reactions in most Evoli. On bad days, they seal the buildings from outside air and circulate purified air through large, roomy vents. You and I will set off the smoke bombs from above the ballroom while Sher grabs Eris in the melee."

Nyx crossed her arms. "And what about the weapon Damocles got from Eris? He'll use it to frame her. Like Rhea said."

Ariadne gave a cough and everyone turned toward the youngest. "I'll find it," she said. "The problem is I'd have to access the Tholosian mainframe through one of the royal fleet. The blaster won't be labeled in the mainframe, but it has internal coding for the sequencer that requires access to the Tholosian system. If Damocles brought it to Laguna, I'll know where." She swallowed. Nyx felt a surge of protectiveness. The kid was putting on a good front, but she was scared shitless.

"*That* I think can also help with," Rhea said with a smile, wiggling her fingers. She'd felled Cato with a touch, but he'd been injured and sick from infection. They all had to hope it worked on Oracle-coded soldiers who were at full health.

"Once we're in the system, it shouldn't take long," Ariadne said, clearly aiming for more confidence than she felt. "Hopefully."

"Good," Kyla said. "Because looking at the manifest of ships coming to Laguna, this seems a likely candidate for storing the blaster and the ichor." She drew up schematics of *Eleuther*. "It's the fueling craft coming in with Damocles's fleet, and it's one of the biggest ships coming in to dock. You can access the nearest mainframe computer through the east storage bay. I'll send you and Rhea the layout."

"What if despite all of this, the plague is still released?" Rhea asked.

Clo let out a breath. "Me and Ariadne talked about that." She held up small devices—metal circles the size of her palm.

Sher raised his eyebrows. "You stole my spharias?"

Nyx was damn impressed. Spharias were dead handy and hard to get ahold of. Nyx had used them before when her quadrant needed to take refuge somewhere uninhabitable. Set up in a circle, they created a mini atmosphere for a few hours. Useful when people needed to do work on a planet or moon with thin or no oxygen but didn't want a bulky suit. How in the flames had the Novantae managed to get ahold of these?

"I *borrowed* your spharias," Clo corrected. "We can make a perimeter around the area to lock in the epidemic. Hopefully, it won't come to that, but it means the rest of Laguna might survive."

"Remind me to give you a raise," Sher said.

"In that case, why don't we start with a new ship?" Clo said, pocketing her spharias. "Ariadne blasted mine and then it jumped down a wormhole."

Ariadne turned from her computer and gave a sheepish smile. "You did give me permission. Anyway, from the monitors, it looked like *Asteria* was already pretty beaten up."

Clo looked offended.

"Nyx and Cato," Sher said, thankfully before Clo could start ranting about her beloved blasted *Asteria* again. "You take the spharias and create the perimeter, then go into the palace for backup duty. If Ariadne warns us the weapon is in the ceremonial ballroom, steal it, cause a scene, I don't care. Just prevent the ichor from being released. Clear?"

Nyx nodded, already deciding which weapons she might be able to sneak in under her delegate silks. She had a few things the scans wouldn't pick up.

A *beep* sounded from the computers.

Ariadne hurried over to the screens. "The shifters are all set!" She held up the devices. "Who's going first?"

———

Their ship was hailed easily into Laguna.

Spacecrafts had gathered from all over the galaxy to celebrate the truce, and each one was carefully scanned and searched for weapons. The only difference between those ships and this was the kind treatment given to the delegates' stolen faces.

Clo let out a soft whistle as she navigated them toward the Laguna palace's hangar. "Look at that."

Light drones glittered across the night sky and formed the shapes and patterns of birds in flight—symbols of freedom and peace. They lit up the thousands upon thousands of revelers, their burning torches casting a smoky, orange glow across the landscape. This was not to be a formal, somber setting for a truce. It was a celebration on such a massive scale that Nyx could barely see the ground through the throng of people. As they flew in, the beat of drums and ecstatic song grew loud enough to penetrate the metal of the ship.

"All these people," Rhea whispered. Nyx knew her unspoken words: if they failed, so many of them would die.

"Focus." Nyx was glad the word sounded confident. She tried to project certainty rather than her fear and unease.

Clo landed *Lysicrates* inside the hangar and expelled a breath. "Okay. Let's do this."

Outside, the crush of people felt as thick as the throes of battle. If Nyx were carrying guns at her belt and the heavy military coat around her shoulders, she would have felt more at ease. But her clothes were the flimsy, formal silks of the upper class. Too light, odd against her skin. She hated how easily air flowed through when she moved.

The crowds around them whooped with glee, thousands of voices rising up in a song she didn't recognize. She was overwhelmed by the bright colors of Evoli clothing, by the flashes of bronzed skin, the streams of lights overhead that lit up the walkway to the palace. Paper lanterns burned bright in the sky as they rose up to the triple moons that felt aligned for this very occasion.

Apparently, the Evoli viewed the sign of alignment as a symbol of great changes to come. To the Tholosians, it was an omen of terrible things. The God of Death would be seeking satisfaction tonight.

"Well, I've never been in a crowd before, and now I can definitively say that I do. Not. Like. Them," Ariadne said.

Her delegate was a woman a decade older than Ariadne, and the kid pitched her voice slightly deeper in an effort to sound older. Her disguise wouldn't mask her age to anyone who cared to look closely enough.

"Neither do I," Kyla added.

Sher seemed nonchalant. "Feels a lot safer than a battle." He leaned closer to Ariadne. "I don't like crowds either."

Nyx guessed that being wanted on hundreds of planets for crimes could definitely make a person feel uneasy among too many people. Her priority was Ariadne, the girl who had lived her entire life sequestered in the Temple with only artificial intelligence for company.

<Deep breaths, kid,> Nyx said. <Inhale on a three count, exhale on a three count, and focus on that asshole's back. The one wearing purple.>

Nyx watched Ariadne as they inched down the walkway. The crowd grew thicker as people cleared different checkpoints. They would have to split up soon, but not before the worst hit.

Ariadne took a deep, deep breath and exhaled, just like Nyx had instructed. <That's it,> Nyx said. <One, two, three. One, two, three.>

Ariadne's hand found hers and squeezed. Nyx wasn't someone who comforted. No one came to her if they wanted to feel less afraid. She was thorny and prickly and not . . . good. Or kind. Not like the others. Not like Rhea.

But godsdamn it, when that kid looked up at her with a grateful smile and said, "Thank you," Nyx understood why people did shit for each other. For comfort. For that look. For trust.

"Rhea, you make sure to take care of her," Nyx said.

A pat on her back. A flow of comfort. "With my life. And she'll take care of me."

Nyx didn't respond. She knew that Rhea would do what she could, but Rhea wasn't a soldier. That mind manipulation might work for an untrained guard, but anyone who had gone through a round of mental resistance techniques might be able to block it.

Nyx shook her head. *Focus, soldier.*

They were nearing the crowd coming in from the docking bay, which meant they were about to split up.

Clo's voice sounded through the Pathos. *<Almost showtime, bermholes.>*

Nyx let out a breath. *<Nice rousing speech there.>*

<Very encouraging,> Kyla added dryly.

<The troops might need more positivity, Alesca,> Sher said.

<Good luck, don't fail, don't die,> Clo said. *<There's your rousing speech. Nyx, you know where to drop the spharias, right?>*

<Got the map burned in my retinas,> Nyx said. *<Rhea, Ari, once you find out where that weapon is, you haul ass back to the ship, you understand? Same for Clo and Kyla.>*

<You don't want us in the palace?> Rhea asked.

<No. The less people we have in that room, the better. Because if I see an opening to take out Damocles, I'm doing it.>

Like Nyx, Clo seemed at ease with the people around them, the crush of the throng. Ariadne still held Nyx's hand, so overly focused on her breathing that Nyx wondered if she heard them speaking at all.

<Just letting you know,> Clo said to Nyx, *<if I sense a mire, I'm going in that ballroom after you. Understood?>*

Nyx nodded and turned to Ariadne. "Okay, kid. Time to go."

Ariadne's hand tightened in hers and she swallowed. "All right." Her voice was faint.

"Hey." Nyx reluctantly released Ariadne's hand. "Rhea's got you. Stop shaking. Be brave." She wished she had better words than that, things that didn't sound like commands.

Rhea smiled down at Ariadne, as serene as ever. Nyx envied that, how even when Rhea was worried, she managed to comfort those around her so easily. Nyx was all thorns and instinct.

<You both be careful,> Nyx told Kyla and Clo. *<I don't want to mourn any one of you.>*

Goodbyes were too much for her. Without waiting for a response, Nyx turned on her heel and merged with the rest of the crowd. She didn't bother pausing to see if Sher or that annoying pilot were following.

Cato caught up with her. "That was almost maternal for you."

She didn't look at him. "Shut up."

Sher hesitated before he separated from them. "Finish the spharia perimeter. I'm going to see if I can grab Eris and stop Damocles from getting anywhere near that dais. If I can't, wait for my signal in the ballroom."

Nyx nodded and let out a breath. "Let's do this."

50.

Present day

Ariadne felt like she was crawling out of her skin. In contrast, Rhea was as cool and composed as a statue. Sensing her agitation, Rhea reached out and took her hand, squeezing once before she released it. The touch soothed the itching beneath Ariadne's skin like a balm. The fear was still there, but she could choose to ignore it.

"I wish I could do this myself," Ariadne whispered. "It must be nice not to feel afraid all the time."

"The rest of us put up a good performance," Rhea said, with a new tension lurking in her eyes, "but we're afraid too. There's no shame in asking for help."

They were quiet as Ariadne turned Rhea's words over in her mind, trying to block out the roar of the crowd around them. Then she squeezed Rhea's hand. "Thank you," she said quietly.

Rhea nodded once with a small smile. "Come on, now. Chin up. Pretend you belong."

Ariadne's delegate had been three inches taller, so there were lifts in her shoes—the mods could only do so much. It was strange to be that tall, to have mods alter her body. She wasn't certain she liked the fit.

Ariadne hoped that no one recognized their stolen faces as they made their way down the path to where the Tholosian military ships would be parked. A safe-enough distance from the palace. Completely unarmed ships, or so the Tholosians pretended.

The uniforms they wore reminded Ariadne too much of her own wardrobe in the Temple. She could almost taste the sludge the Oracle gave her for every meal. Ariadne tried to breathe through it, like Nyx had taught her, but the filters in her nose itched. The one in her throat was tight and scratchy. She wasn't fully convinced these would protect them against the ichor's spores, but since they didn't even know where to start trying to develop an antidote, Cato said they were their best shot.

As they drew closer to the security checkpoints, Rhea and Ariadne fell into their role: they walked with immaculate poise, hands clasped behind their backs. Perfect, professional delegates.

They passed through several security scans, and Ariadne's manufactured identity cards worked each time. She still held her breath, certain that they'd see right through her. She'd never been a soldier. She'd just been another tool for the Oracle to use. Each checkpoint brought them closer to her tormentor.

Ariadne knew she'd have to challenge the Oracle. Face her maker.

She was still reeling from the team's panicked escape from Macella. Gods, she thought she'd grown so strong. But the short glimmer of One's presence on the screens around the framework had turned Ariadne into a small child again, cowering at the commands of an AI who acted as the only mother she had ever known. Rhea's touch had given her courage, but Ariadne knew One would not risk losing again.

The Oracle would be planning One's next move.

Watching, waiting for the opportunity.

Rhea subtly nudged her; Ariadne's posture had wilted. With effort, she forced herself upright again and made eye contact with the soldiers, offering that imperceptible nod they gave each other.

She'd made these soldiers, just as surely as the Oracle had. How many of them would recognize her voice without its disguise? It had been her voice over the comm on every ship, in every home. It had been her voice crooning in their minds as they slept, urging them to lie back, close their eyes, clear their minds, just before One ripped through their neurons and made them perfect killers.

The Oracle hadn't wanted a distinct voice, even when Ariadne suggested it. No, One had learned Ariadne's own voice—her inflections, her tics, even the rhythm of her breathing—and kept it as One's own. Stolen it and turned it cold.

Ariadne fought to keep her expression even.

Rhea must have noticed, because she brushed her shoulder against Ariadne's. "I don't know about you," she said casually, "but after this, I'm planning another dance party."

Ariadne choked back a laugh. "You mean where you make out with Clo the whole time?"

"We didn't make out. We—"

"Gazed deeply into each other's eyes?"

Rhea smiled slowly. "She does have lovely eyes, doesn't she?"

"You should see the way she looks at you when she thinks you're not paying attention. All worshipful-like. I love it."

"I love it too." Rhea sighed. "I'm gone for her."

"I know," Ariadne said. They were both quiet as they continued through the ships, and Ariadne felt her anxiety mounting again. "Thank you. For trying to distract me."

"We'll get through this," Rhea said, voice barely above a whisper. "We'll stop it."

They neared their quarry: *Eleuther.* The ship carrying the fuel for the military fleet. Ariadne had designed the sleep programming on all the soldiers who boarded any ship dispatched to military zones. She knew its system and how the Oracle appeared on the interface.

There were only skeleton crews guarding the ships. Most Tholosians were closer to the palace, unarmed but still around to lend help if anything went wrong. With luck, nothing would. In and out, galaxy crisis averted.

The soldier guarding the ship snapped to attention as they approached. "Delegates aren't supposed to be back here," he said, studying their uniforms.

Rhea gave a perfect Tholosian salute. "We're extra security sent from Commander Octavia," she said. Ariadne wondered if Rhea had purposely used the name of Talley's partner on Ismara.

He frowned. "I don't have any orders."

"It's above your clearance," Rhea said, then before he could respond, she reached out and pressed a pressure point at his wrist. "Relax, soldier. You look tired."

"I am," he murmured, his eyes never leaving hers.

"Of course you are," Rhea crooned. "They work you so hard here, don't they? You've been scanning ships, organizing security . . ."

"Yes. No rest."

Rhea made a sympathetic noise. "Avern, you poor thing. You must want to lie down and sleep."

He shook his head, fighting her influence. "But—"

"Sleep." Ariadne watched as Rhea pressed her fingers harder, her eyes narrowing. "*Sleep*." The soldier collapsed against Rhea and she grunted. "Gods, he's heavy. Help me with him."

Ariadne scanned her tag and helped Rhea drag him into one of the docking bay's supply closets; together, they bound his hands and feet, and gagged him with an old oil rag.

"That was close," Ariadne said as she fitted her scrambler on the door of *Eleuther*'s storage hull. They had to be quiet. There would be other soldiers on board, and Rhea couldn't make them all fall asleep.

"He was trained," Rhea whispered, "so he won't stay unconscious long. We have to hurry."

Ariadne nodded and keyed the code into the scrambler. She had designed it to help seal the ship off from its comrades and prevent the Oracle from counteracting any commands she made.

"What are you doing?" Rhea asked, coming up behind her.

"For now, making sure there are no mistakes in the coding. *If* I did it correctly, I should have complete control over the system and the ship's surveillance in the storage bay. Which means I can also access the Tholosian mainframe to locate the weapon."

Ariadne had looked at the code from all angles, testing for any flaw, any way the Oracle would be able to slither through. If she failed, the rest of the crew would know the moment Rhea and Ariadne boarded. They would be caught, imprisoned, and probably executed.

It'll hold, she told herself. But she wasn't like the Oracle; she didn't have the infinite energy of an artificial intelligence to sort out lines of code. She grew tired. She required sustenance.

They were human needs the Oracle considered obsolete.

"*If?*" Rhea hissed.

"I didn't exactly have time to perfect it, Rhea. I barely slept, okay?"

Rhea nodded. "Right. I'm sorry."

Ariadne drew up one of the wall panels, scrolling through the ship's information. According to the manifest, there were five other soldiers in the storage bay. A skeleton staff simply keeping watch on supplies.

"Can you handle that many?" Ariadne asked Rhea.

"I've never tried. Let's hope I can."

Rhea shut her eyes, her body going entirely still. Ariadne was spared the full effect, but even so, she began to feel sleepy. At least the exhaustion helped with the fear.

Rhea pulled her abilities back and rocked on her feet. "Done."

"Are you—"

"I'm fine." She was breathing hard. "It's more difficult through metal. Hurry now."

When they entered *Eleuther*'s storage bay, the other five soldiers were asleep. Rhea and Ariadne tied them up and took their seats in front of the vid-screens. They kept low; if any soldier out guarding the other ships noticed them through the window . . .

The mainframe, Ari, she reminded herself.

So far, the screens on the walls had stayed idle. Ariadne felt no presence of the Oracle. Not that she should—One was an AI, a program. Only . . . when Ariadne wove her way through the wires of her surroundings, she could swear she felt One, like a shadow or a ghost.

Watching.

Waiting.

The fear spiraled again, taking away her breath. Her skin was cool and clammy, her nerves electrified. Rhea reached out to clasp her arm, drawing Ariadne back from the brink. It helped, but it wasn't enough. Too many memories. Plain foods and so much hunger. Old vids and her shelves of Named Things for comfort. The wall of succulents and plants and rocks that she had given monikers—all collected from places she had never seen, ordered by a computer program that didn't understand a child's needs.

But the Temple hadn't been a home; it had been a prison.

"Ari," Rhea said. "There isn't much time."

"I know. I know." She took another deep breath, squared her soldiers. She could do this. She was strong. The Oracle did not have sway over her anymore.

She keyed in the code, and patched herself into the mainframe.

It was bad news: The blaster had been on this ship, as Kyla had suspected, but had already been offloaded. The notes only had random acronyms she didn't recognize. She stared at them, hard, as if they'd assemble themselves into words that made sense from the power of her glare.

"The weapon isn't here anymore," Ariadne told Rhea. "I'm going to keep searching and track it down."

Rhea nodded and placed a soft hand between Ariadne's shoulder blades. Calm muffled her anxiety, but not completely.

"I'm going to drink during our dance party," Ariadne said, striving for a brightness she didn't feel. "I've always wanted to try wine. Do you think I'll like it?"

She kept up a steady babble as she continued to work, describing silly things to Rhea. Digging just a little deeper, searching for signs that the blaster had linked up with the mainframe. As she ran her search, she distracted herself by describing decorations and music, the drinks they would serve. Silly little details that helped calm her down, that helped her think of a future beyond these screens.

Rhea hummed and agreed when she needed to, keeping a sharp eye out the window of the storage hull. Ariadne noticed Rhea's shoulders slumping. Rhea looked. . . . exhausted.

"Ari," Rhea breathed, shaking her head as if to clear it. "Hurry."

Oh. Ohhh. Ariadne felt so foolish. While she was describing her dance party and trying to locate the weapon, Rhea had been using her abilities to influence soldiers to ignore the ship.

Ariadne typed faster. Just a little longer now. Just a little—

"Ari," Rhea said, swaying on her feet slightly. She looked nauseated. "We need to go."

"But I haven't found the—"

Rhea grasped her shoulder, her strange eyes fevered. "I am so close to losing my grip on those guards outside. We have to go, or we won't make it out of here."

While half of Ariadne yearned for the safety of their own ship, the guilt was a pang. She hadn't found her weapon. She couldn't fail. Not tonight. "Just give me a second. Please."

Rhea shut her eyes. "Hurry." Her voice was a desperate plea.

Hurry, hurry, hurry. One last command.

Ariadne keyed it in; her fingers felt so slow, so clumsy. Her eyes scanned the code, praying to all the gods of death and war and the others she wished were real: goddesses of hope, light and love.

Yes! Tracking coordinates. Where did they point to? Where—

Silence seemed to echo through the ship.

<Hello, daughter,> the Oracle said. *<One has been looking for you.>* One's face, sharp and so real, appeared before them. Ariadne stumbled back in shock; the Oracle had never shown a face on the screens. Not ever.

And like One's voice, the Oracle's face was identical to Ariadne's own.

The lights within the ship extinguished, leaving them in the gloom.

51.

Present day

Clo and Kyla made their way to the exterior of the grand ball-room. They used the crush of a queuing crowd to dart into an empty hallway when guards weren't looking.

Clo turned on the pendant Ariadne had designed, a device that sent out a pulse as they moved through the building to create a digital map. It wasn't to scale, but Ariadne had given it to Clo just in case the Evoli hid something in the blueprints. Clo would know where the cameras and sentries were, and all sorts of secrets hidden behind the walls.

"This little baby is *lovely*," Clo murmured. "I don't think I'm giving this back to Ari."

Kyla rolled her eyes. "Thieving again, wee slumrat?"

"Only in my spare time, Commander."

With the pendant's help, they found an empty room. Kyla planted one of Ariadne's scramblers on the wall panel, which would keep the footage of the abandoned hallway on a loop. Ariadne could have been beyond filthy rich if she'd decided to go into the black market instead of the resistance.

Quickly, Clo took out the bits of her toolkit that Rhea had cleverly sewn into her shirt. Clo and Kyla peeled off their finery to reveal dark jumpsuits. The clothes folded down to small cubes they attached to their belt.

Everything in the palace was made by the Evoli, who had different design aesthetics from the Tholosians. There were no ornate carvings to provide discreet handholds—the Evoli preferred their walls smooth and opalescent, as if they'd been built with finely crushed pearls. Beautiful, yes, but that complicated Clo's plan. On the ceiling were the thin slats of a vent, but Clo couldn't see a way to access it or how to pry it off the wall so they could get inside and burrow into the belly of the building.

Kyla clicked her tongue against her teeth as she considered their ascent into the vents. "No hope for it. We're going to have to leave evidence behind."

She reached down to her shoes and peeled off the outer layer of their soles to reveal the rough, sticky under layer. Similarly treated gloves from the bag at her waist that contained the smoke orbs followed. Clo did the same, wincing as her skin pinched against her prosthetic. She wished she'd had these when she and Ariadne had crawled through the dusty vents of the palace on Macella.

Kyla hadn't asked about Clo's leg—the commander didn't know how much it could hurt sometimes. When Clo had sent her report on crawling through Macella's vents and jumping off a damn building, she had made it seem fully functional, a minor inconvenience at most. Clo hoped it wouldn't betray her.

With impressive aim, Kyla sent up a small grappling hook by the vent, wedged into the cornices of the ceiling. Then they began to climb.

Immediately, Clo wished the Evoli weren't so fond of high ceilings and open spaces. The cables helped take some of the pressure off, and the soles and gloves held their weight, but everything hurt. Every footprint and handprint showed on the walls after them, leaving a clear trail of where they were going, like the salamanders that had crawled along the walls of the slums of Myndalia.

<That's bad,> Clo commented.

<We can't do anything about it now,> Kyla replied. *<Come on. Time to crawl.>*

They set off through the vents. Every fifteen seconds, the pendant against Clo's chest buzzed, mapping another section of the palace as she moved.

Clo tried to reach Ariadne to make sure the building was mapping correctly. No response.

"Is something wrong with my Pathos?" Clo whispered to Kyla. "I can't get through."

A pause. "No luck for me, either." Another pause. "The building might be blocking the signal." But Kyla didn't sound convinced. A Pathos's signal could reach the ground from a ship in orbit.

Clo followed the map on her pendant until they reached the ballroom. The slats were wide enough to peer below. The ballroom was a riot of color: gold brocade, iridescent blues and greens. Clo couldn't help but watch as people milled around the ballroom in their fine gowns and suits. They held flutes of sparkling wine, or cocktails with winged insects that fanned on the brim of the glass. Normally, Clo would have scoffed at such a display of extravagance, but she had work to do.

"I don't see Sher," she whispered to Kyla as she felt for the orbs at her belt. She lined them neatly below the vent. They'd chosen ones in reds, yellows, oranges, and blacks. A distraction that resembled firesmoke.

"Then we wait," Kyla said simply. She stared intently at the revelers below. "Make sure your filters are secure. He'll give us the signal if he needs us."

More people arrived in a steady stream; from up there, Clo could feel the heat of bodies close together. If that contagion were released, everyone in this damn ballroom was a goner.

God of Survival, Salutem, don't let me die, she thought.

Clo and Kyla camped out. Clo's bad leg ached, but she'd rather be up in the vents than down in the ballroom rubbing shoulders with the top dipwells of the Empire, smiling at them and pretending they were in any way on the same side.

The dais, where the Archon and the Ascendant would sign the treaty, was still empty. The thrones for the leaders were raised high enough to look down on their combined people.

In the ballroom, the Evoli kept a physical distance from Tholosians, and the two sides didn't speak or mingle more than they had to. In contrast to the music, the decorations, and the grandeur, these were enemies who had been fighting bitterly for hundreds of years. Generals from both sides—all present—had ordered countless deaths.

Beneath the glitter and perfume was the memory of smoke and blood, the sound of battle hidden behind the fake smiles and gentle laughter. Hands kept straying to where weapons would be. A hip, the small of the back.

Clo shifted, grunting softly with effort. Her knee was holding up as well as could be expected, but the skin was rubbing badly. If she wasn't careful, she'd have to keep the prosthetic off the next few days while her sores healed. But she'd take that over the alternative.

The music grew into a proper fanfare. The Tholosian royals and higher-ups of the Empire and the Evoli Ascended and Oversouls made their way to the dais.

Where the Tholosians sparkled and glimmered over every inch of their bodies, the Evoli were sleeker. They wore billowing robes in pastels, belted tight about their waists. Yet while their garb was simple, the Oversouls wore ornate, elaborate headpieces that resembled woven antlers, encrusted with jewels and delicate chains of precious metals. They were taller than the Archon's crown, which must have salted him off no end.

"Oh, gods," Kyla breathed. "Eris."

Clo peered down, her nose pressed to the grate of the vent, but she couldn't see the small, dark-haired infuriating woman that had gotten herself kidnapped. Kyla's hand lay heavy on Clo's shoulder. "Behind Damocles."

A jolt went through Clo. They'd changed Eris's face back to Discordia's: the pale blond hair, her golden eyes almost luminous beneath the lights. Small, doll-like features that gave the false impression of being delicate, vulnerable. Her headdress was an echo of the Evoli's but darker, flaming opals glittering along the wicked points.

Clo had seen those features broadcast on icons all over the galaxy. It was the face that had stared down at Clo the night she lost her leg. It was the face of a woman Eris had left behind years before. And Damocles had forced Eris to wear that woman's face.

Clo was fucking *furious*.

"I'm going to *kill* him," Clo hissed.

Kyla waved a hand. "Shhh."

The music was so loud, they could only catch parts of what Damocles said. They each picked up a smoke orb and put on goggles to protect their eyes from the stinging.

"Now?" Clo asked.

"Not until Sher gives the signal," Kyla said, but she sounded uncertain.

Clo checked as Damocles gestured to the crowd below him, his acting skills far too good. What was he saying? Clo could barely concentrate on anything but Eris's face: the vacant stare, skin that appeared ashen beneath the face powder. Gods, what had Damocles done to her? What the flames had he done?

Then Eris opened her mouth to reveal an empty, dark maw.

Clo stifled a gasp. *Oh gods. Oh gods.*

Kyla shook with rage. Clo felt horror curl through every part of her. What scared her more than the missing tongue was Eris's body language.

She looked . . . defeated.

The Novan commander shook herself, breathing hard. "They're giving each other their votive gifts. Where the hell is Sher?" Kyla asked, almost to herself. "He should be in place by now."

The Evoli inclined their heads gravely at the Tholosians. The Archon looked ancient in his throne, for all his attempts to appear younger. It was strange to actually see the man who had led the Tholosian Empire for so long. The man who knew the horrible conditions of the slums in Myndalia and didn't give a damn. So many deaths under his rule.

Clo wanted to throttle him with the expensive tassels dangling from his coat. Then she'd go for Damocles. Doing that would throw everything into disarray and chaos, but she didn't care.

<Ariadne?> Clo tried one more time on her Pathos. *<Any word on the weapon?>*

Nothing.

Silt.

Clo clutched the cold metal of the orb tighter as the Archon gave the Evoli their gifts: elaborate, glittering opals that resembled those in Eris's oversized headdress.

They were about to sign the truce. Clo squinted at the faces, still desperately searching for Sher in the face of his stolen Delegate.

"Fuck it," Kyla said, ready to twist the orb. "We'll have to do it and hope Cato and Nyx can get her. Ready?"

Clo started to nod and then froze as something cold as the end of a Mors blaster pressed into the back of her head.

"Stop," said a voice she knew far too well.

52.

Present day

The Oracle blinked at them both, One's face a mirror image of Ariadne's own visage—but a soulless rendition of it. Perhaps if Rhea hadn't known Ariadne, she would have been impressed by the lifelike image, but all she saw was a poor imitation of her friend.

The Oracle possessed none of the spark that made Ariadne *her*.

Rhea recoiled, shifting closer to Ariadne. The girl was stiff, terrified. How would any of them feel if they were confronted with the face of their abuser? Especially when that face was a darkened mirror to her own? A nightmare made into a projected ghost that could be anywhere. Anywhere at all.

This was but a small splinter of the Oracle. One would be spread out through all the Tholosian ships docked on Laguna, in the many still circling the planet. One was back on Tholos, in the Temple where Ariadne had been kept prisoner.

One was on every planet in the Empire, watching the many citizens and servants, pretending benevolence when the system was rotten to the core.

So many places to torment anyone the Oracle chose. Like Ariadne. One's little Engineer.

"One had wondered where One's child had gone," the Oracle said in Ariadne's voice, the pitch an attempt at Ariadne's singsong inflections.

Rhea winced. It was too saccharine. All wrong.

The holographic cameras within the storage bay turned on, shining pinpoints of light into the space in front of Rhea and Ariadne. The Oracle emerged from the screen, taller, so much taller than either of them. The Oracle was so lifelike, almost tangible. If not for the slight transparency to the projection, Rhea might have been fooled into thinking One had a body of One's own.

Rhea grasped Ariadne's hand and pulled her backward.

"One has made such progress since One's child left," the Oracle said with a cruel, cold smile that looked wrong on a face so like Ariadne's. "But now it's time to come back into the code, Daughter. To become One's will."

"No." Ariadne's voice trembled. "My friends—"

"Will be executed." The Oracle's voice was cold, entirely devoid of emotion. "The prince has assured me that you, my child, will be spared. There's still so much to be done in our Temple." The Oracle's head tilted to one side. "It's time to bring you home."

One's simulated lips puckered in a kiss.

The screen showed Ariadne's last command. The coordinates of the weapon had morphed onto a map. It pointed to the ballroom of the Evoli palace.

The weapon was on the royal dais.

Rhea grabbed Ariadne's hand and pulled, but Ariadne was frozen. Rhea tried to pry apart the younger girl's shock and fear—to shift it into anger, to action—but it was like trying to move a boulder. Rhea had used so much energy already, she was trembling to stay upright.

No. You can't rest. You have to be strong.

"Ari," Rhea urged insistently, her grip on the girl tightening. *"Ari."*

Ariadne didn't respond.

"Come, child," the Oracle said.

One's voice attempted to be cajoling, nurturing in Ariadne's own sweet voice. A contrast to One's projected visage: a cold expression Rhea knew Ariadne was not capable of.

"Damn it, Ari." Rhea was desperate. "Focus!"

Her touch wasn't helping. She had to do something *now*.

Rhea lunged through the hologram. Ariadne cried out at seeing her friend move through her parent, her teacher, her tormentor. Rhea grabbed the Mors near the guard's chair and aimed for the computers. *Bang!* Sparks flew. The whole system began to power down.

"*Come on!*" Rhea seized Ariadne again, and Ariadne's legs finally moved.

"You know your place is by the Oracle," the AI said, One's voice distorting and deepening. "One helped build you, just as you helped build One."

Rhea aimed the Mors at the wall panel by the exit of the hull and fired. The ship well and truly shut down this time. Rhea tried to pull the girl up, but she couldn't move. Ariadne's body was as tense and cold as metal.

"Ari?" Rhea dropped to her knees, putting her palms on either side of Ariadne's face. "Ari, I need you to move."

Ariadne's emotions were so clear through Rhea's touch: a whirl of anxiety and fear and a pitiful wish to please the Oracle, even now that One was gone.

"I can't," she said, shaking her head. "I can't."

"Yes, you can," Rhea insisted. "Let me help you. Let me try."

Ariadne gave a small nod.

Rhea grasped Ariadne's hand firmly. She used the dwindling vestiges of her abilities to dull Ariadne's emotions and spur her into motion. Even that small amount made Rhea's vision blur.

Just a little further. Stay awake.

They fled *Eleuther*'s storage hull, speeding past the broken screens where One had taunted them. Outside, Rhea could hear the chatter of soldiers, even through the thick metal hull of the ship. She readied herself to use what abilities she had left.

Rhea had to survive this. She had to get her friend out.

She had made Nyx a promise. She had made *Ariadne* a promise.

<*Damocles has the weapon,*> Rhea sent through the Pathos to the others as they exited the ship. She propelled Ariadne forward, pretending as if they had someplace to be in a hurry. <*He has it and might not wait until the truce is over. Get Eris and get out of there.*>

No response.

Through the massive windows of the docking bay, the palace was lit up like a jewel at the top of the sloping hill, surrounded by the emerald green hills. At any moment, so many people could die.

"I failed, Rhea," Ariadne said from beside her. "I failed them all."

No, you didn't. She wanted to say the words to console her friend, but there was no time. If they stopped now, they might not make it.

"Just keep walking, Ari. Don't think about it." Rhea sent the girl a flow of reassurance through their fingertips, but there wasn't time for any additional comfort.

With each step, though, Ariadne seemed to come back to herself. Her fear still hit Rhea like droplets of cold water, but they both pushed forward. Just before the checkpoint, Rhea straightened, smoothed her face into a haughty confidence. She held her breath and tried to control her trembling.

"Straighten your shoulders," she told Ariadne. "Wipe your cheeks. I have to let go of you now."

Ariadne nodded and whisked away her tears.

There were six soldiers on guard: all Tholosians. Rhea breathed a sigh of relief; they would be easier to influence than the Evoli. Rhea used her abilities like a whip, lashing out and pushing her authority on them so strongly, they had no choice but to step into line.

"Get us a mechanic for that ship," she said. Her voice was clipped even as another wave of dizziness went through her. "It's been tampered with and the hull controls are damaged. I'm reporting higher up."

With another push of her abilities, they accepted her words. A few ran into the ship to assess the damage and others hurried off to find mechanics.

Rhea had never used her abilities so forcefully before. What else could she do? Who else could she influence? She couldn't stop to consider it; her vision was darkening at the edges. Her legs were unsteady. Rhea gritted her teeth and kept herself upright.

They had to survive.

Rhea tried the Pathos once again. *<Clo, Kyla? Anyone?>*

Ariadne and Rhea clutched each other as they heard only silence. They had no choice but to keep moving.

53.

Present day

The world existed through a haze of light and color.

Discordia squinted at the mural on the far wall, unable to make out its contents. Didn't matter. She was still on her brother's ship, and now she couldn't run. The crook of her left elbow—where the medic had injected a drug to keep her docile—stung as someone else dressed her. Hands wrapped her tightly in red and black silks, until Discordia felt as if she couldn't breathe.

"Look up," a voice commanded softly.

Discordia heard the *click* of a cosmetics kit.

It was a woman wearing the colors of a Pleasure Garden courtesan. She'd heard her brother handpicked at least three dona for his personal spacecrafts.

She tried to ask this woman if she knew Rhea. She didn't know why she wanted such a small comfort.

Discordia's mouth pulsed, the area where her tongue used to be screaming with a pain she could no longer speak.

The courtesan gently pressed powder to Discordia's shoulders and arms, something that made them glisten with different colors in the light.

"You're very brave," this woman whose name Discordia didn't know whispered in a voice barely above a breath. "No matter how this turns out, I had to say this to you."

Discordia's head hurt. Everything hurt. She could barely concentrate on the other woman's words, but she heard them. She heard them, and they meant everything.

The courtesan reached into a wooden box and pulled out a head-dress. Curved, like a crown of antlers, studded with dark, glimmering jewels. Fire opals. Common on warm, desert planets, like Nova. When she placed it on Discordia's head, the weight of it made her head bow.

The courtesan pulled away and studied her work with a flicker of sadness in her gaze. "All done," she said.

Before she turned away, Discordia reached out for her arm, but was too slow. She only grasped the woman's sleeve. The movement hurt. Everything *hurt*.

At the courtesan's questioning look, Discordia pressed her fingertips to the courtesan's chest, then her own.

Name, she mouthed.

The other woman let out a breath. "Katala, Your Majesty."

Discordia nodded. She wanted to know the names of the people who had depended on her to lead them once. The people she had failed.

Wordlessly, she followed Katala into the hall of the ship. The weight of the headdress made her see stars.

––––

The path from Damocles's ship to the Laguna Palace had been paved over with gleaming jewels. They hurt Discordia's eyes as she walked—or tottered. Damocles kept a grip on her arm that would leave bruises on her skin. Her tongue was still a throbbing fire. Her arm was sore from a dose of the ichor antidote and from the drug injections they'd been giving her. If death was coming for this planet, she'd witness it all. Damocles wanted her to live with her failure.

When her head cleared enough that she managed to pull away, her brother turned her roughly toward him.

"Look at me."

Discordia met Damocles's harsh gaze. He put his hands on her face and drew an eyelid open. "Her pupils aren't enlarged enough," he said to someone behind her. "Give her another dose."

The medic cleared his throat. "Any more might be too much, General. She could collapse."

Her brother's smile was harsh. "Oh, I think she'll fight not to. Won't you, Discordia?" She didn't respond—couldn't—and the realization seemed to please him. "Dose her," he told the medic. "I don't want her to even think without my command."

Discordia couldn't move as the medic grasped her arm and pulled it taut.

The needle slid home and it was one morsel of pain too much. If she'd had a tongue, Damocles would have had his wish. She would have bitten it off to keep from screaming.

54.

Present day

The blaster was cold and hard against the bare skin of Clo's neck.

She chanced turning her head. Clo had been so focused on opening the vents to release the smoke orb that she hadn't even heard Kyla go down.

Lost focus of my surroundings. Amateur fucking mistake.

The Commander was trapped in a web against the wall of the vent—a newer Novantae invention that splattered a sticky polymer on the target without hurting them. The webbing covered Kyla from mouth to toes, and she looked angry enough to spit as she wriggled beneath her bonds.

"Back up, Alesca."

Clo saw his boots first. Scuffed beneath the polish. The formal trousers, the embroidered jacket she'd seen just a few hours before. Sher.

The co-commander of the resistance.

Time slowed, shrinking into a small pinpoint.

"Sher," Clo said, carefully. "What are you doing?"

"What I have to," he said, voice flat. "Hands by your side."

She complied slowly, her mind whirring. This was the man whose life her mother had saved. Who had taken her in when she had no one. The one who'd taught her the importance of resistance, of fighting even when it seemed evil had threaded its way through every corner of the galaxy.

"Sher," she tried again. "I'm carrying out your orders."

"Your orders have changed. It's no longer in our best interests." Clo was astonished at how emotionless his expression was, how cold. "We have a chance to kill the Archon and the Evoli Oversouls. Burn down an empire. We need the resources."

Clo blanched. The man Clo knew would never sacrifice thousands of people and think that was for the greater good. Not Sher. He'd die first.

Kyla was the ruthless one, the one who made difficult calls to sacrifice the few to benefit the many. But even she would never do something like this.

Think, think. Clo's mind spun.

Eris had been right about Nova being compromised. Gods, she'd even told Clo that they needed to go dark. Looks like they shouldn't even have included the co-commanders of the entire damn resistance.

"You're the one who's been feeding Damocles information." At his silence, she shook her head in disbelief. "You betrayed your own spies? You betrayed *us*?"

Kyla paused in shock at Clo's words. Then she struggled again, the webbing slipping slightly from her face. It was only meant to be temporary—a weapon to pin down someone long enough for them to be shot or tied more securely. If Kyla kept struggling, she could loosen the hold. She locked eyes with Clo. Kyla gave the barest nod, wriggling with renewed vigor.

Clo had to keep Sher talking.

His jaw set. "I did what I had to."

"No, you did what *Damocles* asked you to." When the blaster pressed harder against her, Clo let out a soft noise. "You're not going to shoot me in the back of the head. You're a lot of things, but you're not a coward. I'm going to turn around. All right?"

"No screaming," he said, "or we're all dead."

"We're all dead anyway, aren't we?" Damocles would release the ichor. Take down enemies on the Evoli side and within his own command. He probably had the blaster hidden beneath that voluminous cloak, close enough that none of them ever had any hope of getting it.

"Your filters will work," Sher said. "You'll survive."

"So, you're not going to let all your agents die right away. I guess that's nice of you."

"You'll understand when I have more time to explain. The Archon has been downplaying the destruction at Charon, Clo. Those fancy dinners? The lavish displays? All to hide the fact that there's not enough stockpiled food to go around. It's this or famine. At least the people here will die fast."

"In agony," Clo snapped.

"I never said it was a mercy. Do you want the resistance to starve? Our provisions are stolen from the Empire."

"Oh, fuck you. This doesn't help the resistance." She tamped down the urge to glance over Sher's shoulder at Kyla. "Damocles will change nothing. The status quo continues. And the Evoli? If they ever figure out the Novantae were behind creating the prototype, we'd have them on our asses. *Think*, Sher."

Sher's body language was stiff, tight. "This is what we have to do, Alesca. You'll see this is the right way."

This was all wrong. Clo's mouth went slack. She should have seen it. The different body language, the stilted language. As if he were . . . a Tholosian soldier.

He wore his hair longer this last year or so, no longer buzzed as short as Clo's. There could be an implant beneath that dark hair. If she brushed those strands back from behind his ear, she knew what she would find.

"The Oracle got to you," Clo whispered. Behind Sher, Kyla struggled anew.

Sher jerked back as if she'd slapped him. "Don't even joke about that. This is *me*, Clo. I'm making the difficult decisions for the good of our people. Burn it all down, or we starve." His hand gripped her upper arm hard. "Do you understand me?"

Clo looked down at his hand, then met his eyes. They were as dead as a soldier's. "I know the signs," she said, struggling to keep her voice even. "I've seen Ari's work. I saw Cato. These thoughts aren't your own; you'd never think mass murder was the answer. You'd realize that made you just as twisted as the Tholosians. I've known you since I was fifteen years old. *I know you.*"

Kyla broke free from the remnants of the web. She grabbed the gun from the small of her back.

Clo ducked just as she aimed and fired at Sher.

He fell, tumbling to the ground with a metallic crash. No chance to worry whether anyone down below could hear the sound over the music.

"*Sher!*" Clo crouched beside him, her shaking hands seeking a pulse. She found one, his heart still beating. "Thank the gods, he's not dead. When I saw you shoot . . ."

"It's just a heavy stun," Kyla said calmly. "I'll finish the job."

Clo couldn't watch him die. She grabbed Kyla roughly. "No."

Kyla winced. "He's my cohort. We've fought together for decades and saved each other's lives countless times. You think this isn't hard for me?" Her voice caught. "But we can't risk—"

"Then we'll drag his ass back to Nova for a deprogramming, but we are *not* killing Sher."

"There's no time," Kyla said. Clo grabbed Sher's hand anyway, prepared to drag him her own damn self, but Kyla stopped her. "*Clo.* He'll slow us down. We need to release the smoke and get out of here."

"We can't just *leave* him—"

The Commander shook her head. "We have to."

Clo held back her tears, knowing she'd have to leave the man who had been her only family since her mother died. "I need to see," she told Kyla. "I need to be sure."

Clo turned Sher over, pushing up the hair at the back of his head.

There. A tiny implant, no bigger than so many cogs she'd fit into engines. She took the locket Ari gave her and pried open the back. Kyla didn't ask what she was doing. The grief emanated off her so strongly, Clo didn't need to be an empath like Rhea to feel it.

Clo used a wire from the locket and pressed it to the edge of the chip.

"Doing that without a precision laser will kill him just as surely as a Mors," Kyla said.

"The odds are better. If it cuts him off from the Oracle, he might be able to resist the rest of his programming."

"Or it'll paralyze him."

"Choose, Kyla. A blast or this?"

Kyla hitched in a ragged breath. "Do it."

Clo held her breath and fried the chip. Sher twitched, then went limp. His heart still beat, but who knew what she'd done to the machinery within his skull. Her heart hurt. She'd lost both of the men who had brought her into the Novantae.

"Now, Clo," Kyla said, steel in her voice. "Leave him."

Clo did as her commander instructed.

They started moving along the vent and Kyla froze, her face contorting in a grimace as she glanced down at the ballroom. They'd missed some of the ceremony. Had the rulers signed the treaty? Clo couldn't tell. Damocles leaned over to Eris and whispered in her ear. Kyla reached in her bag. Clo understood and grabbed two smoke orbs.

Wordlessly, they pulled out the pins and tossed the orbs through the vents. The smoke released and obscured the revelers below. Clo prayed that Nyx and Cato managed to grab Eris in the confusion.

This was their only chance.

55.

NYX

Present day

Battles were easier than this. There was a cacophonous symphony to war; everyone had a place, movements were carefully coordinated and planned and executed. Nyx was used to exhausting her body, to punishing it with pain. She was very good at killing.

She did not like espionage, or playing a part, or pretending to be of any station above the one she had been designated. The robes she wore were so soft that she felt naked. The filters up her nose and down her throat itched something awful. The soft, musical accents of upper-class Tholosians and Evoli chafed her ears.

As they moved through the gardens and deposited the spharias amid the vast grounds, Nyx and Cato pretended to gawk like tourists. In truth, Nyx was counting how many Evoli and Tholosians were inside the perimeter of the spharias' quarantine—people who would die if Damocles loosed the plague. The revelers beyond the palace grounds would be spared. That was all they could do.

Nyx and Cato headed back to the palace, and the scan checked them through to the main ballroom.

Beside her, Cato let out a breath. "Now what?"

Nyx wound her way through the crowd, taking care to appear

casual rather than purposeful. "We wait for Sher and the distraction," she said through her teeth.

Beside her, Cato's movements were as stiff and awkward as one of those mech androids on planets without many gerulae.

"Look *natural*, you fuckwit." Nyx put up a hand as if she were rubbing her nose. "Avert your face or cover your mouth when you speak. Evoli are good lip readers. And for god's sake, try not to feel panicked. All they have to do is touch you and they'll sense everything." Nyx scanned the room, eyes darting from person to person. "Plenty of security—"

An Evoli soldier across the room caught her gaze, then he glanced behind her.

Someone brushed her shoulder softly—a quick, light touch, as if by accident. But Nyx felt a quick probe of empathic abilities. It was different from Rhea—the courtesan was so subtle that Nyx hadn't noticed it before Ismara. This was a more blatant nudge. Like a barb. An invasion.

Nyx couldn't fake emotions of joy or delight, because she didn't feel those things. They were foreign to her. So, she tried for contentment instead, what she felt when Ariadne had held her hand earlier.

The touch disappeared and she heard a muttered apology. Across the room, the soldier still watched her.

Nyx put a hand up to hide her lips. "Dance with me," she breathed to Cato.

"Oh," he said. "Do I have to?"

Nyx rolled her eyes. "Shut up and dance."

Reluctantly, Cato pulled Nyx closer. It was a Tholosian royal dance, one familiar to Nyx only because she had been forced to perform it during the military's grand tour after the Battle of the Garnet. The steps between them were uneven, not cohesive at all. More about the performance than the actual movement.

The music slid through the crowd, mingling with the tinkling of jewels, the scuff of expensive shoes. Half a dozen perfumes blended into an overwhelming scent. It reminded her so much of other balls she'd been to—so many over the years. All of them in celebration of victory, the blood of battle only just recently washed away.

This one felt like a sign of death to come.

Cato hid his face in Nyx's shoulder. "Any sight of the general or Eris?"

"No." Nyx kept her voice deliberately low. "If Sher doesn't manage to intercept him, Damocles will wait for the right moment."

"The right moment?"

"Yes. Remember what Rhea said? The maximum effect."

A new song began, some steady tattoo that kept the pace of a heart-beat. An Evoli song; she was certain of it. She remembered hearing such drums on the battlefield in the distant Evoli camps.

The sound of it made her blood stir—too many memories. It brought her right back to being a soldier, fighting for her ruler, her planet, her empire.

Stop, she told herself. *Not your emperor, not your planet, not your empire. You fight for Ariadne. For Rhea. For the rest of the crew. Even Eris. Even yourself.*

Another Tholosian song began. A strong, strident and deep thrum that wove itself with the beat of the Evoli instruments. Both echoed off the walls, intended to be a song of unity, of a new, harmonious future.

Nyx fought her memories, her programming, her upbringing. When she looked at Cato, she knew he felt the same. Cato had deeper pro-gramming, and he wasn't as resistant. His eyes were closed, his expres-sion relaxed. Nyx remembered this. In the communal room with her cohort, they played this song and they all closed their eyes in prayer. Some pressed their hands to their hearts.

"Cato." She gripped his arm, leaned into him. "Listen to my voice."

"I hear you." His voice was faint.

Rhea and Ariadne might have deprogrammed him, but the lure was still there. The drug-like comfort of not questioning, not rebelling, of letting everything be decided. So easy.

The Evoli drums quickened.

The Tholosian anthem grew louder.

Cato's eyes fluttered shut.

Nyx sank her fingernails into his arm, relieved to see him wince.

"Eris," Nyx gritted. "She might need our help. If you can't handle this, I'm leaving your ass right here."

"Eris?" He sounded dazed.

Before Nyx could respond, the drums and the anthem stopped. The dais at the far end of the room was lit in a blazing light that cast the Evoli Ascendant and the Archon in the different colors of a nebula. Projected stars scattered across their features, a symbol in both empires of hope and peace.

The Evoli Ascendant and the Tholosian Archon rose to stand next to each other as they addressed the crowd. Her long robes were deceptively simple compared to the Archon in his full military dress. She wore a headdress that was as delicate as lace, in contrast to the heavy crown slanted across his brow. A goddess, a god—both of them able to change the course of the future with this one meeting.

The room was quiet, rapt.

"Welcome, All Souls," the Ascendant said, using the formal address for Evoli citizens. Even with her words artificially projected, she sounded quiet, her voice ringing lovely as a chime.

"And loyal Tholosians," the Archon added with a single, stern nod.

There was a hunched line to his shoulders and a weariness in his voice. Nyx had always heard that when the Archon finally aged, it caught up all at once.

The Ascendant lifted her chin. "For the last five hundred years, our great empires have been at war. Each victory has been overshadowed by devastating loss, and we agree the cost of this has become too great. It cannot continue."

The Archon added his voice to hers: "We acknowledge this newfound accord will not come easily to some. A declaration cannot undo our pasts, but my hope is that it will clear a peaceful path going forward. A future that will be ensured and continued by my son and Heir, General Damocles."

The Archon nodded to a door off to the side, and Nyx dug her fingers into Cato's arm as the general strode forward to join his father on the dais.

Eris wasn't with him.

"Shit," Nyx muttered.

Where was she? Had Commander Sher managed to get her out without their help?

The treaty was projected toward the dais in a dappling of colors and lettering across the features of both ruling families. It had been translated into both Imperial Tholosian and Evolian, the symbols merging together in a pact that could not be mistaken: from this day forward, the future of their empires would intertwine.

The Ascendant slid her fingertips across the letters of the treaty, until the ridges of her prints had left their impression across the projection. The Archon added his own in a firm smear of a line. He nodded to his son to do the same.

Nyx held her breath as she crept forward, dragging Cato behind her. She had to move slowly, as if she were edging closer for a better look.

Too slow.

She waited, trying to slow the cadence of her breath, the beat of her heart. She had to be careful. Nyx watched as Damocles strode toward the signing table. The crowd erupted in applause.

No, something was wrong. Nyx kept her eyes on Damocles as she moved forward, faster. Where was Sher? He had to do *something*—

Damocles lifted a hand and the crowd quieted. "Before I sign, I'd like to say a few words. In celebration of this treaty, I've come with offerings to reinforce my intent to follow the Archon's legacy." Damocles looked at the Archon and bowed at the waist. "And, of course, a gift for my father." He pointed to the door and beckoned with his fingers. "We have found Princess Discordia, former Heir Apparent."

Nyx froze and watched as Eris swept into the room wearing all the finery of royalty. A heavy dress in red and black, and embroidered with the scythes of Tholos. Dark feathers were sewn into her bodice, their iridescence catching the light. Red cabochons set in black metal glimmered at her throat and ears, one jewel fastened to her forehead like a third eye. She wore a curved headdress that was dotted with fire opals.

Eris also wore her old face, the fine-boned features of the Servant of Death.

Why wasn't Eris doing anything? She didn't even seem distressed or panicked. Had Nyx's fears been true? Had she betrayed them?

Nyx mentally reached for her Pathos. *<Sher? Eris is on the dais and she's not moving. Tell me you've got a plan.>*

Silence.

Her heartbeat echoed in her throat. What were her orders?

"Why the hell isn't she doing anything?" Nyx hissed.

Cato grasped Nyx's arm. "Look at her eyes. She's drugged."

Even from where Nyx stood, Eris's pupils were so dilated the irises looked black. Her expression was blank. Like a beautiful doll, and just as easily manipulated. Drugged to the gills. She gripped a box in her hands, as red and dark and intricate as her clothes.

"She has a votive gift for our Ascendant Oversoul," Damocles said smoothly. "An offering for our new future."

"Son of a bitch," Nyx said, noticing the box Eris was carrying. "Move. We need to move."

"Why?"

"Remember what Rhea said? Damocles won't take the fall for this. He's got Eris holding the godsdamned weapon."

56.

PRINCESS DISCORDIA

Present day

Discordia's vision was a tunnel of stars. It was bright around the edges, as if she were walking into a dream. She heard voices. They sounded like a flurry of birds taking off into the sky—
One voice was clear.

Damocles's voice was a whisper in her ear, a vibration through her bones. It was heat in her bloodstream, straight to her brain. A terse command was lodged there, one she couldn't hear yet.

But she was supposed to follow him until then. Focus on his light, on his features. His fingers beckoned her forward.

A gift. Discordia carried a gift. A box in her hands.

It was important, she knew. Somewhere in the back of her mind—buried so, so deep—a warning sounded. So small, the buzzing of a pest.

Damocles called her name, and she batted the warning away.

The voices went quiet as she moved forward. She looked out at them, at this sea of colors and light and—were they . . . people? Where was she? She couldn't remember. Her head hurt too much. The pain in her mouth pulsed in time with her heart.

"Discordia?"

That voice. She knew that voice.

Hands gripped her arms. She stared at a man she recognized from deep in her memories.

"Father," she tried to say, but the only thing that came out of her mouth was a rough croak, a pathetic sound. They'd used nanites to staunch the blood, but Discordia could still taste iron.

His eyes were as sharp as she remembered, like roughly cut gemstones. "General, if you've brought me another pretender . . ." His fingers tightened and Discordia almost cried out. Her skin hurt. Everything hurt.

"Her DNA is a perfect match," Damocles said, as if from a great distance. "I wouldn't sully such an important occasion with false hope."

The crowd's whispers grew to hisses. Questioning shouts rose, hushed by the steady, calm tenor of the Evoli Ascendant. "What a gift to have such a reunion," she said. "But unexpected and unforeseen in our negotiations. Will your true Heir honor our truce?"

True Heir. Discordia saw how much this chafed her brother. His jaw tightened. "She's not in a position to be Heir to anything," Damocles snapped.

Father barely appeared to listen. "What's wrong with her?" he asked Damocles.

"Drugged and broken by the Novantae," Damocles said. To any onlooker, his tone would have sounded indifferent; Discordia heard the hint of satisfaction in it. Of victory. "So, now you know why the resistance have made such impressive strikes against the Empire. They had her help."

The Archon barely seemed to hear his son. He lifted Discordia's chin. She knew every line of that face. She had spent so much of her life trying to please him. Hadn't she? "I thought you were dead. So many came to me—but they weren't you."

His voice—softer than she remembered—came to Discordia as if from the bowels of a ship. Echoing. Distorted. His face was blurred, and she shook her head to focus.

Give the gift, an inner voice said. No. Her brother's. He'd given that command back on the ship, and the drugs they'd put in her made it so difficult to resist. It pounded through her head like a klaxon.

No. *No.* Something was wrong. She couldn't remember.

She shook her head, opened her mouth to speak again.

"Oh, did I mention?" Damocles couldn't hide his sense of victory. "Her tongue's been cut out."

A hush went through the room. Her vision was beginning to clear. She met her father's shocked gaze.

Do something, she willed herself. But her body wasn't her own. It waited for a command.

Her arm still stung from the needle. The drug coursed through her veins. Her body felt like it was floating. The box was heavy, the only thing weighing her to the ground.

"Discordia?" the Archon asked, gaze searching hers. "Did they break you?"

"I told you she wasn't as strong as you believed," Damocles said. "When I found her, she was giving the Novantae information on how to destroy us. I had to control her myself, and now she can barely resist a command. Watch." He turned to Discordia. "You have an offering for the Ascendant, don't you, sister? Give it to them." He glanced at the Ascendant.

No. Discordia was shaking her head. Something wasn't right. What was it? *What was it?*

Someone called her by another name, one she'd chosen. Or had she imagined that familiar voice in the crowd?

The Evoli soldiers stepped forward to accept the gift.

"Discordia." Damocles's voice again, so loud that it pounded through her head. Was that her name? "Open the box. Let them see." He delighted in ordering her around, as if she were nothing more than a pet.

Open. Open, open, *open*. The command was so loud, she was powerless against it.

She set the box down on the table between the Archon and the Ascendant, and lifted the lid.

A gasp went through the crowd.

The jewels glittered in the light. The necklace, the orb, and the scepter were nestled in the fabric. Each one was beautifully polished, highlighting the reds, blues, and oranges of the stones that gave the fire opals their name. A match to the jewels nestled among the branching antlers of her headdress.

The guards stepped forward to take the box from her. She watched as they inspected the jewelry, deemed it acceptable, and gave it to the Ascendant.

The Ascendant murmured kind words in her language and allowed a guard to fasten the necklace. It looked beautiful against her shining, opalescent skin. So much like Rhea's.

Rhea.

Discordia's mind caught on the name like a pebble in a stream before it washed away again. The two Oversouls—priests to the Ascendant—accepted their gifts of orb and scepter with their thanks and a nod.

The smile Damocles gave Discordia made her freeze in place.

Her command was finished. Discordia had served her purpose. The buzzing in her head cleared.

And Eris remembered.

She had seen Damocles hide the blaster beneath the velvet lining of the box. He had let her watch as he carefully arranged the jewels on top.

Eris had delivered the weapon intended to kill the Evoli.

Stop! She tried to shout the word, but all that came out was an awful noise, more animal than human. She lunged forward to grab the box, but Damocles seized her by the arm.

Eris struggled against him, her vision clouding. The blood pulsing through her veins burned, but she clawed at Damocles. Her scream was savage.

"*Say it,* Father," Damocles demanded. "Admit that after all your training, your daughter failed you. Admit it. You made a mistake in declaring her your Heir."

The Evoli Ascendant watched with unblinking eyes. How much did she and the Oversouls feel? Had Eris's guard been lowered enough that they could sense her fear? What did they think about sordid family secrets unleashed in the middle of a peace ceremony? Their expressions betrayed nothing.

The Archon's gaze was sharp. His voice was so low, Eris barely heard him over the ringing panic in her mind. "I apologize for this upset,

Ascendant and Oversouls. Sign the treaty, Damocles. It's the future we must dwell on, not the past."

Damocles's smile was slow. The Archon had not cast him aside. Had not welcomed Discordia back with open arms. Had not made her the Heir. The realization opened something raw inside her, old wounds she'd thought had closed so long ago. She didn't know her father could still hurt her.

Damocles slid his fingerprints across the treaty next to his father's. In her drugged state, Eris thought they were as red as blood.

Damocles looked at Eris with triumph. "The treaty is signed. We shall have peace."

The Evoli on the dais closed their eyes, pressing their palms flat to their chests. Even Eris could feel their relief that the bloodshed was over. The crowd burst into cheers. The clapping was only background noise as Damocles leaned closer to Eris.

He pressed a kiss to her cheek. "*Occidit rex regina,*" Damocles breathed into her ear.

King kills Queen.

Eris was helpless against the command. She didn't know what Damocles had dosed her with. She tried to resist. She tried to open her mouth to scream.

She couldn't. Her body was trapped, rigid. Programmed to do only what he had commanded.

Eris reached for the carved chest again, and no one stopped her. She pushed aside the velvet covering and the metal of the blaster underneath was cold. She picked it up, her hands on the trigger. *Stop, Eris. Stop, stop!*

The Archon's eyes widened. The Ascendants stepped back in unison, turned as if to flee.

The air filled with smoke, hissing through the vents. Reds, oranges, yellows. Within moments, the ballroom was hazy, impossible to see anything. Eris's mind whirred, desperate to throw off Damocles's command.

Ariadne.

Another name stuck to her mind. Ariadne had created a failsafe. How many shots had Ariadne said would cause the weapon to jam?

Three? Four? Could Eris fire it at the ceiling, or would the spores release and drift down on the guests anyway?

The smoke made her cough. Eris fell to the ground, heaving, the weapon tumbling from her hands. She pulled up the gossamer under-shirt of her dress and wrapped it around the lower half of her face, her ruined mouth, unsure if it would even help.

A horrible sound cut through the confused mutterings of the crowd. A hiss, a shot, a sizzle of a blaster.

Another.

One more.

The smoke cleared, and Eris stared at the frightened, fleeing Tholo-sians and Evoli through a film of reddish orange. Her hands were empty, the blaster four steps away. She had not fired it. She couldn't have.

Could she?

Her head throbbed, her tongue was seared with pain. The world was still hazy and uncertain, her mind still cobwebbed.

The Oversouls, the Ascendant, and the Archon had collapsed to the ground. Their cries pierced Eris's ears. Her vision sharpened and her mind was clearer and—

Oh, the God of Death would be pleased this day. He would have bathed in the blood of his sacrifice. The guards ran to help the Oversoul and the Ascendant; Tholosian guards rushed to her father, but the plague was already manifesting. The ichor spores had been released. They, too, collapsed from skin contact. Their screams rose as they fell to the floor and writhed in agony. Blood would soon slide from their eyes, their noses, their mouths. They'd be dead in days, if they were lucky. Most would die in mere hours.

There was no help for them.

Eris backed away, her hand to her lips. She barely registered her brother fleeing the room with his own guards. Her thoughts were slow, unfocused. *Remember. What happened?* Had Damocles taken the blaster from her? Fired at their enemies and then his own father?

Or had he made Eris pull the trigger for him?

Gods, had she killed these people?

All was chaos. Tholosians and Evoli fell. Their vomited blood cov-ered the floor of the dais.

"Eris!" Hands turned her roughly around. Strangers. Faces she didn't recognize.

"Pick her up, pilot," the strange woman commanded.

Pilot? *Nyx. Cato.* Eris tried to speak, but all that came out was an ugly, strained sound. Desperate.

"Pick her up," Nyx commanded Cato again.

"Wait." Another voice. Eris looked down to see her father staring up at her. His face was streaked with blood. "*Discordia.*"

He met her gaze but could barely move. She saw the tiny puncture where the ichor had blasted through his uniform. *Your fault,* she told herself. As Zoe she had blithely mentioned, the sequencer could target multiple strands of DNA—and Damocles must have imputed both Evoli *and* the Archon's genetic material.

It astonished Eris that such a small blast could bring down the ruler of the entire galaxy. He'd defeated whole armies. He'd seemed invincible. Impenetrable.

"A soldier's death," her father whispered. "Please." The last word sounded as if it pained him to say.

Amid the chaos, Eris kneeled beside her father. *I'm sorry,* she mouthed.

He shook his head, shutting his eyes. "You should be," he breathed.

And Eris knew he thought she was responsible—just as Damocles intended. Everyone had watched her pick up that weapon. Everyone was going to watch her stab him. Her father was going to die hating her. Yet here he was, asking her to give him a last modicum of dignity.

She deserved this.

Eris took a breath and slid the sharp pin from her hair—the only weapon she had. She plunged it through her father's neck, piercing right through his carotid artery. His death, like so many of her others, would be quick, merciful, better than most of her sacrifices to Letum.

I'm sorry, she mouthed again. *I'm so sorry.*

Cato scooped Eris up into his arms. He fled with Nyx through the crowd of people heading out of the ballroom.

"Eris!" someone called. Eris lifted her head to see Clo limping through the crowd, Kyla at her side. Eris felt relief—their faces were their own. "This way!"

Clo pointed to a door. Around them people were dropping, dropping, falling like trees in a forest. So much faster than that first manifestation on Ismara. Honed into a weapon. Spreading like wildfire.

"I thought you said you were going back to the ship," Nyx was saying. Eris barely heard them.

"I said if there was trouble, I would come back to save your arse." Clo gestured to the fleeing crowd, the bodies on the ground. "I'd say this is the fluming definition of trouble, wouldn't you? Now follow me."

"Where's Sher?" Nyx asked Kyla.

Kyla said nothing, her head down.

"Dead?" Nyx asked.

"He chose the wrong side." Kyla's words were heavy as stones. "I'll explain later."

Her words took a moment to filter through the discord of Eris's thoughts. *Sher.* He'd betrayed them.

Emotions like betrayal and failure and grief could wait until after escape.

Clo led them through the door and down a hallway. The jarring movement of Cato's body nauseated Eris. She still reeled with pain and remnants of the drugs, and Cato's hard grip on Eris burned her skin. She was so tired. *Keep your eyes open. Stay awake.*

Clo took them through a supply room. She swept aside a window curtain to reveal a hidden door that led to the servant's wing. They all hurried down the next hall.

Eris reached out to touch Clo's arm. *Thank you,* she mouthed.

"You're welcome," Clo said, striding next to Cato. She reached into her coat and pressed a heavy cloth into Eris's hands. "I brought your piece of junk. Apparently, this ancient silted scrap slips through security."

Eris unwrapped the cloth to find her old, treasured blaster nestled in the center. *Thank the gods.* The familiar weight of it felt like coming home.

Bang! Bang! Bang!

They all froze. Outside, the shouting began anew. Screams echoed in the night.

"What *is* that?" Clo stopped at one of the windows and swung it open.

Nyx was impatient. "We don't have time—"

"Oh my gods." Clo's hand covered her mouth. "*Oh my gods.*"

Eris struggled in Cato's grip until he wordlessly released her. They all gathered around the window and looked outside. There, she could see some of Damocles's guards, out of uniform, forming a human chain to march on the crowd, attacking any Evoli stragglers uninfected by the ichor.

They were spreading the disease faster.

They had found a way to replicate Ariadne's weapon, the failsafe useless. They'd made it look ornate, cruelly beautiful. The Tholosians loved making death into art.

"In Discordia's name," the soldiers shouted, spraying the crowd with weaponized ichor propellants. People fell. They screamed for help, to be spared.

But there was no God of Mercy.

Eris made a sound in her throat. Despite all of Ariadne's efforts, Damocles must have reproduced it before Zoe came back with the updated model. He now had documentation that she'd invented it under the false name of Zoe Eirene-X-2 with the intent to completely massacre every Evoli. This would erase any doubt that she was involved, any doubt at all.

In Discordia's name.

"We have to go," Nyx said, urgent.

"No," Clo shook her head, her eyes filled with tears. "*No.* We can't just leave them. They're using—" Her breath hitched. "Godsdamn it, this is my responsibility."

"No, it isn't. We can't do anything for them, Clo. Most of them are probably already infected."

"And the ones who aren't?"

"They're in the perimeter. They're dead anyway." Nyx's mouth compressed into a grim line. "We have to go. Gods, I hope Rhea and Ariadne somehow survived this."

"Don't tell Ari," Clo whispered. "If she's alive . . . don't tell her about this. It would break her."

Eris struggled toward the massacre. To stop it. She had to stop it.

"Come on," Cato said to Eris. "Nyx is right. There's nothing more we can do here."

The fight left her. Eris leaned heavily against Cato as they hurried through the halls. Her vision wove in and out, and she felt as if she were floating. Cato practically carried her down the back steps deeper into the palace. It was empty—everyone there would have attended the ceremony. They had all been commanded to. It had been ordained.

And it would lead to their murder.

The sound of running made Eris look up. It was Rhea, sprinting at top speed. Her arms flung wide as she crashed into Clo, nearly toppling her.

"Rhea," Clo said, running her hands over the other woman's tear-streaked face.

Rhea stuttered over her words. Her Evoli-like skin was glowing beneath the dirt. Eris realized the other woman must have felt the slaughter outside—the emotions and suffering of thousands of people dying. Her hold on Clo seemed to be the only thing keeping her upright.

"Ship," Rhea managed, pointing toward the docking bay.

"Is Ariadne all right?" Nyx asked.

Rhea managed a nod.

Eris tried shutting her eyes. She could hear the death, smell it; she didn't want to see any more—but no. She lifted her lids. She had to bear witness.

She deserved it.

Nyx fired at the guards to clear a path. Outside, the crowds started to bang on the heavy metal doors. "Discordia!" they shouted, several breaking through the shield of guards. Damocles's people let them go.

They wanted the mob to tear their princess limb from limb.

Eris's group sprinted toward a ship she didn't recognize—*Lysicrates*. Cato secured his grip on Eris, and she hated that she couldn't even rely on her two legs. They made it there seconds before the horde.

Nyx raised the door. People from the crowd tried to scramble up, their screams echoing in a cacophony of noise. Nyx shot at them, clearing stragglers as the door slid shut. Hands hammered on the outside. Shots from the guards skittered along the hull. If they broke into *Lysicrates*, the mob of desperate citizens would not be kind.

"Hurry!" Ariadne said over the comms of the ship. "Clo! Cato! I don't know how to fly this thing!"

Cato sprinted from the hold. Clo stayed.

A screech, and the purr of another engine sounded in the hangar. Eris's head snapped up in time. Damocles and his close guards were hurrying to their own ship.

At her side, Clo snarled, "That lentic spawn of a caiman's balls."

Eris shoved Clo roughly aside. He was hers. *Hers.*

With renewed energy, Eris ran for one of the smaller hatches. Clo shouted her name, but she ignored it. Damocles had to die for what he had done. She didn't care how many people would see her do it. He had already made her look like a villainess, a traitor. Let her be guilty for ending him. What would his death change? Nothing. *Nothing.*

Everything.

She opened the hatch and dropped to the ground, crawling forward on hands and knees with her blaster gripped in a sweaty palm. Damocles had almost reached his ship. She could see his feet. This was Eris's last chance, and she wanted him to know it was her. Pain seared at the base of her tongue like Morsfire.

She emerged on the left side of the ship. As she broke cover, Eris screamed. It sounded almost strangled, her rage so thick she could have choked on it.

Damocles stopped and looked over his shoulder at her.

His mistake.

With the drug pulsing through Eris's system, she could still feel him curled through the edges of her mind. She pushed back. Long ago, she had told him emotion was a weakness. But she was wrong. It made her stronger.

And he was no match.

Eris pointed her blaster and pulled the trigger.

The blast curved. It traveled through the air between them. On target. Perfect.

She shot Damocles right through the eye.

As Damocles fell, memories burst through Eris's mind. Her brother's face, younger, less twisted with hatred. His intense concentration as they played a game of war and he decided his next move on the board. She remembered his first kill, the one she took from him. She remembered being forced to take Xander, too. She remembered every brother she killed.

Damocles was the last name on her list.

Clo reached Eris, dragging her back toward the hatch as guards shot at them. Below the ship, Damocles's body was still visible, his face toward them, his eye weeping crimson.

"You did it," Clo said, breathless. "You fucking did it."

Eris tried to pull away from Clo. She had to be sure. His mods could take so much damage—too much. His guards were already dragging him to safety. She had to finish him off, *now*. She *had to*.

Nyx roughly hauled her up through the hatch. "We have to go."

Eris bucked against Nyx's hold, but the other woman held tight. She let out a cry, strangled, but the drugs were still in her system. She wasn't strong enough to overpower the larger woman as Nyx pulled her deeper into the hold.

She was already losing consciousness as Clo told everyone that Damocles was dead.

But Eris knew better. She could feel it in her bones.

Damocles was still alive, and he was going to make them all pay.

57.

Present day

Nyx watched as Cato tended to everyone's wounds.

She sat, curled up in the corner, with the biggest damn glass of hooch she could find—they'd emptied the supplies off *Lysicrates* before returning to *Zelus*.

Zelus was their ship. They'd made it a home.

In the corner of the room, Eris was still passed out and attached to the monitors as the drugs left her system. She'd come out of this the worst by far.

Or—maybe the resistance had. After Sher's betrayal, the Novantae were fucked. Completely burned. All their secrets out there for the Oracle to sift through. Ariadne had set up an encrypted line, and the rebels were packing up and leaving Nova. Many were going dark. Their small rebellion had become even smaller.

After all her scheming, Nyx would never set foot on Nova sand in the end. It upset her in a way she didn't understand—the lost potential. That plan she, Rhea, and Ariadne had worked for over the course of a year. A life she could have lived, but would never happen.

Now it would be something else.

Or maybe nothing at all.

Nyx downed more hooch. The world was getting a little softer around the edges. Her senses dulled. Her mind was less sharp.

It made it easier to deal with the pain.

"What are you going to do about her wounds?" Nyx asked Cato, tilting her chin at Eris.

"Stabilize for now. Let her heal. If she wants the face she wore in the resistance, between me and Ari, we could manage. Not so sure about the tongue."

"If she got it back, I wonder what she'd say," Nyx said.

"She'd have a few choice swear words, that's for damn sure," Cato said, with an easy smile that didn't reach his eyes.

"No going back from here, pilot," Nyx said. "You're stuck with the most wanted crew in the Iona Galaxy, blamed for the deaths of thousands." She raised her glass. "Cheers to a clusterfuck."

Guilt flashed in Cato's features, but he shook his head. "At least the rest of Laguna was able to evacuate. No one outside of the perimeter was infected and the spores were contained in the spharias. We saved close to a million lives, plus the millions off planet. All of the Evoli, many Tholosians. That's not nothing."

Nyx found a smile. "Silver lining. Well done."

Nyx went up to the top of the ship, a small room that reminded her of her barracks back on Tholos. She could look straight up through a porthole at the stars above.

Stars didn't judge.

In the privacy of that room, Nyx coughed into her hand. Her palm was speckled with blood. Her whole body burned, like splinters were growing in her muscles.

The others hadn't showed any signs of infection. But she'd felt this illness before she'd landed on Laguna, if she were honest with herself. She'd felt it not long after Ismara. She'd stumbled against the walls of the ichor in that underground crypt. Her hand against the rough rock, the tear in her suit. The tiny scrape. Small enough she'd thought nothing of it. Large enough for endospores in the rock to infect her.

With the first speck of blood, she'd known.

The others were safe from her. It was the first strain, the one that had taken Talley. Not infectious, or the rest of her team would have shown symptoms before they even came close to Laguna. She didn't know how long she had.

There was no honor in this. No battle. Just a slow, painful ebb into nothing.

Nyx lay back, shooting herself up with an antitoxin when Cato wasn't looking.

She knew it was useless. There was no cure, or at least not one they could access or develop quickly enough. So, she'd enjoy what little time she had left. It could be days. Weeks. Months. Years.

She'd do what she could to destroy the Empire before the end.

EPILOGUE

Two Weeks Later

Prince Damocles's broadcast went out across the galaxy. To every planet in the Evoli and Tholosian Empires. Every corner, every nook, every quadrant.

And it reached a ship adrift in the darkest parts of space, one that had powered down and hidden itself. There, seven of the most wanted people in the galaxy watched the broadcast.

The newly crowned Archon wore his ceremonial Tholosian cloak and a collar reminiscent of an Evoli's Oversoul collar in a show of good faith. The Oversouls were a collective until the new Ascendant could be chosen. He was an honorary, though closely watched, member of the council.

He had one final new addition.

An eye patch of smooth gold, covering the ruin of his left eye.

When he spoke, it was in a solemn, steady tone. "After the senseless attack on both Evoli and Tholosian citizens at Laguna, our Empires are united in a common cause. I am relieved to report that through the work of myself and my soldiers, the population of Laguna that was not at the site of the treaty were spared the effects of the contagion. These million Evoli lives show how committed I am to this treaty, this peace."

Clo's garbled shout of outrage echoed through the command center. "Are you fluming kidding me? *He took credit?*"

Ariadne glared. "That was my idea, you stupid man. That was all *our* work." She took off her slipper and threw it at the screen as he spoke again. All four quadrants had seen the images of Discordia holding the weapon before the smoke had flooded the ballroom. The footage was glitchy from the presence of ichor, but it was unmistakably the lost Heir, returned as if Avern itself had spat her back out.

"In the future," Damocles continued, "we will build our civilizations alongside one another, but for now, our purpose is simple: to find and execute those responsible for the murder of my father, the Ascendant, and the Oversouls.

"Led by my sister Princess Discordia, they have devoted themselves to eradicating our way of life, our truce, and our peaceful path going forward. Anyone who aligns themselves with these seven criminals are accessories to aggression against our united Empire, led by Archon and Ascendant, once they are chosen. As we move into this new era, anyone who harbors and aids these individuals will be tried for treason. They created weapons unlike anything we have seen before. We must remain committed against our common enemy. Rest assured, they will be found, punished, and executed."

"Seven devils, we're screwed," Nyx muttered.

Ariadne grinned, as if Damocles's words bounced off her like a child's rubber ball. "Hey, I like that. Seven of us, and we're devilishly clever." She gave a clap. "I hereby dub this our team name."

"Really? You're going to name us after a curse?" Clo asked. Then she paused, considered it, and gave a half-shrug. "Actually, it's not bad."

"So sacrilegious," Rhea said, though she sounded amused more than offended.

"See?" Ariadne said. "*Devils*. It's wicked."

"Seven of us," Eris murmured, the metal of her new bionic tongue heavy in her mouth, looking at each of them in turn. A disgraced princess, a mechanic, a soldier, an engineer, a courtesan, a pilot, a leader of the resistance. Yet they were all so much more than that. "Seven devils."

She looked out at the stars and planned her next game.

Queens kill king.

ACKNOWLEDGMENTS

Seven Devils came about somewhat flippantly: Elizabeth had a dream that she and Laura wrote *Mad Max: Fury Road* in space. Laura said: "let's do it!" That was in 2015. It was a long road from idea to book, with bits of drafts written while we worked on respective solo projects. But we believed in this group of rebellious women desperate to topple an empire, and we are so grateful you get to read about them.

A huge team assembled to help us make the book you're holding:

First, it was our agents, Russ Galen, Juliet Mushens, and Heather Baror, who supported our furious ladies in space and put them in front of publishers around the world. Two of those publishers included the magnificent teams at DAW Books in the US and Gollancz in the UK. Rachel Winterbottom, Betsy Wollheim, and Leah Spann formed the tremendous editorial team for this book, pushing and inspiring both of us into making this story bigger, better, and more badass. Shoutout to Richard Shealy, our eagle-eyed copyeditor, who saved us from a few embarrassing passages. We're so grateful for the marketing and publicity teams at both DAW and Gollancz for getting this book out to our readers! Especially Will O'Mullane at Gollancz, and Alexis Nixon and Jessica Plummer at DAW.

Moral support is so important while drafting, so we'd like to give a massive thanks to our mutual friends Hannah Kaner and Julia Ember for reading and cheering us on at every stage.

Laura would additionally like to thank her mother, Sally Baxter, and her husband, Craig Lam, as ever, for their support. To the Ladies of

Literary License and the Asshole Writing Club, and all her friends who deal with her whinging about writing with relative good grace. To the Edinburgh Napier Creative Writing MA, both colleagues and students.

Elizabeth would first like to thank her husband, Mr. May: come give me a hug when you read this! And as always, to Tess Sharpe, who is the most inspiring, brilliant friend and one of the best writers she knows.

She also has a *lot* of people she'd like to thank for supporting her back in 2018 during a really rough health scare, but especially: Todd DeDecker, Raoul Borges, Clara Lee, Matt Miller, William Mauritzen, Michael Grunert, Morgan Folsom, Kendra Floyd, Michael Weatherford, James Holland, James White, Maja Baek, Alek Dembowski, Kendra Hoffman, Michael Gates, Rob Meijer, Enrique Robles, Aneli Aguillon, Susan Davis, Tracy Robinson, Sean Carroll, Jo Henn, John Scalzi, Larissa O'Brien, Kaitlin McCaw, Noah Richards, Allen Clark, D Franklin, Paul Kremer, Rebecca Zanzig, Alexandra Bracken, Parris P McBride-Martin, the wonderful people on the SFWA EMF Committee, and especially Cat Rambo. Thank you, every last one of you—including those not listed here—for your immense kindness. Thank you, thank you, thank you.

Lastly, we would both like to thank you, readers, for stepping into our universe and following the Seven Devils Smash the Patriarchy In Space.